Poppies

Written by

Deena Thomson

Poppies

For information:
http://www3.sympatico.ca/deenathomson.menard/

ISBN: 978-1-84728-096-1
Printed in the United States of America

To my boys

Dream, darlings, dream…

— Acknowledgments —

One of the reasons I wrote this book was because I dared to follow a dream I had. It started out with a few sentences fresh from my sleeping mind.
Soon I had my first draft of about hundred or so pages. Wondering if it was even interesting, I let a friend read it. I would like to thank Cathy Lalonde for being that person and saying, "This looks good, you should do something with it." That was the seed needed to grow into **POPPIES**.

I would also like to thank the following persons whose help was immeasurable. Joanne Ederer, for being the first person to edit my book and spend so much time going over it. Stacie Johnson who spent countless hours "fine tuning": Your advice for perfecting the book was greatly appreciated. You have been a good friend. Jennifer Merrill Thompson for leading me. My husband, Todd, and son, Anthony, for believing in me and putting up with my time spent on the computer. My mother, Pam Thomson and Jeff Edginton. And last, but not least, the rest of my family and friends for encouraging me and rooting for me along the way.

— Prologue —

"...you guys are gonna look
like Poppies in a field of daisies."
-Adam to Alan

She is dreaming.

Mama and Pappy are smiling as the train rolls down the track Mama is so beautiful and happy. Strands of her golden hair have fallen from her usually well-kept bun. She looks over at Pappy. He smiles lovingly at his wife and brushes a wisp of loose hair out of her clear, hazel eyes.

"Jobeth will be so surprised," Pappy says in a faraway voice. His dark eyes twinkle, full of life.

The conductor is walking up the aisle.

"MAMA! PAPPY! RUN! GET OUT OF THE TRAIN!"

The conductor is an elderly gentleman of about seventy years. He is dressed in black trousers and a matching black blazer. A black cap rests comfortably on his balding, pale head. His shiny black shoes stop at Mama and Pappy's seat.

"YOU ARE RUNNING OUT OF TIME! RUN! RUN!"

The conductor tips his hat and smiles at Mama, his lips becoming smooth and unwrinkled.

"Is there a problem?" Pappy asks curiously.

The noise in the train is getting louder. A baby held to a plump breast in the next coach cannot be quieted and continues to cry in protest. The baby's fists are balled up and it's face is scrunched up in anger, fighting off some menacing creature no one else can see.

The conductor places a blue-veined hand on the red velvet seat. Blood seems to billow around his knobby digits. Mouth gaping open, he looks out the window beside Mama.

"HURRY--IT IS ALMOST TOO LATE! HURRY--GET OUT! MAMA! PAPPY!"

The noise is increasing. The baby continues to cry louder and louder. The mother, frustrated, makes noises into the wiggling baby's red face. She cannot understand her child's behavior.

Two gentlemen dressed in dark suits look up from the card game they are enjoying. They turn toward their window, mouths opened in surprise.

Or is it fear?

The noise in the coach is getting louder. There is an odd smell clinging to the air. A sweet, sickly smell. The smell of doom. The smell of certain death.

"What is the problem?" Mama asks. Concern creases her smooth brow. She stands up in her seat and glances around frantically.

Pappy reaches for her arm to soothe her. The conductor raises his old hand. It is shaking and blood is streaming down his arm, sliding into the waiting hole of his sleeve. His rumpled lips flap up and down like sheets on a clothesline. He defiantly shakes his raised hand at the window. Droplets of blood sprinkle Pappy's clean white shirt and Mama's hair. They do not notice the blood. They are looking at the old man's fixed gaze.

"MAMA! PAPPY! NO! NO!"

Terror fills their eyes. The train reeks of fear. It is a fear that emanates from the very soul of each person on the train. They are going to die--they are going to die horribly and they know it.

Mama looks at Pappy sadly and clutches his hand tightly.

"I love you, Constance." Pappy says above the whirling noise.

"I love you, too, Michael" Mama mouths, her voice lost amongst the jumble of other fearful voices. "Jobeth . . . " Mama chokes out. A tear rolls from Pappy's dark eyes as he embraces his wife.

"God help her." Pappy breathes into Mama's hair. He buries his face into her shoulder and squeezes Mama tight, knowing it would be the last time he would ever feel his wife again.

Suddenly the train is lifted off the tracks. Screams echo through the compartments as the occupants are tossed around like misfit rag dolls that a spoiled child no longer wants.

The hurricane sweeps the train into its vortex like a toy, crushing the conductor, crushing the card-playing gentlemen, crushing the now-silent baby.

As quickly as it began, it ends. Everything is silent. There is no noise to be heard, except the crackle of flames starting to grow from the engine. The bodies of the passengers are twisted and mangled together, indistinguishable from one another. Blood flows freely from wounds and misshapen bodies.

There is Mama. Pappy is nowhere to be seen. Her leg is twisted at an impossible angle. Debris covers her midsection. She is blanketed in blood. Her eyes are closed. A choking sound gurgles out of her bloody throat. Her fingers reach out into a mushy mass of severed arms and legs, searching for someone who is not there. She reaches in vain. Her broken fingernails dig into wet gore, aching for a comforting touch.

Suddenly she feels the deep rumble that fills the air. Mama opens her one good eye in panic It rolls madly around in its socket searching futilely. Mama sees it coming directly toward her. A fiery ball of angry orange rolls quickly over the train. A wet bubble of a scream squeaks out of her blood-soaked throat just before she is consumed by the inferno's sphere of death.

— Chapter 1 —

Part 1

In the beginning

"Wake up Jobeth! Wake up!"

There is something shaking me, the girl thought. She opened her eyes to the threatening pull. Glaring down at her with steel-gray eyes was Mother Tomalina, a large woman who could never have been thought of as anything but homely. Even as a young woman, she had been nothing to look at. She had narrow eyes and no eyebrows or eyelashes. Folds of skin between them made them appear even closer together than they were. She had a long crooked nose, courtesy of her charming husband, Father James.

Tomalina Johnston, at the age of fifty-two, had not had an easy life. Her father forced her, to marry forty-year-old James Johnston when she was twenty-five years old. He claimed she should count herself damn lucky anyone would marry her ugly mug in the first place as he sent her on her way. She went to James Johnston, a man who repulsed and sickened her, married him and bedded with him begrudgingly, always with bile in her throat.

James Johnston, who found Tomalina unattractive, took amusement and sexual pleasure over her distaste in copulating with him. This caused him to frequently lift her gown and fondle between her frigid legs. If Mother Tomalina refused Father James, she would be faced with even more pain and humiliation: a nice black eye or a broken nose. Once he even broke a couple of ribs. With time, Mother Tomalina, who had never been a warm very person to begin with, became a bitter old woman. Her heart filled with hate and contempt. Her thin lips were usually pursed into a pucker. The beginnings of a road map of wrinkles covered her face. Her gray hair was always pulled tightly back from her long thin face, so tight that it seemed the roots would pop out and all that would be left was a handful of scant bun.

Mother Tomalina savagely grabbed the girl lying on the cot and dropped her like a lump of coal onto the cold cement floor. Jobeth felt no pain as she fell, only shame. Shame for the wet spot between her legs and on her nightgown.

She had wet herself again.

Her mind started racing with the things to come.

He would come now, and she feared him much more than she feared Mother Tomalina. She closed her eyes and swallowed.

How did she end up here? How did she, the daughter of Constance and Michael Roberts, end up on a cement floor, soiled and humiliated, awaiting a beating by people she had never even imagined could be so cruel. A lump formed in the back of her throat. Jobeth had once had such a good life, a happy life. Why did it seem a lifetime ago?

The hurricane.

It all started (or ended depending on how she looked at it) with the hurricane.

Her parents had been killed it on their journey home, after a getaway in Louisiana It was far from their Northern dwelling, but it was a much needed trip for Constance and Michael. Jobeth had stayed home because she had not wanted to miss school, and she felt her parents needed some time alone to heal some wounds. Six month's prior, her younger brother Paul had been killed. As a rambunctious eight year old, he had been the apple of his parents' and sister's eyes.

Jobeth's parents had given up all hope of ever having another child after their daughter's birth. Each pregnancy ended by the fourth month in a painful miscarriage, sending Constance Roberts, sick and depressed, to her bed. By the time Jobeth was six years old, her Pappy had beseeched with his wife not to go through with the pregnancy she had just become aware of.

"Michael, God's will shall be done. I will not destroy this gift." Constance said calmly but firmly to her panicked husband.

"But Constance, if you lose this one, we may lose you also. Is it God's will that Jobeth and I live without you?" Michael asked in despair.

"I do not wish to discuss the matter anymore. This child will come when it is ready or not. But it will be born when it decides and not beforehand." Constance stood firmly, not looking at him. She rarely disagreed with her husband, but when she did there was no changing her mind. Michael knew there would be no arguing with her and he feared for his beloved wife's life, hating the child in her womb that threatened her.

Several months later at a birth that nearly killed Constance, Paul was born, big and healthy. As soon as Michael's wailing, squirmy son was placed into his arms, all hate he had for the boy left and love took over. Jobeth, seeing that her mother was going to live and that the child she'd been carrying was also going to live, quickly forgot about her former feelings and became excited that she was no longer an only child.

Since his birth, Pauli, a name adopted by Jobeth, was a child everyone, including his big sister, doted on. The little boy with light brown hair and sea-green eyes was aware of his family's affections and knew that he could do no wrong. So, often he got himself into trouble knowing he would be forgiven. This was his mindset when he climbed the tree in the backyard of their home. He had been warned many times by his parents and Jobeth that it was too high and he could seriously hurt himself should he fall. Pauli felt he could do it. He had climbed many trees in his eight years and this beast of a tree would prove that he was the best tree climber around. He had done well until he reached the top branch. The twigs up this high were brittle and bark flaked off easily under his thick-soled boots, crumbling to the ground far below. Pauli had to clutch tightly to the main torso of the tree several times to balance himself. As he looked up, the leaves of the tree spiraled up to the sun, letting only glimpses of sunshine through. He felt triumph. He had conquered the beast. He raised his right hand high into the coiled green and let out a victory cry. His hand slapped against a branch. It moved and let in some of the sun's blinding rays. Squinting, he became temporarily blinded. His hand instinctively went to shield his eyes, causing him to lose his footing on the branch. It happened so fast. Pauli never knew what hit him. He never even felt his neck snap, sounding eerily like the branches that fell underneath him, as he hit the ground and landed on his head.

He was killed instantly.

Jobeth and her parents were devastated after the death of little Pauli.

Although they clung to each other for support, the emptiness would always be in their hearts.

Jobeth felt relief when her parents had left on the train to a popular resort located on the coast of Louisiana. She had visited there many times with her parents and brother. It was a favored place to vacation in 1893. The dark circles that seemed to haunt both her beloved parents' eyes seemed to be just a tiny bit faded. She knew this was just what the doctor had ordered.

She had been studying quietly in the parlor, curled up in Pappy's favorite velvet chair when she heard the knock on the door. Sitting up, she folded her notebook and absent-mindly placed it on a nearby end table. Shivering, and feeling as though something was wrong, she walked to the door. Rich aromas hung thick and delicious in the air. She had prepared her Pappy's favorite: roast suckling pig with potatoes and baby carrots, topped with a thick rich gravy. Her mouth began to water with anticipation of her parents' arrival. They were due any time now and she could not wait to see them. It had been lonely while they were away and a little frightening at night with all the shadows dancing around on the wall. One night she was certain Pauli's ghost had returned to get her, angry because she had not saved him from his fall from the tree. She knew she was being silly. But still she hid, quivering under her covers, fearful Pauli would come, his head sitting on his shoulders in an unnatural way.

Jobeth quickened her step to the foyer, figuring that maybe it was her parents so loaded down with parcels that they could not get the door. She smiled broadly and skipped excitedly to the entrance.

Opening the door, her joy was quickly dashed. Isaiah Hyman the old Jewish man who was her family's closest neighbor was standing in the doorway. He twisted his yarmulke nervously in his rough, old hands, his leathery face drawn and sad.

"Mr. Hyman, what is it? Is there something wrong?" Jobeth's heart suddenly began to race. Mr. Hyman was not a man to smile much. He never had any type of expression on his face, only a neighborly wave and a "How do you do?"

Frightened, Jobeth began to twist her hands together. Maybe something had happened to his sweet wife Sarah?

"Is it Mrs. Hyman?" She reached out and clutched the old man's hand warmly but firmly.

"No Miss Roberts, Mrs. Hyman is doing well, but I do bring bad news." He looked down at the ground, wishing he were not the conveyer of unfortunate tidings. "It is about Mr. and Mrs. Roberts. There has been an accident . . ."

Jobeth could not stop crying. At first it was a guttural deep wounded cry that took her breath away, but as days past, it lessened to silent tears. People from town frequently came to console the young girl, bringing plates of steaming food, but nothing worked. She sat numb, hands limp in her lap, as each person asked the same questions.

"Do you have any other relatives dear?"

"No. They were all I had," she would answer bleakly. Concern for Jobeth's welfare soon became eminent.

Although she was fourteen years old, she could not run a large farm–and it was improper for an unmarried girl to live alone without a guardian.

It was unanimously agreed by the town council that since Jobeth had no living relatives, she would be sent to a nearby town to live with a couple who were known to take in orphaned children.

The arrangements were made immediately and the couple was very accommodating in accepting another mouth to feed. Jobeth's father's farm was auctioned off and his arrears paid off with the proceeds of the auction. The small amount of money left after all the debts were paid was given to the couple taking Jobeth in. This was to help feed her, clothe her and keep her in school until she came of age. All this was done as Jobeth sat back passively and watched her old life slip away.

The house she was sent to was the home of Mother Tomalina and Father James Johnston.

From the moment Jobeth stepped into the filthy shack, she relived her parents' death in dreams. Sometimes Pauli was with them, his neck broken and his head twisted and hanging on his shoulders. When she awoke from the depths of her nightmares, bathed in sweat and panting heavily, she saw that she had wet herself like a child just fresh out of nappies. Although Jobeth was humiliated, she could not seem to stop herself.

Which brought her back to her present predicament: Lying on a filthy cement floor with Mother Tomalina standing over her.

"You filthy girl." Mother Tomalina screeched. Jobeth tried to get up and run But she was too slow as Mother Tomalina's strong hand stopped Jobeth in her tracks with a stinging slap across her soft face, sending her sailing across the room. This time Jobeth felt the pain. She brought her hand up to her throbbing cheek and instantly felt the heat rise from her assaulted countenance. Quickly she wiped away the drops forming in the corner of her eyes.

"Get up and strip." Mother Tomalina said in a dry, dead voice, as she turned her back to Jobeth. The girl stood up, shaking on weak legs, and stared at the large rump bent over the tiny cot. Mother Tomalina quickly removed the gray, soiled sheets.

"I should wipe your nose in it, you filthy girl."

Mother Tomalina hated children, and thanked God that He chose not to implant her womb with any of her husband's demon seed. She knew that it was she who was barren and was grateful for it.

Guilt filled Jobeth as she shivered and slowly started to unbutton her worn night gown. She could not understand why she wet herself nightly. She never had before. Her numb fingers slowly worked on her buttons. She stared down at the faded gown and wondered again as to the fate of her old clothes. She used to have pretty dresses. Blue and pink with lace collars, not these gray sheer nighties she wore now. They were so worn from use that one could see her naked form beneath it *Where had her clothes gone?* She had not seen them since she came to live here. Mother Tomalina had taken them from her the moment Mr. Hyman had left after dropping her off in his buggy.

"You won't be needing these high missy clothes here. You're here to work, not show off your wares." Mother Tomalina sniffed through her nose that first day. Jobeth didn't understand the meaning of those words as she followed the homely older woman down to the cellar, her clothes captive in Mother Tomalina's firm grasp. But they became crystal clear soon after.

"Fourteen years old and still messes the bed. Dogs ain't this bad." Mother Tomalina scowled, scooping the sheets into her arms. She turned to face Jobeth, who was still fumbling with her buttons. "Not only are you as dirty a dog, you are slow as one too." A large hand suddenly reached out from beneath the sheets and grabbed the neckline of the nightie. Jobeth's head snapped up in protest, but before she could say anything Mother Tomalina had ripped her gown viciously off her. She quickly bent down to pick up the pieces of her only night garment and tried in vain to cover her nudity.

Now what will I wear!? Jobeth screamed in her head, not daring to speak her anger aloud.

"Humph." Mother Tomalina clucked, her eyes sinking into the younger girl's naked body. "That modesty of yours will go. There is only one place for the likes of you and that's the streets."

Jobeth wrinkled her forehead in confusion. The streets? What did she mean?

Mother Tomalina twisted her lips into a sour pucker.

"Don't look so innocent to me--within a year you'll be spreading those pretty white thighs to any eager man with a jingle in his pocket. I've seen your type before. You'll end up with a bastard in your belly not knowing who the Pa is or where he went.

Jobeth opened her mouth in protest but Mother Tomalina quickly turned on her heels to leave. She swiveled around suddenly to face the dismayed young girl.

"Father will be down to deal with you shortly. I reckon he'll be mighty mad." She smirked.

Jobeth's blood ran cold in her veins as Mother Tomalina closed the door.

She will do for a while, Mother Tomalina thought to herself. He would leave Tomalina alone for a little while at least, and when he got bored with this one, she'd just find a new one. She groaned under her own weight as she ascended the stairs. She would sleep well tonight.

"How could she say that?" Jobeth's lips quivered "My Mama and Pappy never raised a girl like that." She clutched her gown around her tiny breasts and went to sit down on her cot. The cold, wet gown touched her flat belly.

Goosebumps jumped to the surface of her skin, forcing her thoughts to reality.

Father James would be down soon.

Ice-cold fingers crawled up Jobeth's spine and the hair on the nape of her neck stood on end. He would be dressed in his usual trousers, old and faded from years of use. In his large, hairy hands would lay the belt. The belt that would soon turn into a whip that would lash Jobeth's young flesh.

She was terrified of him.

He was huge and burly with cruel, beady eyes. Never had she met a man like him. Then again, she had never experienced brutality until she had come to the home of the Johnstons.

Jobeth peeked through the strands of her own greasy hair. She had always been clean, but since she was thrown into this prison for some hidden crime she had committed, she had only been allowed one bath per month.

"It's too much trouble to waste time pumping water from the spring," Mother Tomalina said.

Jobeth was not permitted hot water either when it was time to bathe. It was a waste of cooking wood to heat water for a bath.

"We don't have them privileges here." Mother Tomalina would preach, "A cold bath makes for a quick bath, so you can be sure you won't be lazing around soaking in a hot, fancy tub."

Jobeth had to admit the old woman was right about that. The water was always ice cold. She would quickly wash the grime off her skin and be out of the tin barrow before she turned into an ice cube. Once, she was last to take a bath. The water had been warm and greasy from the previous people who used it. This disturbed her more than bathing in freezing water. From then on she volunteered to be first into the tub. It was better to wash in cold water than to bathe in someone else's dirt.

She closed her eyes and cowered on the corner of her cot, waiting. The Johnston's didn't have a large house and with all the children they took in, there was not enough room for everyone to sleep. Jobeth's cot was in a small room dug out in the cellar. All that furnished the room was her cot. The few clothes Mother Tomalina had given her after taking Jobeth's were neatly folded in the corner of her cubbyhole.

Her heart pounded uncontrollably as her eyes darted around the gray room. She would never become accustomed to the degradation of being whipped naked. The first time Father James had come into her room a month ago, she was more upset that he had seen her naked then at the beating. He did not seem to care if she was naked or not. He just grabbed her and beat her and left. Jobeth had cried for hours. No man had ever seen her naked. Not even Pauli or her Pappy. It was just not decent and she felt somehow dirty from it all.

But worse of all was the way Father James looked at her. It was a hungry look. Like a fox about to pounce on it's prey. Bile rose in her throat. Those eyes were far more frightening than the belt ever could be.

Father James stood holding onto the knob of the door.

Inside was the whore.

The whore he must possess. He felt himself harden with desire. Yes, she would be his, just like the others. She would be his. He thought of the greasy little wench inside and a mixture of lust and hate filled him. Scratching his swollen belly, he belched with disgust. All women repulsed him. They reminded him of his mother. As a child his life had been filled with humiliation after humiliation by the very hands of the woman who birthed him. His father would leave for work in the fields and the nightmare would begin.

"JAMES! You lazy good-for-nothing, I told you to get the eggs from the barn." She would yell with such venom. James would duck his curly head down to try to avoid the hard whack across the head, but it didn't matter. Her hand always connected, and if it wasn't her hand, it was something else. Once she had knocked him out with a rock. As he lay semiconscious on the ground, bleeding from the head, she calmly stood over him, her dark eyes looking down at his six-year-old body with disgust and said, "Get up, or just die. I don't' care which one you choose."

The memory flooded Father James with hate and anger. He had endured his mother's torture until he was eighteen. On a cold winter's morning she had woken him to a slap across the head and something snapped. He grabbed her hand and all the anger he had built up inside him broke through like a raging inferno He saw the fear in her eyes as he easily twisted her arm behind her back. She grunted painfully as he forcefully heaved her body next to his. He said nothing as his hand went up and connected full force across her thin face. The joy he felt did not need words. She had cried out, but that only excited him more as he ploughed his fist over and over into her face.

It was the beginning.

The beginning of years of abusing women. First he found pleasure in beating them, but soon that became tiresome. As his beating became more violent, so did his sexual desire. After a while his beatings were accompanied with much more.

He sighed thinking about it. They were all the same. Just like his mother. His mother had died from his abuse, but he had gotten away with it. Who would have suspected a son of beating his mother to death? He always got away with it and he would again with this one... what was her name? He scratched his greasy head and specks of dandruff fell onto his yellow stained shirt. Jo something... Some silly name he had never heard of before. He didn't really care. She would be his to play with in whatever way he wanted. And today he wanted more than to beat her, he wanted to own her.

Father James turned the knob and walked into the tiny room. The girl was huddled into a corner of the bed. She shrank back in fear. The smell of sweat clung to him and consumed the room as he gently shut the door, locking it behind him.

— Chapter 2 —

Puffy white clouds floated across the clear blue sky. It was harvest time and Jobeth was out in the field, picking corn with the other children. She threw a cob into a sack and wiped the freely flowing sweat from her brow. Her face was a mass of black and blue bruises After Father James raped her, he whipped her ruthlessly with the belt. Her entire body was covered with welts and she ached all over.

"I have to leave," Jobeth said under her breath. "I cannot let him come back tomorrow." Visions of the morning filled her mind.

She shivered, feeling as though she were dipped in a pool of ice. The day was sweltering hot, but she felt cold.

"No," she said out loud, "I will not think about it." She shook her swollen head back and forth. Pressure formed in the front of her skull. The ground swirled before her eyes and she felt faint. Jobeth closed her eyes and sat on the ground until the dizziness passed, her fingers raking the gritty dirt beneath her.

"Oh God!" she sobbed, clutching her arms. Tears fell uncontrollably as her nails dug into her already bruised skin. Droplets of blood pooled around her fingers, but she did not feel it.

"Jobeth?" A tiny voice broke through Jobeth's tears. She wiped grimy tears away with her fist and looked up into a small, pale, porcelain face.

Shawna had lived with the Johnstons since she was eight months old Her long platinum blond hair fell limply in her face. Her steel blue eyes stood out strikingly against her unearthly pale skin. She would have been a beautiful child if she had not been so sickly pale and if dark circles did not shadow her haunted blue eyes.

Jobeth slowly stood up, embarrassed to be caught crying, and dusted her dress off.

"Yes, Shawna?" She sniffed trying to compose herself. She had purposely gone deep into the fields to be away from the other children. The thought of anyone seeing her after what happened with Father James appalled her. Surely they could tell she was defiled. She looked down at the tiny girl. Shawna was so small for her five years that it was easy not to have seen her.

"Are yah okay?" Shawna questioned, and blushed, looking at her scruffy shoes.

"Yes." Jobeth lied "Yes."

"You look like yah got it bad." Shawna continued.

"What?" Jobeth uttered too loudly. Her head snapped toward the puny girl. What if Shawna could tell what had happened to her? Did she look soiled now? She surely felt dirty and polluted.

Jobeth cleared her throat and ignored the images forming in her mind. No one could know what happened in that room. No one.

"Sorry," Shawna jumped back frightened, "Your face," she shuddered. "He must 'ave beat yah badly."

Jobeth's hand fluttered to her swollen face. "I'm all right," she said, feeling guilty. The child was as nervous as a newborn colt. She remembered when one of Pappy's mares had given birth to a chestnut colored colt. She had gone to pet its damp nose and it had bolted from her outstretched hand with a comical leap into the air. Shawna reminded Jobeth of that colt. High-strung and skittish, ready to leap into the air at the slightest movement toward her. It had never occurred to Jobeth before that maybe the neglect she was experiencing could be happening to the child before her.

A sinking sensation crawled up her neck and into her face, making her cheeks tingle.

"Shawna," Jobeth said wiping her nose again, "I have to go to the outhouse. So if anyone asks where I am, tell them that, all right?" She had squatted down to the miniature girl's level. Shawna lifted her frail face up to Jobeth and fought back tears welling in her enormous eyes.

Please. Jobeth yelled in her mind. *Do not let me think of you. I have to leave. I cannot worry about you.*

"You know Mother and Father don't like it when we go to the outhouse during work." Shawna wavered. A large drop of salty water formed in the corner of her eye.

"I know, but I have to go badly," Jobeth tried to ignore the tear. She would not feel responsible for a child she hardly knew.

During the time Jobeth had come to live at the home, she had hardly seen Shawna. Only in the fields and the odd times at the dreadful kitchen table. There, Jobeth and the other children would eat the same watery soup and dry bread every mealtime. Sometimes if they were lucky, they would be rewarded with a little butter and the odd glass of milk from one of the many cows that the Johnstons owned. Jobeth' s mouth always watered at the smells of roast beef and other dishes Mother Tomalina prepared for Father James. More than once at the supper table as she stared at their savory foods and ate her soup, she envisioned ways to snatch a leg of lamb or chicken, but was always too frightened of the ever-watchful Mother Tomalina. Maybe at night when everyone slept she would creep up the cellar stairs and steal quietly into the icebox and satisfy the constant hunger that plagued the pit of her stomach But alas, when evening came and everyone slept, Jobeth lay trembling under her gray sheets, picturing the old woman patrolling the icebox with its contents of leftovers.

Shawna looked up at Jobeth beseechingly. It struck her that the child never played. This she knew because Shawna was always working.

"Look, Shawna, I have to go. If I don't go then I will wet myself and soil my clothes. I will be whipped again and I do not need another beating," Jobeth pleaded. This was her chance, her only chance to leave. Mother Tomalina would not be expecting to see Jobeth until the sun was down. If Jobeth left now she would not be missed for hours. This would put plenty of distance between her and the dreaded house.

"Okay." Shawna said, head bent low, turning around slowly. Her little frame looked as though it would blow away like the frail dress whipping angrily around her. Faded and worn, her bony structure was visible through the thin material as it struggled to pull away.

Jobeth took a deep breath, wincing at the pain she felt throughout her entire body. She turned and hurried toward the outhouse. Shawna could be watching. She must not give herself away by going in another direction. She picked up her ratty sweater, half-eaten by moths and tied it around her scrawny waist. She had become increasingly thin living with the Johnstons and the sleeves of the sweater hung limply between her legs, nearly reaching her knees, knees that a couple of hours ago were viciously torn apart to amuse Father James She closed her eyes tight, erasing the images of the morning threatening to play themselves out again in her mind.

Run.

If she ran she would escape what happened in the dank cellar.

Her feet began to move. The sleeves of her sweater twisted between her legs as the sack dragged behind her. She quickly grabbed corn, rhubarb and other vegetables growing in the field and tossed them into the bag. Her chest heaved painfully from the effort and her heart beat frantically for what she was about to do.

"I can't get caught," Jobeth sobbed. The memory of Father James' "purple snake," as hard as a rock, forcing into her, ripping her, humiliating her, flashed before Jobeth's eyes. She rubbed away tears streaming down her grubby face with the palm of her hand.

"I need a bath. Oh God how I need a bath! I have to get his smell off me! How will I ever get his smell off me? " Jobeth stopped in her tracks, her chest heaving up and down and clutched her hands to her mouth. "What has happened to me? What has happened to my life? Things used to be so simple." Jobeth sobbed out loud, her tears streaming freely. She felt her heart would break. "Why did you die Mama, Pappy? Why? How could you do this to me?" She moaned. A grimy strand of hair went into her wet eyes and she absently pushed it behind her ear. The wheat in the fields swayed in the wind, making rustling noises that startled Jobeth. "What am I doing standing here like a fool crying? I have to look out for myself now. There is no one for me anymore. I am alone."

She stood up and breathed deeply. The autumn air felt crisp as it went into her lungs clearing them of the heaviness surrounding her heart.

Jobeth felt light-headed as she looked beyond the rows of wheat. Later, She would have to reflect on everything. Right now she needed to get herself far away from the Johnstons.

She began to run.

Jobeth wrinkled her nose as she reached the rat-infested outhouse. She thought of entering the rotting structure with its cold, splintery seats and decided against it. The smell inside was putrid and she already felt nauseated from the fumes emanating from the open door. If she needed to use the lavatories, she would just go outside. At one time in her life, the thought of relieving herself in public was mortifying, but many things had changed since those days. Jobeth never had to worry about being bitten by rats in her old water closet. Mama and she would always scrub the privy regularly, dousing it with lye. Using the outdoors as a washroom seemed more civilized than the dangerous, infectious outhouse that stood before her now.

"I will never have anything to do with this place again," she said, staring up at the house. She crouched down behind the tall grass. It was not really a nice house. It slanted to the right. The original builder of the house, Mother Tomalina's father, had not been very bright and built it in the winter on frozen ground, so every year during spring, the house shifted and sunk down more to the right. Soon it would sink right through to the bottom of the earth, straight to hell where it belonged. The roof was falling apart and would not be fixed until the cold came and Father James sent one of the young boys up to patch it.

Mother Tomalina was sitting in her usual spot at that time of day, rocking in a stiff old rocking chair given to her by one of the villagers.

"To rock the waifs in," The elderly haired woman who had donated the chair had commented. There was never a waif rocked in that chair or a child who wanted to be held in Mother Tomalina's flabby arms. She always sat like an angel, how she wanted others to see her, but really she was a demon, smirking and rocking at the passing neighbors, looking quite saintly, as she self-righteously perceived herself to be.

"That kind, elderly lady," the ladies of the town would say, while waving at Mother Tomalina as she sat rocking and knitting away. Mother Tomalina would wave back, giving her best sanctified smile and continue to knit.

"It is too bad about her husband, always in town with heathen women," one would say.

"Didn't one of those orphaned girls they took in turn to wicked ways?" the other would say.

"I hear tell Mr. James takes a real liking to her. What a shame for poor Mrs. Johnston. She works so hard to give those children a real home." They would shake their heads sadly.

"To think one of the strays she took under her wing would betray her with her own husband. Two heartbreaks: turning against God and selling herself with the only man known to her as Pa. It is disgraceful."

As soon as they were out of sight of the rocking chair, they would shake their heads and carry on their way forgetting about poor Mrs. Johnston and her wild husband.

Jobeth had seen it before in the store when she had been sent to fetch supplies. The whispers passed from one bonneted lady to the other. She saw the distrustful sneers when a lady walked by with her husband. A protective grasp to their man's arm, as though a mere look from Jobeth would cause their husbands to stray. She had always felt confused by their response. She knew she wasn't as tidy as she had been before her parents' death, but Mother Tomalina refused for other people to see the children in her charge dressed in their usual attire. There was a special dress for the older girls and a pair of slacks and shirt for the older boys for such trips into town. Only one boy and one girl could ever be seen in town together, because there was no other outfit for the rest to wear. Jobeth, who was used to being treated as one of the respected children in town, was now thought of as white trash and shunned by the townspeople. Not used to this treatment, she sometimes forgot herself and would start a conversation with a girl around her age, only to have a protective mother herd her daughter away from the ragamuffin child. Jobeth's ego would be bruised and she would be brought back to the reality of where she was. The girl she had once been, the one with a mother and father and a younger brother, was dead. Just like her parents. Just like her brother. They might as well have all died together.

Had she provoked Father James to do what he had done to her? She shook her head and cleared the impression forming again in her mind and turned from the sight of Mother Tomalina's portrait of a wronged woman. Her eyes searched the expansive area. She spotted Father James in the barn with Dex, a ten-year-old boy who had just come to live at the Johnston's. Jobeth's heart once more began to pound uncontrollably. Her breath came in quick sharp thrusts and she realized that she was nearly panting. She looked at Dex and remembered something one of the older boys had once told her. When a boy turned fourteen, Father James would make him pay for his bed to sleep in and the food he ate. Jobeth had asked if any boy had worked for his bed and measly dinner and the boy had said he'd be fourteen soon and would be gone before he would pay for poorly flavored water and a bug-ridden bed. Jobeth had laughed. The boy, Nick, was nice and she enjoyed having him to talk to. She had been so lonely since her parents had died.

"What about girls, Nick?" Jobeth had asked once in the barn. They had been sent to milk the cow and she stood behind Nick's bent back as he finished squirting milk into a tin bucket. He stood up and faced Jobeth. She was already fourteen so she knew girls did not have to pay for their keep, even though Jobeth felt that the backbreaking work she did in the fields was payment enough. Nick's expression had become dark and he had turned away.

"Nick?" Jobeth asked the dark-haired youth. "What about the girls, do they pay?" Jobeth did not like the way he clammed up. Nick, a rambunctious youth with a glimmer in his smile, was a boy who seldom kept a word to himself. He turned to Jobeth, his bangs hiding his brown eyes.

"They pay, Jobeth. They pay dearly."

"What is that supposed to mean?" Jobeth responded. Her heart skipped a beat for no apparent reason. She suddenly felt like a trapped rabbit. Did she really want to know what he meant?

"They pay with their souls, Jobeth, they all pay with their souls. Leave before yours is taken too." He turned and scooped up his bucket of milk, not saying a word to her. What he said left her surprised, confused, speechless and very afraid.

Shortly after they talked, Nick disappeared. The day before he left, he asked Jobeth to leave with him. She shook her head, afraid. How would she survive out in the world?

Now she wished she had left with Nick. Anything would have been better than the ordeal she had endured that morning. Now she would have to leave on her own. Maybe she could find Nick? Then she wouldn't be alone. But would Nick want to be with her if he knew what Father James had done?

Jobeth rubbed her arms roughly. They ached not only from her beating but also for someone to comfort her and make everything all right. She was so alone. So terribly alone.

Little Shawna's face popped into her mind. Small and pale and so very young.

It dawned on Jobeth that once she was gone, Shawna would be the only girl left. She shivered thinking of the small, frail girl. Again she steadied her head, trying to clear her mind of all thoughts. She could not think about anyone or anything but herself and the urgency of leaving.

Jobeth turned to depart. She had seen enough; there were no second thoughts. She did not want to think what lay ahead; she just wanted to get as far away as possible. She swung her bag over her shoulder and started to walk swiftly away from the house. She didn't notice the small figure materialize before her, until it was too late and she collided with Shawna. Both girls tumbled to the ground. Dust flew high above them and fell slowly, like a baby's blanket coming to rest on top of the fallen girls.

"What are you doing here?" Jobeth sat up, trying to shake the fear that had jumped up into her throat. The thought that she had been caught would not leave her. She stood up and started dusting herself off with her hands.

Shawna mimicked Jobeth, dusting herself off and copying her movements, step by step. She looked up at the older girl, embarrassed, clumsily trying to hide a bulging burlap bag behind her back. The small child knew she had frightened Jobeth terribly and she felt awful about this.

"Are you leaving?" Shawna whispered as Jobeth's face drained of blood.

This cannot be happening, Jobeth thought. She glared up at the angry sun that was determined to bake them alive.

"Please," Shawna begged with desperation, her hands clasped together in prayer, "take me too?" Jobeth looked pale beneath her bruised face, but she was listening.

Shawna struggled to raise the sack she held behind her back. "I won't be a bother, I got food so yah won't have to share. I don't eat much so yah could have most of my food too. Please take me too. I is begging yah." A tear slid from her bleached blue eyes and Jobeth could see something haunted, something she did not want to see. Closing her own weary lids, she tried to block out the little girl's pitiful face.

"Shawna, I can't," Jobeth clenched her teeth. She felt awful and her lips began to quiver as she pleaded with this child she barely knew. Shawna was trembling, ready to erupt into tears. "Can't you see you would hold me back? They would search for you. They have had you for so long."

"Noo," she whimpered, tears rolling freely down her ashen face. Her little hands went up to rub quickly swelling eyes and her lips protruded in a pout. "You don't know. I'll grow up and be a big girl and, and . . . he'll do it to me too, when I'm big like you. I can't stay cause I'll end up like the other big girls."

"What other big girls?" Jobeth grasped Shawna's arm ignoring the child's astonished face. Tall grass swayed on either side of them and she quickly pulled her and Shawna into the safety of it. Time was already ticking against her. If anyone saw the two girls standing and talking to one another, it would be all over for them and Father James would be back to hurt Jobeth.

"What other girls, Shawna?" Jobeth implored, unable to stop herself from shaking the child by the shoulders. If there were other girls, what had happened to them? Jobeth was suddenly desperate to know. Nick had said girls paid with their souls. Did he mean what Father James had done to her? Had Father James done the same thing to other girls?

"The other girls who left." Shawna choked, her head shaking back and forth on her shoulders.

Jobeth's eyes were darting frantically in their sockets, causing Shawna to become frightened. Her reaction reminded Shawna of a trapped doe with starving wolves surrounding it, trying in vain to escape to freedom.

"They weren't ever found, Jobeth, except that one gal. But she wasn't really found--she just went to town and became . . . " Shawna looked around to see if anyone else was listening. Seeing there was no one in sight, she cupped her hands to her mouth and whispered, "a whore."

Jobeth pulled back from Shawna gasping and looked at her disapprovingly. Her hand raked through her greasy hair as she absently pulled it away from her tense face.

Could the stories be true about the prostitute who had once lived at the Johnston home? Father James' favorite? Is this the girl the town talked about?

Their souls?

Nick's words echoed in Jobeth's ear. A cold finger rippled up her spine and goose bumps began to rise on her arms. She rubbed them harshly with the palm of her hands.

"But the other girls weren't found, they won't find us either. Mother and Father never search for runaways long. Only for what looks good in town. When the town folk say its just another ungrateful foundling, Mother and Father stop looking and get another child. It's the truth." Shawna bent to look at Jobeth eagerly.

"What other girls?" Jobeth asked sternly, looking beyond Shawna.

"My sister." Shawna became a grisly white and the shadows under her eyes darkened. She bowed and stared at her worn shoes.

"You have a sister?" Jobeth was surprised. As far as she knew, they were the only girls at the Johnston's home.

"I had me a sister. Her name was Donna. Ain't that a pretty name?" She smiled as she looked up. Jobeth forced her lips to smile back. The child was beautiful when she smiled, even with her ailing waxen color.

"Yes it is very pretty."

"When I have me a baby girl one day, I'm naming her Donna," Shawna said in a faraway voice. Jobeth stood impatiently waiting for Shawna to continue.

"Donna said our real folks loved us. I don't 'member the folks cause I was just a babe in nappies, but Donna 'membered, that being she was eight when our folks up and died of the fever. They took Donna and me away. Our folks were scared we'd get it. That's what Donna told me. I wish I had known them," Shawna said longingly picturing parents she never knew. "We was sent here after they died. First nothing real bad happened. Just always working lots, like now. But then Father started doing his thing with Donna. Just like he done with Melodie. Touching her in places he ain't suppose too. Melodie said she was running away and Donna better get me and her out fast before he come after us. I was just four and so scared."

A tear started to fall down her white cheek leaving a dirty trail behind and her eyes became vacant.

"Donna always said, Don't worry, Pun. I'll never let nothing happen to you.'

"Melodie was fourteen and Donna was twelve when Melodie ran away in the night. Don't know what happened to her. Time passed and Father kept looking at Donna funny and touching her. Donna kept saying, 'Just a little longer, Pun, and I'll have enough money for us to run away. I don't want us to starve.'" I knew where she was gettin' the money. Stealing from peoples' pockets in town. Could have had her hands chopped off if they'd caught her."

Jobeth sighed and placed a grubby hand to her head, wondering where the girl got such an idea into her head.

"Don't think Donna was bad stealin', " Shawna defended her sister, pointing a chicken bone of a finger at Jobeth.

"I don't, Shawna. I don't. She was just thinking how you both were going to survive." Jobeth had not even thought of money. *How was she going to survive?* A scream started to build in bottom of Jobeth stomach. *How was she going to do this?*

"One morning," Shawna continued, more tears falling down her cheeks, "he came into our room wanting more than just touching. Donna told me to hide when he comes burstin' into the room. I did, 'cause I always listen to Donna. She was smart and took care of me. Well, he tore her up bad down there where yah pee. She was bleeding all over. I watched the whole thing while peeking from under the bed. He just kept pushing on her. She screamed and screamed, but he don't listen. No one here listens to screams. I wanted to go help her, but Donna looked over at me and shook her head. She whispered for me to stay under the bed. I knew she was afraid he'd come after me next if he knew I was there. So I stayed under the bed and watched."

Jobeth felt sick.

Images of Father James on top of her, hurting her...

Jobeth clutched her head in her hands and squeezed tightly, holding on for dear life, her dirty hair poking out of her fingers.

No. She wouldn't allow it. She couldn't relive it. It was best to forget and never think it happened.

Shawna sniffed and rubbed her runny nose with the back of her sleeve, her mind recalling the day her sister had been raped.

"When he left, I crawled out from under the bed. Donna was bleeding and crying. She didn't look herself at all. She was all white and her lips were blue. Her teeth kept on chattering together and her body kept jerking. "'Donna let's go away from here now,' I begged her. I ran to our bed and grabbed the blankets on top. She seemed to be real cold, so I put them over her. She looked up at me all glassy-eyed and told me to be brave, and not to be afraid anymore. She told me to get away from here before I got to be a big girl.

"'The money's in the mattress take it, promise me?' Donna said, grabbin' my hand.

"'I will Donna. It's our money when we run away.' I say to her, cryin'. Donna's eyes were open, but they seemed really scary lookin'. Just kept staring at the ceiling. She wouldn't blink or anything. I begged her to stop foolin', but she never moved.

"I stayed with her a long time, till Mother came yelling at us to get to work. She saw me shaking Donna and stopped yelling. She just ran over and put a hand on her chest.

"'Git out of here! Out!' she hollered. I didn't know what to do.

"'What's wrong with Donna?' I asked her.

"'She's dead' Mother said as if it were nothing."

Jobeth's throat started to close up and she could not breathe. She knew only too well the pain and loss that Shawna felt.

"I said to her, 'No. Donna ain't dead. She ain't. We're running away from you and Father so he can't hurt Donna no more.'

"Mother got real angry and grabbed my arm, twistin' it till it hurt.

"'You listen to me if you don't want to end up like your whoring sister. Donna had a high fever she couldn't break, and that's what killed her.'

"'It was Father's pushing on her that kilt her.' I yelled. "He tore her all up and she couldn't stop bleeding.' Mother got so mad she done slapped me real hard across the face.

"'Those are lies.' Mother starts yelling. I ain't never seen Mother so mad before, and I seen her plenty mad.

"'You listen here, you little devil. I'll kill you myself if I hear those foul words from your filthy mouth again. Now get out.'

"I ran out of my room and hid in the barn. When it went night, I figured it would be best I get back to the house before it got too late and I got whipped for being out past the dark time. Donna was gone. I never saw her again. I asked Mother where she was at, and she said that she was in hell where she belonged and not to worry, I'd be there soon to help her shovel coal for the devil." Shawna looked up at Jobeth, cheeks all streaked with tears and dirt. A small fist rubbed viciously across her puny red nose as she sniffled.

Jobeth suddenly realized the reason why this little shell of a girl was just that, a shell. The horror Shawna had faced at such a young age had robbed the child of everything. The pain on her babyish face weakened Jobeth's already broken heart. She ached all over from her brutal rape and the new responsibility of this defeated child before her.

She could not leave Shawna. If she did, she would never be able to live with herself. The girl would come with her. How she would care for her, Jobeth did not know. But if she left Shawna, she would be as dark and monstrous as Father James and Mother Tomalina. She would never be that cruel to anyone, never.

"How will we survive? I have never been on my own," she whispered staring across the yellow fields. A gust of wind tugged at Jobeth's insufficient dress, matting her sweaty, sticky hair.

"I still have the money," Shawna disclosed softly.

Jobeth bent her head down to Shawna's hopeful face. She continued, seeing Jobeth's interest.

"I saved it for when I'd run." She bit her bottom lip, making it paler, and looked at Jobeth under light eyelashes, "I even stole some from Father. He thought it was one of the older boys and beat him real bad." She returned her gaze to her battered shoes, shamefully. Jobeth said nothing. Shawna's lips clasped tightly and stubbornly, together, "I had to. I'm not bad. An I ain't going to go to hell neither. I don't give a dickens what Mother says. Donna ain't in hell, she's in heaven with Mama and Papa and when the Lord calls for me I's guess that's where I'll be headed too."

Jobeth placed a hand on the little girl's bony shoulder. Shawna tilted her wet face up to face of the young woman standing tall and stiff. She began to shiver from the look in Jobeth's eyes and her lips began to tremble uncontrollably.

"You are not bad, Shawna, and no one will ever make you feel that way again." She whispered, "Let's get the hell out of here."

Shawna released her breath and smiled. She didn't realize she had been holding it.

— Chapter 3 —

Jobeth and Shawna ran with their skirts billowing out behind them and their hands held tightly together. They were afraid to look back.

Shawna kept up the best she could with Jobeth, but Jobeth was possessed to run as far as possible from Mother Tomalina and Father James. She would not stop even when her face was beet red under her bruises. Shawna was exhausted but afraid to ask Jobeth to slow down for fear she would be sent back to the Johnstons. She knew Jobeth had not wanted to bring her. There was no where Shawna wanted to be other than with the strong girl running beside her. She never wanted to return from where she came. Never.

Exhausted, Jobeth stopped and stumbled to her knees, dragging an equally exhausted Shawna to her own shins. They were both heaving heavily. Shawna felt her lungs would collapse.

"Look." Jobeth panted pointing straight ahead of them. The little girl squinted but could not see anything. Her eyes were blurry from running in the wind.

"What is it?" Shawna panted, unable to catch her breath. She spit out a stream of saliva.

"It's . . . it's a pond." Jobeth began to laugh oddly. She started to get up. Wiping her sweaty brow with the crook of her arm, Jobeth reached down and grasped Shawna's twig-like arm, lifting the confused child to her feet. She was almost exuberant over finding a pond.

Shawna could not understand this joy as she had never known the need to be clean, having spent most of her five years barely bathing.

Kicking off her ill-fitting shoes, Jobeth walked straight to the stream and bent first to drink the cool water. Shawna followed. Surprised at how thirsty they were, they greedily gulped water from the pond.

"Have you ever tasted water so good, Shawna?" Jobeth spouted between gulps. She cupped her hands together and took another large gulp of water, savoring each drop as it passed her lips. The excess was permitting to dribble down her chin.

"Cain't say as I has." Shawna replied. Jobeth turned and smiled at the clean circle around Shawna's lips. Was that color she saw in the child's face?

"You know, Shawna, it is not proper English to use words like 'cain't'. It is, 'I cannot say that I have.'" Jobeth said sternly. If she was going to be responsible for the young girl, she was not going to have her sounding like an uneducated hick.

Shawna lips dropped into a frown. Her dirty face was streaked with water.

"I's sorry." Shawna whispered, feeling ashamed. She had already offended Jobeth right when she seemed so happy to find this pond. Shawna looked down at her clean, moist palms. Red lines and calluses from long days of working in the fields glared up at her. She was no good. Jobeth would leave her behind. A painful lump began to push its way into her throat, bringing with it pesky, salty tears to fill her eyes. Shawna bit her lip and desperately tried to hold back from crying.

Jobeth felt the heat rise to her cheeks, realizing she had crushed Shawna's tender feelings. She felt awful--like a bully. Couldn't she have just let her enjoy the water, instead of criticizing? .

"No need," Jobeth corrected herself, placing a hand on Shawna's shoulder, "You will learn soon enough. Probably very quickly. You seem quite intelligent. You just need proper guidance. You have never been taught. In fact, when Pauli--my little brother--was five, he did not have quite the understanding you do. So there is nothing to be upset about." She gave Shawna the best smile she could muster.

Shawna sighed with relief. Jobeth thought she was intelligent. She was not sure what the word meant, but it was obvious it was a word that pleased the older girl. The pale child grinned back at Jobeth, her hurt feelings forgotten. Jobeth stood up and reached for Shawna.

"Let's go swimming and see what is under all this dirt."

"I ain't never swam before." Shawna stiffened. Jobeth was going to be hard to please.

"No need to worry, I will show you. But today we don't have time. We'll just clean off," Jobeth said while holding back the urge to correct Shawna's speech again. She walked into the water. Shawna stood on the shore, hesitant to follow. The water felt cool and refreshing. Jobeth sank down to her knees, her dress ballooning around her. She giggled out loud and encouraged Shawna to kneel down too. It felt good to laugh again. Jobeth couldn't remember the last time she had laughed or felt good.

"Take the sand from the bottom of the pond and rub it on your skin." Jobeth grabbed at the cool, grainy floor and started rubbing sand roughly on her neck and arms. She sighed and dunked her head back into the water. The water tickled her ears and she felt herself relaxing just a bit. "My Pappy used to say if you don't have soap and a tub, a pond and sand will do the job just the same."

"Will it clean your hair?" Shawna asked rubbing sand on her arms, amazed that it worked. She looked up at Jobeth for an answer. Shawna always liked how nice her hair felt after being washed. So soft and fresh.

"I don't know. I guess we could try it." Jobeth grabbed a large handful of the muddy substance and plopped it on Shawna's head. She squealed with delight and mashed the sand into her hair. Jobeth laughed and grabbed another handful, plopping it on her own head and grinding it into her scalp. Both girls began to laugh and splash each other as though they had always known each other.

Warmth encased Jobeth's tattered body. Covered in sand, she scoured harder on her arms, legs, chest and stomach. She wanted to rub sand between her legs to wash away the filth Father James had put there, but thought against it. She was already very sore down below.

Shawna, delighted, closed her eyes and splashed the water with her tiny hands, sending beaded droplets up into the air. Jobeth, seeing her chance, quickly and gently rubbed her swollen genitals with her fingers, until she was clean. She did not feel clean, but at least the proof that James had been there was gone.

"We better rinse off." The thought of Father James sobering her. How she longed to stay in that pond. But that was impossible. They had come far that day but not far enough.

"All right." Shawna splashed water over her muddy arms.

"I'll just dive under water and get the sand out of my hair and then I will help you with yours."

In an instant Jobeth was down beneath the surface of the now murky water. When she resurfaced, she was still black and blue, but at least she was clean.

She helped Shawna rinse her hair and they both got out of the pond and sat on the grass to dry off.

"We should eat something to keep up our strength," Jobeth said, combing the tangles out of Shawna's clean hair with her fingers.

Shawna, who had never experienced loving hands brush her hair, basked in the glory of her newfound attention. This day would be etched in her memory forever. In all her five years this was the happiest she'd ever felt. She closed her eyes and smiled to herself as Jobeth continued to detangle her hair. She had been secretly thinking of eating too, but was afraid of ruining the wonderful time and didn't dare to ask. What if Jobeth felt she was too much of a bother, or ate too much? Maybe she would not want to keep Shawna with her. So she kept quiet. A hungry belly she could deal with. But in just the short time she had spent with Jobeth, she knew she could never be without her.

"We will eat one carrot each and a raw cob of corn. Maybe tomorrow we will find something else to eat."

Jobeth stood up and went back to the pond where their sack had been left on the shore. She grabbed two large carrots and cleaned them in the pond. A light breeze caused her damp dress to cling. Walking quickly, Jobeth fretted about where they should go. She could not think of anywhere in particular. Suddenly, she remembered something her father had said to her not too long ago.

They were out in the buggy looking at a fence that needed mending. Jobeth went with her Pappy because she enjoyed the ride and his conversation. She always felt so peaceful sitting beside the father she loved so dearly. The sun began to fall behind the horizon. Pauli had been standing behind them telling tales of fighting pirates, dragons and wizards. Jobeth laughed as Pappy declared that Pauli had the greatest imagination he had ever heard.

"Oh Pappy, it's all just playing," Pauli said, not sure if having an imagination was a good thing or a bad thing.

"Look children," Pappy said, slowing the buggy to a stop. The horses stomped their feet in protest and snorted in disapproval. Jobeth and Pauli looked where their father pointed and saw the reddish yellow of the sun slowly burning out beyond the valley.

"When I had no place to go and was in no hurry to get there, I put my sights toward the sun and let my feet carry me home." Pappy said in a faraway voice.

"You talking about the old days again, Pa?" Pauli asked while leaning over his shoulder, his eyes transfixed by the fiery sun.

"Remember that hymn we sing in church?" Pappy asked as he turned to Jobeth. She looked at him solemnly. "How does it go again? Oh yes. 'I once was lost but now am found. Was blind but now I see…'" Pappy stared at Jobeth making her feel that the moment was very important: something she should remember.

"Yes, Pappy, I remember it. It's Amazing Grace." Jobeth answered, gazing at the horizon.

"When I had no place to go and was in no hurry to get there, I put my sights toward the sun and let my feet carry me home. I once was lost but now am found. Was blind but now I see."

Pappy's eyes were kind and warm, as his words were softly embedded in his daughter's heart. They sat silently for a few moments.

Pauli mouthed the phrases his father had just spoken. He looked in frustration at his father and sister.

"Pappy, I don't get it. What does it mean?"

"Well, it brought me to your mother." Pappy turned around and messed with Pauli's hair.

"But Mama didn't find you, Pappy. I still don't get it," Pauli said, shooing his father's hand away. Michael Roberts looked back at Jobeth and gently took her hand in his. It felt warm and safe.

"One day you will understand. It is not for me to explain it for you," Pappy answered, still looking at Jobeth. She had the strangest feeling he was speaking only to her and not her brother.

"I still don't get it," Pauli said, tossing a piece of grass out of the wagon.

Pappy nickered to the horses and turned toward home, humming the tune of Amazing Grace.

Jobeth felt it was strange that she would remember that evening. Did Pappy know that he would not be around for her when she needed his advice the most? Was Pauli never to understand that night because he would never need to?

Jobeth watched the dying embers of the sun in the horizon. Night, with all its darkness, would come very quickly.

"When I had no place to go and was in no hurry to get there," Jobeth said to herself, "But I am in a hurry Pappy, I am in a really big hurry." She clutched Shawna's hand and began to walk toward the sun, singing Amazing Grace softly to herself.

Night quickly rolled in, casting eerie shadows on the browning grass of fall.

Shawna trembled from the chilling breeze and from the scary shapes hovering in front of them. She squeezed Jobeth's hand tighter and looked up at her face. Was she scared also? Noticing the large, frightened eyes searching her own, Jobeth smiled uneasily at the spooked child.

They will know we are missing now, Jobeth thought. *I wonder how far we have gone. I wonder if it is far enough?* She looked down at the exhausted urchin. She looked as though she would fall asleep standing up. They had not even eaten supper yet. The poor child was probably starving.

Jobeth felt ashamed again.

She was going to have to start thinking about her young charge. As much as Shawna wanted Jobeth to believe she was capable of watching out for herself, she was still only five years old.

"We won't travel tonight," Jobeth said aloud with regret. "We need all the rest we can get so that we can travel farther during the day." She wondered just where they would sleep for the evening. It all seemed so simple when she decided to leave. Only the drive to escape Father James had occupied her thoughts. Now she was dragging a five-year-old child into her mess. Jobeth tried to read Shawna's huge eyes. What lurked behind those hollow dark sockets? She shivered unconsciously.

"Jobeth?" Shawna whispered apprehensively. "Are we's going to sleep outside in the night?"

"Of course, Shawna. Where else would we sleep?" Jobeth looked around at her surroundings. Shadows jumped like phantoms. Trees hung their leaved branches low to the chilled ground, reaching for fallen comrades. It was very frightening and Jobeth shuddered, clutching her sweater around her for warmth. She forced a brave smile for Shawna's sake.

"I guess we could look for some sort of shelter." Jobeth did not want to admit it to herself, but she too was exhausted. "Just in case it rains or something."

Shawna sighed with relief. The night air was chilly, but there was no sign of rain.

Jobeth clasped Shawna's small, pale hand in hers and together they searched for a place to sleep.

It did not take long before they found a small, shallow cave beside a narrow pond. They could both smell the sweet, crisp air emanating from the water and Jobeth smiled, knowing that a swim was a good prospect for the morning.

"I know it looks spooky," She said, coming out of the mouth of the cave after searching it first. She did not want to interrupt any four-legged guests who might already be occupying the establishment. "But at least it is a roof over our heads and we are out of the open." She persuaded Shawna into the dark cave with a stern hand on her hesitant bony back.

"I wish we could see better." Shawna said, walking beside Jobeth into the cave.

Jobeth placed her arm around her companion's thin shoulders.

"We will sleep together for warmth. Here, sit down." Gently she pressed Shawna down into the farthest corner of the cave. It was not a very large cave: just big enough for the two of them. "Use your sack for a pillow," suggested Jobeth as she squatted down beside the child.

Both sacks were quickly arranged as pillows. Shawna slowly lay down. She suddenly felt very tired and the foreign noises outside quickly faded as Jobeth deposited her exhausted form down beside her, cuddling up against her back.

Heads resting on their sacks of food, Jobeth looked at Shawna, who was already breathing in deep rhythmic breaths. For the first time, Jobeth thought that Shawna's pale face looked peaceful.

Thinking of the events that had transpired during the day caused overwhelming emotions of doom and despair to crawl up Jobeth's spine. The images of the morning began to fight their way to the surface of her conscience. Suddenly her chest felt as if a large boulder rested on top of it, crushing the very breath out of her. She sat up, looking around, breathing heavily and trying to catch her breath. Darkness enveloped her, making her heart bang against her scrawny rib cage.

"No," she yelped. Shawna frowned, stirring in her sleep. Jobeth clutched her arms around herself and shivered. "I will not. I cannot think about it ever again. I am free now." Absently, she wiped a tear from the corner of her eye with the back of her hand. "I have more important things to worry about now." She glanced at Shawna, who was breathing evenly again. She took a deep breath and the heaviness on her chest began to slowly disappear. She blew air out of her lungs, releasing all the pent-up emotions. "I have to be strong. There is Shawna to worry about now." She lay back down beside the slumbering child and snuggled up close to her small, warm body. Jobeth ached all over and wondered if she would ever feel normal again.

"So tired," Jobeth mumbled. Overcome with exhaustion, her eyes grew heavy and within minutes she was asleep.

She had been dreaming of Father James, naked, coming to her. Then suddenly she was on the train, walking down the aisle to meet her parents. The baby was crying. She turned to look and noticed everyone looking at her with disgust. When she came to her parents' seats, they glanced at her with abhorrence.

"Mama, Pappy? What? What have I done?" Jobeth was confused. Why was everyone looking at her so strangely?

"How could you, Jobeth?" Mama said turning away repulsed. The back of her head was caked with blood.

"How could you do this to your mother and me?" Pappy glared "Have you no shame?" He went to place his arm on his wife's shoulder to console her, but his arm was only a mangled stump.

"But Pappy..." Jobeth looked around, confused. The woman with the screaming baby avoided her eyes, shielding her crying infant from her. Jobeth felt a menacing breeze, and went to wrap her sweater around herself. There was no sweater. She had no clothes on at all. She was standing in the aisle naked. Red fingerprints covered her breasts and belly, descending down low to her hidden mound. They became redder and redder by the moment. She could hear an evil laugh coming up the aisle behind her. The laugh felt hot against her bareback.

It was him.

He was back again.

"Jobeth, you whore. You're mine forever. Can't you see it? My mark is all over you."

"No!" Jobeth opened her eyes to darkness--a darkness that seemed to swallow her whole. She sat up frightened, not knowing where she was. For a moment she thought she must have died and gone to hell. Then she heard Shawna breathing beside her and remembered the events of the day.

Carefully, Jobeth moved over Shawna's sleeping form and stood to go outside.

The wind nipped at her scantily clad body. It seemed angry at her, trying to blow Jobeth away for all she had done wrong in her life. She wrapped her sweater around her shoulders and gazed out across the dark trees. The wind whipped at her legs, causing goose bumps to rise. She felt a damp chill between her legs. She had not noticed the stinging sensation where the dampness was.

She'd been too caught up in the surrounding darkness and the memories of her dream. She touched the wet spot on the ragged dress.

Tears gripped her. Suffocating fear caused Jobeth to suddenly want to run away. Maybe if she ran, the nightmare would end.

I am safe now. I am safe now. Jobeth heaved trying to control the shakiness in her knees and the beating of her heart. Could her heart take any more of this emotional turmoil? She began to remove her dress, repeating to herself that she was safe. Once her dress was off, she repeated the process over again until she was standing naked in the moonlight, clutching her urine-soaked clothing. Her head hung low as she gripped her clothing to her. She sniffed the air and savagely wiped her nose with her knuckles.

"I am going to just rinse these," she said lifting her face to the stars. Tears streamed down her face but she did not bother wiping them away. "I will never be frightened again. I will clean these clothes and no one will ever know what happened. Mama, Pappy, I will never disappoint you again. I know I am no longer the girl you have raised and I have disappointed you in the worst possible way. I did not want Father James to do what he did to me. I know I must have done something to cause him to fornicate with me. I just don't know what. I will never entice a man to do it again. I promise. From this day forward I will be strong and never again think of how I lost my virtue."

Slowly Jobeth walked naked to the small pond. She crouched down and began to rinse her clothes by the shore.

The sun rose and shone in Jobeth's eyes, causing her to squint and shield them with her hand. She sat up, confused as to where she was. She must have dozed off. She looked down at her thin, naked body. Her bony rib cage glared fiercely up at her. The brisk morning air caused her bruised nipples to stand erect. She winced with pain. Her whole body felt as though it had been trampled by a horse.

Embarrassed that she had fallen asleep on a rock naked, she jumped up and snatched the clothes she had carefully laid out to dry the night before. They were still damp. The sun warmed Jobeth's bare back. She looked longingly at the stream and turned to the cave. There were no movements from within its dark mouth. Carefully, she put her damp clothes back on the rock. She glanced once again toward the cave and listened for Shawna.

Nothing.

She slipped into the cool stream, letting the water envelop her. She swam a few strokes toward the center, her beaten body relaxing in the icy water, which was refreshing her and making her feel reborn. Jobeth became entranced with the swim. She felt like she was being transported away from the world and the responsibilities thrust upon her. She sighed deeply and plunged under the water. Its healing powers encased her.

Wrapped up in her indulgent swim, Jobeth did not notice Shawna stumble from the cave. Fuzzy from sleep and, if possible, paler than ever before, the poor girl looked as though she might faint.

Jobeth surfaced and reluctantly started swimming toward the shore. She would have to wake Shawna and start on their way soon. Just because they had not been caught yet did not mean they were out of danger. People could still be looking for them and with the seed of freedom now planted in Jobeth, she would rather die than return to the prison she had just escaped.

She stood up, placing her foot solidly on the sand bed beneath her. Kneading water out of her eyes she turned to face the cave.

Shawna was frantic searching for her.

"Shawna!" Jobeth called out, an arm protectively covering her bosom.

Shawna whirled around. Jobeth looked like an angel, submerged to her waist in water, arms modestly covering her front. Tears flowed from Shawna's eyes but when she saw Jobeth, relief flooded her completely.

"What on earth is wrong?" Jobeth questioned. Embarrassed, she quickly came out of the water and hastily dressed.

"I thought yah left me." Shawna said bowing her head. She knew Jobeth was flustered because she had caught her swimming naked. Shawna couldn't help noticing the teeth marks on Jobeth's breasts and the fingerprints covering every inch of her body. She didn't need to guessed what had happened to Jobeth. She'd seen it too many times before. She felt sorry for her -- but at least she was alive. The ordeal had not killed her, as it had Donna.

Beads of water dripped down Jobeth's face. Her dress, which had finally dried thanks to the sun, clung to her wet body. Jobeth wondered again if color ever entered Shawna's face. She smiled weakly at the ghostly child and grabbed for her hand.

Shawna placed her waxen palm meekly in Jobeth's and gazed up with anguish into the older girl's face.

No child should ever have that look, thought Jobeth. *No child should be this frightened.*

"We are together now. From now on it's you and I. You do not have to worry about me leaving you behind. I won't do that to you, Shawna, you must believe me. Can you stand being with me all the time?" Jobeth maintained her composure, trying to sound strong.

Shawna beamed, "I don't want to be with anyone else."

— Chapter 4 —

Jobeth and Shawna tracked up the dirt road, exhausted from a long day's travel. Sweaty and covered with dust, they stopped to rest, collapsing at the side of the powdery brown road.

Breathing heavily, Jobeth wiped her grimy brow and glanced at Shawna. The wee child lay on her back with her eyes closed, her chest rising evenly up and down. A small hand rested on her sooty forehead. Color had quickly come to Shawna's pale cheeks during the four weeks they had been on the run. Traveling had transformed the little girl into a healthy five year old.

Jobeth sighed with contentment. She was not regretting her decision to take Shawna with her. From the moment she had decided that the little girl was to be her responsibility, the child had become dearer and dearer to her. In the month they had traveled together, Jobeth came to realize that she needed Shawna as much as Shawna needed her.

Time wandering in the wilderness had faded the bruises that blackened Jobeth's body; but the bruises that surrounded her heart were still painful and tender to the touch. If she had not been responsible for Shawna, she would have given up a long time ago. When she was too exhausted to walk any farther, Shawna would look at her with such hope and admiration that Jobeth would rather die than disillusion her young charge. So she trudged on, dragging both weary feet forward, always wondering where they would sleep that night.

Since they had escaped from Father James and Mother Tomalina, the girls slept in barns and fields--any place that was warm and dry. Miraculously, the second week out on the road to freedom, Jobeth stopped soiling herself at night. Although she still had the nightmares of her parent's death, they were not as frequent as they had been at the home of the Johnston's.

Jobeth lay down beside Shawna and looked up into the blue sky. There was not a cloud to be seen and it amazed her again how quickly the sunny day could turn dark and cold. The weather was changing; winter was just around the corner and they would need permanent shelter from the elements during the days when the earth would be covered with snow.

Once she thought she had found a place to stay for the winter.

It was their third week traveling and they had come across a small shack that seemed to be abandoned. There was a small wood stove that could keep them warm through the cold days and nights ahead. It had seemed perfect for their immediate needs.

Jobeth happily roasted a rabbit that was caught earlier that morning in a snare she made. Shawna sat by her feet cleaning some wild onions and the remainder of their carrots. Jobeth was telling Shawna another story about her family, how her Pappy taught her how to make traps and how to live off the land Shawna listened wide-eyed, envious of Jobeth because she had known her parents, whereas Shawna had not. Jobeth seemed to have endless stories about her rugged frontier father and the woman he fell in love with.

She was listening intently to Jobeth's tales when the door of the shack crashed open—both girls jumped up with a start.

"Hey yah brats. Git outta ma house!" bellowed a burly bearded man dressed from head to toe in furs.

Both girls leapt to their feet and clung to each other.

The rabbit, forgotten, fell into the fire. Spitting juicy fat, it began to burn.

Shawna whimpered, hiding behind Jobeth's skirt. Shaken by the sight of the first person she had seen since running away, Jobeth nearly lost her legs. Bile rose in her throat and she prayed she would not vomit.

"I says, git!" the fur-clad man roared, barreling toward them.

Startled into action, Jobeth grabbed Shawna and their bag of meager belongings and quickly swung them around the man and out the door.

The man grunted and bent to remove the burning rabbit from the stove. He ripped off a side of meat from the tender carcass and popped the flesh into his mouth, smiling.

He was hungry and the meat tasted good.

Jobeth continued to run with Shawna clinging to her tightly. She ran until her lungs screamed out in pain and the weight of the small child's arms around her neck began to feel like a noose slowing her down. Finally Jobeth stopped and placed the sobbing girl down.

Unable to control the churning of her belly, Jobeth turned from Shawna and let go of the yellow acidic contents of her stomach. She continued to dry heave, her insides contracting painfully, and wondered again how they would go on. Drops of sweat beaded on Jobeth's forehead, and she absently wiped them away with a shaking hand. The world wavered before her. Dropping painfully to her knees, she closed her eyes, willing the dizziness and nausea to go away.

Hiccupping, Shawna crawled on all fours up beside Jobeth.

"Was, he going to kill us?"

"No, no one will ever hurt us again." Jobeth struggled to whisper and began to vomit the foul-tasting bile again.

Jobeth breathed deeply of the autumn air, clearing her mind briefly. It had been over a week since they encountered the fur-clad man. The problem of where they would stay for winter was still unanswered.

"Come on, Shawna. We best be on our way. We need to find a place to sleep tonight," Jobeth said.

Shawna had fallen into a light sleep. She sat up and rubbed her eyes, yawning.

Without a word of complaint, she stood up and dusted herself off. She sensed Jobeth was panicking, but did not say a word. Shawna had never been happier in her life. Jobeth showered love upon the lonely child, a love she had only experienced once before--with her sister, Donna. But even Donna's love was shadowed by the coldness that enveloped the house of Mother Tomalina and Father James. To remember Donna was to remember how her sister died and the ugliness that shadowed their lives.

So now she followed Jobeth, trusting and faithful. Now that she had experienced love and felt its healing power, Shawna could not live without it.

They walked for what seemed like an hour when they saw a barn and a house up ahead. Most of the windows were broken and the place looked ready to fall down upon itself.

"This looks like home for the night." Jobeth sighed, exhausted. All she wanted to do was lie down and sleep an eternity of sleep. She had never felt so tired in her life.

Slowly, they dragged their battered bodies up the rotten stairs in front of the house. Brown grass sprang through a hole in one of the steps, enticing an unsuspecting foot to break through. Jobeth grabbed Shawna under her arm to prevent her from going through the decayed step.

"It's scary." Shawna spoke softly as Jobeth opened the door. It let out a painful thin squeal. She hesitantly put a foot forward, taking Shawna with her. The floor groaned in protest. Walking through the bitterly cold house, stale air assaulted their nostrils. Huge dark walls loomed before them, dwarfing the two girls.

"It's not eerie, Shawna. Why, look at these rooms! This was probably once a beautiful, rich home," Jobeth said with as much enthusiasm as she could muster. The truth was if the old dwelling had once been beautiful, it was a very long time ago. Shawna gulped and held fast to Jobeth's hand.

"I guess you're right." The tiny voice said hoarsely, her eyes wide with only a hint of the haunted girl in them.

"Of course I'm right." Jobeth said, trying to convince herself as she walked forward.

They crept all over the house looking into spider-webbed rooms with broken floors and corners filled with mouse droppings. Finally, Jobeth opened the door to a small room that was fairly clean compared to the rest of the house. There were five dirty straw mattresses littering the floor.

"This is home for the night." Jobeth said, crawling onto the largest one. Shawna mouth clamped tight, looked behind her shoulder at the darkness beyond and quickly jumped in beside Jobeth.

They cuddled close together.

The mattress was soft and comfortable compared to the sleeping arrangements to which they had grown accustomed.

Exhausted, Jobeth closed her eyes and tried not to think about the soft down bed she once slept in, in another life. It was best to erase the memory of her mother tucking bright, clean quilts around her--quilts she helped make.

"Sweet dreams, Jobeth," her mother's soft voice would say as she blew out the lamp. "And remember, God is always watching over you. He is always there to protect you."

Jobeth would nod drowsily, feeling happy and content. She had no reason to disbelieve her mama. Life was filled with happiness and love. And life had always been that way.

She sniffed. A single tear squeezed out from her closed eye.

Where is God now, Mama? Jobeth screamed in her head. *Why isn't He protecting me anymore?*

Angry voices woke Jobeth from a deep, dreamless sleep. She fought to awake from the darkness that had swallowed her. Shawna was already awake and clinging to Jobeth for dear life. Her fingers dug into Jobeth's arm like tiny needles, forcing her to come back from the darkness of her mind.

"It's all right, Shawna," Jobeth put her arm around the trembling little girl.

She was shaky and disoriented herself. Looking up toward the noise to see what or whom they were about to face, she felt fear. It had been so long since Jobeth had been in contact with people other than Shawna. They had avoided contact, as much as possible, with other people they saw on the road, hiding in bushes until it was safe. People hurt people, and they could hurt her and Shawna. A heavy feeling pressed down firmly on her chest. People could do worse: they could take Shawna from her, leaving her alone once more.

That was something Jobeth would not let happen. No one would take Shawna from her.

She looked up toward the screaming noises with hooded eyes, prepared to defend herself and her charge.

Crowded around the mattress, like soldiers at a siege, stood six yelling boys and one shrieking girl.

"They ain't got no right in ma house!" caterwauled the girl with jet black, curly hair that frizzed out wildly around her face. Her eyes were like black rubies and seemed to be alive with fire. Her tattered brown dress fit her curvy shape snugly; her breasts heaved angrily, about to pop out of the extremely low-cut neck line.

"Now Tamara, this just ain't the way to act." The boy receiving her fury fumed. He was an odd-looking boy who looked like he was about sixteen or seventeen years of age. He had sandy brown hair and a round, flat face with green cat-like eyes. He stood uncomfortably, gangly with his newly developed height, and stared back at the black-haired beauty.

Jobeth felt numb. She wondered if she should grab Shawna and run. She felt so tired--she did not think she could outrun the group surrounding them.

Another boy, with hair just as dark as the girl's, noticed that the two terrified strangers were awake. Jobeth caught sight of him from the corner of her eyes and flinched back, holding Shawna protectively in her arms. Her heart pounded loudly in her chest, ready to beat out onto the dirty floor at any moment.

"Hello," he said kindly, his deep blue eyes penetrating through Jobeth. Her breath escaped her for a moment. The boy was the most handsome person she had ever seen. Before she had time to compose herself, everyone else in the room was circling her and Shawna with questioning faces.

"My name is Oliver," he said, eyes twinkling. "And the two you just heard fighting over there are Tamara and Alan." Oliver offered his scruffy hand slowly to Jobeth in a friendly manner.

Shawna smiled hesitantly at Jobeth. She could not help herself. Oliver had already won her over with his handsome good looks and his charming smile.

Jobeth twisted her lips as she watched the admiration in Shawna's blushing face and was suddenly angry. Jumping up, she pulled Shawna with her. It didn't matter how tired she was, she was not staying any longer in this house.

Shawna frowned, confused by Jobeth's hostility, and hid behind Jobeth's legs.

Jobeth immediately felt guilty and her anger slipped away as quickly as it had come. She cleared her throat and tried to decide whether to say something.

"I am Jobeth and this is..." she pulled Shawna in front of her, almost defiantly, and glanced at the one called Tamara. At first she thought the black-haired girl was older than she was. But with a closer look, they seemed to bè about the same age. "this is Shawna."

Tamara glared back with distaste. Shaken by the fiery female in front of her, Jobeth straightened her back.

"We've been traveling for weeks," she continued, looking around the room for a reaction. Everyone was quiet and seemed to be listening with interest, with the exception of Tamara, who had turned her back to them all. Her long black hair hung like a jungle of vines to her petite waist. Jobeth had never seen such hair before. She found it quite striking, even if she was taken aback by Tamara's apparent resentment of her.

"We thought the house was empty. We only planned to stay the night and leave in the morning." Jobeth finished.

She looked down on Shawna's platinum head trying hard not to think of the situation they were in. Her eyes stung with fatigue and the fight in her was quickly escaping.

"Well, yah see it ain't empty," Tamara hollered, turning around quickly, her hair flying madly about her. The boy, Alan, nudged her with his elbow, glaring at Tamara angrily. She looked back at him with as much venom.

Jobeth and Shawna both jumped at Tamara's outburst. Straightening her shoulders again, she looked directly at Tamara, whose chest was still heaving angrily. Jobeth felt like crying. She was so tired and felt so sick. Her limbs felt like dead weights hanging helplessly from her shoulders. She simply did not have the energy to battle this stranger.

Her mouth began to water and Jobeth fought back the urge to gag.

"I am terribly sorry if we have caused anyone any inconvenience. We'll just be on our way." Jobeth grasped Shawna's hand and plunged forward, dragging her out of the tension-filled room. Her throat tightened and her eyes began to burn with tears. Every muscle in her body cried out for rest. She was defeated. It was late and too cold to sleep outside.

"Now just hold on there, Jobeth," a male voice interrupted. She stopped in her tracks. Saliva pooled in the inside of her mouth behind her bottom lip, but she didn't dare to do a thing about it. The voice sounded like the odd-looking boy with the round face who had just argued with Tamara.

What is his name?

"Yes?" Jobeth asked. Her back still faced the voice. She squeezed Shawna's hand hard feeling her wince in pain.

Alan stared at the straight, thin back of the peculiar girl as she clutched tightly to the ghostly white child. His chest tightened at her stubborn refusal to turn and face him. He looked to Oliver, questioning him with a raised right eyebrow. Oliver nodded his head, giving Alan the answer he wanted.

"Yah two are welcome to stay here." Alan spoke quickly before the spooked girl ran out of the house with her little waif in tow.

Jobeth closed her mouth and held her breath. She really did not want to stay, but she was so tired and --something she didn't want to admit--she was lonely.

The last person she had spoken to who was her own age was Judith. Judith was Jobeth's best friend before her parents accident. She cried with Jobeth after her parents were killed. She also wept, her red pig-tailed head buried into Jobeth's shoulder, before Jobeth was sent to live with her new foster parents.

"I will never forget you, Jobeth," Judith had pledged the day Jobeth left. They had clung together, two friends never to see each other again, their lives headed in opposite directions.

Jobeth pulled away from Judith's freckled, wet face and climbed into the wagon. Her belongings were packed neatly in a small chest in the back, secured with thick ropes.

"I will never forget you either, Judith," Jobeth promised as the horses pulled away from the sobbing girl. She waved frantically at Judith, but her friend, overcome with grief, ran away, her hands covering her face, unable to bear seeing her friend leave.

She hadn't thought of Judith since she entered the doors of the Johnston home. And she did not want to think of her now.

Judith would be appalled to see what had become of Jobeth's life.

Suddenly Nick came to mind. The boy Jobeth had spoken with at Mother Tomalina and Father James'. He was tough and scarred from battles fought too young in life, but full of life and laughter regardless. Judith would have wrinkled her brown spotted nose at Nick. But Jobeth had rather liked him. She then thought of the ragged lot behind her. They were like Nick. She looked down at her thin, faded dress. She had given Shawna her tattered sweater to keep her warm. It hung down to Shawna's knees, causing her to look lost in the stretched garment, but it at least kept the chill out, if only a little. Jobeth fingered the material of her dress. She would freeze with nothing but its flimsy cover.

Judith would not be caught dead in a rag dress like the one Jobeth wore.

She was like Nick now. She was like the people behind her: tough and scarred, ragged on the inside and out.

No, I am still different, she thought. *I am mostly dead inside. Only the darkness of dreamless sleep soothes my soul.*

"There ain't no place for yah to go and we don't mind the extra company at all. Plus, that there little one don't look like she can go nowheres but bed."

Alan's voice cut into Jobeth's thoughts. He knew Jobeth was seriously weighing his offer. He refrained from mentioning that she looked as though she would drop in her own shoes at any moment.

Finally, turning to the voice speaking to her, Jobeth surveyed Alan. He had strong, green, cat-like eyes. A strand of hair bobbed up and down on his forehead, giving Jobeth the feeling that Alan was a boy fighting in a man's body. She looked away, blushing, feeling she had seen something private and personal about him. The other boys in the room were all smiling at her, trying to make her feel welcomed. Her eyes came to rest and widened on a child's face that sat oddly on a young man's body. He flashed Jobeth a wonderful, bright smile. She could not help staring, speechless. The boy's skin was a deep, rich chocolate brown. Embarrassed by her rudeness, she turned her gaze quickly to the handsome raven-haired Oliver.

"Stay, Jobeth. We'd all like you to stay." Oliver walked over toward the hesitant girl and placed a warm hand on her bony shoulder. Jobeth instinctively pulled back, repulsed, but then relaxed as Oliver gently coaxed them back into the room by taking Shawna's small hand. Unable to help themselves, they both followed Oliver shyly.

Alan stood alone and held his breath. Anger began to burn in his chest. Oliver's smooth talking had again worked its magic. Jobeth glanced back over her shoulder at Alan, who looked lost and awkward. His heart pounded heavily in his ribcage. This new girl was different. He could tell she wasn't like them, even though she looked like it. She had come from better--a flower hidden in the weeds. He smiled awkwardly and blushed because it felt silly and forced. Jobeth grinned weakly back and turned away. Alan lowered his head, feeling like a fool.

"Humph," Tamara smirked, moving to stand beside Alan. He shoved his hands deep into his pockets and tried to compose himself. Tamara stood righteously with her arms tensely crossed over her large breasts. Her exposed cleavage bulged in Alan's face.

"What now, Tamara?" Alan steamed, looking away from her chest and back to Jobeth, who sat quietly listening to Oliver.

"Seems Oliver found a new toy to play with, don't it, Alan?" she asked, nastily pursing her red lips together. She cackled, noticing Alan's red face and walked over to the other side of the room where Jonah, the black boy who had shocked Jobeth, sat. Tamara plunked down beside Jonah as graceful as a lump of clay and continued to smirk at Alan. His attention veered from Tamara, tired of her obnoxious ways, and went back to watching the new girl.

Jobeth was putting Shawna back down on the mattress they had been sleeping on. Oliver was talking a mile a minute and Alan could not help noticing Jobeth shyly smiling back. His heart pounded painfully again. Absently, he reached up and rubbed at the pulsing muscle beneath his chest. His fingers moved up and down in rhythm to his heart. His fingers tingled warmly with the motion.

Jobeth was the most unusual girl he had ever seen.

— Chapter 5 —

As Jobeth sat on the mattress listening intently to Oliver, Shawna slept peacefully in her arms. The child's pale hair fanned out across Jobeth's lap and she absently stroked the silky locks.

"We all just gradually hooked up with one another." Oliver said calmly. His elbows rested comfortably on his lap as his hands dangled freely between his knees. Jobeth could not help noticing Alan looking at Oliver uncomfortably.

She shook off the feeling of animosity and turned her attention back to Oliver.

"So you don't have any parents?" Jobeth inquired, facing him. His eyes danced with amusement.

"Not one of us has a parent. They're either dead or just up and left." He smiled and leaned in closer to Jobeth. "What about you? Where are your parents?"

Jobeth darted her eyes away and began staring at her hands in her lap. Her nails were broken and black and the lines in the palm of her hand were embedded with dirt. She nervously began to stroke Shawna's soft, blond locks. Tears tried to force themselves to the surface, but Jobeth swallowed them back.

"I have no parents. Shawna and I are all alone."

"Is Shawna your sister?" Jonah asked, sitting beside Tamara. He had been silently listening to Jobeth and Oliver.

Jobeth looked up at him, still surprised at his color. She had only seen black people a couple of times around her hometown, and always on the poor side of citizenry. But the blacks and whites never spoke to each other. She was embarrassed to admit it, but she had never paid much attention to the colored folks. They were like apart of the scenery, standing on the corner or in the store. She had never taken notice.

"Yes," she lied, not looking up. It wasn't completely untrue, Shawna felt like a sister.

Alan noticed Jobeth's uneasiness and sensed she was not used to addressing colored folks. Studying her tired face, Alan saw only kindness. She had probably never spoken to a black person before. Once she got to know Jonah, she would love him like everyone else did. Even Tamara, who pretty much hated everyone and everything, loved Jonah.

"I think it's time we let Jobeth sleep," Alan announced, still looking at her.

Relieved, Jobeth's eyes met his. He tried again to smile warmly at her, but it only came out twisted, making him look ridiculous.

"But we want to hear more," Tamara chided, lying back on her side, her head resting snugly on her propped hand. She smiled sweetly.

Jobeth ignored her. She was tired and did not want to answer any more questions. Too many questions would lead to too many truths, and that was the last thing she wanted them to know. Then they would throw her out and keep Shawna. They could never know the truth about what had happened to her. She would never let that happen.

"There's plenty of time to talk," Alan interrupted, scowling at Tamara. "That is, if Jobeth decides to stay with us." He held his breath, afraid of the answer. Alan could not explain it, but he felt the need to protect her and her little sister.

Jobeth stared at Alan, open-mouthed. She hadn't thought of staying permanently.

"Please stay, Jobeth," Oliver repeated leaning even closer to her.

"Well, I don't know..." Jobeth stumbled. She still felt a little frightened of these people. Tamara's face was red with anger. Her friendly smile was now gone. Did she want to spend the whole winter with a girl who obviously did not like her and felt threatened by her? Tamara's expression to Oliver was one of disgust. She flopped herself flat on the mattress, turning her back to Jobeth and Oliver.

"There is no need for her ta answer that question, Oliver," Alan answered for Jobeth. "We all can leave any time we want and so can Jobeth. Stay as long as yah want." He layed down on a mattress and yawned, his eyes never leaving Jobeth. "Lots to do tomorrow, better get some shuteye."

She stared back, grateful. Alan nodded as she snuggled in beside Shawna.

Oliver stood up and went to the mattress Tamara was sleeping on. Lying down beside her, he whispered something into her ear and she elbowed him roughly in the stomach. He chuckled, said something Jobeth could not hear and crawled onto a mattress with another boy.

Jonah, smiling at Oliver's behavior, crept away from the fighting couple and over to Alan's mattress. He laid his large frame down, not noticing the difference between his frame and Alan's lean one.

"I like her," Jonah whispered to Alan's rigid back.

"Me too," Alan whispered back, wide-eyed, staring at Jobeth's already sleeping form. "Me too."

Jobeth awoke refreshed and in good spirits for the first time in a long time. She sat up feeling a little stiff and confused, unable to remember where she was. Suddenly she became frightened. Where was she? Her head spun around from side to side taking in the objects around her. Then the events of the past evening flooded her memory.

Alan and Oliver. Tamara.

It all came back in a rush of events. She turned to check on Shawna and smiled at the sleeping child beside her. The poor thing was still asleep, completely exhausted from all the activities of the past month. Jobeth pulled the blanket Oliver had given her over Shawna's frail shoulders and lightly kissed her warm cheek.

"Good mornin'." boomed a deep voice.

Jobeth spun around to face Jonah. Her hand clasped her heart and she did not know what to do.

Jonah loomed large with broad shoulders over her.

"Good morning," Jobeth said, reserved, her eyes avoiding him.

She had remembered when Mother Tomalina had been offered a black baby. She had refused to take the baby, stating that there was no way she was having one of those kind in her home. Jobeth had not understood the comment. She had been in the kitchen peeling potatoes at the sink when the nice-looking lady with brown hair and a straw hat had come to the door holding the dark, crying infant. The baby was dressed in a darling white crocheted bonnet and dress that flattered the infant's chocolate colored skin.

"But Mrs. Johnston, the child has nowhere to go. You are my last hope," the lady begged.

The baby flailed its tiny feet, knocking off one of the matching white booties and exposing a brown foot with a pinkish underside. Jobeth leaned closer to the door to listen, her knife poised over a half-peeled potato. Mother Tomalina always wanted babies. For reasons unknown to Jobeth, Mother Tomalina had a soft spot for small babies. Maybe it was because they didn't yet have a personality to offend her, or maybe it was because they did not look at her drawn, wrinkled face with disgust. Whatever the reason, it did not last long. As soon as the child was old enough to walk, Mother Tomalina would have nothing to do with it.

"No. Now leave with that--that thing, now." Mother Tomalina ordered the lady out of the house. "Bring me a white child, even an Indian, but never bring those soulless creatures into my home," she ordered. "I will not have the children of Ham under my roof."

The woman left, enraged, and Mother Tomalina went to pray. As soon as Jobeth was sure Mother Tomalina was deep in prayer, she left the potatoes in the sink and went outside. She bent down where the baby had kicked off the bootie and picked it up. The yarn was silky to the touch. Jobeth couldn't' help herself and rubbed the small garment to her cheek, feeling its warm comforting touch.

Before her parents were killed, Jobeth had asked her Mama about the black people.

"Some feel they are different--inferior--to us white people." Mama said while knitting in her favorite chair. "But the white people were the ones who enslaved the blacks, and no one, black or white should be treated like an animal." She put down her knitting, motioning Jobeth to sit down in front of her. Jobeth listened and knelt down. As Constance Roberts began to braid her daughter's long golden brown hair, warmth and safety enveloped Jobeth.

"Remember, my dear, we are all God's children and in the end when we are in heaven, all color fades to a bright light and in that light, there is only love."

Jobeth looked at the little shoe and the warmth she had felt when her mother braided her hair lingered. She gently folded the bootie and placed it in the pocket of her dress.

Jobeth looked at Jonah, ashamed. His size was threatening, but his face and his smile were kind and genuine.

"I owe you an apology Jonah," Jobeth said looking at his confused features.

"Whatever for?" Jonah handed Jobeth some bread.

"I am afraid I have judged you unfairly." Jobeth looked down at her hand holding the bread Jonah had given her.

"Aw, you ain't the first," he smiled brightly, "and you won't be the last. Everyone does at first. It's cause I's so big for my age and I's so dark and all. Least yah say you're sorry. Don't normally gets a 'sorry' from folks."

Jobeth felt her apprehension starting to leave.

"I guess you had a good sleep?" Jonah asked, coming close. He sat on the nearest mattress to Jobeth. "Sit down, Jobeth. Sit down." He patted the mattress beside him.

Jobeth walked over and sat down uneasily beside the massive youth. Too many things had changed in her life in such a short period. It was hard for her to overcome. She had never spoken to a black person before and now she sat inches away from one. She couldn't help feeling dirty around people. After what Father James had done to her--why would anyone want to be around her?

She closed her eyes and took a bite of the dry bread.

I am not going to think about that!

Jonah smiled and chuckled through a mouthful of bread.

"Yah looks like yah got the weight of the world on those little bitty shoulders of yours."

"I do?" She twisted her hands, surprised at her outburst. She nibbled on her bread, angry with herself for revealing too much. "Where is everyone?" Jobeth gazed around the empty room, trying to change the subject.

"They all gone to town," Jonah smiled broadly displaying a mouthful of teeth that seemed to take up his whole face.

She liked his smile. She started to relax again, the images of Father James forced to the back of her mind once more. Mama was right. Everyone was God's child.

"We has to treat the newcomers with class," Jonah continued eating, whipping away breadcrumbs from his mouth with his massive paw of a hand. "Bread won't do for the feast we gonna have tonight." He lifted his crust of bread to Jobeth's face.

Instantly her stomach growled at the mention of a feast. It had been so long since she had eaten a good meal. She wondered if Shawna had ever eaten one. She felt warm inside thinking of the child feasting on good nutritious foods.

"Yah," Jonah continued, noticing the hunger in Jobeth's eyes. "Carter and Adam are at work, but they promise to bring home a little extra for the dinner." He grinned at Jobeth bashfully, his brown eyes twinkling with life. "Are yah hungry, Jobeth?"

She blushed, ashamed that her hunger showed so plainly.

"I am only hungry for Shawna," Jobeth said with little conviction while sweeping the crumbs off her skirt.

"Yah, I know how it is to be hungry for someone else." Jonah laughed.

Jobeth couldn't help herself, she began to chuckle too. She sounded ridiculous. The sides of Jonah's eyes creased and wrinkled with laugh lines. She wondered how old he was. His frame was the size of a man but his face was that of a boy, kind and gentle, not yet ruined from the cruelty of the world.

"Jonah?" Jobeth asked, "How old are you?" She blushed. She felt like her tongue did not belong to her. She had lost all sense of the good manners she had been raised with. Tears burned behind her eyes. Could Jonah not see what a fraud she was? But she suddenly really needed his kindness and offer of friendship.

"You are all so young," she said, trying to recover from her mess-up. Her throat felt tight and it was hard to speak.

"That we are." He stared at the doorway to the rest of the house, lost in thought, unaware that Jobeth felt she had insulted him. He turned from the door and graced her with his beautiful smile. "All babes lost in this great big ol' world. Well, let's see. Carter and Adam are the oldest of the group. They's eighteen and the best of friends you ever saw. Then there is Alan."

Jobeth eased up and felt her throat relax. She could not help noticing the look of worship on Jonah's face at the mention of Alan.

"Alan's sixteen and Oliver the wild cat," Jonah could not help but radiate as he spoke fondly of his only family, "he's fifteen. Todd, he's fourteen. He's also Adam's brother. He's mighty shy, so don't yah be getting upset and hurt if he don't speak to yah." Jonah wagged a finger seriously in Jobeth's face. She shook her head, amused, and forgot her earlier shame.

"And we can't forget Tamara. Beautiful Tamara. She's at the lovely age of fifteen. And I, well I's sixteen too."

Shawna stirred waking up. She rubbed her eyes in the familiar way Jobeth had become accustomed to.

"Well, if the sun hasn't shined right in this very room." Jonah beamed, standing up and walking toward Shawna.

She quickly backed away from him, frightened. She had lived all of her life with Mother Tomalina and Father James. It was hard to remove a lifetime of learned racism in just one night. The messages the Johnston's seeded in Shawna's brain since infancy had taken plant and rooted on her shoulders for so long.

"Now there is nothing to fear from old Jonah, little girl. Now look here."

Jobeth watched curiously as the boy searched in his pants pocket for something.

Shawna eyed him with distrust.

"I saved this just for you," Jonah said, handing Shawna a large, shiny red apple. "Just for yah breakfast. A growing girl such as yourself needs an apple a day to keep the doctah away." He chuckled, handing Shawna the red fruit.

Shawna held the fleshy apple, her eyes feasting on the red color. She looked to Jobeth for approval and Jobeth nodded, smiling. Without a moment's hesitation she took the apple and bit into it.

"Mmmm . . . It's GOOD!" She beamed up at Jonah. Apple juices ran down her chin. "Thank you!" She bit into it again, the sounds of crunching rang through the room and all fears of Jonah vanished with each sweet bite.

"You are welcome. And since you love ma apples, I will bring one for yah every day." Jonah said. He picked up Shawna and walked back to Jobeth.

Jobeth reached her arms out for the little urchin and placed the apple child between the two of them.

"Jobeth?" Jonah asked, handing each of them more bread.

"Yes?" Jobeth placed the bread in her lap. She began to wipe away some breadcrumbs that had fallen onto her dress.

"I always wants to know what a body wants out of this great big ol' world. An' I wants to know what you want too." Jonah asked, looking at Jobeth sincerely.

She knew he was serious with his question and it made her uncomfortable. She had given up all her hopes and expectations of the world.

"What do you want?" Jobeth countered back, teasing, trying to avoid his questioning face.

"Oh, I don't know," Jonah's face puzzled up like an old rotten apple, "I guess I want people to see me and accept me as Jonah. Not the nigger boy. Not the poor black trash. Just Jonah." He looked at Jobeth with wide, wet eyes. "See, I got two strikes against me. I's black and I ain't got no one but a bunch of white kids as family."

"But that is better than being any color and all alone." Jobeth spoke softly.

She felt for the man-child beside her. She knew what loneliness was and it did not discriminate. It attacked everyone it could.

Jonah saw Jobeth's fallen face and the sadness plainly displayed there. People's troubles come in all forms, he thought. He perked up quickly, not wanting to darken this new encounter.

"That's right, Jobeth. I knew yah was meant to be a part of our family. I just knew it. I gots a bad habit of getting down on myself and the group is always at me, reminding me of the good things in life. Just like you just done."

Jobeth laughed and tickled Shawna, who giggled and bit into her half-eaten apple. It felt good to laugh. It had been a long time since she felt like laughing, since it felt safe to laugh. It might not be so bad to stay the winter with these people. They could not tell Father James had raped her. Besides, winter was nearly at the door and it would be good to spend the cold nights talking to Jonah. Maybe with time, she would even become friends with Tamara. She allowed herself to be content, if not happy. Maybe she could put the incident in the Johnston household behind her. Maybe she could forget and go on with her life.

"Now quit tryin' to change the subject. You tell me now what you'd like outta life." Jonah scowled playfully.

"I'd like to be as free as a birdie." Shawna tittered.

Jobeth still could not believe the change in Shawna. She had really transformed into a new little girl.

It was hard to believe that Shawna had once been a frightened little phantom, afraid of her own shadow.

"Me too," Jobeth said dreamily. "I would like to fly away where no one would ever find me. Like a deserted island. I would eat wild berries and drink from a clear crystal stream. Then I would dive into its cool depths and be forever clean." She blushed, embarrassed. Shawna and Jonah listened intently.

Jonah put his hand on Jobeth's knee and clasped her hand. It felt warm and friendly.

"We have the same dreams," he whispered.

Stillness enveloped the room.

"How did you meet up with these people, Jonah?"

Jobeth coughed nervously. The silence between them had grown uncomfortable.

"Well," Jonah began, ripping his bread in two and handing half to Shawna. She took it greedily and began to munch down on it. "I was three when my ma died and a few years later my Pa died of a bad heart. I believe that it was a broken heart. He was always a silent man, but after Ma died of her headaches, he seemed to become even quieter. Into himself. I didn't have no brothers and sisters on account of Ma nearly dying havin' me. Pa said it messed her insides up pretty bad. Anyway, I was just wandering around, nearly starved, when I met up with these boys. Most have the same story. Some different. Some have been on their own as young as Shawna." He ruffled Shawna's hair. Shawna rolled her eyes up at him.

"Yah, Tamara's been on her own since she was seven. I don't know much about Alan. He's pretty quiet about his past."

Jobeth felt queer. Why was the boy Alan so secretive about his past? But then again, she did not want anyone to know about her own sordid history. She pushed the mystery of Alan's previous life out of her mind. What did she care about a boy she did not know? Jobeth had enough to think about with Shawna and herself. She did not need to worry about Alan and his secrets.

The door suddenly burst open, causing the three to jerk clear out of their seats.

"Hey," laughed a slobbering, drunk Oliver. He reeked of booze. Jobeth became frightened and reached for Shawna instinctively.

"No need to dent the roof." He stumbled into the room and nearly fell onto Jobeth. For a brief moment she felt like screaming. A memory of Father James looming above her popped into her mind and just as quickly faded when Alan grabbed Oliver by the collar of his shirt, frowning at him.

"What? What did I do Alan?" Oliver looked confused and a little hurt.

"You better learn how to handle your whisky, Oliver, or I might have to teach yah how." Alan steamed. He had seen the look of terror cover Jobeth's face. She could not help noticing Alan looking at her. She bent her head down and felt her face begin to burn red.

Oliver sulked over toward Tamara who was standing in the doorway frowning down at Jobeth. She had also noticed Jobeth's reaction to Oliver's drunken behavior.

"Hey, baby," Oliver slurred at Tamara. A pink tongue protruded out of his mouth and darted into her small white ear. Tamara's expression revealed that she was not impressed. "How about it honey? I need a little lovin' and I know you can fill it." He leaned over and planted a boozy kiss right on the nape of her neck.

A shiver ran up Tamara's spine. Softening, she gazed down at Oliver's tousled black hair. She had a weak spot for his good looks and exquisite blue eyes. Eyes, she now noticed, trying to focus on the surprised Jobeth. Fury that seemed to always fill her snapped free. Tamara turned around so fast that Oliver did not have time to duck and her hand smashed into the side of his flushed face.

"Pig!" She shrilled so loud that Shawna leapt into Jobeth's lap. "You don't talk to me that way or I will do more than slap yah. I knows how to do that too," Tamara hollered. She stormed over to Alan, who was taking food out of the inside of his jacket.

"Stop it, Oliver!" Alan said, shifting to Tamara. She began to remove food from her coat. Alan avoided looking at Jobeth.

Oliver shook his head, touching the side of his face where Tamara's handprint was already red and noticeable. He went to the nearest mattress and lay down. He did not understand what had come over Tamara.

"We got a ham and a dozen eggs. Carter and Adam got some other stuff. We gotta be careful from now on. They're startin' to watch us closer." Alan spoke to Tamara. "You women can go and begin this ham." Alan avoided Jobeth's fixed look. He could tell the look of disapproval in her eyes and it made him feel small. He was sure Jobeth had never stolen for her supper. It was plain to see in her eyes.

Alan was sure he was right.

She thinks I am trash, he thought, ashamed and humiliated. *She is too good for us, for me.*

"C'mon." Tamara said miserably as she picked up the ham and slung it loosely by her side. She did not even bother looking at Jobeth as she trudged out the door.

Jobeth started to slowly stand up and follow the raven-haired beauty, unsure as to what to do.

"Jobeth?" a small voice questioned. Jobeth wheeled around. She had forgotten about Shawna. The poor thing looked frightened as a scarecrow. Tears had begun to roll out the corners of her eyes and her bottom lip started to tremble.

"Am I a woman? Do I go too?" She choked, trying not to cry.

"Do you want to come?" Jobeth asked. She felt bad; her mind had been on Alan's stealing and Tamara's insolence. Shawna was her responsibility. She should not have concerned herself with how Alan and Tamara lived their lives. Shawna would be eating tonight. Eating until she was completely filled up. What did it matter where the food came from or how it had landed on their plates? It only mattered that it was there. Jobeth could not believe she had let herself forget about the little girl. She was going to have to be more careful. These people were temporary and this place was only a pit stop for the winter. Shawna was permanent—she was her whole future.

Shawna nodded her head up and down, forcing the frown from her lips. She really liked Jonah and the attractive boy Oliver, but she still was not ready to be away from Jobeth.

"Then come along," Jobeth coaxed holding out her hand.

Shawna grinned and jumped up from the mattress, running to Jobeth.

"You's in charge, Shawna," Jonah said, pointing. "Don't let those two diddle-daddle with our feast."

"I won't," Shawna said, feeling better.

Jobeth and Shawna went outside behind the broken-down house.

Tamara was already building a fire. The ground was black and full of ashes. There were burnt twigs and black charcoal rocks placed in a circle. Logs were neatly stacked up against the wooden walls of the building. Tamara had already brought three good-sized logs beside the circle.

"Shawna, honey," Tamara said, surprisingly sweet. The young child looked at her fearfully, grabbing the hem of Jobeth's frayed skirt. "If'n you wanna play, I have some pretty dolls up in the house by my mattress, just waitin' to be played with by some beautiful girl just like you. You see, they happen to be lonely. No one's played with them for a long time."

Shawna's mouth grew into an ecstatic smile. She had never had dolls. Mother Tomalina did not believe in such indulgence. They were a waste of money, in her opinion.

"Go play, Hun'." Jobeth coaxed, thinking maybe Tamara was all bark and no bite.

Shawna giggled and ran off excitedly into the ramshackle house. She quickly returned moments later with three porcelain dolls. They were beautifully made, with real human hair as blond as corn silk. Their faces were delicately painted with happy smiles. The dolls, Jobeth noticed, were well taken care of, their dresses clean and bright. Shawna sat down on the grass a little ways from the other girls and began to play.

Tamara's fire had started to take and she was preparing a spit to roast the ham on.

"If you're gonna stay, you better learn to cook." Tamara said, glaring at Jobeth. She ignored the look. "Everyone has to work. Ain't no room for one livin' off the others here."

"I can work." Jobeth spoke bitterly, poking a stick into the ground. The sight of the ham, which moments ago had caused her stomach to growl, now made it churn. Her breasts began to throb and she wondered if her monthly would soon start. She glanced at Tamara putting the ham on the spit. It looked red and the smell of raw pork began to repulse her. Her mouth began to water and bile rose in her throat suddenly. Turning to the bushes, she quietly spit up her bread that Jonah had given her for breakfast.

Tamara watched out of the corner of her eye. She had been ready to argue with Jobeth for leaving her duties when she noticed her throwing up. Tamara turned back to her cooking. She hated being sick, but she was only briefly concerned for Jobeth. She didn't like the scrawny gal invading her home. The little one, Shawna, was all right. She knew only too well what it was like to be so young and alone.

"Sorry," Jobeth said returning back to Tamara, wiping her mouth with the back of her hand. "I haven't been around solid food so long that I'm afraid my stomach can't handle it."

Tamara nodded, not bothering to look at Jobeth's waxen face. Oliver paid too much attention to the gaunt, stringy-haired girl. She couldn't understand his attraction to her. She thought Jobeth's hazel eyes were too big. Her hair was too straight and an awful mousy color. Although Jobeth's dress was barely being held together, she had no body to contend with. She was built like a skinny child, compared to Tamara's curvy frame. Tamara knew she turned all men's and even some women's eyes. She always had. People had always fantasized about her and lusted after her. And Oliver had been no different.

She let him have her a few times. What did it matter to her? Sex was nothing new. She had always been surrounded by it.

She was born in a brothel. Her mother, a black-haired beauty like Tamara, had been the favored prostitute of the establishment. Madame Keisha, the painted, red-haired woman who owned the pleasure hotel, had pulled the bloody, screaming Tamara from between the quivering legs of Lorraine, Tamara's mother. It had been a cold winter night and the room was so frigid that a hazy mist steamed from Tamara's wet body. Her balled-up fist struck out angrily at the world. Madame Kiesha placed the infant on her mother's working bed, the very bed Tamara had been conceived on, and looked up at Lorraine, who was exhausted. It had been a hard and long labor. Madame Keisha expected both mother and child to die. She was still afraid that her most popular girl would. Her business would not be as prosperous without Lorraine. She had the beauty the clients only dreamed of having, but would pay highly to have, if only for the night.

"It's a girl," Madame Keisha said, looking down at the squirming infant shivering in the cold. Little puffs of cool air blew out of her wailing blue lips.

"She should have died," Lorraine whispered weakly on her side. A tear ran down her sweaty, pasty face. "Who will marry a whore's daughter? She will be a whore too. Like mother, like daughter," Lorraine sobbed. Madame Keisha lifted the wiggling Tamara to her mother's breast. Lorraine wished she could have feelings for the child. The child was from her body, but she just could not love her. She did not even know who the child's pa was. He could be any of the foul-smelling rogues who frequented the establishment. The thought of the men who came to pleasure themselves on her made Lorraine sick. This child was a product of one of those encounters. Lorraine had hoped that maybe it had been one of the wealthier clients. Maybe even one of the young virgin boys whose daddy or older brother had treated them on a birthday. She was an expensive product. It was something to relax her mind for a moment. But there were the few scoundrels who, captivated by her beauty, spent a month's salary just to pump her for a few moments of pleasure. The thought that one of these men could have fathered her child sickened her.

The baby cried angrily, begging to be fed. Lorraine placed a hard nipple into the child's mouth to stop the fury of the infant. She laid her head down upon her pillow, feeling her child feed from her and cried.

Tamara grew up watching her mother with countless men. She always craved the love Lorraine seemed to give them and not her. Only when Tamara had been sick would Lorraine sit by Tamara's small bed that was beside her mother's and feed her soup, humming a tuneless hymn.

When Tamara was seven, her mother was killed. She had told a favored customer that she was pregnant. The man was enraged and strangled Lorraine while Tamara slept peacefully beside them.

Tamara never cried when Madame Keisha and two of the other girls who worked for her removed her mother's limp corpse from the stained sheets of the bed. Madame Keisha pulled Tamara aside after her mother's body had been taken away.

"Tamara, your mother has left us, child. It is a great loss to my business. But she did have you and you will garner a great price. The beautiful daughter of Lorraine, even more beautiful than she, and still pure. You will be my greatest profit." The heavily made-up woman spoke, her eyes visibly calculating the income that would come in with the price of Tamara's virginity. "I will auction you off to the highest bidder. The gentlemen will bid high, very high for your young beauty and unspoiled body."

Tamara said nothing. She was aware of the virgin auctions. She had no intention of having the filthy creatures who groaned naked over her mother do the same to her. That very night when the brothel was packed with customers and laughter, Tamara slipped out of the establishment when everyone was too busy to notice. Madame Kiesha never saw her again.

Tamara shook her head. That was a long time ago. She had survived. Sometimes by the very means she had run away from. Men seemed to desire her, wanted to possess her. Tamara just shrugged it off. They could have her body if she needed the money, but they would never possess her.

Eventually, years later, she met Carter, Adam and Todd. They treated her like one of them. For the first time in her life, she felt she belonged to a family. Others joined the group. Some left, some stayed. Although there were the few boys who felt they could have Tamara, she had never allowed it. Not until Oliver showed up, so handsome and charming. She never minded lying in his arms. In fact, she loved the way he touched and caressed her.

She glanced over at Jobeth and noticed her pallor.

"What do you have against me, Tamara?" Jobeth breathed heavily, the back of her hand pressed against her moist mouth.

"Nothin'." Tamara stiffly turned away. Guilt kept surfacing in her conscience. She turned the ham, which had begun to release a delicious aroma.

"Don't lie, Tamara. You don't like me. If you just got to know me, we could be friends."

It would be better for the two girls to be friends. When Jobeth's monthly started, she would like a girlfriend to confide in about womanly woes.

"We are living together. I just thought we might as well get along with each other instead of being at each other throats."

A cruel laugh escaped Tamara's lips. Her anger had returned. She placed her hands on her rounded hips and spread her legs apart.

"Hell, I don't need to like you." Her lips curved into a hateful grin. Black hair swept out behind her in defiance. Tamara was indeed an enchantress. One that Jobeth knew she would never be. Not that Jobeth was ugly. She had her own special qualities, but Tamara was a gorgeous creature.

"If yah want to know why I don't like yah, well, I'll tell yah. Yah nearly fainted when I swore. Yah think you're all high and mighty with your proper English. I bet yah even went to school." Tamara was wild. She had seen Jobeth's type before. Even though Jobeth was dressed worse than her, she knew her type: the type of girls who whispered and laughed about Tamara. The type of girls who called her names, names for people like her mother. Jobeth was like those girls and that was what attracted Oliver.

Jobeth was no whore's daughter.

"You don't belong with us! You ain't one of us! Go back wherever you came from!" The ham started to burn unattended, giving off a charcoal smell. Smoke swirled up from the fire, mingling with Jobeth's tears, blinding her vision.

"No!" She shrieked with all the force she had. Shawna and Tamara both jumped in union. Shawna dropped the dolls she was playing with and ran over to Jobeth, trembling like a leaf. Jobeth bent down and hugged her tight to her swollen breast. "I cannot. We can't ever go back. I am like you. I went to school when Mama and Pappy were alive. Yes, I liked it, but when they died and I went to live--" Jobeth stopped. Shawna was sobbing holding tightly to her waist. She took a deep breath and looked straight into Tamara's surprised face. "I have not been to school since my parents died. That was a lifetime ago. I was another person. Please try and like me. I want us to be friends. I am not high and mighty-- I am far from high and mighty. We can't leave. We just can't. And you will just have to live with that whether you want to or not."

Jobeth's back felt naked as she stretched herself straight. Tamara would not defeat her. She would never be defeated by anyone again.

She hugged Shawna defensively and began to whisper comforts into her ear. Shawna had become the little sister she never had. The little sister to replace the little brother she had lost. If only Tamara knew what had happened to them, to Jobeth. Maybe she would be more understanding.

Maybe Tamara wouldn't be so mean. Jobeth tightened her lips angrily. She would never tell anyone about the horrors of her recent past, especially Tamara.

Tamara looked at Shawna whimpering and clutching Jobeth around the neck. She was astonished by Jobeth's outburst and a little amused. Jobeth might have guts after all.

"Stop crying, Shawna." Tamara said softly. "I guess I can try to get along with your skinny old bones."

She began to turn the burning ham, avoiding the two clinging figures behind her.

"I guess it ain't your fault the way yah are. Just don't get all mushy on me. I just can't stand that."

"Thank you," Jobeth swelled, smiling comfortingly to Shawna.

— Chapter 6 —

The transformation in Shawna was amazing. The days at Mother Tomalina and Father James' quickly faded into an old nightmare. Children are astonishing in that respect, able to flourish after a terrible ordeal. She no longer clung to Jobeth's skirts. Shawna thrived in the love and affection showered on her by the group. She went everywhere with Tamara and the boys. She loved fishing with Carter or Todd for dinner, or collecting wood with Adam and Jonah. The boys would take her into town to the local store and buy her candy and ribbons for her well-kept hair. Shawna's small face would light up with joy as she sucked reverently on a candy piece. She was no longer a pale shell of a child, but a rosy-cheeked, bright-eyed girl.

Jonah loved to throw Shawna high into the air, catching her safely in his strong arms. Jobeth smiled as she sat in the tall green grass, watching as Shawna let out full belly giggles. Everyone loved her. She was an inspiration to them all. Maybe it was because so many of them had been alone when they were her age or maybe it was simply the need to protect the five year old from the hurt they had experienced. Whatever the reason, Shawna was the inspiration for the small group of children to fix up the old house. To make it a home.

"A child shouldn't live in a shack. Especially one about to fall in on itself," Alan announced one evening about two weeks after Jobeth and Shawna had come to live with them. He directed his speech to everyone as he stood up from the tattered dinner table. Secretly he wanted a nice home for both Shawna and Jobeth.

"I agree," Tamara said with her arms folded tightly across her chest. She pushed herself away from the table, leaving her half-eaten stew. Everyone turned to her, surprised. Tamara's affections toward Shawna continued to amaze the boys. This warm and tender spirit was not the girl they knew. "And she needs clothes. I could sew her some pretty dresses, if I had some material."

"We'll get some." Alan said, firmly placing his hands on the table while carefully avoiding splinters. "We will get some material so all the girls can have new dresses."

Tamara's head snapped up in response to Alan. Her eyes narrowed, but she said nothing. She had longed for new dresses for some time, but no one had seemed to notice.

"An' apples," Jonah smiled, bouncing Shawna on his lap. "I wants to plant an apple tree right in front, so's me and Shawna can pick an apple for breakfast every mornin'."

"Well, Jonah," Alan chuckled feeling proud of himself, "I'll leave the planting to you."

"That's just fine by me." Jonah smacked the palm of his hand on his free leg. "We'll have a great big ol' tree just drippin' with fat, juicy apples."

"Yummy!" squealed Shawna as she hugged Jonah around the neck. Her white face pressed firmly onto Jonah's dark one.

She looked like the porcelain doll Adam brought home one afternoon. It was a beautiful doll that resembled Shawna, with long, blonde hair as soft as silk and bright blue eyes that closed when you laid her down. She had a dress of royal blue velvet that billowed around her porcelain knees. The dress was trimmed in white lace and matching blue ribbons went in her hair. The doll must have cost a small fortune, which Jobeth knew Adam did not have. She could not help wondering how he had been able to get the beautiful doll for the child who had never owned anything so wonderful before in her life.

"I am naming her Donna," Shawna squealed kissing Adam squarely on his cheek.

Jobeth swallowed the lump growing in her throat. It did not matter how Adam got the doll. Shawna deserved it. She thanked him kindly, causing him to blush red.

They all seemed to shower the little girl with gifts. On another day Alan brought home an old, small trunk. He sanded it down and gave it to Shawna to keep her dolls and their clothes in. Shawna had never had anything so beautiful. She touched the smooth surface and began to cry softly.

"Thank you, Alan," the child said and hugged him around the waist tightly. Alan stiffened, unsure how to react to the child's affection. But her thin little arms felt so warm and trusting that he relaxed and hugged her back.

As the days past Tamara and Jobeth slowly became friends, if not close friends. True to his word, Alan bought material for Jobeth and Tamara. They made clothes together and Jobeth had to admit that Tamara was an excellent seamstress. She fashioned Shawna the prettiest dresses Jobeth had ever seen, with matching ribbons to go in her hair. Jobeth loved seeing Shawna prance around in her new frocks, ribbons bouncing in two long braids down her back Tamara would clap her hands with glee while Shawna would twirl around and around, her petticoats flying high.

Jobeth could not help loving her own dresses. She made high-collared, puff-sleeved dresses that were a little extravagant, but it had been so long since she had anything nice, let alone new, that she could not hold back from the latest styles.

Tamara's dresses were very low-cut and exposed most of her cleavage. Jobeth was mortified when Tamara returned home with a small bottle of red dye. She intended to dye her beautiful modest blue dress a brilliant red. Jobeth could not help wondering where Tamara had acquired her flamboyant taste.

All three girls blossomed in the glory of their new apparel. The boys had to admit that the women of the house looked too classy for a bunch of scallywag boys.

Jobeth liked living with the boys and Tamara. They were not her parents and Pauli, but they were the next best thing. She tried to disregard the time spent with the Johnstons. She did not want to destroy the small comforts she had escaped to.

It was a hot early morning and Jobeth and Tamara were busy washing their clothing in the lake when Jobeth's head began to swim dizzily. She stopped scrubbing Alan's shirt on a rock and wiped her sweaty brow with the back of her hand.

"Another spell?" Tamara asked off-handily, her hands never stopped scrubbing. She did not want to sound concerned.

Since the first day Tamara and Jobeth had locked horns, Tamara had witnessed the thin girl trying to hide her sickness more than once. Even though she hated to admit it, she had become fond of Jobeth. She was beginning to get worried. Jobeth was the only girlfriend she had ever had.

"Huh?" Jobeth had forgotten Tamara was beside her. "Oh, yes."

"Well, I think it's time for a doctor," Tamara said, casually banging Oliver's slacks across the rocks. "Damn soap, can never get this crap out of the clothes."

Jobeth smiled weakly. Tamara's cursing did not offend her any longer. She found Tamara's outbursts amusing.

"Here, give them to me." Jobeth reached for the pants and began wringing the soap out. "You can cook up a storm and you sew better than anyone I have ever seen, but you are the worst clothes washer in history, Tamara." Jobeth breathed trying to ignore the waves of dizziness.

"Well, we can't all be perfect," Tamara scowled, grabbing one of Shawna's soiled dresses from the basket of dirty clothes. She fingered the dress absently, stealing a quick glance at Jobeth. "You think I sew good?"

"Yes, the very best." Jobeth replied fighting back the wooziness. "You could be a seamstress."

"You don't look so good." Jobeth's skin had become colorless.

"Thanks. Remind me never to give you a compliment again." Jobeth wiped loose strands of her bun from her sweaty face.

"No, you look sick." Tamara continued as she dipped the dress into the cool water. Jobeth stopped her scrubbing and turned her head to see Shawna's pigtailed head bent over her dolls in the grass near by.

"Well, I have to admit I have not felt quite like myself lately," Jobeth confided, her eyes downcast. Her hands in her lap were wet and soapy and she began to rub them on her skirt to dry them.

"Yah know," Tamara tittered, slapping her hand on Jobeth's back, "if you weren't such a goody-two-shoes, I'd think you was in the family way."

Blood drained from Jobeth's face and she clutched the other girl's arm. Tamara drew back as she watched Jobeth's pale face turn an even ghastlier white.

"Jobeth, I was just foolin'." Tamara fretted. She grabbed a rag from the pile of clean clothes and damped it in the stream, placing it on Jobeth's fevered brow.

Jobeth looked at Tamara's fearful face. Her eyes rolled back into her head and everything went black.

"Jobeth! Jobeth!"

She could feel someone tapping her face, but Jobeth would not open her eyes.

Shawna, distracted by the commotion, put her dolls down and went over to the stream where Tamara was hovering over Jobeth.

"What is wrong with Jobeth?" Shawna asked, patting Tamara's shoulder. Fear began to crawl up Shawna's spine. Jobeth looked like she was sleeping, but the panic rising from Tamara reminded Shawna of Donna and how she had went to sleep and never woke up.

"Shawna, go get someone quick!" Tamara did not know what to do and she was as frightened as the platinum-haired child. Shawna stood frozen to the spot not moving, her eyes fixed on Jobeth's gray face.

In a panic, Tamara screamed, "Move it, quick!"
Shawna jumped into action and started scrambling up the hill to the house.
Jonah and Alan were outside testing the new steps they had just built.
Alan patted Jonah's shoulder proudly, "Very good, old boy, if I do say so myself."
"Not bad, not bad." Jonah replied, hooking his thumbs into his suspenders.
Running up the hill madly, Shawna spotted them.
"Alan . . . Jonah!" She heaved trying to catch her breath. They turned, surprised to see Shawna's flushed face.
Jonah bent to the exhausted girl. "Slow down, little one, what's the matter?"
"Jobeth . . ."
"What about her?" Alan jumped in, his heart starting to beat fast. He looked where Shawna had come from and could see nothing.
"At the lake . . . she is sleeping and won't get up," Shawna finally spit out bent over, trying to catch her breath.
Jonah gently took Shawna's hand in his large dark one. "You show us where she is, all right sweetheart? Yah done a good job so far, but yah gots to show us where Jobeth is." He glanced up at Alan, hoping he had been listening to him too. He was aware of Alan's feelings for Jobeth and did not want him to fly off the handle. Alan paid no attention to Jonah as he shifted from one leg to the other, impatiently.
Shawna, her breath coming back to her, pulled at Jonah's hand to lead them back to Jobeth.
The lake was only down a small hill behind the house and within moments they were beside Tamara and Jobeth, who was still unconscious. Alan rushed up to them and quickly scooped up Jobeth's frail body in his arms. She had gained some weight since she came to live with them, but she was still as light as a feather.
"Jobeth?" Alan whispered into her ear. Her head rested on his shoulder and he could feel her even breath against his cheek, warm and alive.
She stirred and let out a mumble.
"She's coming to." Alan called over his shoulder to the relief of the three standing there.
Alan began to soothe Jobeth with soft whispers, "Jobeth, it's Alan. Wake up."
Weak as a kitten, she lifted her head from his comforting shoulder. She squinted while trying to open her eyes against the bright sun.
"Alan?"
"Yes?" Alan's voice was husky and felt trapped in his throat.
"What happened?" Jobeth looked around her. The last thing she remembered was washing clothes with Tamara.
Tamara looked down at Jobeth's pale face, relieved she was alive. "Yah fainted. Never had anyone faint on account of my bad mouth."
Jobeth felt ridiculous. She looked up at Alan, abashed, and struggled to sit up.
."I am so sorry," she said, feebly trying to compose herself.
"Are you all right?" Alan's voice was full of emotion. The smell of Jobeth's hair, crisp and clean like the lake, lingered in his nostrils. He wanted to hold her light-brown locks up to his nose and inhale deeply. His heart ached for his sweet

Jobeth. He was desolate. If anything happened to her, he wouldn't know what to do.

Jobeth gazed into Alan's strange green eyes; genuine concern for her welfare flooded through him so strongly she felt overwhelmed and ashamed.

"I am fine," she murmured, avoiding those feline eyes. She tried to stand up, feeling undeserving of Alan's affection. She didn't deserve anyone's care. Not with the realization of what was wrong with her. It all made sense. Her recurring sickness and dizziness. Her missed monthlies. How long had it been since she had menstruated? At least three months. Her waist had been slowly disappearing.

How could she not know? Mama had explained what happened to a woman when she was to become a mother. Why had Jobeth not known?

Tamara had guessed, but dismissed the very notion because she believed Jobeth to be pure. Tamara was wrong about her.

"Let's bring our sick girl to the house," Jonah said, hovering behind Alan like a mother hen.

Alan nodded and held on firmly to Jobeth's shaking arms.

"No. I am able to finish my chores. Let me go please." She pulled away abruptly. Alan flinched aware of how close he was to her.

"Jobeth, I can do the wash fine by myself. I was doin' it alone for a long time," Tamara said, afraid Jobeth would faint again.

Jobeth stood up straight, her legs feeling wobbly. She walked over to Shawna and gave her a reassuring pat on the head.

"I am fine. It was just the heat," Jobeth said, not facing the worried people in front of her. "I refuse to go and lie down when there is work to be done. Quit worrying about me and get back to your own chores." She walked over to the laundry, grabbed the garment she had been cleaning before she fainted and continued where she left off, not daring to look at the open-mouthed group behind her.

Tamara looked to Jobeth in disbelief. She shrugged her shoulders at Alan and Jonah, who stood bewildered.

"You heard her, back to work," Tamara squawked, shooing the two baffled boys away. Not knowing what to do or how to protest, they reluctantly turned around and began to ascend the hill.

Tamara went back to smacking clothes on the rocks, glancing every few minutes back at Jobeth.

"Stop mothering over me, Tamara," Jobeth said, without pausing for a break.

Shawna, satisfied that Jobeth was all right, went back to her dolls. She gently sat down on her quilt littered with porcelain babies and was instantly lost in her make-believe land once again.

Tamara bent her head down low and sneaked a peek out of the corner of her eye.

"I ain't motherin' no one."

"Humph, could have fooled me," Jobeth sniffed, pushing a strand of hair behind her ear. She attacked the garment she was washing with fervor.

Tamara raised her eyebrow, but pretended not to hear as she too went about her duties.

Both girls continued to work in silence.

Jobeth felt Tamara's eyes burning into her back. Guilt flooded her entire body. The heat of her eyes burned straight to Jobeth's flat belly. It felt hot and heavy. Could everyone tell she was with child? She thought of Alan's round face full of concern. Jobeth banged the piece of clothing harder onto to the rock, trying to beat out the frustration she felt. A savage scream filled her mind, causing her to slump over, exhausted. She stared down at the beaten shirt, unable to swallow this new discovery. She did not want to leave the people she had come to love in the last two months. She did not want to take Shawna from the only family she had ever known. Jobeth pressed her fingers to her head and squeezed; she could see no other alternative.

Jobeth watched as Shawna continued playing with her dolls, unaware of the new situation thrust upon her charge. Her cheeks radiated color and health. Her tiny voice tinkled on the wind with the innocence of childhood naivety. Was it fair to remove the child from her new home?

Jobeth's throat tightened. She could not take Shawna when she left. She Couldn't steal her childhood away again. Pain tore at her heart and her chest felt as though it would cave in. Life would be unbearable without little Shawna.

A tear trickled down her face and Jobeth wiped it away unconsciously. She would never be happy again. She looked to the sky. It was a beautiful day. Her eyes went longingly to the hill and the house she now called home. She squinted, shielding her vision with her hand.

A lone figure was running towards them. Jobeth stood up and looked closer.

It was Jonah with a look of dread on his face.

He stumbled to the ground and jumped up, brushing the dust off of himself. Jonah was yelling something, but Jobeth could not understand what he was trying to say. She turned to Tamara, who had stood up, confused.

"What the hell is wrong with him?"

"The sheriff! The sheriff! They's after us! They's after us!" Jonah yelled, coming closer.

Tamara started walking towards Jonah, but stopped in her tracks upon hearing the words come out of his mouth. Jonah finally reached them, panting as he bent over, supporting himself on Tamara's shoulder. She grabbed him under the arm to keep him from falling onto his face.

"Jonah, what are you talking about?" Jobeth asked, lifting Shawna up. The child had run to her when Jonah ran down the hill.

"The sheriff . . ." Jonah panted. "They done found us out." He looked as though someone had poured a bucket of ice-cold water on his head "Ole man Willard caught us stealin' at the store today. Todd and Oliver gots away from him, but he done got the sheriff after us." He stopped and looked at Tamara. His friendly ginger eyes were wide with fear. "We gotta split." Jonah began to shiver.

Tamara placed her arm around him protectively. "And yah knows what'll happen to me," he said, wide-eyed. Tamara frowned. "I am hung. Ol' man Willard said it before. And I bet yah I will! I will!"

"Damn it to hell," Tamara's old voice boomed. Whimpering sounds escaped Jonah's pink lips. "I don't want Jonah to hang, Jobeth," Shawna crushed her pale fist into her eyes.

Jobeth felt helpless. She did not want Jonah to hang either. Feeling as though the wind were let out of her sails, She began to gather the clothes up into a heap.

Everything was moving fast. Her mind whirled trying to absorb all the new information flooding it.

"Don't just stand there like you don't have a brain in yah head, move Jobeth! Move!" Tamara grabbed the damp clothes clutched tightly in Jobeth's arms. "Get Shawna's dolls and stuff into her trunk and get to the house!"

Relieved, Jobeth jumped into action

Anxious faces turned to the lone figure standing in the kitchen. Light filtered through the windows giving Adam an ominous glow.

"Alright," he said calmly, "Here's what we'll do. The sheriff will be looking for a large group of us. We would be caught like a coyote in a chicken coop if we were all together."

Jobeth felt as though she were being torn apart. All her wrenching over what to do about her pregnancy was for nothing. She was going to have to leave her new family anyway. Grief filled her heart and soul as she fought back the urge to cry. All their belongings were quickly packed and tied to their backs in makeshift packs. It had taken only minutes to get their meager belongings together.

"We will have to split up," Adam finally revealed. He twisted his cap in his hands, nervously. "Todd, Carter and I will go together. Tamara and Oliver will be together and Alan, Jonah, Jobeth and Shawna will be together - nobody will be alone. When it's possible, we'll get together again."

"Where?" yelled Tamara, standing beside Oliver and looked as though she might cry. Oliver looked miserable as he placed a hand on her shoulder in comfort.

"Hell, Tamara, I don't know," Adam choked, running his hand through his sandy blond hair.

"What yah really mean is we isn't ever gonna see each other again." Tamara cried. Huge tears fell freely from her ebony eyes.

"Yes, we will," Adam stammered, uncertain if he spoke the truth. He had never seen Tamara cry or look so vulnerable. The effect was quite unsettling and he could not look at the beautiful, red-eyed girl without wanting to cry too. For the first time Tamara looked like an angel sent straight from heaven with all the sorrows of the world on her feathered shoulders. "All I know is we have to. God help us. But we can't be worrying about that now. We gotta get outta here fast." He went and stood beside Carter who was staring at the ground, kicking dirt angrily with the toe of his boot.

Oliver encircled Tamara in his arms as she willingly succumbed, sobbing hard.

"We're gonna be alright, Tamara," he whispered, brushing his hand through her silky curls. "I'll take care of yah. Don't worry."

Tamara sobbed and hugged Oliver closer.

"Everything's gonna be all right," he said without conviction as he saw the look of despair in his fellow friends' faces. It was written just as plainly on their faces as if it had been printed in the newspaper. The likelihood of them ever seeing each other again was doubtful.

Jobeth shifted the weight of her sack. It was slightly heavier than when she had arrived three months earlier with only the clothing on her back. She shivered and squeezed Shawna's hand. Would she ever see her new friends again? At least she had Alan and Jonah with her this time. She would not be alone with the responsibilities. The thought of the baby she was carrying flashed through her mind like a hurricane. She quickly erased it. For the moment there were more important things to worry about.

They ran as fast as they could from the others who had, just a short time ago, been part of them. The three groups separated and went in three different directions. Jobeth turned towards the direction Tamara and Oliver had gone.

Their hands were clasped together, Tamara's jet black hair streamed out behind them. The image quickly faded. Soon all she could see were two black dots.

Why do I always lose the people I love? Jobeth screamed in her head. For she felt love for the people she had just left. The wind ripped viciously at her face, blowing away the tears as they started to fall.

Alan carried Shawna in his arms. Her little legs clutched tightly to his waist. She wondered how he could run with Shawna's full weight burdening him.

He looked over at Jobeth who was nestled safely between Jonah and himself.

He told Adam and Carter that he wanted Jobeth, Shawna and Jonah with him. Adam had not liked the idea of the four of them together. It would have been more reasonable for Jonah to go with Oliver and Tamara.

"No." Alan had said strongly, taking no other answer. "He comes with me and so do Jobeth and Shawna."

Adam nodded giving in to Alan. There was no time to argue. The sheriff would be there at any moment and they needed to get away. Sheriff Duncan Migel was a cruel man who had been waiting for just this moment to get Adam and his crew behind bars. Adam shivered. They needed to get out of there fast.

"All right, Alan, he goes with you. But be careful--you guys are gonna look like Poppies in a field of daisies."

"I'll take that chance." Alan replied, his face stone cold.

They were running so fast, Jobeth feared she would fall behind. Jonah firmly grabbed hold of her arm, helping her keep pace. She smiled at him and was thankful as they continued on.

When dusk came, they stumbled into a field and fell asleep exhausted. Jobeth woke to the sun shining in her face. For a moment she was confused as to where she was. Then she saw the frosted yellow grass around her. She sat up and faced Jonah. He was squatting a short distance from Jobeth, his elbows resting on his knees and his index finger was playing with his front teeth.

Rubbing the remainder of sleep out of her eyes, she stood up feeling as though her legs would give out from under her.

"Jonah," she said, her legs crying out in pain from the journey the day before.

"Jobeth," he said through a weak smile. He stood up and came over toward her, gently taking her arm. "Legs a little wobbly from running?"

"It would seem that way." Jobeth grabbed his helpful hand. Wincing, she pressed her free hand to her spine.

"Yah better try and walk it off because as soon as Alan comes back, we will be heading out again."

"Where is he?" Jobeth asked while walking in circles with Jonah. The pain in her legs was slowly turning into a dull throb.

"He took Shawna out with him to hunt up some food." Jonah searched the clouded sky with his eyes.

"Are you all right Jonah?"

"Oh yah," Jonah grinned, "I just worried about the others. They's like my family is all. I hates to lose more family."

Jobeth nodded. She understood more than he knew.

"They will be all right, Jonah."

"Yah, I guess you's right." They stood silently side-by-side, Jonah holding Jobeth's arm protectively. Neither spoke for a long time.

Alan and Shawna found them still standing in the same position. Shawna was giggling about the rabbit they caught together. When they came upon Jobeth and Jonah, they stopped for a moment, afraid to break the peace emanating from the two stone figures. Alan coughed, embarrassed, and sat down on the ground by the dead fire. He removed his hunting knife and began to gut the rabbit.

"What's the problem?" he asked trying to sound casual.

"Ah, nothin'," Jonah said, breaking the silence. He bent down and grabbed a burlap sack beside the bundle of belongings and removed some potatoes. The food had been divided into three portions before they had left the others.

"Let's start a fire for that delicious rabbit you caught," Jobeth said cheerfully to Shawna.

Shawna jumped up. Tiny wood chips clung to her dress and she absently brushed them off as she skipped towards Jobeth. Alan watched out of the corner of his eye as Jobeth and Shawna disappeared into the tall grass.

"Winter is just about here," Alan said as he peeled the soft fur from the rabbit. He would keep the fur and make Shawna some mittens.

Jonah nodded, not saying a word. He sensed Alan had something on his mind he needed to get off.

"Jobeth and Shawna need a home. A real home." Alan continued, never pausing in his butchering, "I have to give them that."

"You will, you will." Jonah agreed while starting to peel potatoes.

"I have to," he said firmly, looking off into the horizon, lost in his own thoughts. After a quick breakfast they packed up the remainder of their food and started on their way again—this time walking. They were going farther from the people they loved and further into an uncertain future.

Jobeth wondered about the rest of her new family.

This continued to be in her thoughts as the four traveled on. Each time she awoke to the sun shining in her face, she wondered about them. Each time she fell asleep under the vast black sky with its many eyes glaring down at her, she wondered where the others were, and if she would ever see them again.

Wild Tamara, so angry and untamed. Oliver with his piercing blue eyes and irresistible charm. Shy Todd who barely said a word but always had a special pocket full of treats for a little five-year-old girl. Carter, the shadow of his best friend, Adam. And Adam, the brave leader of them all.

Were they all right?

Did they sleep well last evening, alone for the first time in who knew how long? Were they as scared as she? It was something she knew she would always worry about and she wished that they were all safe and back together at the old abandoned house they had made home.

— Chapter 7 —

"We better find shelter," Alan said to Jobeth, who stood beside him. She was exhausted and chilled to the bone. A month of traveling had taken a toll on her already frail body. All that day she had been experiencing sharp pains in her small, rounded belly. Instinctively she rested the palm of her hand on her growing mound, feeling the quickening movements of the child growing inside her.

Alan watched Jobeth closely. He noticed that Jobeth seemed to be getting thicker around her middle, but could not understand why. Their diet was meager.

They had all lost weight while traveling on the road. Jobeth's face and arms were rail thin and she had a gaunt look to her, like an animal with parasites. He was concerned for the frail girl. She seemed to always be in a great deal of discomfort. He wondered if she had gotten worms from one of their too-hurriedly cooked meals. He had seen sick kittens with gaunt frames, little bellies distended from parasitic infections, and Jobeth's appearance reminded him of them. He worried and wished he knew what to do.

"Are you all right, Jobeth?"

"What?" She asked. She had forgotten that Alan was beside her. "Oh, I'm fine," she lied, feeling another sharp pain. She wrapped her shawl around her shoulders tightly. The days were getting increasingly colder and she could smell snow on the wind.

"Are you sure?" Alan whispered, placing his hand on the middle of Jobeth's back.

Jobeth smiled up at Alan's worried face. "Yes, Alan. Let's find some shelter. I smell snow coming."

Alan turned toward the town up ahead and started to walk with her. Jonah and Shawna followed closely behind. He took a deep breath of crisp air and exhaled. Jobeth was right. There was a distinct smell of snow in the air.

It wasn't until evening when they found a small shack on the outskirts of town. It was old and rotted and by the next year it would probably only be a termite-infested wood heap, but to the four weary wanderers, it was home for the night.

Jonah opened the door. They could hear the scurry of tiny animals running across the floorboards. He shook his head. "Lots of cleanin' needs to be done here."

Swiping cobwebs away from her face, Jobeth said, "That is an understatement."

She followed Jonah into the one-room shack.

Alan popped his head in after Jobeth was safely inside. Shawna lay fast asleep in his arms. Anger filled him. He had failed once again.

"The girls can't sleep here," Alan said, voicing his thoughts. He would not budge inside the door. Jobeth and Jonah turned to face him in disbelief. They were cold, hungry and exhausted. Jonah began to stutter, unable to believe what Alan said.

"But Alan, we can't find nothin' else." The weather outside was getting colder and a light flurry had begun. They needed to start a fire and get the chill out of their bones. He looked over at Jobeth whose hand was on her tiny ball of a stomach. His brow wrinkled with concern. Jonah knew what Alan did not.

He knew Jobeth was pregnant and was in serious pain.

After Jonah's father died, he had stayed with a neighboring black family for a while, helping the husband on the farm. When his wife was only half way through her pregnancy, she had already experienced problems. The midwife told her she could not do her chores on the farm until the baby was born. Jonah had been looking for work in the town when he came across Mr. Jackson. They worked out an arrangement. Jonah would help work the farm for food and shelter until Mrs. Jackson had the baby and was again strong enough to work.

It had been good at the Jackson farm and Jonah liked the family very much.

He watched Mrs. Jackson with a belly just like Jobeth's grow into a larger one, until the day came when she had her son. He knew the symptoms Jobeth was having. They were the symptoms Mrs. Jackson had experienced. He also knew that her pains were not good and she needed to rest.

He had left the Jackson's shortly after the baby was born. They were sorry that he could not stay but they were poor and could not afford an extra mouth to feed. Jonah understood and was grateful for their kindness. He was again alone, left to fend for himself.

Alan glanced at Jonah's pleading look and could not help noticing how the bigger boy looked anxiously at Jobeth.

"Alan, I have slept in worse places than this," Jobeth sighed, rubbing the ache in her belly. She was feeling a little resentful toward Alan. Did he think she was a piece of glass so easily broken? If he only knew the predicament she was in, he would not be so worried where she slept. Jobeth was not kidding herself any longer. She was going to have a baby and she could not hide it much longer.

"Besides, it has started to snow. Where do you think we should sleep in such weather?" she asked a little crossly. She plunked herself down onto the filthy floor. Fluffy cobweb like balls few up into the air and then fell gently back down, landing on Jobeth's skirts.

Alan could not answer. He did not know where they should sleep.

Reluctantly, he walked into the shack, sensing Jobeth's hostility.

"We will just put our blankets on the floor and use our sweaters to keep warm," Jobeth said, very much needing to lie down. The child growing inside her did a somersault, causing her to let out a gasp. It was the first solid movement she had felt, instead of the fluttery feelings she had recently experienced.

Alan's eyes darted to Jobeth. His face turned red with embarrassment. She was angry at his stupidity. She would never think of him as a good provider, a man worthy of her and her sister, Downcast, he handed over the sleeping Shawna to Jonah and began preparing the bedding for the night.

Jobeth watched Alan's forlorn look and wondered if he could tell that she had just felt her child move inside her. Blushing deeply, she busied herself, helping Alan make their beds. She did not notice Jonah's eyes following her every move nor how his brow creased with fear for her and her baby.

I wonder where the Pa is? Jonah thought as he sat down cradling Shawna in his large arms. He didn't remember Jobeth mentioning being married. Then again, he knew you did not have to be married to have a baby.

The thought of Jobeth having a baby out of wedlock did not seem likely to Jonah. She was too well bred and moralistic. Maybe the reason she ran off was because she married the wrong man? Maybe he was mean and beat her? Jonah had heard of women doing that when their husbands were nasty. He knew her parents had been killed, but that was it. She didn't like to talk about life before she met Alan and him. If she were married to a cruel man, she would have taken Shawna and herself away to safety. Jonah could understand. Jobeth probably didn't know she was with child then, but she must know by now. He could not understand why she was keeping her condition a secret. He shrugged his shoulders and placed Shawna down on the blankets. Whatever Jobeth's reasons were for not telling them about the baby, she would not be able to keep the secret much longer. With that, Jonah lay down beside Shawna and went to sleep.

Alan awoke early the next morning. Jobeth and Jonah were already up and starting the daily routine of getting breakfast ready with whatever meager remains they had left from the day before. He jumped out of his blankets quickly.

"Going to check out the town. See if we can stick around a bit or if we need to keep going." Alan ran a hand through his brown hair and swiftly opened the door to leave.

Outside, the world was gray with a light blanket of snow covering everything the eye could see. Alan shivered in his flimsy sweater. His breath streamed out in front of him.

He hoped that he could find a job and make some kind of living. If he did find a job, he could build Jobeth a pretty house, like the ones he had seen other people living in. He never had desires before to change the way he existed. He always liked the adventure of moving from one town to the other. But, since meeting Jobeth, things had changed. He wanted her to have a real home that was always warm and cozy, and nice clothes she would never be ashamed of. He wanted Jobeth never to worry where they would sleep next. Shawna was a bright girl; a girl Alan wanted to see in school, laughing with classmates. If they kept up like this, before long, Shawna would end up a street-rat and miss out on being a normal child. He didn't want that for Shawna—for her to be hard from living too long on the streets. He wanted her sweet and kind as she was now.

He smiled, picturing Jobeth cooking him dinner in their home. She would smile lovingly when he and Shawna returned from work and school, both starving.

Jonah would greet him at the door telling Alan about their vegetable garden and how their cow had just calved. Jonah loved working around the house doing farm work. He would run the farm, while Alan worked in town. They would have everything they needed. At night they would all sit down together around their own dinner table and eat the feast Jobeth made. The kitchen would be warm and smell of home cooking. It was a beautiful dream. A dream he felt he had to make happen.

Alan pulled his sweater tighter around himself, trying to prevent the cold from cutting through him. He began to brood as he walked closer to town.

What if this was the same as the last town?

Alan opened the door of the variety store and instantly felt the heat penetrate his cold bones.

Behind the counter a bored, middle-aged woman looked up from a small list in front of her.

"Can I help you?" The store was packed with jam preserves and fresh vegetables and fruit. Farming material lined almost every wall.

"Yah... er...I mean, yes," Alan said, removing his cap clumsily. He cleared his throat and walked toward the leery lady.

Her fingers began rapping on the wooden counter, causing Alan to become nervous.

"You ain't from these parts." She gave Alan the once-over. He was not an ugly boy, but he had a peculiar look. She was a stern Christian who distrusted anything peculiar. His clothes looked poor and unkempt as if he had been sleeping in them, but that was not uncommon in these parts. Hygiene was not top of the list in importance. She placed her hands on her plump hips and glared into Alan's green feline eyes.

Trying not to show his nervousness, Alan remembered how Jobeth would answer this crotchety old lady. He did not want to sound ignorant.

"No, Ma'am, I am not."

"Well. What can I do yah for?" she asked, folding her arms across her large breasts. Alan stared at the brooch the woman wore under her high collar. It was a pale pink oval with a silhouette of a lady in the center. It was pretty and the type of broach that Jobeth should be wearing. He straightened his shoulders, summoning his courage.

"I was wondering if there are any jobs around here."

"Nope," the woman puckered, "besides we don't hire strangers around here."

"Oh," Alan blushed once again defeated, "then I will be picking up some supplies."

"Very well. What do yah need?" the woman asked quickly, coming around the counter. "And we don't give credit to strangers neither."

"No, Ma'am. I have money," Alan said sadly, sure he had some money but it was quickly running out.

He paid for his groceries, throwing a couple of sticks of candy in for the others and collected his bags.

Standing back out in the cold holding his bag of groceries limply in his arms, Alan felt condemned. He stood glancing around at the small, growing town. Everywhere he looked a building was in construction. Hastily he began to walk toward the sheriff's building in hopes that maybe he could give him some guidance about a job. People passed by him and he nodded politely as they looked at him oddly. One day, he thought, one day, I will be a respected man in town, one Jobeth would be proud to be seen with.

"Hello Mr. and Mrs. Benson, fine day is it not? Hope today is seeing you well," they would say in passing. Alan would nod and Jobeth would smile demurely.

He felt himself warming at the thought of Jobeth being his wife. Just then, he noticed that he had reached the wooden door of the sheriff's building. There were brown sheets of papers pasted to the unfinished wall. Glancing at them, Alan's mouth dropped opened.

The brown papers were "Wanted" posters. On one there was a face sketched of his likeness. There was one of Jonah, Adam, Carter, Todd, Oliver and Tamara. There was even a sketch of Shawna. The only face not sketched was Jobeth's. Alan figured this was because she had never ventured into the town they had left. He swiftly turned on his heels and started back to the small shack. Winter or no winter, they would have to leave. It was not safe in this town.

Jobeth stood beside the makeshift fire Jonah had built in the corner of the shack. She was making a stew from the remains of a squirrel Jonah had caught the day before. She cut up carrots and potatoes, the last of their supplies, and plopped them into the simmering brew.

Jonah and Shawna were playing a silly game about naming objects of certain colors. They sat on the grimy wooden floor laughing and playing as Jobeth stirred their supper, enjoying the sounds of their voices tinkling in the air.

Alan stood outside holding onto the door handle, wondering how he was going to break the news to the group inside. He took a deep breath and barged inside--regardless of how they felt, they couldn't stay. All three inside stopped what they were doing to look anxiously at Alan's distraught face.

Jonah stood up and took the bag of food Alan clutched in his arms.

"What's wrong? Yah, I mean, you, look like you have seen a ghost," Jonah corrected himself. They were all trying to speak better with the help of Jobeth.

"They have posters of us," he said, uncontrollably running his hands through his straight brown hair. Jobeth felt a queer feeling pass through her as she watched the gestures Alan made. Heat began to rise in her face, making her look flushed. Alan noticed and was mortified.

"I am sorry Jo-Beth. I sometimes forget I am in the presence of a lady," He was flustered and ashamed. The feeling of helplessness enveloped him. Why couldn't he just get it right for once? "Not that I could forget you are a lady," he stammered. "It's just that they even have a drawing of Shawna."

Jobeth's head bobbed up and her mouth dropped open. Her neck would suffer from having wrenched it so quickly.

Shawna skirted over to Jobeth and gave her a frightened look. Bending down to her level, Jobeth put a reassuring arm around her small shoulders. Feeling safe in Jobeth's embrace, Shawna's shivering subsided a little.

"But she is only a baby," Jobeth stormed, suddenly very angry. She held Shawna's cornflower head close to her chest.

"Well, it seems she was spotted in the store with one of us. The rest I'm sure you can figure out," Alan said, previous conversation forgotten.

"No," a soft, spooked voice said out of nowhere. Jobeth turned to Jonah. He was staring vacant eyed, down at the dirty floor, his full lips quivering and mouthing the word no.

"No," he repeated, louder, in a strange voice far away.

"Jonah," Alan said calmly going over to stand beside the gentle giant. "We are going to be all right."

"No, we ain't," Jonah argued, his gaze fixed to the floor. "They are after us and they gonna hang me till my eyes bulge out of my head, that's what ol' man Wilson said and he weren't foolin'."

Jobeth, unable to help herself, pulled away from Shawna's embrace and went to Jonah.

"Jonah," she begged. But he wouldn't listen. He began to bounce around mumbling about hangings. She tried to grip his shoulders, but he slipped through her hands. Alan and Shawna stood back from the scene wide-eyed, mouths agape.

"Then all the white folks watching are gonna laugh and sing, 'nigra's dead, hung dead!'" Jonah was becoming hysterical. Jobeth did not know what to do.

Before she realized it, she had reached out the palm of her hand and slapped Jonah's wet face with all her might. Startled, she swiftly withdrew her hand as quickly as she had struck and covered her mouth.

Jonah stopped bouncing on his huge feet. Large tears slid down his reddened cheek.

"I am so sorry, Jonah," Jobeth sobbed, disgusted with herself. "I didn't know what else to do."

Helpless, Alan stared in disbelief, protectively shielding a weeping Shawna.

Jobeth watched as Jonah placed a shaking hand on her shoulder. She looked into his distorted face, his lips still trembling. Tears fell freely down Jobeth's face as she reached out to touch Jonah's swollen cheek. His dark hand cupped her pale one. Slowly, Jobeth's hand encircled his neck as she pulled his woolly head to her. Willingly he went to her, wrapping his arms around her thickening waist like a child.

"It's going to be all right, Jonah," Jobeth cried, cradling his curly head in her arms. "We won't let anyone harm you." Jonah felt Jobeth's baby kick him through her garments.

"How?" he asked, pulling away from her comforting grip. He grabbed her hands in his. His eyes grew large with frustration. "How can you do that? You ain't black. Yah don't know how it feels. Yah don't know and yah never will know how it feels to have folks hate yah because your skin is a darker color than theirs."

She knew he was right and wished she could give him the answers he wanted.

Feeling helpless and weak, Jonah released Jobeth's hands and let them fall to her side. He turned his back to walk away as Jobeth looked beseechingly after him. He slowly rotated around to her.

"Yah know, Jobeth, I hate being black."

"Don't ever say that!"

Jobeth and Jonah both leapt into the air, startled. Alan, who had been silent through the whole episode, now stood solidly in front of them. His face was filled with a rage neither of them had ever seen.

"Don't ever say that again, do you hear me, Jonah?" Alan waved his finger in the larger boy's face, surprising both Jonah and Jobeth. "Don't you know anything?" Alan said, trying to calm himself. He had not meant to fly off the handle as he had. "They are all just threatened by you. They don't understand the difference between you and them and it scares them. It makes them question themselves. It makes you different," Alan said, full of emotion. He put his arm around Jonah's massive shoulder, having to step on tiptoe to do so.

"And those no-good, no-accounts know it and prey on it. Don't ever be ashamed of who you are. Be proud of yourself, because you ain't ever going to be anyone else." Jonah looked at Alan and rubbed his swollen bronze eyes with the back of his hand.

Jobeth watched passively as Jonah threw himself into Alan's arms and hugged him tightly. Shawna tiptoed over to the two hugging boys, her tiny hands twisting and turning in front of her. She reached up to Jonah and pulled his shirt hanging from his pants.

"I love you just the way you are, Jonah, and I think yah skin is pretty," she said with all the innocent wisdom of a five year old. Jobeth swelled ready to burst open with emotion. Out of the mouths of babes comes the honest truth.

Jonah bent down and picked Shawna up in his arms, nestling his head into her tiny shoulder. She looked like a porcelain doll in his large embrace. He breathed deeply of her innocence, kissing the nape of her white neck.

The child stung his aching heart. He had let her down by showing his fear when he had promised to protect her when she cried in the night.

"Oh, little girl, I think Jonah let yah down. I luv yah too much to do it again. Jonah's not gonna let himself get all crazy no more."

"Good," Shawna said, pressing her warm cheek to his.

"Guess I scared yah, huh?" he asked taking a deep cleansing breath. He felt Shawna's soft cheek go up and down.

"Won't do it again."

"Promise?"

"I promise." Jonah chuckled feeling a little like his old self. "Ol' Jonah has a time of it some days, running off at the mouth like a fool. But we all act a little touched sometimes."

They ate the stew in silence and just as quietly left with the sun falling behind horizon. Fortunately, the morning snow had melted and the evening air warmed a little. The three eldest felt leery of the changed weather. They knew it was only a matter of time before winter would finally make a permanent appearance. They needed to find winter shelter before the cold settled in or they would not survive.

They trudged on in weather that became harder and harder to bear, sleeping in whatever shelter they could find: abandoned sheds, overturned wagons, caves and once two large boulders with a blanket as a roof. The weather was beginning to show its affect on them, Jobeth in particular.

As much as she tried to ignore her pregnancy, at nearly six months along she could no longer deny her condition.

At night, when she thought everyone was sleeping, she let the waist out of her dresses. Her numb fingers worked by firelight, diligently creating a dress that hid her growing frame.

She tried not to think of her pregnancy often. If she did, which usually happened when she felt the child move inside her, she became panicked and guilt-ridden.

As Jobeth's waist grew, her strength continued to wane. Her slender face had begun to look pinched. Her eyes were framed with dark circles and her arms and legs had wasted away to thin sticks. Her body constantly ached from the cold and traveling; she suffered an almost constant pain in her abdomen. She knew the baby was in danger but refused to think of the outcome. It was all too much to think of and stay sane.

They finally came to another city several weeks after leaving the last. This one was smaller--just starting to develop. Small wooden buildings littered the landscape, not yet completely digested with homes and business. This was a good sign. The smaller the town, the better chance that news of distant cities had not reached it.

Upon seeing the town ahead of them, Alan felt like crying out in relief. He was very worried about Jobeth and her deteriorating appearance. She needed to see a doctor and she needed a warm place where she could heal and feel better.

He still didn't realize that she was pregnant. She had done herself justice with her dresses. Covered in layers of clothing as they all were, it was hard to see her belly increasing in size. Wearing what they owned to keep warm, their blankets wrapped around them for shelter from the cold, it was almost impossible to tell she was with child.

Jonah knew, though. He had watched quietly from his sleeping area while Jobeth squinted by the fire fixing her garments. He figured out that she did not want anyone to know of her condition and started to wonder if Jobeth cared to have the child at all. What were her secrets?

Jonah only hoped that they would soon come to a town, or else he was afraid neither Jobeth nor her unborn child would make it. After searching for an hour, they found an abandoned house with only minor damage caused by neglect. They entered the house and slept where they fell, all too exhausted to bother with a fire or removing their layers of clothing.

Jobeth slept late the next morning and when she awoke Alan had already left for town.

She yawned, giving a fleeting look to Jonah and Shawna who sat on the floor talking in whispers. Not wanting to disturb her, they had been quiet knowing she needed her rest.

"He's gone to look for work," Jonah said, noticing that Jobeth looked a little better from her long sleep. "Gonna be no more stealing around here. We gonna live like good folks and give Shawna a real home." Jonah nodded his head and gave the child one of his famous smiles full of teeth.

"We might actually stay?" Jobeth stretched, her body crying out in pain.

Jonah nodded again, not looking at Jobeth. He wanted to tell her he knew about the baby, but he did not know how to go about it. Every time he looked at her, he could not keep his eyes from resting on her small, round belly.

"Alan says we stay for the winter whether he finds work or not. We ain't runnin' no more this winter."

Jobeth sighed with relief and lay back down exhausted, and instantly fell fast asleep.

"Well, Shawna, I guess we should clean up around here. It looks like we gonna be here for awhile." He stood up and began to tidy things, while Shawna shadowed him and Jobeth slept.

Later in the day, Jobeth, feeling a little better, turned a rabbit Jonah and Shawna had recently caught over a fresh fire. She listened mutely as Shawna bragged about catching the rabbit when Alan came into the clean room.

Jobeth brightened when he entered. She fluffed up her skirt unconsciously. She had begun to worry about him. He had been gone a long time.

Shawna ran to Alan and jumped into his arms. The reserved phantom child she had once been at Mother Tomalina and Father James' had completely disappeared. Alan, Jonah and Jobeth were her family now, fading the memories of her early life.

"Hello!" Alan said, Shawna beaming in his arms. Jobeth noticed Alan slipping a piece of candy into the child's small hand. Not putting Shawna down, he placed his hat on an old chair. A grim expression contorted his face as he turned to Jobeth and Jonah.

"What is wrong?" Jonah asked, fear pinching his own features.

"Nothing. It's just..." He paused for effect and thought about his trip to town.

The town was small but was beginning to build up. It would take years before it became very populated. Competition for work was little. Alan had traipsed up to the one and only carpentry building in the place and was instantly greeted with a friendly handshake and a job offer.

Beaming, he could not keep his good news to himself any longer.

"I got a job in town at the mill and this house is ours." He swung Shawna into the air, making her giggle uncontrollably, then ran over to Jobeth and planted a kiss firmly on her cheek, Shawna still in his protective arms. He then went to Jonah and proceeded to play fight, Shawna now riding on his back. All of them hooting and laughing loudly. The air was filled with excitement and happiness.

Jobeth stood by the pot, smiling and holding the side of her cheek.

Alan kissed her.

— Chapter 8 —

Alan woke the next morning with a hop in his step and a whistle on his lips. He had done it--he could now give Jobeth the life she deserved! He washed his face in a warm pot of water Jobeth had heated for him. Out of the corner of his eye, he noticed her narrow back and grimaced. She was so very thin. But still, he thought, she was very well groomed with her hair piled up in the latest twist.

"Here you go," Jobeth smiled, handing Alan his lunch wrapped up in a burlap bag. They had been using it to carry their food in when they had been on the road. "It's leftovers from last night."

"Thanks," Alan said, drying his face with an old towel.

Jobeth stood uncomfortably before him, trying not to meet his gaze. She cleared her throat and started busying herself by tidying up the main room.

There was a smaller room off to the side where Shawna and Jonah slept on the floor in blankets. Above was a loft the length of the house.

"Are you nervous?" Jobeth asked while dusting the only chair in the room with a rag. She couldn't look at Alan's round, flat face.

"Not really. I'm used to carpentry work," Alan returned.

This was the first time he had ever been totally alone with Jobeth and he felt at a loss for words. Each time he opened his mouth his tongue felt thick and heavy.

"Well," Jobeth said, having no choice but to look at him.

He stood awkwardly with his lunch clasped in his hands. "You don't want to be late for your first day."

"No," Alan said, wide-eyed. He grabbed his hat off the chair where he had left it the night before and started for the door.

"Jobeth?" He paused, keeping his back to the girl behind him.

"Yes?" she asked with her hands clasped together. Her heart began to pound anxiously. Had Alan noticed her condition now that she was not layered down with clothes?

"Uh," the boy faltered not knowing how to tell Jobeth what he needed to say. He pressed his lips tightly together. It had to be done. It was the best for everyone.

The blood drained from Jobeth's face. Alan had to know. She would be out in the cold once again. Maybe he would let her stay the winter, please God.

"No one knows you and Jonah are here. I didn't think they should know." Alan said looking embarrassed. This was the fly in the ointment. The one thing he could not give Jobeth still.

"Why not?" Jobeth asked, surprised and a little relieved. "What about Shawna?"

Alan stood in the doorway feeling like a failure once again. Just when he thought he might succeed in her eyes, another obstacle was put in his way.

"These people . . . listen, we have been on the road for two months. Finally we can live in a real house that ain't about to fall in on us, and it's ours. Not some shack we steal into in the night and sneak out of during the day. I am paying for it monthly at the bank in town. I set it up with this Mr. Myers, he is some big shot at the bank. He said this place was for sale. With my job we could get a horse, maybe even a buggy. Shawna can go to school and be educated like them other proper girls. We can have real food--not these meager bits of scrap we been living on. But if you and Jonah are found out . . ." he stuttered, feeling ashamed. Could he ask so much of Jonah and Jobeth?

"Why?" Jobeth protested, her hands gripping the back of the chair. She wanted to lead a normal life again. The baby kicked her hard, a reminder of her present situation and she blushed, shutting her mouth tightly. She had no right to a normal life any longer, let alone to be seen in public.

"Because," Alan said, annoyed by Jobeth's red face. He just could not stop disappointing her. He breathed hard, running his hand up the side of the rough wooden wall and gazed down at the floor. "They don't like blacks in this town, Jobeth. Blacks are considered the lowest humans around here."

Remembering the events of the day before, he continued, "I was in town at the lumber yard where I got my job. I was talking to the owner of the shop when this black man walked by. The owner called him 'boy' and asked him what he was doing walking by his shop. The black man had fear in his eyes. The type of fear that has seen too much trouble and knows what could happen if he just walks in the wrong place." His eyes darted from the sight of Jobeth's gaping mouth.

"I told them I had a small sister, Shawna, who would be attending the school. Tonight after work I am gonna sign her up and later I am going to the store and get some credit so she can have dresses. I won't have the other kids laughing at her because she is dressed in rags. She ain't going to be ashamed of where she comes from."

Jobeth nodded and wrapped her arms around herself protectively. "We won't be noticed."

"Good." Alan turned back to the door again, "You're a good kid, Jobeth." And he left, leaving Jobeth standing in the doorway watching after him. She placed a hand on her budding tummy, feeling the occupant inside twisting and turning, and wondered what she was going to do.

Life settled down as the winter hit full force. Shawna started school dressed like an angel in her new clothes that Jobeth and Jonah made. Alan had even splurged on a store-bought dress for Shawna. Jobeth was disappointed with his extravagance and said so one morning.

"Why waste money on store-bought dresses when I can make the exact same dress for half the price?" Jobeth scowled at the humbled Alan. "Besides, the other children will think she is too high-class for them."

She stomped off to the room she shared with Shawna and threw herself onto the straw bed Jonah had built for them.

Alan, confused at Jobeth's outburst, turned red and clumsily left the house. He walked a few feet from the house and began kicking stones around.

He bought the dress to make up to Jobeth for forcing her to stay hidden from the rest of the world. He felt terrible that she could not lead a normal life, a life he felt she deserved. Again he had failed.

Alan looked toward town and contemplated leaving early for work. He did not want to see Jobeth's disappointed face. Shrugging his shoulders, defeated, he began walking down the worn path. A hand on his shoulder stopped him in his tracks and he turned to face Jobeth's crestfallen image.

"I will return the dress. I wasn't thinking right in the head." Alan fumbled, his hands jammed into his pockets.

"No, Alan." Jobeth shook her head. He looked at her, wide-eyed, fearing he had done yet another thing wrong. "I am the one who should be apologizing. I acted horribly and for no reason. Please forgive me. The dress was a beautiful idea and Shawna loves it. She will be the envy of her schoolmates."

Alan became red in the face, completely confused. As long as he lived, he would never understand women.

"I...I know things ain't been fair for you and Jonah, with being hidden up here," Alan said.

Jobeth lifted a pale hand in protest.

"Alan, please. You have been trying so hard to give us a proper life. Jonah and I don't mind just staying around here. At least we have each other for company, and there is plenty of work around here to keep us busy." Jobeth winced, clamping her hand down upon her stomach. The familiar cramping across her middle ripped through her. She wondered if it was normal and wished she could talk to someone about the changes occurring in her body.

Alan couldn't help but notice Jobeth's pained expression.

He went to her and placed an arm protectively around her shoulders. Her face became very pale and her hand gripped her small swollen belly, harder.

"You're not well," Alan said. Jobeth scanned Alan, liking the way his strong jaw was set firmly with concern.

"Something I ate," she cringed, pain rippling through her. It was stronger and harder. She needed to lie down and said so, panting.

"Of course, of course," Alan supported her back with his hand as they walked into the warm house.

Jonah and Shawna were sitting at the newly built table and chairs. Jonah, it turned out, was an excellent carpenter. His handiwork was showing up everywhere in the dwelling, making the small home very cozy.

He and Shawna both directed their attention to the door when Alan came bursting through it practically carrying Jobeth. Jonah bounced up, knowing full well what was wrong with her.

She must be further along then I first thought, Jonah thought to himself. He bolted to Alan, grabbing the other side of Jobeth. She grasped his hand painfully, her hazel eyes saturated with panic.

"Get Alan and Shawna off. I don't want them to be late," she whispered to Jonah. He nodded in complete understanding. Jobeth did not want Alan and Shawna to witness the birth of her child.

"Must have been that cabbage we ate, Jobeth. I gots the same bellyache."

Alan looked at Jonah, questioningly. He did not look sick. "Me and Jobeth done ate a cabbage we weren't sure of was good or bad. Guess it weren't." Jonah put his hand on his own belly and groaned. Alan looked suspicious at the two crumpled forms beside him.

"Yup, what we need to do is lay down till it passes. Gonna end up in the outhouse all day. No work gonna be done today. No, not today. You and Shawna be no help to us sick ones. Better get yourselves off to your business. Nothing can be done for us with you here," Jonah shook his head scooting the bewildered Alan and Shawna out the door.

"Jobeth, I told you, you shouldn't have eaten so much of that old cabbage,"

Jonah eyed Alan. "See, Jobeth ate most of it. I guess that's why it is getting back at her worse than me."

Hunched over in agony, Jobeth couldn't understand why Jonah was lying for her, but she was grateful. The pain began to subside.

"Alan, please get to work. You and Shawna are already late. I will be fine. I already feel a little better. I just need to lie down for a bit." She straightened her rail thin frame and walked, alone, to the bedroom.

"If you think so..." Alan hesitated. Jobeth suddenly seemed better. Again, he shrugged, not knowing what to do. He couldn't miss any work. If he did, he would lose a day's wages, wages that were needed. He could see Jonah helping Jobeth to her room. The two boys now slept in the upstairs loft together. "Come on, Shawna," Alan said to the mystified child.

She obediently grabbed hold of his hand.

"Is Jobeth gonna be all right?" Shawna asked in her tiny voice.

"Yes. She just ate something that didn't agree with her. Jonah will take good care of her." Alan stood in the doorway ready to leave, where Jobeth lay.

"I'm leaving!" He yelled. From the bedroom he could hear Jonah saying goodbye and a strained farewell from Jobeth. Suddenly he felt he should stay. There seemed more to the situation than met the eye. Alan's free hand raked through his brown hair: a habit he had when he was nervous and confused. Jonah did not really seem sick and Jobeth would be in good hands. There was no reason for him to stay behind. It was just a feeling in his gut. But then again, Jobeth had seemed in a hurry for them to leave. Not knowing what to do, he turned away from the warm room with Shawna in tow and closed the door gently behind him. Jobeth did not seem to want him around anyway. She seemed quite happy to have Jonah with her.

Jonah sat anxiously beside Jobeth. She writhed on the bed in pain, clutching her extended abdomen. There was a silent click from outside as Alan shut the door. The coast was clear and Jonah looked into Jobeth's twisted pale face.

"It looks like your baby is gonna come, Jobeth," Jonah said tenderly, smoothing the hair from her sweaty brow. Jobeth's eyes darted, surprised.

"Does Alan know?" Fear mingled with her pain as she clutched her belly.

"Naw, he don't know, but he gonna have to know soon," Jonah said, rubbing her arm.

Jobeth moaned, menstrual-like cramps boring through her again.

"It's gonna be all right, Jobeth. I am figuring the reason yah don't tell us about the baby is because you married a bad man. Makes sense you take yourself away from those bad types," Jonah soothed patiently, trying to reassure her.

Jobeth started to cry. How could she tell Jonah she was not married?

"Now don't cry. It'll be all right," Jonah comforted, glancing at Jobeth's hard belly. "You sure is small for your time to come."

"That's because I'm not at my time. I'm only a little over six months along." Jobeth wheezed through clenched teeth. Her body felt possessed as though it wanted to turn inside out. Hard as she tried to stop it, her body was doing its own thing. It was awful. The worst pain she had ever experienced. When another contraction seized her, she let out a loud wail.

Jonah began to worry. Six months was too early for the child to come. How would it survive? He frowned on the whimpering Jobeth, who howled while holding tightly to her belly.

"I'm gonna get some blankets to wrap the babe in and some water to wash him." Jonah stood from the bed, his head hanging sadly. Jobeth's baby could not possibly survive.

"Jonah, don't leave me," Jobeth sobbed reaching out and grabbing the sleeve of his shirt. "I know it's too soon. Please stay."

Jonah closed his eyes and squeezed his full lips together. He nodded and held Jobeth's hand tight.

"Aaaah!" Jobeth gasped, her contractions becoming one constant pain. "Talk to me Jonah. Please!" she panted. Sweat started to run down her face and she held her breath and strained as the urge to push consumed her body.

"Maybe you should bear down if you have the urge," Jonah said, wiping Jobeth's face with a corner of the quilt she lay on. There was a basin of water beside the bed for Jobeth and Shawna to clean up in the morning. With all the commotion, Jobeth had not had time to change the water. Jonah looked around for a cloth and grabbed a damp towel resting on the floor. He quickly dunked it into the water basin and placed the wet towel on Jobeth's streaming forehead.

"Thank you," Jobeth breathed and let out a blood-curdling cry. Jonah reached behind her back and helped Jobeth situate herself, her chest pressing forcefully on her bent thighs.

Jobeth pushed, her veins pumping furiously from her forehead. A warm gush of fluid poured from between her legs, soaking her and the bed.

"Did I wet myself?" she asked, embarrassed. Jonah, who was now supporting her back from behind whispered into Jobeth's ear.

"No, Jobeth, your water broke. The baby is coming." He sighed. It was too late to go back now. The child would have to be born.

Jobeth screamed in agony for two hours as Jonah slowly coaxed her into allowing him to see if the baby was starting to come out. At first she had refused, mortified. But with each contraction the pressure became too much and soon she relented, just wanting it to finally be over.

"I see the head," Jonah cried excitedly, looking up from between Jobeth's trembling legs and into her fevered face.

A tiny head, the size of an apple, all covered in black curly hair, slithered out. Jonah turned the child's face upward and inserted his pinky finger into its small mouth, clearing the mucous.

"One more push, Jobeth. Just one more," He said holding firmly to the miniature head. Jobeth tightened her grip on her legs and closed her eyes, trying to gather all of her strength. She was exhausted and could not take much more.

"You can do it, Jobeth. Please, one more push," Jonah cried out, noticing how fatigued she was. Jobeth braced herself and, straining with all her might, pushed.

Jonah held the incredibly small baby as it slipped out.

Infinitesimally small hands and feet flailed weakly. Never had Jonah seen anything so small. Jobeth collapsed onto the bed, exhausted, breathing heavily.

It was over.

Jonah cut the cord and wrapped the baby in a blanket, wiping the fluids from the birth off him. The baby was a boy and he was alive.

“What is it?” Jobeth asked without emotion. A frail meowing noise came from the blanket Jonah held. Almost like a cry of protest over his mother’s rejection. Something pulled at Jobeth’s heart. The child was her baby. It was not his fault how he had been created.

“He’s a boy,” Jonah said sadly, noticing the tiny infant struggling for air. His small scrawny chest heaved uncontrollably up and down.

“Let me hold my son,” Jobeth said gravely, a tear sliding down her face.

Jonah placed the baby into her arms. She quickly uncovered him and undid the buttons of her blouse. Tiny dark eyes looked up at Jobeth lovingly. Her heart melted as she loosened a breast from her stays. She placed a nipple, darkened from pregnancy, into his small gaping mouth. Her breast was nearly the size of the child. The infant tried to suckle but did not have the strength. Jobeth hummed a lullaby and rocked her wee son as he tried to feed from his mother. Jonah, holding himself, looked on with tears in his eyes. The baby’s chest was jumping in spasms.

“I am naming him Jonah after you,” Jobeth sobbed, touching the soft curly down on the baby’s head. She was not blind. She could see the irregular movement of the baby’s chest. His lungs just were not developed enough. The child was literally gasping for air.

“Oh, that is too kind,” Jonah choked out, unable to contain his emotions as he watched mother and child. The baby, although small, was the most beautiful infant Jonah had ever seen.

“You are my best friend, Jonah. It would be an honor to me and my son if you accepted.” Jobeth smiled through her tears. She reached out her hand to him. Jonah received it and bent beside her and the small newborn.

He reached out his dark finger and placed it on the infant’s small transparent cheek. His finger took up most of the child’s face.

The baby looked at Jonah, as though he recognized his namesake and his little chest stopped rising painfully. Jonah felt his tiny life leave. Jobeth let out a wail, the sound of a wounded animal, as she felt the baby’s lips fall from her breast lifelessly. She clutched the dead child close to her chest wanting to squeeze him back into her body where he was alive and well.

“I want my child,” she cried out in pure agony. Jonah, overcome with emotion encircled his arms around Jobeth and the baby, scooping the two into the safety of his embrace. He rocked her back and forth in his arms as she cried, broken-hearted, for her son.

They buried the infant Jonah, in a tiny coffin that the senior Jonah built in haste. He had prepared the wood earlier, planning to surprise Jobeth with a cradle. Tears fell freely as he nailed the lid of the small coffin over the wrapped body of the baby. Jobeth had enshrouded the child tenderly and lovingly in a soft blue and pink quilt that she had made just recently for Shawna. Tears fell silently as she kissed her son’s curly head and handed the child to Jonah to place in the miniscule coffin.

Weak as Jobeth was from the terrible ordeal of childbirth, she walked stiffly beside Jonah, out into the backfield. She wore a shawl wrapped around her for warmth and it hung limply, dragging on the icy ground.

Jonah stopped at a clearing and looked at Jobeth questioningly. She gazed around slowly, feeling a clean breeze brush her wet cheeks.

"This is a good place," Jobeth said with little emotion.

Wild flowers would sway gently in the breeze and the flutter of small wings would bustle out from hiding spots in the tall grass when spring came. She could imagine how it would be alive with nature. The place would be lovely. But for now, because it was winter, the tall grass pictured in her mind was standing yellow poking out of its white winter blanket, waiting for spring and the warmth of summer to be reborn. Jonah placed a quilt on the tightly packed snow. Gently he placed the coffin down and retrieved his shovel. It would be hard work breaking the frozen ground, but Jobeth had insisted that the baby be buried that day.

She sat the coffin down beside her and lovingly placed her hand on the smooth surface, rubbing the grain of the wood.

Jonah worked with a fever all afternoon, digging the grave for his namesake. Tears refused to stop falling and he could not look at the figure of Jobeth draped protectively over the wooden box. His heart ached to comfort her, but she didn't want comfort, she wanted the baby buried. So he continued to dig into the frozen ground, blinded by his own tears.

When the grave had been dug deep enough, Jonah gently removed Jobeth's exhausted form that was clenched tightly to the little crate. Jobeth then watched with vacant eyes and a heart as cold as ice, as he placed the coffin into the hole.

She struggled to stand up, her strength completely wasted. Jonah went to her and helped her stand, his large hand supporting Jobeth under her arm. She was weak as a newborn fawn and as light as the snow that fell to the ground.

Together they walked to the foot of the grave, looking across the white field.

Jonah cleared his throat and tried to think of a proper farewell for little Jonah.

"Go with the angels, little Jonah. You won't feel pain ever again. God has got you now. No one is ever gonna hurt yah, little one. You will always be in our hearts and one day we will meet again." Jonah spoke directly to the sky, as though he truly believed he was speaking to the babe in heaven.

Jobeth gazed up into Jonah's dark wet eyes, her own eyes dry and distant.

"I do not want anyone to know about little Jonah."

The words came out icy, in a voice Jonah did not recognize. Not believing his ears, he stared at Jobeth in shock.

"Why not?"

"I was not married, Jonah. My foster father made me . . . forced me to be with him." Jobeth stammered on her words. She had never said them out loud before. "I have committed a great sin and God has punished me by taking my son. I didn't deserve to have little Jonah and I do not deserve to grieve for him aloud. He was conceived in violence and I hated him and his father. I had wished my child never to be born and now I will have to live my life as though he never was."

She turned stiffly from Jonah's stunned face and headed back toward the house, leaving him to stare after her, baffled.

"Oh, girl, you done nothing wrong," Jonah said out loud to himself. "But you got a lot of wrong done to you. God help yah with the blame you got nestled up inside. It's gonna eat you alive . . . God help yah."

He shook his head and rubbed his face with his hanky. It had been quite a day. A day he was not likely to forget anytime soon. He scratched his head and began slowly to fill the smallest grave he had ever beheld. He winced, repulsed at the sound of the cold earth thudding sickly onto the coffin.

— Chapter 9 —

Alan noticed the change in Jobeth immediately.

She had been in bed when they returned home that evening. He assumed she was still not feeling well, but by the end of the following day, she still had not emerged from the room she shared with Shawna. He became concerned.

"I better get a doctor up here," Alan said at the dinner table. Jobeth had refused supper again for the third night in a row. The remaining three sat silently eating the meal Jonah had prepared.

He placed his hands on the table, bracing himself to get up. His intent was on going to town to fetch the doctor. It didn't matter if they had to leave when Jobeth and Jonah were discovered. She was sick and he could not let her go without medical attention.

"Alan," Jonah said softly, looking up from his plate of vegetable stew, "no doctor can help Jobeth. She gotta sickness of the heart that only she can heal."

"Now what the hell is that supposed to mean?" Alan stormed angrily, his face displaying a look of disgust.

"Alan, don't be asking me something I can't tell yah," Jonah said to the red-faced youth. "There's gonna come a time when you gonna have to listen with your heart and not your ears."

This just made Alan angrier. He could not understand what Jonah was talking about.

"And I know yah getting hot under the collar, but that is too bad. If you want to help Jobeth, you sit down and finish your supper. She will be up and at it tomorrow. We is gonna let her be for tonight," Jonah said with finality. He lifted his spoon and shoved it into his mouth forcefully. He chewed his food without actually tasting it.

Alan was too stunned for words. He sat down in his chair and stared resentfully at his half-eaten stew.

"Now tell Jonah about your day at school. You learning to read?" Jonah said changing the subject. He listened intently while eating his dinner as Shawna chatted about daily activities and a girl at school who was mean to all the other children. Jonah listened intently as Alan, defeated, began to eat again. His eyes stayed transfixed on the bedroom door where Jobeth slumbered deep in mourning.

The next day, after Alan and Shawna had left, Jonah walked hesitantly to the door of Jobeth's retreat. Shawna had been sleeping in the loft with him and Alan since Jobeth began hibernating. He paused, dreading what he had to do. Knowing he could not put it off any longer, he walked into the dark, dank room. It smelled stale and slightly sour. Swiftly, he crossed the area between himself and the window and pushed open the curtains. Sunlight bathed the room, exposing the pale, dark-eyed form collapsed on the bed. Jobeth turned and buried her head into the pillow, protesting. Jonah placed his strong young hands on his hips and glared on her frail body as she withered under his angry eyes.

"You can lay there and slowly die if you want, but you are needed around here. You got a bad loss that come to you, but life has many bellyaches to hand out to us all," Jonah growled, hating himself. "We need you and we are the living.

Little Jonah is gone. I am ashamed that he is looking down from heaven with the angels and seeing that his ma's a quitter. She done let herself get so consumed with misery that she neglecting the living that loves and needs her." He shook his head sadly.

"There will be tears in heaven right now, 'cause you done forgot about us and how we needs yah." He turned to leave trying not to see Jobeth's red-rimmed eyes. "There is lots of work to be done around here and I can't do it alone. I need my best friend to help me." And he walked out of the room, closing the door behind him.

Lifting her head from her pillow, Jobeth gazed toward the window, her eyes squinting from the bright light. Tears she thought were all dried up fell anew. She wiped them away with the back of her hand and slowly sat up, every inch of her body feeling bone weary. She swiveled her head to the door of the bedroom and mustered all of her strength.

"The least you can do is draw me a bath," she roared with all her might. Jonah leaned behind the door and held his breath as his hands tightly clasped the door handle. He smiled, released his firm hold on the handle and went to get the washtub.

"I suppose I could do that by myself," he responded.

Alan was surprised when Jobeth finally surfaced, weak as a kitten, but seemingly better after her ordeal. Jonah had been right; it was just a matter of time before she came around. He still did not understand what had happened to cause her to hide from view for nearly a week, but he trusted Jonah and obeyed his wishes. Jobeth had lost a lot of weight and the dark circles under her eyes worried him. She seemed very sad but at least she was not sick. As time passed, the circles that ringed her eyes began to fade just as the snow began to melt and spring started to bloom.

Jobeth ached for her dead son, but her heart started to heal slowly with the love of the two boys and Shawna. She seldom spoke to Jonah about the baby, but felt a great bond with the young man who was decades older than his sixteen years. Then again, she too was much wiser than her own age of fifteen.

The two frequently went to visit the tiny grave. They would sit silently, absorbed in the tranquil atmosphere. When the snow finally melted, just as Jobeth had envisioned, the grass grew tall, alive with small animals and birds. Tiny budded heads pressed out of the earth and soon the field was speckled with multicolored wildflowers.

"It is nice here," Jobeth said, smelling a small, red flower she had carefully uprooted. She planned to replant it onto the child's grave. Jonah turned from placing the small cross he had constructed on the ground. He wiped his sweaty brow and breathed deeply of the spring smells bursting forth around him.

"Good place," he sighed looking around him. "Feels like God is right here."

Jobeth agreed.

"Jonah?"

"Yes?" He continued with the work at hand. He would have to dig a hole deep enough to support the wooden crucifix. Jobeth stared at his naked dark back rippling and glistening with sweat. He had removed his shirt when the heat became unbearable. She could not help admiring his beauty. Jonah was a very handsome man.

"Thank you."

"For what?" Jonah asked, facing her again, shovel in hand.

"For everything," she pretended exasperation. She stood up and walked to him. "I love you, all right." And she kissed him squarely on the lips.

"Ah, heck," Jonah said embarrassed, turning his back to her. "I love you, too." He blushed under his dark skin.

Jobeth fell backwards, giggling, until her stomach ached from laughing so hard.

"What is so funny?" he said, pretending to be offended.

"You," she giggled, sat up and rubbed tears out of her eyes. She had not laughed so hard in ages. In fact, she could not remember ever laughing so hard. "What would I ever do without you, Jonah?"

"You would be just fine," Jonah smiled, trying to hide his own urge to laugh. It felt good to see Jobeth smile with color in her face.

"Aren't we an unlikely pair?"

"You know it," Jonah laughed out loud in his deep, rich voice. Hearing Jonah laugh started Jobeth up again and they both continued to snicker together.

A week later the two were cooking supper when Alan ran into the house after finishing his work at the mill. The house was fully furnished, thanks to Jonah's carpentry work, and looked like a very comfortable, modest home.

Jonah and Jobeth had worked hard to create the type of home they wished to live in and they had succeeded.

"Jobeth! Jonah!" Alan yelled from the doorway, "Come see what I brought home." He was very excited and Jobeth could not help the smile that broke over her face. Her heart fluttered when she thought of him. Jonah noticed how

Jobeth flushed over Alan and smiled. He saw the same look on Alan's face every time he was near Jobeth. She wiped her hands on her apron and removed the cooking chicken from the fireplace.

"Come on, Jobeth, move," Jonah squealed, grabbing her hand and dragging her outside.

Both stopped in their tracks as they reached the front veranda. Jobeth's mouth dropped open and she covered it with her hands.

There on the lawn was a cow. It was a small cow, spotted black and white and it stood lazily, chewing grass. Shawna stood beside it holding the leathery lead rope.

"Wow!" Jonah yelped, jumping down from the porch. "A cow!" He went up to the beast and began to pet it.

"Milk and butter and cream and . . ." Jobeth started to laugh, jumping down from her domain. "Alan, how wonderful!"

Alan stood back proudly. This had been a dream of his.

"We cannot have a home without a cow. Shawna, show her." Jobeth faced the blonde child with anticipation as the waif laughed, pulling out small packages from behind her back.

"Seeds!" Shawna squealed. Jobeth grabbed the small packages from her tiny hands and recited the writing on them.

"Radishes, potatoes, carrots." She squeezed the envelopes to her chest. "Vegetables! Vegetables! Finally, some vegetables!"

"Are you happy?" Alan asked, suddenly standing beside her. A strong desire moved through him to sweep her lithe body up into his and touch her lips longingly with his own. His heart pounded and the scent of her freshly washed hair made him dizzy for her.

"Very," Jobeth whispered, very much aware of his strong male presence. She gazed into his eyes, her breath failing her. "Thank you." She placed her hand on his warm cheek and without thinking leaned over and kissed him softly on his smooth lips

Alan's hand instantly encircled her wrist by his face and he breathed in her breath. It was sweet and fresh.

Jobeth's eyes were closed and a surge of heat tingled up from her toes to her head. She opened her eyes and stared into his piercing gaze. Embarrassed, she pulled away and covered her mouth with the back of her hand.

Alan was confused, feeling he had offended her. One moment he had felt joy as he had never felt before and the next he felt as though he had committed some heinous crime.

He looked directly into Jobeth's eyes and breathed deeply of her essence. Not knowing what else to do, he squeezed her hand and went to Shawna and Jonah, who were too involved with the cow to have noticed them.

"What we gonna name her?" Alan yelled running down to where Shawna and Jonah stood patting the cow. Jobeth stood still, her heart pounding rapidly in her chest, staring after Alan and wondering what she had done.

"How about Edna?" Jonah roared, picking Shawna up and placing her on the cow's back.

"Edna?" Shawna and Alan questioned in chorus.

"Yes." Jonah puffed up his chest, faking hurt feelings. "I had an aunt named Edna once. Yup, Aunt Edna. If I remember right, she looked just like this here old cow." Shawna and Alan began to laugh hastily at Jonah. Jobeth could not stop a giggle from escaping her lips as she gazed upon Alan's strong young back.

She felt confused. She had enjoyed kissing him and would have liked to kiss him more. How was that possible? When Father James had kissed her, she hated it. She cringed with disgust at his very touch. But Alan had been different--he was gentle and his lips were soft and caring.

After Edna and the new seeds came into their lives, Jonah and Jobeth had more to occupy their busy days. Jobeth did not miss going into town. Jonah was more than enough company for her during the day, and in the evenings she had all three of them to absorb her time. She felt very loved and needed once again.

Life seemed livable.

Jonah and Jobeth quickly set themselves to work fixing a barn for Edna and starting a garden. Fortunately, her mother had taught Jobeth at an early age how to make dairy products. So Edna became a great luxury in their lives.

"Jobeth, a girl has to know how to make edible foods with what she has," her mama would say, looking down at the little girl.

She no longer cried when she thought about her parents and the life they once shared together. She was only thankful that they had taught her well. The knowledge her parents had bestowed upon her before they died had proven to be very useful. Jobeth thought of them now with loving memories. They had served her well.

Every time Jobeth milked Edna or was making butter or cheese, she would remember her mother and her calm voice telling her how to do this or that. It was just like when she had been on the run with Shawna. She remembered her Pappy's strong voice telling her how to build a fire or make a snare. They left Jobeth prepared to survive alone and for that, Jobeth was forever grateful. Her parents were still protecting her and watching out for her.

Alan kept surprising them with gifts.

A month after Edna's arrival, Alan came home with two live hens, a rooster, some flour and two pigs. But the best surprise of all was Queenie, a little puppy Alan and Shawna found half-starved and abandoned by a creek. They brought her home and nursed the light brown mutt back to health.

Everything was going well. The four had everything they could hope for. They had a real home full of love and kindness, something most of them had never experienced before. And they had livestock to sustain them. They even had a watchdog.

Fall rolled around quickly, changing the green leaves of summer to bright red and yellow. The warm air began once again to turn cool and crisp.

A year had passed since the four left the other members of their little family.

Early one morning Jobeth and Jonah started pulling out the remaining vegetables from their garden. They had harvested enough for winter and were storing the food in a cellar Jonah had built behind the house during the past summer.

"Jonah, do you ever wonder what happened to the others?" Jobeth asked while brushing dirt from a carrot with her gloved hand. The garden had thrived under their care and she was very pleased. Gardening was becoming a passion of hers. Little seeds bursting forth with life never seemed to bore her. She could spend hours in her vegetable garden unaware of time passing. Next spring she planned to add a flowerbed.

Jonah stopped what he was doing and looked at his dirty hands. He did not like to use gloves. He said he liked to get his hands right into the earth. It made him feel closer to nature. He truly believed that was why the vegetables grew so well. He was a firm believer in coddling the garden, treating it with loving care. He and Jobeth were so alike in many ways.

"Yes. All the time," he said, arching his back. He had been bent over digging and picking potatoes for a while and a stitch had begun to gnaw on his spine.

"I just hope they have fared as well as we have," Jonah replied, testing his new vocabulary. Jobeth and Shawna had been teaching him and Alan how to read and write; during this time their slang was disappearing, much to both Alan's and Jonah's pleasure.

"I guess we will never know." Jonah continued picking potatoes. He felt suddenly sad. The others rested heavily on his chest. He felt guilty for the fine life he was living. The likelihood that the others had done as well was unlikely.

"You don't mean that, do you? We will find them some day."

Jonah looked up into the sky. "It is not for us to know. God willing, they will be back in our graces. But there is no use letting dreams like that eat at your mind.

Some things in life happen that we don't much like, but life doesn't have to be fair."

"That is something I do know," Jobeth spoke softly.

"That is something we all know," Jonah replied, returning to the potatoes at hand.

Jobeth sat by the roaring fire after dinner, lazily working on some mending.

The nights were getting cooler and the mornings were filled with a world covered in frost. She felt content being inside the warm little house. Shawna was fast asleep in their bed and Alan and Jonah sat at the dinner table figuring out the accounts.

Queenie, who had been sleeping by Jobeth's feet, stood up and began to growl. She was not fully grown yet and was already taller than the largest pig they owned. Alan looked up from the table and Jobeth put her sewing down, glancing at the door.

Someone knocked abruptly and insistently.

Queenie began to growl louder and Jobeth placed her hand on the dog's back. Her ears went down and she began to whine. The knock came again, louder.

"Alan?" asked a deep voice behind the door. "It's me, Simpson." He knocked again, a little more forcefully.

Alan, close to hysteria, stood up and pointed for Jonah and Jobeth to disappear.

"The loft, go!" he whispered in a panic. Jobeth and Jonah obeyed by jumping up and climbing quickly to the loft.

Messing his hair, Alan yelled out, "Coming." He opened the door pretending to tuck his shirt in. "Come in," Alan said, moving away from the door. His heart pounded and he fought the urge to look up at the loft. Two men followed behind the person named Simpson.

"Kurt, Dean," Alan said, nodding to the other men. The two in question looked younger than the man Simpson, but they all looked quite similar, with closely cropped brown hair and blue eyes. They all were a bit overfed and wore similar brown felt hats.

"What is the meaning of such a surprise?" Alan laughed nervously patting the middle-aged Simpson's back.

"Alan," Simpson replied, looking around the neatly kept room, his eyes resting briefly on the basket of half-finished mending. "Sorry to have to bother you like this. I hope we did not wake your little sister." He continued to look around the room.

Jobeth spied down quietly at the men, her heart beating against her rib cage uncontrollably.

"The boys and I needed to have a talk with you," Simpson said, looking back at Alan. The other two men examined the house with their eyes, searching for something. They turned on cue when Simpson spoke and sat down uninvited at the table. Alan took the money he and Jonah had been counting and placed it in a container on the shelf. He sat down with the other three men. Queenie, seeing that Alan sat calmly with the strangers, settled back at the fire and went to sleep.

"Nice little home you got here, Alan," one of the men said. He was running his finger across the fibers of the wooden table and admiring the handiwork. "How did you fix it up so good while working?" He looked up, smirking at Alan.

"I manage," Alan replied a little coolly. "Shawna helps a lot." He started tapping his fingers on his knees under the table. Jobeth looked at Jonah crouched beside her under his bed. She placed her arm around his shaking shoulders. He tried to smile confidently at her, but failed.

"Alan," Simpson said seriously, "the reason why we're here is because my little girl, Amy, she is in school with your sister, well she says when she walked by here the other day, she saw a nigger and a white girl running around."

Simpson stared at Alan hoping to see him falter. "Rumor around town is that you and your sister aren't the only ones living up here."

Jonah and Jobeth clutched each other tightly in the loft.

"Is there a nigger and a girl here?" Simpson asked point blank.

Alan stood up angrily.

"Does it look like I have anyone else around here?" He glared at the faces of the three men he worked with. He felt the heat rise on the back of his neck as anger and dread enveloped him. Everything was going so well. Jobeth even seemed to be happy. Nothing else had happened between them since the kiss, but she was always kind and sweet with him. He did not want things to change and the three before him only posed problems. He had to think quickly.

"I only wish I had a girl up here." Alan laughed, causing the other three men to laugh with him.

Jobeth did not find it funny. She felt fear rising in her throat, and she squeezed Jonah for comfort.

"Yah, don't we all?" laughed one of the other men. "A real saloon gal. Yee-Hah!" he wallowed.

"Well, my Amy don't lie." Simpson said.

Jobeth and Jonah swallowed a lump forming in each of their throats.

"But the doc thinks she might need specs," Simpson said, standing up from his chair as the other men followed suit. "If there is something going on up here," he said calmly to Alan, "I'd put a stop to it right away. We are God-fearing, good folks. We don't want no messing around going on in our town."

He looked straight into Alan's green eyes, telling him his true feelings.

"Sorry to disturb you, Alan, but this is the way things are." He paused, trying to lighten the mood. "Listen, there is a country dance at the Mackenzie's on Saturday. Young Miss Jossie's gonna be there. A young man like yourself aught to be thinking of settling down, especially with a little sister to think of. She needs a female around to teach her how to be a good wife and mother. Miss Jossie would be a mighty good catch and I know she has an eye for you."

Alan blushed deeply. Miss Jossie was Simpson's niece and not at all his type. She was a mindless creature who constantly hung out at the lumberyard bringing him refreshments and baked goods. Alan was fully aware of her intentions and was not at all interested.

"That seems fine," Alan lied. "I will have to look into it."

"Good . . . Good," Simpson said. "Jossie will be glad to hear it."

Jobeth felt sudden outrage. Who was Jossie? Did Alan like her? What if he did?

Then she felt fear. What if Alan did want to settle down? What would happen then? How would she fit into the picture? It had never occurred to her that Alan might want to marry. But then why wouldn't he want to get married and have his own life? She was a fool to think he would always be there to protect and care for her. One day he would want to move on. Maybe he already wanted to with this Jossie.

"Well, boys, come on. Let's get a move on before the women folks start to fret. Good-bye, Alan, and mind what I say. We like you and want to keep it that way." Simpson said opening the door, looking serious.

"Don't worry," Alan said too loudly as he watched them walk away. Jobeth could tell he was jittery and her heart went out to him. Alan was always concerned about how she and Jonah felt about being hidden away. They had never even thought how hard it might be for him to pretend they were not there. It must have been torture to lead two different lives. Jobeth had been so content that It had never occurred to her.

"Come on down," Alan said, after a bit of time had passed. Jobeth let out a long sigh and relaxed.

"That was too close for comfort," Jonah said, helping her down the ladder.

"You're telling me," Alan replied, absently. His mind was a mile away.

Something told Jobeth things were going to change once again.

— Chapter 10 —

Alan went to work as usual the next morning, but he couldn't shake feeling restless and nervous. Something deep in his bones told him to pick up everything and everyone and run. When he voiced his thoughts out loud to Jonah, he was surprised at his reaction.

"Alan, we could be jumping to conclusions. We got ourselves a nice little life here and I am tired of running."

Alan, feeling defeated, nodded. He too was tired of running. He stood beside his friend, wanting him to take the burden he suddenly felt off of his shoulders.

"Be careful today," Alan said as he held Shawna in his arms. She was beginning to be too big to carry. Her long legs dangled over Alan's hips as she clutched her slender arms around his neck.

"We will," Jonah replied. Jobeth came up from behind him.

"Good. Give Shawna a kiss and we'll be off." Alan smiled. Shawna stretched her arms out to Jobeth and she hugged and kissed the six year old.

Once Alan and Shawna left, she went to the water basin sitting beside the dinner table and began to wash up. Edna needed to be milked and she wanted to make Jonah's favorite dish for supper: roast pork with potatoes and carrots in with thick gravy.

Later, Jobeth sat humming on a stool, tugging Edna's teats. Milk squirted into the pail making a pleasant hissing sound.

Jonah was behind the house down by the creek slaughtering one of the largest pigs for supper. It would supply the meat for many meals to come.

Suddenly a thundering roar pierced the air, causing the world around Jobeth to vibrate. Edna stumbled backwards and mooed kicking the pail of milk over. Jobeth jumped up, her heart leaping into her throat. Her hands raced to her neck as dread filled her. Something terrible had happened.

She ran outside to see where the noise came from, looking out toward the creek. There was a man who looked like the fellow Simpson, with a shotgun, running away. Jobeth's eyes darted one way and then another as she started to run in slow motion.

"Where is Jonah?" Jobeth asked through clenched teeth. She turned to the side of the house and noticed two lumps slumped on the ground. They were not moving.

Jobeth gasped and sped up her pace. "Jonah!" she screamed as she drew closer to the figure hunched beside the butchered pig.

"Oh no..." She moaned as she fell beside his crumpled form. A dark pool of blood encased him. The source of the blood was a deep wound in his stomach.

"Noooo..." Jobeth cried, tears falling uncontrollably. Panic overwhelmed her as she gently touched Jonah's sweaty brow.

"Jobeth," he whispered, spitting blood through stained red teeth.

"Oh no, Jonah," she whimpered, picking his head up and cradling it in her lap.

"I am dying," he winced--his eyes were bloodshot and yellow.

"No," Jobeth whined, "I won't let you." She hugged his limp head close to her heaving chest.

"Jobeth . . . you have to listen." Jonah wheezed again. His head felt fuzzy and he had a hard time thinking straight.

"Jonah!" Jobeth wailed, her heart breaking. "You are my brother and I won't let another brother die! The people I love can't always die! How much do I have to lose for the sins I have committed?"

Jonah sputtered, spitting up fresh blood. "Listen to me . . . remember what I said about life not always giving you what you want." Jobeth wiped a tear from her eye with her fingers. A crumpling frown crossed her face.

"Shut up!" she yelled. "Life is not fair. How could this be happening?" Her tears fell on Jonah's paling face.

"I have to say what is on my mind before I meet my maker," Jonah's eyes became wide, the black orbs drilling into Jobeth. "I don't want you to mope around after I'm gone. I will be with God and baby Jonah. I am not sad to go to them." Weakly he reached above his head and grabbed Jobeth's hand, squeezing with all his strength.

"And I will always be with you."

Blood bubbled from the wound in his belly.

"You gotta be strong for Alan and Shawna . . . They need you."
Jobeth was bawling, but she continued to listen. She was covered in Jonah's blood as she clung to him, hoping her love for him would keep him with her.

"Alan," he spat, his voice becoming weak. "He loves you so much. He wants to do good by you and Shawna." He closed his eyes, his chest not moving.

"Jonah!" Jobeth screamed in terror. His eyes fluttered open and looked around aimlessly, unable to focus.

"Don't cry, Jobeth," Jonah smiled a bloody smile. His eyes seemed fixed, gazing at the sky. "I'll be watching over little Jonah, telling him his ma loved him."

"Don't say that, I need you here with me," Jobeth cried, rubbing her bloody hand across her already blood-smeared face. She hugged Jonah's heavy head harder to herself. "I love you. You are the best friend I have ever had. You make me want to go on when I don't want to. Who will help me run the house or help Shawna and Alan? We need you here."

"I love you, too, but it is time for you to go on alone without me. You don't need my hand to hold anymore." He smiled peacefully. "Tell Alan I love him and our girl Shawna." Jonah squeaked in a high voice.

"I will Jonah," Jobeth sobbed.

He grabbed Jobeth's arms, embracing her body, weakly.

"I can't see! I can't see..."

"Oh, Jonah!" Jobeth cried, hugging his limp body. "Please don't die. Please . . . please don't die."

"The living needs you, not the dead. Don't make me cry when I am gone cause you dying down here," Jonah barely whispered. "You promise me," he strained.

She lifted his face and gently cupped it in her blood stained hands.

Tenderly, she placed an upside down kiss on Jonah's bloody wet lips, her forehead resting on his chin.

"I promise," she said closing her eyes. She felt Jonah give one final sigh on her cheek, warm and moist, and threw back her head and howled mournfully.

She wailed out her pain to the clear blue sky as she held tight to the lifeless body of her friend.

That night, Alan walked into the small house feeling dread. Something was wrong. It was too quiet.

"Go to your room and play," he said to Shawna. She looked at him with puzzled blue eyes. "Git." He said softly but lovingly. He shooed her off with his hands and she skipped off to play with her dolls, grabbing an apple out of the basket on the table.

Alan looked around the empty room. It was neat and tidy—it looked like what he usually returned home to, but there was no smell of dinner perfuming the air. Jobeth was nowhere to be seen, when she normally would be bustling around setting the table with Jonah chatting around her.

Something was terribly wrong. Alan felt it the moment he'd walked into work that morning. Simpson was not there until later in the day, which was unusual. He acted strange and distant to Alan once he returned.

Fear enveloped him. Something was just not right. He immediately ran out the door.

Shawna, sitting on her and Jobeth's bed, listened to the door slam shut. She clutched her doll close to her small chest watching the entrance to her room.

Something was very wrong.

It did not take Alan long to spot Jobeth slumped over Jonah's dead body.

He ran up to her, panting. Grief spread over his face instantly and a moan escaped his throat. Jobeth lifted her blood-streaked face to Alan's tortured one.

"He's gone." She said hoarsely reaching her hand out to him.

Alan's knees gave out from under him and he fell beside Jonah and Jobeth, a sob caught in his throat.

He placed a hand over the open, glazed eyes of Jonah and closed them, searching Jobeth's grief-stricken face for questions he already knew the answers to.

"It's my fault," he choked, his words barely audible. Tears formed in his beautiful eyes.

Jobeth gently took his hand away from Jonah's eyes, and held it tightly.

"No," she said through a stuffy nose. "Not your fault," she repeated, shaking her head. She took a deep breath and rubbed tears out of her eyes.

Alan looked at Jobeth with quivering lips. He began to cry.

Jobeth embraced him and stroked his soft brown hair, lovingly.

Jonah had been right again. Alan and Shawna would need her even more now.

"I should have moved us last year when I thought there might be danger," Alan cried, holding on to Jobeth for life.

"No, Alan," Jobeth soothed softly. "It was winter and we were freezing. You did what you had to do. For us. And we were so happy, if just for a little while."

"But," Alan said, red-eyed, "I knew I should have stayed home today."

"No, Alan," Jobeth whispered, her fingers running through his hair. She could not help noticing Jonah's dried blood coated her fingers. "No one knew this would happen. The fault for Jonah lying here is that Simpson and his prejudice! His fear of Jonah, not yours, and Jonah knew that."

"How could he?" Alan begged, wanting the guilt that plagued him to leave.

"He told me, and he told me he loved you." Jobeth smiled, giving birth to fresh tears. "He loved us all and he wasn't afraid to die anymore. He said there are many waiting for him in heaven so he won't be alone." Jobeth sighed and looked down at Jonah. It did not even look like the boy she had loved and lived with. It was just an empty shell. Jonah was already gone. She cupped her hand to her mouth trying to control the urge to burst out crying. Alan needed her to be strong for him. Later she could mourn for her beloved friend, in private.

"He told me we were not to cry for him. We had to be strong for each other. That we still had each other and Shawna."

Alan placed his head in Jobeth's lap and cried. She put her arms protectively around him and rested her head on his back as Alan shook with grief.

"We have to be strong for each other," she cried, Jonah's words ringing in her ears. "Jonah was a very wise man. One of the wisest men I have ever had the pleasure to know . . . I promised him we would be strong Alan . . . I promised."

She held him and cried with him until night fell across the land and the cold became unbearable.

"Shawna will start to look for us." Alan sniffed, releasing his grip on Jobeth.

She nodded, trying to fix her hair.

"I will have to clean up before she sees me." Jobeth stood up on sore, cramped legs. She had been crouched in the same position since finding Jonah that morning.

"What do I tell her?" Alan choked back a sob about to release again.

"The truth . . . the truth," Jobeth said turning to the creek.

She walked away slowly, like a mythical creature of the forest, leaving Alan standing and staring after her.

"I am so in love with her Jonah," Alan whispered to the air.

Jobeth's form faded out of sight.

An unseasonably warm breeze blew over him, blowing into his ear. He could have sworn he heard, "I know," in its warmth.

He looked down at the empty body of Jonah.

"I will miss you," Alan said numbly. "More than you know."

Leaves rustled in the trees behind Alan. He turned back, confused. There were no leaves on the trees. They had fallen off days before.

They buried Jonah the next day beside Jobeth's son. Alan was confused by Jobeth's insistence as to where Jonah was to rest.

"I want him there. It is very beautiful and peaceful in the summer. Jonah once told me it was like God was right there," Jobeth said, trying to avoid Alan's questioning eyes.

"All right then. That is where he would probably want to be buried."

When the three mourners reached the sight of the burial, Alan looked at the cross already placed in the ground.

"It looks like someone else thought this was a good place," he said to Jobeth.

She looked away from him, guilt flooding her soul. She wanted to tell Alan that it was her son that lay beneath the tiny grave marker. She wanted to reveal to him how Jonah had asked to be buried here, beside his namesake, but she was afraid--afraid she would lose Alan if he knew the truth. It was a chance she was not going to take.

Alan began digging as Jobeth and Shawna stood back, teary-eyed and watched.

They cried openly without reservation as Alan began to scoop dirt over the wooden coffin. No more deep laughter echoing through the day. No more talks. No more Jonah. He was gone forever.

Jobeth stood staring at the two crosses erect in the cool air. Alan was on one side of her and Shawna on the other.

"Good-bye, dear friend. I will miss you forever. Take care of mine in heaven. My life will always have a hole without you in it. We have been blessed to have you in our lives, if just for a short time. Sleep well and one day we will all be together again," Jobeth said, looking at both crosses. "I will never forget you," she said to both crucifixes. Alan placed a warm arm around her shoulder and she smiled at him as she clutched Shawna's hand.

"We'll be all right," Jobeth coaxed Alan.

"If anything should happen to you two . . ." Alan breathed, bending his face into Jobeth's loose hair.

"Shhh," Jobeth placed her index finger to Alan's moist lips. "Nothing is going to happen to us." She hugged the two sobbing people, holding them dearly to her.

"Please," she prayed in her mind, *"please don't take them from me too. That would be too cruel to bear."*

Alan went into town later in the day to sell the livestock, while Jobeth and Shawna packed their belongings.

"Don't open the door for anyone," he said to Jobeth before he left.

"I won't," Jobeth said, cupping Alan's face in her hands. They felt warm and smooth. He smiled warmly into her kind face, hating to leave, but having no choice. Winter was nearly upon them and he wanted to purchase a horse and covered wagon to protect them from the elements. He did not want to travel on foot again. It had nearly killed them the last time. They had come too far to regress back to the beginning. They were not the same people they had been a year ago.

"Jobeth?" Shawna asked, handing the older girl some of her dresses. They were in their bedroom sorting through their belongings. It was the last room to pack.

"Yes," Jobeth said absently folding cloths.

"At school . . ." Shawna stopped, afraid of the answer she would receive.

"What is it Shawna?" Jobeth looked up from her folding. Shawna's blonde head was lowered and her two braids hung down on each side of her small shoulders.

"Well, the children said I would be taken away," Shawna's eyes looked beseechingly at Jobeth. Sympathy filled Jobeth and she reached out, grasping Shawna's light form, bringing the child into her comforting embrace.

"No one will ever take you away from me, Shawna. No one," she said earnestly. Queenie jumped up from her resting place on the floor and began to growl. A shiver ran up Jobeth's spine. Both she and Shawna turned to the door.

"Stay here," she ordered, standing up. Queenie stood protectively beside Jobeth, teeth bared.

"Jobeth," Shawna squealed. Jobeth put her palm up to silence the frightened child and crept to the locked front door leading outside.

"Come on out, you whore!" came a female voice from behind the entrance.

"We don't want trash like you around our children!" yelled another female voice.

A chorus of approval rang out. Jobeth peeked out the window and saw about twenty women with small children held tight to their sides. One plump, middle-aged woman with a toddler in her arms lifted a rock from the ground and hurled it at the window. The glass shattered, causing Jobeth to jump, screaming as her hands covered her ears. Shawna came running out of the room, terrified.

"Jobeth!" she squealed, frightened.

"The loft! Go to the loft and hide under the bed!" Jobeth said, running to Shawna. Queenie started to bark as rocks began to pelt against the little house, crashing through windows and denting the sides.

Shawna scurried up the stairs and looked down at Jobeth with wide, frightened eyes.

"Send out the child, whore," came an angry voice from outside. Jobeth grabbed the snarling Queenie and wrapped her arm protectively around the furry neck. The dog licked Jobeth's face, whining and growling, baring her teeth menacingly at the door.

"It's all right girl," Jobeth soothed. "Come on Alan, hurry back."

She glued her eyes to the door and did not move, knowing Shawna would be scared up in the loft alone. Jobeth wrung her hands together, feeling guilty. She was not there to comfort the poor child.

"Go upstairs, Queenie. Go see Shawna." Jobeth spoke into the animal's ear.

The dog whined turning to go up the stairs. She looked back at Jobeth, ears alert.

"Go see Shawna," Jobeth hissed, grabbing a chair to place under the door handle. Queenie obeyed and went to the waiting arms of the little girl. Shawna was relieved to have the dog's warm furry body with her.

"If you think you can whore around our town, you got another think coming!" yelled another voice.

Jobeth grabbed a log from the woodpile and stood in a defensive pose, ready. She would do what she had to, to protect herself and Shawna. No one was taking Shawna from her, and no one was going to hurt either one of them again.

"Alan, please hurry back," Jobeth whispered, afraid more than she had ever been in her life. "Hurry..."

That afternoon, Alan rode up the familiar path to the house he had shared with Jobeth, Jonah and Shawna for more than a year. He was seated on the front bench of a covered wagon. A brown mare and a spotted brown and white filly pulled the cart easily up the path. He reached the house and noticed the battered appearance. Glass was shattered everywhere and rocks littered the once immaculate entrance. Jobeth and Jonah had cleared out the weeds and branches that littered the path, taking care to give it a simple, yet appealing exterior. Now it was unrecognizable. Panic seized him.

"Whoa!" He reined in the horses, which gave a startled snort. Alan dropped the reins and jumped off the wagon, running to the sealed door. It was jammed and he pushed full force with his shoulder trying to get in.

"Jobeth, Shawna!" he yelled frantically, pushing the door slightly ajar.

"Alan?" he heard from the other side. Relief filled his soul. He could hear Jobeth moving objects away from the door.

"Oh, Alan!" she cried, opening the door to his bewildered face. She had never felt so glad to see him as she flung herself into his arms and hugged him tightly, afraid that his husky presence might not be real.

"Where is Shawna?" he peered over Jobeth's shoulder. Rocks and glass littered the once tidy room.

"I'm here!" Shawna chimed over the railing of the loft.

"Thank God," he panted, squeezing Jobeth back.

"Oh, Alan, we were so frightened. They called me horrible names and they threw stones. They came to take Shawna."

"Don't cry. They're gone now," Alan soothed, patting the back of Jobeth's long loose hair. Jobeth pulled away from Alan's strong embrace.

"Did you get the wagon?" Jobeth asked. He nodded. Tears filled her eyes. The reality of leaving their beloved little home flooded her. Jonah was here. Her baby was here.

"Why?" she wailed angrily. "Why did they have to kill Jonah? Why did they steal him away from us? Why did they have to ruin our home? Why?" She sobbed, unable to stop. "I loved him so much. I loved our home." Jobeth fell to the floor crying into the palms of her hands. She was leaving so much behind.

"Jobeth," Alan pleaded. "Please, Jobeth . . ." He bent down and placed his large, strong hands around her tear-streaked face. Jobeth looked at him, sniffling.

"We have to leave. I don't want to leave Jonah either, but we have too." He looked at the debris thrown aggressively across the floor and Jobeth could see his eyes water. "What they did to Jonah . . ."

"Alan," Jobeth felt ashamed by her outburst.

"No," Alan jumped up, glaring at Jobeth. She shivered. Alan had never before acted this way. "Jobeth don't. You understand what they could do to us, to Shawna?"

Shawna gasped, clinging onto Queenie's neck.

Jobeth stood up. Jonah's last words, to be strong, rang in her ears. She patted her messy hair down, looking up to the loft with a forced smile.

"Come on down, honey, and help me pack," Jobeth said to the silent child whose eyes were big with worry. Goosebumps crawled over Jobeth's skin. For a moment, the child looking down was that same haunted child Jobeth had escaped with so long ago.

Slowly, Shawna crawled down the stairs and grabbed Jobeth's hand tightly. Reassuringly, Jobeth squeezed it back.

"Did you have trouble selling the animals?" Jobeth asked Alan.

"No, we had good animals. They just want us out of their town. I sold them quickly." He smiled shyly at Jobeth, wanting to kiss her. "Wait till you see the horses. They are beautiful."

"Well then," Jobeth forced a grin, "let's see them."

They ate in silence and then packed their belongings in the wagon. Jobeth made up a bed in the back, putting the fatigued Shawna down to sleep. It was getting late and they wanted to be on their way.

They stopped at the grave one last time to say good-bye. Standing beside Alan, she stared at the stark crosses: the only reminders that the two buried beneath had existed in this world. She wished they were coming with them.

She bent down and fingered the dried red flowers on her son's grave. Her heart ached at leaving them behind, but Jonah had been right, as always. Alan and Shawna needed her and they were alive. She felt she would never get over losing Jonah or her son, but she would live and love. She had to; She had promised Jonah and it was the only way she could survive.

"Are you ready?" Alan questioned, watching her caress the dried seed heads.

Jobeth was almost sixteen and had already lived a life far beyond her years.

She had lost her parents, her child and her best friend all in a little more than two years. The pain was there. It probably always would be. She looked at the man beside her and her sad heart lightened. She snapped one of the flowers into her hand. She would take a part of them with her. Somewhere, someday she would plant those seeds. She placed a mittened hand on his arm and smiled peacefully at him.

"Now I am ready," she said.

Seated back in the wagon, Alan clicked his tongue and slapped the reins down onto the horses' backs. The wagon began to move forward.

Alan was worth going on for. He was only seventeen years old and worked harder than any man she knew. She turned and faced the road. The sky had turned gray and cool. She snuggled into her wrap and sighed, clutching the dried flower in her hand. They would make it. They had to make it.

— Chapter 11 —

They moved on until late in the night. Exhausted, Alan tied the horses to a tree and the two went to sleep in the back of the wagon. Jobeth slept snuggled up to Shawna while Alan lay alone in a roll on the floor. The wagon had become their new home.

In the morning Alan caught a rabbit for breakfast. They had plenty of food: the meat dried for winter and their store of vegetables and dried fruits and grains, but there was no reason to dip into their supplies when food was plenty off the land.

Jobeth tried to push aside the pictures that came to her mind, but she could not stop the images of Jonah arguing with Shawna over who caught the rabbit or of him standing next to her chatting away while helping her prepare the evening meal. She wanted to cry when she thought of him but tears were a luxury she could not afford at the moment.

Landscape passed by without Jobeth noticing. She easily conformed to traveling again and figured she would never be settled in one spot. Something would always happen to uproot them again. The difference this time was she had no urges to lay down roots. She had all she needed and that was Alan and Shawna.

They passed town after town in their covered wagon. Alan knew eventually they would have to stop. Shawna needed to be in school and Jobeth needed her own home, whether she believed it or not.

He knew this and still continued pushing the horses on.

As they moved farther south, the weather warmed. Even though winter had begun, traveling was not a problem. Covered in warm blankets at night and dressed in cozy clothing, there was no reason not to continue on their journey.

How nice it was now that they had the leisure of the horses. They became healthier and stronger as their hearts and souls healed.

"Jobeth?" Alan asked, flicking the horse's reins.

"Yes?" Jobeth responded, seated snugly beside him in the front seat of the wagon. Evening was creeping up on them. Soon they would need to stop for dinner. The gray sky was cool and the bare trees swayed in the breeze. Alan and Jobeth could hear Shawna playing contentedly in the back with her dolls. Her small voice in harmony with nature's music.

"We are gonna have to stop soon," Alan said, looking at the gravel road. It was well-worn, a telltale sign that a town lay ahead.

"Yes, Shawna must be hungry." Jobeth clasped her mittened hands together, shivering. The night air was unusually cool.

"No, that is not what I mean," Alan continued.

Jobeth pulled the dark brown woolen cloak she wore tightly around her ears and bent her covered head down.

"I know you don't feel ready yet, but it has been three months since Jonah..."

"I know, Alan," Jobeth sighed, looking at him. She sniffed, wondering if her nose was as red as his. "It's just hard. I'm not sure I am ready to start again."

"Shawna needs school, friends, a home. We all do," Alan said, staring out at the starlit sky. He understood how Jobeth felt. He too didn't feel ready to stop moving yet. The last three months had been so peaceful. He pushed out his breath, loosely between his lips, causing the air to steam up in front of him like smoke.

"You are right. I know you're right," Jobeth nodded, her heart fluttering. Alan grinned and absently placed a mittened hand on her blanket-covered lap.

"Soon, just not yet," he said, patting her leg reassuringly.

The next morning, Jobeth was sleeping soundly as Queenie lay curled up protectively beside her.

"Jobeth wake up!" A male voice called from the back of the wagon.

"Alan?" Jobeth groaned in protest, turning over and hiding her face in the quilts.

The sun was beaming bright into the wagon, stinging Jobeth's unadjusted eyes.

"I am exhausted," she moaned, noticing the wagon was not swaying with movement. Alan must have stopped for some reason.

"Now honey, I want you to see this house with me," Alan said in an excited voice.

"Honey?" She sat up abruptly.

Alan was holding the canvas of the wagon open, his body shielding most of the sun's rays from penetrating inside the dark retreat. He beamed at Jobeth, winking at her.

Confused, she quickly arranged her hair. Alan held his hand out, imploring.

"Please play along?" he whispered into her ear as she jumped down from the step. Squinting from the bright rays, she adjusted her eyes and looked around.

The wagon was stopped in front of a little white house. A couple in their early sixties was standing respectfully by the horses, waiting it seemed, for her and Alan.

"This is my wife, Jobeth," Alan presented to the elderly couple. He placed his arm around her waist and gave a light squeeze, causing a shiver to bolt up Jobeth's spine.

The couple walked over, hands outstretched in greeting.

"You two look young to be married," the man said, squinting his gray eyes.

He was a handsome man with a mane of snow-white hair and a strong tanned build, made hard by work in the sun.

"Oh, stop it, George. I married you when I was just sixteen," said the small woman beside him. She pushed him aside easily in spite of the difference in their sizes and raised her hand out toward Jobeth, warmly.

"Hello, dearie. I am Diana and this big old lug is my husband, George."

"Hello," Jobeth replied rather shyly, wanting to hide behind Alan. Diana was the first new person she had spoken to in over a year. She felt nervous, but Diana had a kind face with light blue shimmering eyes and soft blonde hair showing only the slightest gray. She accepted the older woman's hand and was pleased how soft and warm it felt.

"Well," Alan said clapping his hands together if in prayer, "I guess we can see the house now," Jobeth looked at Alan questioningly.

"Of course." Diana smiled sincerely, gently dropping Jobeth's hands and turning towards the little white building.

"Where is Shawna?" Jobeth asked searching for the little girl. With all the confusion she had forgotten about her little charge.

As her eyes scanned the area, she could not believe the magnificent view. Two large oak trees towered over a little two-story house. That was what it was, but to say it was merely a house would be an understatement. The dwelling screamed out "home." A swing hung from one of the oak tree's branches. In the summer the grass would cover the front lawn in a counterpane of green with flowers trimming the edges of the house.

"Shawna is in the back yard playing with our grandbabies," Diana said, linking her arm in Jobeth's, comfortably. She began to lead her toward the house.

"Your husband here says you are newlyweds. Big responsibility having to raise a little sister on top of just becoming a wife. Once the babies start coming, you are going to have your hands full." Diana exclaimed.

Jobeth's heart jumped.

Suddenly she felt frightened and didn't understand why. She looked back beseechingly to Alan who was engrossed in his conversation with George.

He did not notice the anxiety in Jobeth's eyes.

"Shawna is no trouble to Alan or me. We love her dearly," Jobeth said a bit defensively. "She is a blessing."

Diana looked at the young girl's wounded face. This couple did seem awfully green to her. But what tugged at Diana's heart most was the sorrow in Jobeth's eyes. She had seen that look before in ones who had beheld and lost too much in life. Diana also saw how those same pained eyes would glow lovingly at the boy, Alan. He shined just as brightly at Jobeth.

"Children are all a blessing," Diana smiled kindly. Jobeth forced her lips into a grin and followed Diana into the little house.

It was beautiful. It had two separate bedrooms plus a loft. There was a secluded room for cooking and eating, plus another room for sitting and relaxing. This room boasted two chairs and a couch jacketed in a rich burgundy material.

Best of all was the outhouse. It was indoors! An odd-looking chain hung from a tank attached to the wall. When you pulled it, the waste was flushed away. It was truly amazing. Jobeth and Alan had never imagined such a device. Diana and George laughed at the young couple's disbelief and had to demonstrate how it worked.

"They are called toilets and they are the wave of the future. Soon every home will have one," exclaimed Diana, her hands clutched to her full chest. "Now that you have seen our little place, what do you think?"

"It is the most beautiful residence I have ever seen," Jobeth was unable to hide her awe. Alan smiled proudly at her excited face.

"There is the barn too, and a few animals," George said, holding the hand of his bride of fifty years. "You don't have to start from scratch. We know how hard it is to start a home when you are newlyweds."

"Do you want the house, Jobeth?" Alan asked, clutching her hands tightly in his.

"Of course," Jobeth commented in disbelief. She had never dreamed of such luxuries. "But how? You don't even have a job?"

"I got a good paying job in town while you were sleeping. In fact, after I was hired, I asked around if there was a house I could buy and was told about George and Diana. All we need to do is trade Diana and George our horses and wagon, plus a hundred dollars."

Jobeth couldn't believe their luck. Could it be possible the beautiful house could be theirs?

"That is it?" She squeaked. A hundred dollars was a lot of money. It was all the money Alan had saved. A near fortune. But a home such as George and Diana's was a dream comes true.

"Yes," Diana chuckled, placing a hand on a bewildered Jobeth's shoulder.

"George and I want a change. The children are grown and have families of their own. Now it is our time. Like when we were first married."

George reddened and coughed, embarrassed. It had been his dream, when they first got married, to travel across the country, but Diana kept having one baby after the other. Now, finally his dream was coming true. All he wanted was Diana by his side and leather reins in his calloused hands.

"The horses are fine beasts. We aren't really giving you a deal, Miss."

Jobeth nodded kindly to the older man. If he only knew how they had started out. This house was too much to ever dream of.

"Alan says you have been traveling for months and it is beautiful," George said, excited. His adventure was about to begin. He would never have guessed at sixty-eight years of age his life's wish would come true.

"Wonderful," Jobeth cooed, remembering the therapeutic power of the open plains. Yes, her heart was forever changed with the loss of Jonah and her baby, but the journey to this little town had begun to heal the wound their deaths had left.

"Well, Jobeth?" Alan asked, staring into her hazel eyes, looking incredibly handsome. Jobeth's blood felt warm in her veins and her heart fluttered uncontrollably. "Do we take it?"

"I would be a fool if I said no," she said, overcome with joy, "Yes, we'll take it."

Jobeth spun around, arms outstretch like a gleeful child in the center of the family room.

"Oh, Alan!" she cried out happily.

George and Diana needed a week to pack and say their farewells to their children. Alan and Jobeth used that time to enroll Shawna in the local school, and to become accustomed to their new surroundings.

Diana and George were dears, always there to help the younger couple with whatever they needed. Jobeth felt it was all too soon when the older couple sat in the buggy, glowing about their impending future. They wished Jobeth and Alan well and said their good-byes with warm embraces.

"We are so lucky to get this house!" Jobeth said, jumping into Alan's arms, laughing. Shawna sat on the couch with her dolls. She could not sit by and quietly watch Alan and Jobeth's enthusiasm. Bouncing off her seat and sending her dolls tumbling to the plush rug, the bright child joined in the excitement, running into Jobeth and Alan's waiting arms.

"Are you happy, Jobeth?" Alan asked, holding her close to his strong chest.

"Yes," she breathed, deeply conscious of her breast pressed firmly against Alan. Tingling sensations rippled through her nipples and she felt them harden. Confused, she pulled away slightly.

Alan was conscious of his effect on Jobeth and gripped her tighter to him.

"Now that I have told everyone we are married, you won't have to hide like before. Shawna can have friends at the house and you can, too." He said in a husky voice. He looked deeply into Jobeth's flushed face. His eyes dove into the depths of her soul. She felt a warmth between her legs and she pulled abruptly away from his embrace.

"Let's go see our animals." Jobeth bent down to the giggling Shawna and lifted her onto her hip. She avoided Alan's eyes, confused with these new emotions.

"You heard your sister, Shawna, let's go!" Alan clapped. He reached over and retrieved Shawna from Jobeth's grasp easily placing the squirming six year old on his broad shoulders. Nothing was going to ruin his good mood, not even Jobeth's hesitance towards him.

He watched the back of her head as she demurely walked in front of him. Her long sandy hair was loose and it bounced softly down to her narrow waist.

"We are going to like it here!" he roared, full of life, clasping Shawna's legs firmly around his neck. The child wrapped her small hands under Alan's stubbly chin and held on tight.

"Go! Go! Go!" She squealed, roughly kicking Alan in the chest with little bare feet. Jobeth glanced over her shoulder shyly, unable to keep her heart from fluttering uncontrollably at the sight of Alan and Shawna so content together.

"You heard our girl, Jobeth. Let's go, go, go!" Alan teased, speeding past her.

Shawna's squeals trailed behind them.

Jobeth blushed, turning a scarlet shade. She took a deep breath and exhaled, pausing a moment before she continued on. She needed to compose herself before she faced Alan again.

Outside there was a small barn with a chicken coop nestled right beside it where chickens scurried to escape a bullying roaster.

"Oh look," Shawna pointed, "baby chickies!"

Alan put the excited youngster down and opened the door to let her in.

Shawna ran inside and began to chase the yellow, chirping puffballs. The mother hen, angered by Shawna's pursuit of her offspring, pecked furiously at her exposed ankles.

"Ouch!" giggled Shawna, gently pushing the mother chicken aside with her foot.

Jobeth chuckled to herself. Shawna looked beautiful standing amongst the clucking fowl, her face animated. The child bent and retrieved a squeaking chick and nestled it to her cheek lovingly. Jobeth fondly remembered similar events that had happened in her own childhood at about the same age. She took a deep refreshing breath. It was good to know Shawna would have memories of the softness of a baby chicks' down rubbed against a cheek. Maybe it would help to erase all the bad ones she had accumulated over her short lifetime.

"Let's go see the other animals," Alan said over Jobeth's shoulder. She could feel his breath warm on her neck, as goose bumps jumped forth from her skin like seedlings springing out of the newly dampened earth after a rain. Jobeth nodded, hesitantly rubbing the goose bumps on her arms. For some reason she didn't yet understand, she was suddenly uncomfortable being alone with Alan.

"Shawna, are you staying here?" Alan asked, leading Jobeth towards the barn.

"Yes!" she grinned as a furry chick pecked at her hand. Jobeth laughed despite her apprehension. The sight of Shawna being attacked by chickens was too funny not to respond. She sighed nervously and followed Alan obediently towards the barn, feeling rather foolish.

This was Alan, what was there to be afraid of?

Inside the barn a medium size brown cow and her calf greeted them. The beast mooed lazily in response to their arrival and continued to chew on the yellow hay littering the barn floor. Her calf ignored the visitors and suckled busily from its mother's udders.

"We will have to get some pigs," Alan said, walking over to the stall to examining the cow. "Maybe even a horse and carriage."

Queenie sauntered into the barn, her tail wagging playfully. She bent down low on her front legs and yipped at the mother cow. The cow, unmoved by Queenie, mooed back at the dog. Queenie, insulted, turned on her haunches and ran out the door, barking once more in defiance over her furry shoulder.

Alan and Jobeth both began to laugh, the earlier tension between them melting away.

Jobeth smiled warmly as she bent down and shooed the little brown calf away from its mother's milk supply. Everything was going to be all right.

"This is my dream house," Jobeth said to Alan later that evening. They sat side by side on the couch, Jobeth admiring the handiwork of the furniture. Diana must have worked hard to make the cushions fit the carved wood frames. She traced her finger down the tightly sewn seams of the flush wine cushions, her eyes focusing on Shawna, who lay fast asleep on a matching chair.

"Ever since Shawna and I ran away..." Jobeth stopped herself. She didn't want to remember those times. Too much pain would surface, with the memory of other times. One bad memory would lead to another and another. This was a happy time. She had to learn to let go of the past and all that happened in it.

"What?" Alan asked. He had always been curious about what had happened to Jobeth before he found her asleep on the dirty mattress with Shawna held tight in her grip.

"Nothing," she stood up, avoiding Alan's eyes. "Shawna is asleep and we should put her to bed. Which room will be ours?" She reached down to pick up the sleeping body. Shawna's pale blonde hair haloed her angelic face causing Jobeth's heart to swell with love. She bent and kissed the warm, flushed cheek like a mother would a favored child.

Alan stared at Jobeth, holding his breath. He couldn't stand not to touch her any longer. He stood up and quietly walked behind her. Nervously he reached out, placing a gentle hand on her slender shoulder. Jobeth turned her hazel eyes upon him, and then quickly shifted her gaze down to her shoes.

Alan summoned all his courage. She had responded to him in the barn. She had. It wasn't his imagination.

Jobeth began to shake uncontrollably. She was torn between fear and something else she could not explain. Something warm and good.

"I thought..." Alan said, slowly caressing Jobeth's arm with his finger. His breath became heavier and his heart pounded uncontrollably. "Since everyone thinks we are married..." He hesitated then leaned over and softly kissed the nape of Jobeth's neck. A shiver raced through her whole body, like the rumble of thunder. Alan felt the goose bumps rise beneath his lips and continued to softly kiss her neck, savoring the tiny bumps.

She was torn between pleasure and fear. Against her will, her hands combed through Alan's soft chestnut hair, pulling his head closer to her waiting neck.

Alan, encouraged by Jobeth's grip on his head, kissed her straight, fine-boned jaw. She let out a sigh as Alan, unable to hold back, cupped her face in his hands and kissed her hard on the mouth. She acknowledged his touch, grasping him to her heaving chest like a starved person finally handed food
He slid his tongue between her parted lips and without hesitation she opened her mouth and received him greedily.

"Oh, Jobeth," Alan moaned, clutching her savagely to him, afraid she would suddenly vanish and leave his arms empty, "I have wanted this for so long."

"Alan..." Jobeth sighed arching her head back allowing him to kiss her throat and collarbone. Warmth permeated Jobeth. She didn't want his kisses to stop. Each time his lips touched her skin, she felt electrical current crackle through her. She felt Alan's hand unbutton her blouse and his warm wet kisses cover her chest, slowly creeping to her breast held tight in her corset. The stays were quickly loosened and her perky breasts fell free from their imprisonment.

Alan swallowed hard at the perfect beauty of the round flesh, with small rosebud nipples.

"Oh Jobeth, I love you so," he exhaled in a husky voice. His hand caressed the circular form. The nipple instantly became erect. Unable to leave the other bare he gently stroked it with his bottom lip.

Jobeth, completely enthralled, held Alan's head to her breast, wanting to cry out with delight. She jumped as she felt Alan's lips encircle her raised nipple. It was moist and good. He began to suck gently and then with more fervor.

Alan felt the uncomfortable confinement of his enlarging groin. His hands encircled Jobeth's back and he pulled her to him, eagerly pressing her to his throbbing member hidden behind his trousers.

She went into his arms willingly, pressing her pulsing body to Alan's hard one. He rubbed against her intensely and Jobeth gasped.

Suddenly Father James stood before her, fat and ugly, his purple snake enveloped in mangy black curly hair. Memories of him forcing that vile stick savagely into her flooded her mind. Revolted, she pulled away clutching her blouse over her exposed breast.

"No!" Jobeth began to cry, horrified at what was happening between them.

Alan stood stunned, his erection becoming increasingly painful in his pants.

"Jobeth?" He reached out to her.

"Stay away from me," she yelled, not seeing Alan any longer, but Father James. She had been transported back in time to the house that had caused her so much pain.

"Give me the whip, Father James. I don't want to play these games. I promise I will never wet the bed again." Jobeth fell to the ground, crying hysterically, pounding it viciously with closed fists.

Alan, dumbfounded, dropped behind Jobeth and grabbed her arms, trying to prevent her from hurting herself. Everything was going terribly wrong.

"Jobeth you are safe. It's me Alan," he reassured her, holding on for dear life. She fell into his arms heaving and sobbing, burying her face in her hands. The nightmare had passed. She was again with Alan in their new home. It was Alan: sweet, kind Alan, not Father James.

"What happened to you?" Alan

"Nothing," Jobeth shrieked, clutching her arms protectively around her unbuttoned blouse. Alan sat down wearily beside Jobeth. Shame coursed through his heated body, all desire leaving him. He was nothing more than a selfish rogue. Why would Jobeth just give herself to him freely? They weren't really married.

"Who is Father James? Is he a priest?'

Jobeth's head jerked up surprised. "How do you?" She shook her head confused. "Am I going crazy?"

"Jobeth," Alan lightly touched her damp arm. She pulled away, causing him to blush, embarrassed. He sat back some distance, giving her the space she wanted. He loved her so much; he felt he would die without her in his life. Now all his hopes for them were shattered. "Did this Father James do something to hurt you?"

"Why should I tell you?" She cried, hunched into the corner of the couch. She knew this time would come. The time to expose what had happened with Father James and the outcome of that union, her son.

Tears formed in the corners of her eyes. Her precious, tiny baby. Oh how her heart ached to hold him one more time!

Images of his tiny grave littered with red flowers played itself out behind her closed eyes.

Jonah was with him; he was not alone and by now the little flowers would have crept over onto his grave as well, blanketing them both with her love.

She opened her eyes. It was time to reveal her shame and her heartache. It was time for her baby to be recognized.

"I don't know a thing about your past," she said lamely trying one more time to avoid the inevitable. Alan would never want to live with her after he knew the truth. He would probably even find her unfit to care for Shawna.

Fear enveloped Jobeth; she could not lose them too.

"All right," Alan jumped up from his seat.

Shawna moaned in her sleep.

Alan savagely raked his fingers through his hair, a habit Jobeth had come to recognize meant he was troubled about something.

"Stay here. I will put Shawna to bed and then we are going to talk. It's time we got everything out in the open."

How strange the night had turned on him. Teasing him to believe Jobeth was his. At least Shawna did not change, he thought. She was still the sweet little girl she always was. She was always happy to see him and never disappointed if he did something wrong. He sighed as he looked at her in his arms, then laid her on her bed and kissed her warm brow, tucking the slumbering child under her blankets. Quietly, he stood and left the room, shutting the door behind him.

Jobeth was still huddled in the corner of the couch, sniffing. She watched Alan as he sat down on the opposite side and felt sad. He looked defeated and Jobeth knew she was responsible. Alan always tried so hard and she made him feel like a failure every time.

I am not worthy of him, she thought, staring at Alan's pained expression. It was time to be honest. At least Alan would not feel responsible for her outbursts any more.

Alan looked to the ceiling and could not help but admire the white, smooth surface. He took a deep breath and glanced down at his rough knuckles.

"I am not an orphan," he began. Jobeth startled, sat up straight. "My parents are alive."

"What?"

"Let me finish," he said, not looking up. He did not want to tell this story. It was all a distant memory. A memory he cared not to remember, but if it would help Jobeth convey her own bad memories, then he would do it.

"My parents, they were terrible. They drank moonshine all the time and beat me when they were liquored up. They told me I was nothing but a freeloader and wished I was never born." He choked, refusing to look at Jobeth' sympathetic eyes.

"Anyway, when I was eight years old, one day they up and went to town. I was glad because I could have some peace for a bit. Well, they never returned. I did not know what to do. I was just a little thing. Days passed and I was starving. I wandered through the house crying out for help, but no one answered."

Alan paused remembering the fear he had felt as a boy. The pain resurfaced as fresh as if his parents had left him only the day before.

"The nights were the worst. The night sounds...I used to hide under the bed, thinking every sound was a monster coming to eat me up. Finally, because I was starving, I went out on the streets and begged for food. I even hoped I would see my parents and ask them to take me back. I could handle the beatings but I could not stand being all alone." He glanced at Jobeth and quickly turned away.

She could feel his pain from the experiences he had endured as a child. How horrible it must have been to be abandoned by your parents! She had been lucky to have her parents for the short time she did.

"The street folks took me in as one of their own. Especially one--Eddy."

Jobeth thought she heard Alan's voice break slightly.

"We decided to make it big on our own. We hopped on a train and we did all right. We weren't rich by any means, but we had a home and a little money put aside. Eddy was the first real family I had ever had. I had only lived with beatings and hatred before. Eddy gave me love and comfort. He gave me everything.

"Everything was going well until my parents came and took me away. I still don't know how they found me. I told them I hated them and that I would not go with them. Damn, I was already ten by then and the only time I had ever been happy was with Eddy. He was my father in my heart and the only parent I needed," a tear rolled down Alan's cheek. "I asked them where they had been the last two years. They never answered me and took me anyway. They threatened Eddy and me, telling us they would have the sheriff arrest and hang

Eddy for kidnapping. I had no choice but to go. Eddy cried when I left and I cried too. He was so good to me, Jobeth. No one had ever been so good to me. I knew what it was like to love and be loved in return. I was never allowed to see Eddy ever again. Two months later, he died." Alan covered his face with his hands, his emotions taking control of him. It had been a long time since he had thought of Eddy and he was surprised how fresh the pain still was for losing his only father figure.

"Eddy was old. That was true, and he was the kindest man I ever knew. My time with him was the best part of my childhood. I suppose that is why my parents took me from him. They could not stand to see me happy, especially with someone like Eddy. You see Eddy was black, and there was no way their son was going to be raised by a nigger."

Jobeth looked up at Alan. Jonah's gentle face jumped into her mind. Oh how she missed him.

"I despised these two people who claimed to be my parents. They hadn't changed. They continuously insulted me and beat me within an inch of my life on more than one occasion. They drank day and night; if I ever saw them sober I couldn't tell you. I don't remember it. It was harder living with them the second time. Maybe it was because they kept badgering me for living with a black man, or maybe it was because I now knew what it was like to be loved. I had never known before. Eddy taught me I was good enough to love. That I was someone. That is so important to a child and something I plan for my own children to always know. I will never let them feel like they aren't worth loving... Anyway, my parents were cruel.

"When I was twelve I left to go to town and decided I would never go back. I met Todd and Adam on the road. We met up with others. Some stayed for a while and others left. I remember when we met Jonah." Alan shook his head remembering and laughed sadly, "He was nearly dead when we found him. He reminded me of Eddy. Not just because he was black but also because he was like him: Kind and funny with a good heart. Now they are both gone. I used to believe Jonah was Eddy. Stupid, eh?"

"No," Jobeth said weakly, wanting to reach out and comfort Alan. He looked so lost sitting on the other side of the couch. It broke her heart to see him in such pain. It had never occurred to her that maybe he too had experienced such horrible events in his young life.

"Now you know," Alan said, wiping his face with a hanky he retrieved from his pants pocket. Jobeth looked at him mutely, not knowing what to say.

She did not have time to say anything. Alan leaned forward a bit and looked straight into Jobeth's eyes with his slanted feline ones.

"I want to know what happened to you. I was honest with you, now it is time for you to be honest with me."

"I'm afraid to tell you," Jobeth uttered barely louder than a whisper. Her hand clutched the sides of the cushions, digging in with all her strength.

"Jobeth," Alan said coming and sitting beside her. He pried her hand free from its death grip and lifted her chin to face him. Jobeth closed her eyes and turned her face away, tears beginning to form. He pulled her face towards him again, forcing her to look at him. "Jobeth, you don't need to be afraid. I will never think badly of you." He blushed in all honesty, the love plainly written in his face.

"Oh, Alan, you will loathe me. I just know it and I can't bear for you to hate me." She couldn't stand to look into his loving eyes and see the shock in them when she revealed her sordid story.

"How could I hate you? I love you more than I have ever loved anyone or anything before," Alan confessed.

Jobeth looked into his strange, wondrous eyes. She had once thought they were unusual and odd. Now she saw the truth in them. He loved her and she knew without a doubt she also loved him.

Closing her eyes, her heart started to deaden. How could Alan love her after she told him about herself?

"Alan, I feel the same. I do and that is why I am so afraid of telling you."

"Jobeth," Alan beamed, grasping her hands to his firm chest. His very soul was singing. "This is the most wonderful news I have ever heard."

"Alan, no." Jobeth cut him off, placing the palm of her hand over his moist lips.

He grabbed it and kissed the smooth surface. She gently pulled it away, not wanting to look at his face, the face she had grown to love so dearly.

"I am an orphan," she started. She had to tell him the truth, he deserved to know. If they were to have any future together, she was going to have to come clean about her past. Whatever happened, she would deal with the consequences. The weight of her secret was too heavy to keep any longer.

"A few months before I met you and the others, my parents were killed in a train accident," Jobeth breathed deeply, dreading to tell the rest of her story.

Alan listened patiently, his face void of any signs of emotion. He knew Jobeth would watch closely to see if his expressions would change.

She started by telling him about Pauli, and the tragic accident that took him from their family. Then about the loss of her parents, and her nightmares of how the hurricane had wiped out everyone on the train. Her chest tightened at the recollection of the horrible way her parents died. Jobeth couldn't believe how it still hurt to think of it. It was nearly two years since their deaths. It suddenly dawned on her that she never spoke about how they had died to anyone before.

"I loved my parents dearly." She swallowed; a lump had begun to form in her throat. "They were good folks. Our lives together were happy.

After their terrible deaths I was sent to a home for orphans. I had no living relatives to go and stay with.

The people who ran the home were Mother Tomalina and Father..." Jobeth could not bring herself to say his name out loud.

"Father James?" Alan asked, holding on tightly to her hand. He was beginning to see where Jobeth's story was going.

"Yes." Jobeth whispered, her eyes fixed and blankly staring into space. Her throat felt so tight she could not swallow.

"Was he a priest?" Alan asked. It would not be the first time it had happened with a man of the cloth.

"No," Jobeth said miserably. "We just had to call him that."

"Did he force himself on you?" Alan asked, focusing his eyes on Jobeth's hand held firmly in his.

Hearing the words spoken out loud, Jobeth could not hold back and burst into tears.

Alan caught the agony about to release in his own throat. His arms automatically went around Jobeth and he held her shaking body tightly.

"You don't have to worry. I won't ever hurt you," he whispered into Jobeth's hair as he stroked her thin back. He lifted her chin with his hands so she could look into his eyes. "I love you. The moment I saw you and Shawna asleep on that old mattress, I fell in love with you. Nothing will ever change that."

"But, Alan," Jobeth sobbed, "what happened between--"

"Jobeth," Alan soothed, "he forced you. My darling, how could you blame yourself?" He gathered her into his arms as she sobbed like a child.

"Alan, he said I provoked him, led him on. I didn't think I did, honestly. The man had always repulsed me." Jobeth broke into fresh tears. It was like a dam had been released inside of her and she could not stop the outpour.

"Shh now, I know." Alan patted her head, reassuringly. "If I ever see the animal, I will kill him for what he did to you." He did not want Jobeth to know the anger he truly felt over her rape. The thought of Jobeth's virginity being ripped away from her by another man and the thought of that man touching her and taking something of hers freely without permission made Alan barely able to see straight.

He shook his head, clearing his mind of the horrible vision.

"There is more, Alan," Jobeth sobbed, holding him tight. Alan felt his own eyes burn with tears. He could barely stand to hear what she had to say next.

"What is it darling? You can tell me," he lied, hating every word she uttered.

"I had--" she stuttered, remembering the tiny infant weighing barely more than a stick of butter, so small in her loving arms. "I had a son."

Alan pulled Jobeth abruptly away from him.

"What?" he gasped, speechless and unable to hide the emotion flooding to his face.

Jobeth began to wail.

"Oh, Jobeth, I am sorry. I'm not angry. Please, you just surprised me." He grasped her tightly to his chest again, feeling her tremble uncontrollably.

Fear seized him. Where was the child? It didn't make sense. Jobeth had said her parents died only a few months before they had met.

"I ran away after the first time." Jobeth wept. "I didn't know I was pregnant until that time when I fainted at the lake with Tamara."

Alan remembered the incident and how frightened he had been for her.

The pieces started to come together. He stupidly thought that Jobeth's growing belly was caused by parasites and her deteriorating health during their first travels.

"What happened to the baby?" he was confused. The child would have been born. Where was it and how could he have not known?

"You and Shawna were gone to town," Jobeth sniffed, wiping her red nose. "It was too early for him to be born. Jonah delivered him and he died shortly after. We buried him in the field. The same place where we buried Jonah."

Jobeth held her breath, waiting for a response from Alan. The truth was out. It was too late to turn back.

"Is that why you insisted Jonah be buried there?" Alan asked trying to soak up all the shocking information. How could he have been so blind? He remembered how once for nearly a week Jobeth would not leave her room.

When she did, her waist had shrunk away. Jonah had said Jobeth did not need a doctor that the doctor could not help the sickness she had. It all made sense to Alan now. Jobeth had been grieving the death of her child. How could they have kept it from him? He bent his head, aghast at the horrifying news.

"Yes. Jonah wanted to be buried there, as did I. We named my little son after him." Jobeth's eyes began to tear again. "I did not want my baby, but when I held my little boy, I loved him as much as a mother could love her child. I will always miss him and the man he might have been. But I had Jonah and he was such a support for me. He saved my soul and now they are both gone."

"Why didn't you tell me? I would have been there for you, too," Alan said, numbed.

"I was afraid you would have nothing to do with me. I thought you would find me disgusting. I did not want to lose the only family I still had," Jobeth hiccupped--the horror of the past had already begun to lift.

"You never need to worry about telling me something, Jobeth. I will always listen and never would I leave you," Alan whispered afraid to let her hand go.

"I am so sorry about your son. I cannot imagine your loss."

"I feel so awful. I hated the man who raped me, but I loved the son that was produced from it. Am I that sinful? I don't deserve anything."

"No. Jobeth, you did no wrong. You loved your child, like all mothers should. You cannot punish yourself any longer. You have committed no sin."

Jobeth, now released from her guilt, clung to Alan.

"What about Shawna?" He asked, stroking Jobeth's hair. His feelings were hurt that she had not felt comfortable confiding in him sooner, but he kept his feelings to himself and concentrated on the baffling story being told. Jobeth had lived an entire life without him even realizing it and something told him there was more, meaning Shawna. He had always wondered how the two could be sisters. Besides the age difference, they looked incredibly different from one and other.

"Is she really your sister?"

"In my heart, yes, but no," Jobeth said looking up at Alan. He looked down at Jobeth with more love than she felt she deserved. "Not by blood that is. She was one of the children at the home. Her sister was killed." Jobeth stopped remembering how she had feared the same fate awaited her and Shawna.

"He raped her."

The blood drained from Alan's face.

"I never knew her until I was going to run away. She begged me to take her with me. I almost didn't. I was afraid she would slow me down. She ended up being the reason I kept going. No matter what, I needed to keep going for her."

"I remember what she looked like when I first saw the two of you." Alan said. Jobeth's head was cradled in the nook of his shoulder. "A frightened little lamb. No wonder, the poor thing . . . She was never raped?" Alan asked a few minutes later, afraid to hear the answer.

"No, he seemed to prefer them a little older than her." Jobeth sighed, starting to feel sleepy. It had been an exhausting night.

"Will I ever be forgiven?" She still feared damnation, but not as strongly as before.

"You never needed to be forgiven, Jobeth," Alan yawned too. "You have suffered enough loss. You don't need to be forgiven. You did nothing wrong."

His eyelids drooped and he could hear Jobeth's steady rhythmic breathing. He held her tighter, feeling drowsy.

"I love you, Jobeth, and I will wait forever for you," Alan whispered falling asleep.

The next morning, Jobeth awoke in his muscular arms. She got up and went outside to the chicken coop to get eggs for breakfast. The air felt cool and crisp as she walked back to the house. For the first time in a very long time, Jobeth felt peace in her soul. She stopped and gazed around at the view. The ground was frozen with a sheet of ice that covered everything. Wind blew her waist length hair out behind her and she looked the picture of an ice maiden standing in her frosty domain. Everything sparkled with life and promise. Alan loved her. He knew everything and still loved her. Finally, the weight on her soul was removed. She had nothing else to hide.

She searched the sky. The morning sun shone down on her fresh up-turned face. She grinned and closed her eyes.

"Oh, Jonah, I do miss you and I always will. As always, your words of wisdom have once again rung true. Please watch over my little one. Tell him I love him. Mama, Pappy, I am sorry, but I did not ask for what Father James did to me. I will not apologize for my son any longer. I love you, please watch over my boys and give them the love I cannot right now. I must say good bye and start living my life fresh again." She looked away from the sky and continued walking toward the house. Right beside the door nestled in the corner, she spotted something red buried deep beneath the grass and other vegetation. She bent down pushing away the greenery to expose the tiny red flower trying desperately to shove through. Blood coursed through her warm and alive. It was the same red flower she had planted on her baby boy's grave. The same flower which now covered both Jonah's and the baby's resting place. She thought of the dried seed head she had wrapped tenderly in a hanky in her drawer. They were still with her, they were always with her. Smiling down on the tiny flower, she thought of how she would weed out the other plants to let the flower grow and multiply. She stood up, dusted herself off and opened the door to where Shawna and Alan waited for her.

— Chapter 12 —

The next day Jobeth tended to the chores as usual. She was surprised how easy it was to fall back into old routines. Spring was just around the corner and soon it would be time to plant. Standing outside in front of the mound of dirt that would soon be her garden, she took a deep breath. The taste of spring lingered in her throat. Oh, how she loved this time of year! It was a period for fresh beginnings, and this year it was quite appropriate with her new life spread before her. She examined her garden with an expert's eye. She could easily picture carrots, onions, lettuce and various other vegetables sprouting forth green and luscious.

Noise from the front of the house disrupted Jobeth's thoughts. Curious and a little apprehensive, she went to investigate. Walking around the corner of the building, she stopped short. A buggy full of women was pulling up toward the dwelling. Her heart began to pound, thinking of the vision of the last group of woman she had encountered. Feeling exposed, Jobeth felt a desperate urge to hide. The carriage moved closer and closer toward its destination. Sweat began to form on her brow. What should she do? Where should she hide?

"Hello," waved a pretty brunette. Her other hand held the leather reins, controlling the two horses that pulled the wagon full of women.

It was too late. They had already spotted her.

"Hello," Jobeth stood nervously and walked toward the buggy that had now stopped.

The women began to emerge from the wagon, chatting amongst themselves.

"Did we come at a bad time?" asked the same brunette. She looked to be about twenty years old.

"No. No," Jobeth said, clutching her shawl around her shoulders. Her nerves starting to settle. Held proudly in each woman's lap were baskets loaded down with goodies. Delicious smells raised and mixed together to form a welcoming atmosphere. There was no reason for her to fear these women or anyone else

"Would you like to come in for refreshments?" she asked shyly, not used to entertaining. She was not the same young girl she had once been. It felt strange and a little frightening to be participating in activities long thought gone.

"Well, if you are sure we are not interrupting?" a young blonde, about eighteen, asked. Jobeth looked them over cautiously, soaking their very essences in. There were four of them, all about her age. They seemed friendly enough.

Friends.

It had been so long since she had a girlfriend.

"No, you are not interrupting at all. Just give me a minute to clean up," Jobeth ushered them toward the house. The four young women followed suit, with welcome baskets held snugly in their arms. Walking with her back straight,

She couldn't help but smile to herself. Spring was indeed in the air.

Jobeth nervously poured hot water from her kettle into matching blue cups. Tiny white flowers embroidered the bottom, giving them a dainty, feminine feel.

The four women had seated themselves around the kitchen table; their baskets full of treats were now laid out before them. The four women were as diverse in appearance as were their choices in treats. Sara, the small blonde who had spoken outside, was seventeen and had been married for a year. She had brought homemade bread with pickled eggs. Mandy was a little plump eighteen-year-old woman with thick red hair pulled back into a modern twist that she had adopted since her marriage. She proudly displayed her famous cinnamon muffins topped with melted white icing. Heather was the youngest at sixteen and was expecting her first child. From her basket she removed smaller bowls and the plaid towels that covered them, exposing the colorful berries inside. Each bowl held a different color of berry. Twenty-year-old Lorie was the tall, thin, attractive brunette who had driven the wagon full of greeters to Jobeth's door. From her basket she gently removed two candles finely crafted into a delicate design. Jobeth was in awe of the intricate artistry. The wax seemed alive with movement. Each piece of wax delicately interwove with the other forming a beautiful sculpture. Lorie, seeing Jobeth's expression, was pleased in her choice of gifts. Her candles were her passion and up until she married two months ago, she sold her candles at the local store. Now she made them for herself. Her husband would not allow her to sell them for money. Afraid people would think he could not provide for his new bride. It embarrassed him. Lori sighed, trying to push aside the memory of the joy she had in selling her prize candles to her fellow neighbors and reveling in their complements. She was married now and had to listen to her husband's requests.

"Larry said a new young couple had moved into George and Diana's house and the girls and I decided to make a visit," Lorie spoke, the self-proclaimed leader of the small group. The other girls nodded in unison.

"Do you like it here so far?" asked Sara, sipping her tea. Her eyebrows knitted together in anticipation of Jobeth's answer. She was curious about the frail-looking young woman who bustled about the kitchen trying to scratch up some edible snacks of her own.

"Yes." Jobeth looked back toward the table, enjoying the banter between the girls. Sara smiled supportively. She liked Jobeth's pretty face and knew they would become fast friends.

"Well, you will just have to go into town with us next week and meet the rest of the girls. We all go to Max's Café." Mandy proclaimed, feeling important to be the one to tell Jobeth about Max's. It was a favorite place to gossip and escape the monotony of housework.

"You will just love it. It is just like cafes in France. Jean-Claude, the restaurant's owner, is adorable. He is a short little man with a thin twisted moustache that twitches when he talks rapidly in his accent. It is so European. You will just love it." Mandy squealed, "Our town is just wonderfully modern."

"I feel like I already love it," Jobeth said in all honesty. For the first time since her parents had past away, she felt normal. It felt good to be back in her old skin. Better. She was no longer a young, naive girl. She was a grown woman with the experiences of a lifetime behind her.

"I hear your husband's sister lives with you." Heather beamed across the table at Jobeth. Like Sara, she immediately liked Jobeth.

Jobeth nodded, lowering her eyes. She could not look Heather in the face and lie. She was certain she would see that her marriage to Alan was a hoax, plainly written all over her face.

"Does it bother you?" Heather leaned forward in her chair. The other three followed suit. All eyes were upon Jobeth. She looked up at them shyly and smiled a warm smile. If they only knew how much little Shawna meant to her and how the blonde little girl had come into her life. It was funny how Alan had continued the charade that Shawna was his sister. It just showed Jobeth how much the child meant to him.

"No," said Jobeth strongly, and firmly. "She is like my sister and I love her as such."

"Well it is always good to get along with one's in-laws," proclaimed Lorie. She was thinking of Larry's younger sister whom Lorie did not like. The sister felt Lorie was too old to marry her brother. Cecilia was a constant thorn in Lorie's side and she could not help but notice the love in Jobeth's eyes for her sister-in-law. Lorie felt envious. Jobeth seemed to have everything.

"She is just a little thing, isn't she Jobeth?" she asked.

"She is." Jobeth smiled thinking how much Shawna had seen in her short years. Too much. But things were changing. They were starting a new life again. There were no more secrets. Not really. Jobeth thought of Alan and the warm safe feeling enveloped her once again. It was her Alan feeling: safe and secure. She felt married to Alan. He loved her and she loved him. There was no more shame. Alan had taken the shame away by continuing to love her, even after knowing the truth. They had a chance to begin once more. Jonah had been right. She could move on from her past and love.

"Would anyone care for more tea?" Jobeth stood up to get the kettle. Yes these women would become her friends but they would not be Jonah. No friend could take Jonah's place. She picked up the kettle still hot from the fire and pushing the sadness from Jonah's death down deeper into her body, she waited patiently for a reply.

"Oh yes, me." Mandy piped up. "Jobeth, do tell, what are you going to plant in that glorious garden?"

"I have plenty of plans," Jobeth said, looking out the window and beyond. "Plenty of plans." She turned to her guest, kettle in hand. Life was going to be different here. She was counting on it.

— Chapter 13 —

Jobeth easily fit in with the social elite of the town. She was a young, pretty and kind woman. The local inhabitants drank her up. Jobeth was a perfect hostess when she entertained guests. Her table was always decorated with fabulous chocolate cakes and scrumptious gingersnap cookies, muffins always dripping with sweet icing and other delicious snacks.

As the months passed, Jobeth's teas had become quite the social event for the ladies of the small town. Shawna was instantly a popular friend among her peers. They were constantly under Jobeth's feet begging for yummy treats.

Alan laughed happily seeing his "ladies" become such a success. Life was shining on them and Jobeth could hardly believe it as she basked in their newfound glory. The past they had lived seemed like another lifetime ago or someone else's nightmare. At dinner every night sitting around the supper table, Jobeth would say thanks to God, holding tight to Alan and Shawna's hands. Their lives had turned around for the better and she was so grateful.

On a bright summer day, Jobeth was again socializing with her four closest friends. These were the same four young women she had met that first winter day, sixteen months ago.

They sat around the familiar kitchen nibbling on peanut butter cookies, gossiping about the latest news in town. Jobeth, now very acquainted with the daily coming and goings of the town, joined in whole-heartedly. Her shy reservations had long ago melted away.

Mandy, the one who always knew the latest bits of information, turned to the girls with a twinkle in her eye.

"Guess what?" she asked distastefully screwing her face up. Jobeth and the others leaned in closer to hear. Jobeth was excited. She had news of her own she wanted to tell. Mrs. Black at the general store had told Jobeth that they would be getting telephones soon. The very thought of being able to talk to someone from their home to hers dumbfounded Jobeth. Modern technology excited and frightened her. What would they think of next?

She hoped Mandy did not know about the telephones. Mrs. Black had promised not to tell Jobeth's four favorite comrades, knowing the young woman wanted to be the one to share the details with them. Like everyone else in town, Mrs. Black adored Jobeth and her little family.

Mandy sat back and wrinkled her spotted nose.

"Someone moved into that old house down on Bayer's Road."

"Oh, really?" Jobeth asked, delighted. Her piece of gossip had not been revealed. She knotted her brows confused. She was familiar with this road and couldn't think of any houses along its unkempt grassy lane. It was in the poorest part of town and she was baffled as to who would want to live down there. "Oh well, the more the merrier," she shrugged. She quickly thought of what to bring the new family. Peanut butter cookies? Or maybe sandwiches made with thick homemade bread?

She looked up at the four pairs of eyes glaring at her disapprovingly. Taken aback, she sat silent, confused at what she had done wrong.

"Yes, I heard," Lorie snorted disgusted. Jobeth was becoming increasingly perplexed. This person who had moved onto Bayer Road was apparently someone of distaste to her friends.

"She is a whore, Jobeth. Not a person you go greeting." Heather said, patting Jobeth's hand like a confused child. She could not help noticing Jobeth's puzzlement and felt she needed to save her naive pal further discomfort.

"She lives there with a baby and no husband. The father, whoever he is, ran out on her when she was pregnant."

Jobeth's face turned red. The little baby boy she had delivered popped into her mind. He had been so small and so sweet. It broke her heart to remember him gasping in vain for air. She had no husband when he was viciously conceived. There was so much her friends didn't know about her.

"Yes," grunted Sara, pushing her blonde hair away from her face. It had been neatly wrapped in a bun, but some strands had escaped in her fury to speak her mind. Her eyes became angry little slits. "Do you blame the father? No proper girl would get herself in a marrying way."

"Serves the trash right," snipped Lorie as she stood up for another cup of tea. Ridged with anger, she turned when her cup was full and she sat back down with a thump.

"And do you want to know something else?" she boomed. The three other women looked wide-eyed in anticipation. Jobeth sat back, her face a crimson red. The others assumed that the conversation was embarrassing her.
Sara and Heather almost felt they too should blush. Only a proper girl would turn the cardinal color Jobeth had.

"I even heard that once she lived with a group of boys and she was the only girl."

Jobeth turned pale and swallowed hard, her throat becoming increasingly dry. She took a drink of her tea, looking at her friends who had transformed into a den of lionesses. If they knew Jobeth's past they would be appalled. But they would never know her. "I bet she doesn't even know who the father is.

Can you imagine?" Sara gasped, looking quite horrified.

Heather put a protective hand over her once again enormous stomach. She had become pregnant right after the birth of her daughter.

"Oh that poor little baby girl! What fate awaits her? That innocent child in the care of that hussy. The shame on that baby when she starts to get older. She will end up just like her mother." All the women nodded with certainty. Jobeth could do nothing but stare at them in disbelief.

"I think someone should get the baby away from that woman before she does it any more harm," Lorie glared, feeling a twisting in the pit of her gut. It was not fair for this tramp to have a child when she so wanted one herself. It was starting to become apparent that she might be barren. Larry and she had been trying to have a child for two years without success. A tear formed in the corner of her eye. She wiped it away, covertly, not wanting her audience to see just how upset she was. Larry's sister made comments all the time about Lorie's inability to produce children. She said it was because Lorie had waited too long to snag herself a husband. Lorie would retaliate, telling her sister-in-law that she was not yet twenty-two and that woman had children much later than that in their lives.

"Yes, but their first?" Cecilia would answer cruelly.

Lorie squeezed her lips tightly together causing the blood to drain away, leaving them a grayish-pink color.

"You don't really mean to take this woman's child do you?" Jobeth interrupted. She had to speak up. The pain of losing her own son was still too fresh to keep quiet.

"Taking her baby?"

"She doesn't deserve a baby!" cried Heather in an emotional outbreak so common for her. Jobeth was not sure if it was the pregnancy or if she was just prone to outbursts. She had never seen Heather when she was not with child.

"That baby deserves better than that trollop. Someone like Lorie and Larry!" Heather continued. They all knew how much Lorie wanted a child. Jobeth had been a confidante a few times to Lorie's monthly disappointments. Lorie felt that since Jobeth was not yet pregnant herself after a year of marriage, she would understand her pain the most.

Jobeth noticed a glimmer of hope in Lorie's eyes. She wanted the woman's baby for herself.

"That woman Tamara doesn't deserve a baby. She should belong to Lorie." Sara said, repeating what Heather said. She felt proud of herself. She had discovered the perfect solution for the baby and her friend.

"Tamara?" Jobeth whispered, knocking her cup and spilling her tea all over the table. Lorie jumped to the rescue grabbing a rag from the counter. Jobeth took it from her, embarrassed, and began to wipe up her mess. She could feel the eyes of her friends drilling into her back.

"Jobeth, is something wrong?" Lorie asked. "I know the subject is horrible, but dear," Lorie said tenderly, "such things do happen in the world. You must not be so sensitive."

"Nothing is wrong," Jobeth lied, mopping up the tea before it stained the lace tablecloth. She concentrated on the work at hand, not wanting them to see her deceit.

Tamara was here? This could not be happening. Not now when things were going so well.

The women left some time later and Jobeth was glad to see them go. They eventually stopped talking about Tamara and had moved onto more pleasant conversation, like who was getting married and who was having babies. Jobeth told her news about the telephones and tried to act excited, but the accounts of Tamara plagued her mind. She had to know if this woman was the same Tamara she knew.

Jobeth dreaded what she already knew was the answer. The Tamara she had known had lived with a group of boys. The same boys she herself had lived with.

She sat down to finish a quilt she had been working on for Heather's new baby. Her mind kept wandering, causing her to make mistakes. She put her work down and grabbed a shawl, throwing it carelessly over her shoulders. Staring at the door, she wondered what she was doing. If the woman was Tamara, her comfortable life would be over. Did she want to risk it all, this life she and Alan had created for themselves? And for what? A girl who had never been very nice to her.

"She is family," Jobeth said out loud, ashamed of herself. Even though

Tamara had fought hard to make Jobeth feel unwelcome, in the end they had come to some kind of truce. Jobeth looked around her spotless home. It smelled of happiness and comfort. A rag doll sat sideways on a cushioned chair waiting for its owner to return home to play. Jobeth's quilting lay slumped in her basket. Alan's pants were hidden beneath waiting to be mended. This was her home with Alan and Shawna. She signed, opened the door and walked out.

Plenty of thoughts ran through her mind as she walked down the overgrown path. Once she even turned to go back, but changed her mind continuing on.

She had to know if the girl was Tamara. Jobeth kept remembering the day she had fainted while washing clothes with the wild, black-haired beauty. Tamara had been frantic with fear. She had cared for Jobeth when Jobeth felt no one cared. If this woman was Tamara, she couldn't turn her back on her. Jonah had not turned on Jobeth when he found out the ugly truth about her. Neither had Alan. She was stronger for their love and devotion. How could she even think of not doing the same for Tamara?

Jobeth continued down the path to the only house on the road. It was a rundown shack. The type of place they might have stayed in, in the old days. A chill ran up her spine. She was suddenly afraid of ending up in one of these shacks once again.

She took a deep breath, shaking off the creeping sensations and knocked on the gray wooden door. Inside, shuffling could be heard as Jobeth held her breath, afraid to move.

The door swung open fiercely, exposing a pale, dreadfully gaunt woman with blazing black hair. Jobeth gasped at how awful the woman looked, dressed in a ragged red dress that showed off too much of her thin breasts. Dark angry eyes glared fire, in expectation of a fight. Her nostrils flared. It could only be Tamara.

"Hello," Jobeth said weakly, swallowing back her surprise. Even though she had expected the creature in front of her to be Tamara, she was not prepared for what she saw. Skin just concealed her bones. Dark circles smudged the bottom of her hollowed eyes.

What has happened to you? Jobeth thought, feeling guilty. She was the picture of health. Life had been good in the past year and it showed on her, just as it showed how hard it had been on Tamara.

Jobeth had gained weight and turned into a slender woman instead of the scrawny girl she had once been. Tamara was ghastly white where as Jobeth's complexion was tanned and healthy from hours spent in her garden. Her hair was bright and shiny in the latest style, piled high off her neck. Although her clothes were modest, they were stylish, clean and new. It seemed her misgiving about the group of people they had parted ways with so long ago had come true.

The concerns she had were answered in the skeletal woman before her. They had not done so well.

"Have you come to make shit?" Tamara steamed in her familiar voice.

Some things did not change. Tamara was still as feisty as ever.

"Well take your Miss Priss ass outta here. I ain't gonna listen to your 'save the soul' crap."

For such a frail looking creature, Tamara was still full of vinegar.

"Tamara, don't you recognize me?" Jobeth asked, knowing very well she looked different. "It's me, Jobeth."

Tamara took a closer look. She did not recognize the sanctimonious individual before her.

"I was with Alan and Jo . . ." She stopped and took a deep breath, not knowing why she suddenly felt as though she had run all the way there. "And Jonah . . . Remember, I was with a little girl name Shawna?"

It all seemed so long ago. Jonah's beautiful face saturated Jobeth's mind, as it often did. She quickly brushed the thought aside. There would be time later to think of him. As Jonah would say, "The living need you, Jobeth."

"Jobeth?" Tamara whispered, a sparkle of light flickered in her dark eyes for a moment and just as quickly died out. "What do yah want?" she answered coolly.

For a moment Tamara had felt hope and then, examining Jobeth's appearance, had dismissed it. This was not the same person she had encountered years ago.

"Can I please come in? It's cold out here," Jobeth lied. She was not cold but she could see Tamara shiver and could tell she had nothing beneath her thin garment. Her dark nipples stood erect through her dress, causing Jobeth to avert her eyes from the sight.

Tamara moved out of the way for Jobeth to enter, not once taking notice of her embarrassment.

The inside of the shack was drafty, damp and filthy. There was no furniture to be seen, only a crumpled mound of clothing in the middle of the dirty floor.

In the corner stood a solitary cradle, Jobeth could not help eyeing.

"How long have you lived here?" Jobeth asked, forcing herself to look around the rest of the room. Tamara crossed her arms over her breasts. She began to walk around Jobeth, circling her like a vulture. Resentment was plainly written on her face.

"Just came," she snipped.

Jobeth could not help but feel pity for the bony mortal before her. Never had she saw someone so pathetic and so in need.

"Looks like yah headed in the right way," Tamara conveyed in her twangy voice. It had been a long time since Jobeth had heard such ragged speech. She had prided herself on correcting Alan and Shawna's broken dialect. "When did you leave Alan and Jonah?" Tamara presumed, giving Jobeth a critical look.

There was no way Jobeth had stayed with them. She looked too much like a "society" woman. Somehow Jobeth had picked herself up and got back to the life she had obviously lived before, dumping Alan and Jonah the first chance she had.

"I didn't leave them," Jobeth said, feeling the air go suddenly thick and stale. She could not breathe and worried about the infant she assumed was in the cradle.

"Yah mean you still with them?" Tamara sounded surprised.

"Well--" Jobeth stalled, dreading telling Tamara about Jonah. She had always been tender toward him.

"I knew it, they--" Tamara stifled a laugh with the back of her catlike hand. "Alan and Jonah dumped you."

"Shawna and I are still with Alan," Jobeth swallowed, trying to rid her throat of the familiar ball that formed every time she thought of her dead friend.

"What about Jonah?" Tamara shrieked, looking like a caged animal ready to attack. "You didn't leave him alone did you?"

"Of course not!" Jobeth countered back, appalled. "Do you think I would do that to him?"

A sad, pitiful wail broke the increasing tension mounting between the two women.

Tamara and Jobeth both turned at the same time toward the bassinet where the cries originated.

"Way to go, you woke the kid." Tamara stormed toward the cradle and roughly picked up the infant inside. She was dressed in a ratty, gray sleeper that had a damp spot growing near her bottom. Jobeth's heart skipped a beat. The baby had black curly hair plastered to her small wet head.

"My baby," she whispered, remembering her tiny son with the same black curly hair. Her chest hurt and she didn't know why. All she did know is that she had to see the child.

"Can I hold her?" she asked Tamara. The child seemed pitiful in her mother's skeletal arms.

Resting the squirming infant into the crook of her arm, Tamara could not help noticing Jobeth's look of longing. She was confused. Why was Jobeth here? What did she want?

"Why are you acting like this, Tamara?" Jobeth asked coolly, her eyes not leaving the wailing newborn. Small fists belted the air, with a fury equal to the child's mothers.

"I haven't seen or heard from you in two years. We shouldn't be fighting," Jobeth said, focusing hungrily on the baby.

Tamara slowly approached Jobeth, the babe still crying in her arms. Jobeth feared Tamara would drop the child, she was so frail looking.

"Why on God's big old earth would I ever be happy to see the likes of you?"

Tamara threw back her head and laughed. With quick sudden movements, she popped out a pale breast and began to nurse the baby. The infant sucked forcefully from the flat, pallid bosom, scrunching her face up and turning red. The offered breast did not look like it could nourish the child and from the looks of anguish on the newborn's face, it wasn't far from the truth.

"I didn't even like you. You just here to look good in front of your friends? Helping the whore to save her soul, are yah now, Jobeth?" Tamara cooed, ignoring the child.

"Stop it!" Jobeth collapsed to the dirty floor causing dust to fly up around her and gently tumble down onto her clean skirt. She did not know why she dropped to the ground so theatrically. She just did and she looked to Tamara beseechingly. No tears fell from her eyes, but she could see water droplets forming in Tamara's dark orbs.

"Please, Tamara, I am here to help. Don't be a fool and let your pride get in the way. We are family. The only family either of us have. We must stick together and not fight."

Something in Tamara's tough shell cracked. She had been alone and ridiculed for so long. Now here was Jobeth, a woman of respect, on the ground begging for Tamara's friendship. Calling her kin. A sob escaped her chapped lips. She bent down defeated beside Jobeth onto the dirty floor. Someone wanted her, wanted to love her. She hugged the baby close to her exposed chest and began to cry. She was so alone. Jobeth wrapped loving arms around the scrawny shoulders shaking with emotion. She held Tamara tightly, comforting her.

"Don't worry any more, Tamara," Jobeth said, stroking the black mass of curly hair. It felt surprisingly soft. "You are home now. You are home."

— Chapter 14 —

"You will stay with us," Alan stated as he stared at the ghostly figure that resembled the Tamara he had known. They were seated around the kitchen table, awkward with each other. Tamara seemed uncomfortable in the warm, sunny kitchen. She couldn't remember if she had ever been in such a place.

The brothel she had grown up in had a large agreeable kitchen, but this one she sat in was someone's home. The brothel was not. She looked down at her narrow fingers, examining the dirt beneath her broken nails.

"You know that will cause problems for you all. I ain't married and I have a young 'un."

"Tamara," Jobeth reached across the table and grabbed the girl's hand reassuringly. "You are family. We want you and the baby with us. It does not matter what others think."

Tamara smiled weakly and took another bite of the stew Jobeth had given her. It was her third bowl. She had to admit that Jobeth was a good cook. The stew hit the spot in her empty stomach. It felt good to be in Alan and Jobeth's home. She stared at their concerned faces and put down her spoon.

"Well," she said, sipping some of the hot tea Jobeth had placed in front of her. Jobeth is determined, Tamara thought, to pump me full of food. "I guess you all are wondering how I got ma self in such a state."

"Whenever you're ready, Tamara." Alan said softly, unable to look at her.

Guilt engulfed him as it had Jobeth. He was proud of how he had changed their lives for the better. Seeing Tamara brought back bad times when things were so difficult. Had the rest of their little group done as poorly as Tamara? He hoped not.

"If yah all are willing to have me and the kid, I feel it's only proper to tell you how I got the whelp." Tamara took another bite of stew and tried to prevent the juices from dribbling down her mouth.

"When we all split up back at the old house, Oliver and I headed out and pretended we was married . . . seemed the proper thing to do when we was in towns and stuff. Well, Oliver," Tamara snickered, the love in her eyes plain to see, "he took the pretending as real. I suppose I am to blame for going along with the little devil." She looked at Jobeth and felt a twang of jealousy.

Jobeth had a good life with Alan. Oliver had turned into a drunk and would never amount to much, but they had some wild times gambling and making love. They had fooled no one with their marriage facade. No one believed Tamara and Oliver were wed. She looked too much like a saloon girl and he was a typical gambler.

"But a girl needs some lovin' once in awhile and Oliver sure did feel good," Tamara said with a twinkle in her eye, remembering their crazy times together. It had been a roller coaster of emotions. One day they were flying high and just as quickly the next day, crashing low.

Jobeth flushed and looked toward the bedroom where Shawna sat on the bed with the baby. She breathed a sigh of relief. Shawna had not overheard Tamara talking. The bright child was too excited about the baby with the dark curly hair, so much like Tamara's, to be concerned with the adults' conversation in the kitchen.

Tamara could not help but notice how she embarrassed Jobeth. Normally she loved to shock people like Jobeth, but a wave of remorse filled her. She had been starving when Jobeth found her. It had become so bad that Tamara had decided to let some of the stinking men who knocked on her door bed her for money.

News of her arrival had spread fast. The husbands of the good town had come with hats in hand feebly asking for her services. She was disgusted at how they ogled her, as all men did, and sent them away, saying it was still too soon after the birth. Now her money and her food had run out. She planned to let the next man who came calling into her door. In fact, she thought it was a customer when Jobeth arrived. Jobeth didn't know it, but she had saved Tamara from selling herself. Saved her from a fate worse than her mother's. Her mother had at least had a clean, fancy brothel to live in with warmth and food. There was always the company of the other girls to fight off the loneliness and despair. If the townspeople shunned them, they at least had each other for comfort and it did not seem as hurtful when surrounded by your peers.

Tamara shook her head. Alan and Jobeth had no idea how hard it was going to be now that they had taken her and the baby in. They would be frowned on by their neighbors, especially the men. Tamara was familiar with half of the men folk. They had looked forward to her speedy recovery from childbirth.

When they found out that the town whore was staying with one of the respected citizens of the community, all hell would break loose. It was all right if Tamara knew who each man was, but an entirely different story if she spoke up to Alan and Jobeth. It was not going to be easy, but they seemed willing to deal with whatever came about. Alan and Jobeth were not fools. They knew what the town thought of her and what would happen to their social status once it became apparent that they called her family.

"Anyway," Tamara continued, "Oliver had a habit of leaving for days. Usually he spent the time drinking or gambling our money away. I was used to his whoring around, but the last time he left a week went by, then another, and he still didn't come back. By then I had learned about the tot. I thought no babe of mine is gonna have a drunk for a daddy who's never there for her ma. So I left."

"Did you love Oliver?" Jobeth asked, remembering the boy with the beautiful blue eyes and brute personality. He was definitely a charmer with his sweet-talking ways. Jobeth glanced at Alan and warmth filled her heart. He was no Oliver. Alan was so reliable, so sweet. He would never abandon her or Shawna.

"I still do," Tamara said matter-of-factly, staring blankly into space. Her eyes glazed over and one had to wonder what secrets lurked behind those dark pupils. In the next room the baby began to cry. Tamara's eyes slowly focused.

Jobeth stood automatically, her body instantly responding to the child's sad wail and went to the other room to retrieve her.

"I think she's hungry," Shawna said, leaning over the beaten cradle Jobeth had dragged over from Tamara's shack.

"There, there little one." Jobeth gently picked up the tiny infant and cradled her to her chest. The smell of soiled diapers and baby vomit lingered in her nostrils. She made a mental note to bathe the baby after Tamara fed her. Jobeth smiled. She had some baby clothes she had sewn for Heather's impending birth in her dresser. She had just laundered them so they would be ready to give to Heather when needed. Jobeth could not keep her heart from skipping a beat thinking how lovely Tamara's baby girl would look in them. She even thought Shawna might have some diapers from her dolls that would fit the infant.

"Tamara?" Jobeth beamed, coming out of the room, cradling the baby in her arms. Shawna followed close behind. Tamara glanced briefly up from her bowl of food to Jobeth, who stood with the child comfortably in the crook of her arm. The infant seemed content for a change. "I have all sorts of baby clothes here that will fit this precious darling. If you wouldn't mind, it would please me to let the baby have them." Jobeth proudly placed the squiggling child into Tamara's arms, where she proceeded to pull out a sagging breast to feed her.

"Sure." Tamara shrugged, uninterested. Alan turned away red-faced and coughed. Tamara, choosing to ignore him, paid no attention to Alan's embarrassment.

"I have chores," he said uncomfortably, getting up from his chair.

"All right," Jobeth clapped her hands together trying to cover up his discomfort. Alan hastily left the house and Jobeth sat back down in his chair. Her eyes were unable to leave the sight of the child hungrily nursing from her mother.

"What's her name?" Jobeth asked as the baby's eyes opened and looked toward her. Oliver's exquisite blue orbs stared out of the tiny face. Jobeth could not believe how beautiful the infant was.

"Haven't named her yet," Tamara said a little frostily.

"How old is she?"

"A month. Hey," Tamara said, changing the subject, "where is Jonah?"

Jobeth tilted her head down, dreading what was to come next. It was going to be hard telling Tamara the awful news about Jonah.

Tamara seeing Jobeth's reaction instantly became nervous and the baby fussed at her breast.

"Tamara, there is no easy way to say this. I have terrible news . . ." Jobeth began. Tamara listened with no emotion showing on her face as Jobeth told her the details of the last years. She recounted with sorrow, the events leading to Jonah's death, omitting the facts that Jonah had helped her deliver her son and consequently bury him. There were certain subjects she did not wish to share about her life. Subjects that would always be personal to just her.

When Jobeth finished, Tamara looked blankly with no trace of emotion.

"I need to lie down," she responded dully. Jobeth nodded and showed her to a room. The frail woman sank into bed exhausted, leaving the baby in Jobeth's care. She did not come out of the room for the rest of the night. Jobeth had to send Alan to a neighbor's in search of a bottle to feed the hungry infant.

She was relieved no questions were asked of him. There would be plenty of interrogation later. Jobeth just wanted to settle Tamara and the baby in first.

Later that evening the baby woke. She cried for sometime before Jobeth went to get her. As she opened the door quietly, she was assaulted by the smell of dirty diapers. Tamara slept like the dead, not even stirring as her daughter cried out in hunger. She picked up the soaked, squirming bundle and quietly changed her so as not to wake Tamara. Jobeth then went to rock the baby in the other room. She hummed as she fed the infant a warm bottle of goat's milk; her heart feeling full as she looked down on the content babe gulping from the bottle. She couldn't help but to love the child instantly. It wouldn't matter what the town's people said, Jobeth wouldn't lose this baby too.

Tamara was staying.

Tamara did not do much but stay in the room given to her. She was like a ghost that only showed herself at dinner. Every morning Jobeth would peek into the room Tamara shared with the baby and without fail Tamara would be staring out the window from her bed, her dark eyes no longer flashing with fire, but dull, the fire extinguished.

She immediately began neglecting the baby from the first night, letting her cry until Jobeth came to rescue her. It was Jobeth who would change and feed the infant. Tamara seemed to be finished with breastfeeding, just as her milk, which had been weak to begin with, went dry.

Jobeth didn't mind. She loved caring for the child Tamara and Oliver had created. She could sit for hours looking at the blue-eyed beauty, touching her tiny toes and fingers. Every moment with Tamara's child was like a lost moment with Jobeth's son.

As much as they hated to create more lies, Alan and Jobeth made up a story to tell everyone. They said Tamara was Alan's cousin they had not seen for many years. She was family and they could not turn her away. Although Jobeth's friends said they understood the situation she and Alan were in, the friends Jobeth had once longed for stopped coming over. She was no longer invited to any social gatherings in return.

Shawna too was shunned, no longer popular with her peers. The parents of the children did not want them associating with a child whose cousin was a woman of ill repute. It was apparent to Jobeth that her family was no longer accepted in town. It bothered her at first, but then she would look at the smiling baby cooing in her arms and know she had made the right choice.

Shawna adored the baby, too, making the sacrifice of losing her friends worth the pain.

"She is such a joy, Jobeth. This baby has brought so much joy to our home," Shawna would say every time she saw the smiling cherub. Jobeth agreed.

The only thing that bothered Jobeth was that Tamara still had not named the baby. The infant was three months old and they still did not know what to call her.

Shawna was the one who began to name the baby unofficially. While leaving for school she would come over to the plump child sleeping in Jobeth's arms, rosy lips all puckered up, and kiss the healthy infant's cheek.

"Good-bye, little Joy," Shawna would whisper as the baby stirred in her sleep.

Three months later, Jobeth woke as she always did. She turned over carefully, so as not to disturb Shawna who was sleeping peacefully beside her. Shawna's hands were tucked safely under her chin with her long blonde hair fanned out on the pillow like gossamer.

"Shawna, time to wake up, sweetie," Jobeth whispered, gently getting out of bed. Shawna moaned, trying to wake up. This was a familiar pattern for the child in the morning. Jobeth smiled lovingly as she watched Shawna struggle with sleep. She patted the little rump reassuringly and went to wake Alan in the loft.

She placed her hand on the bottom of the wooden ladder and called up to him.

"Alan! Morning!"

There was no response.

Jobeth began ascending the ladder, knowing full well he would not budge from bed till she was all the way up.

"Alan." Jobeth stepped off the ladder and padded over to him. He was asleep on his bed with his back toward her. "Time to wake up, sleepy head." She sat down on his bed anticipating what was to come next. Alan turned around and encircled her waist in a great big bear hug. She fell into his arms willingly.

"How I love being awakened by you," he muttered, kissing her softly on the neck.

"How I love you," Jobeth giggled, kissing him playfully on the lips.

This had become their morning routine. Although they had not proceeded past kissing and petting, Alan and Jobeth were more in love than ever.

"Lay with me?" he asked, patting the blankets beside him. Jobeth shook her head.

"I need to get to Joy. She is probably starving and soaking wet by now."

Bending down, she kissed Alan one more time. "I will meet you downstairs for breakfast."

"Abandoned by the woman I love, and for what?" he jested, lying back on his cot. His naked chest glistened with morning sweat. "A dimple-faced baby who melts my heart with a gurgling smile. Uuuhh." He sighed. "The women in my life!"

Jobeth laughed at him as she proceeded to descend the stairs toward Tamara's room. She had not felt right taking the baby out of her mother's room, even though it was apparent Tamara was going to have nothing to do with her daughter.

She walked up to the door and stopped. It seemed awfully quiet behind the shut entrance. Feeling nervous for some unfathomable reason, she grasped the round metal knob with a sensation of foreboding. Opening the door she felt her mouth fall open and heard the baby begin to cry. Next thing she knew Alan was beside her, looking frantic.

Jobeth was screaming.

— Chapter 15 —

Hanging from the ceiling beams with chicken wire around her neck, Tamara's dangling body hovered above them.

Shawna ran into the room after hearing Jobeth's screams and collided with Tamara's swaying body. The chicken wire had cut deep into her skin causing blood to drip from her neck. Some landed on Shawna's face. Unable to stop herself, Shawna gazed up in horror into Tamara's bulging, dead eyes and fainted. Alan instantly lifted the small limp body and took her from the horrible scene. Jobeth stood, frozen, staring at the swinging corpse in disbelief.

The baby was crying from behind Tamara's frame. Snapping out of her shock, Jobeth squeezed past the corpse's hanging legs, trying in vain not to touch the bloody body.

"It's okay, baby. It's okay." Jobeth cooed, lifting the sobbing infant to her. The baby buried her head in Jobeth's shoulder, calmed by the familiar voice.

"Jobeth?" Alan shouted from outside the room.

"I'm in here, Alan," Jobeth called back, rocking baby Joy. She couldn't turn toward his voice. To do so would mean facing those dreadful swaying legs.

"Are you all right?" Alan asked, appearing beside Tamara's hanging body.

Jobeth shook her head, refusing to look his way. She kissed the top of the baby's soft black hair and fought back the urge to cry.

"Alan?" she asked, not knowing what else to say. "Now what?"

"Pass me the baby, Jobeth." Alan said, reaching out his hands. Jobeth walked over and placed Joy into his arms. The baby stretched out her hand and grabbed instinctually onto the hem of Tamara's nightgown, causing the body to teeter on the wire that suspended her.

"No, Joy!" Jobeth pulled the baby's hand roughly away, causing her to wail.

"Get out of there, Jobeth," Alan beseeched, reaching a hand toward her.

Jobeth took it, pinching herself through the doorway again, careful not to touch Tamara.

When she was safely through, Alan handed the baby back.

"Go to Shawna. She needs you. This is going to mess her up for a long time," Alan raked his hand through his hair, clenching his teeth.

"Damn her . . . Damn her for doing this to Shawna . . . to us."

"Alan?" Jobeth asked, lost beside his shoulder. He shifted around and grasped her and the baby in his arms.

"Don't worry, Jobeth. I'll take care of it. I'll take care of everything." He kissed her forehead and looked into her bloodshot eyes.

Jobeth was trying hard to hold herself together.

"Go to Shawna. Go." He gently turned her in the direction of the other room down the hall. Jobeth, clutching the baby tightly, went in a daze to Shawna.

Alan began the gruesome chore of taking Tamara's body down from the beams. He wrapped her in a clean sheet and laid her on the floor. Arrangements would have to be made to bury her. He would say she died of a broken heart after losing her husband before the baby was born. No one needed to know that Tamara had killed herself. As he started to clean up the blood that had dripped onto the floor, Alan noticed a piece of paper on the night table. He lifted it up and started to read it. His shoulders shook, overcome with emotion, as he read Tamara's last words, sad now that Jobeth and Shawna had started teaching her to read and write.

Tamara was buried in the town cemetery, inside the church graveyard.

The lie Alan and Jobeth told about Tamara's death would keep her out of the shunned cemetery. They could not stand the thought of Tamara spending eternity disdained as she was in life.

Jobeth's friends were at the burial, proclaiming their regrets over her family's loss. She thanked them, clinging to Tamara's orphaned child and to Shawna's ghostly pale hand. They exited the cemetery, huddled together, getting strength from one another.

Shawna could not sleep at night anymore. Nightmares plagued her. Tamara had left them all scared.

"It will be all right, Jobeth," Alan said, clutching her shoulder. Jobeth nodded in response.

"I will be fine as long as I have you and the girls."

"She left a note about the baby, Jobeth."

"Alan, I just can't right now. I am too angry with her to listen to what she had to say. What she did to Shawna . . . to the baby . . . to us." Jobeth waved her hand in the air dismissively.

"When you're ready then." Alan kissed her cheek warmly.

"I don't know when I will be ready. She left Joy, mother- and fatherless. She left Shawna haunted." Jobeth shook her head frustrated. "I am angry, Alan. Very angry."

"I understand."

Later that evening at dinner, Jobeth looked across the table at Alan. He ate his portion of roast chicken silently. The baby was asleep in Jobeth and Shawna's room.

It had been a long day and she felt emotionally exhausted.

She watched Shawna pick at her food. The little girl had not spoken since she walked innocently into Tamara's lifeless form. Jobeth reached across the table and grabbed hold of Shawna's hand, searching for a response from the catatonic child. Shawna did nothing but continue to stare at her uneaten food.

"Okay . . . I will read the letter." Jobeth's eyes did not waver from Shawna's pale face.

Both Alan and the child looked up together and gaped at Jobeth unexpectedly.

Alan quickly pushed back his chair and stood up, absentmindedly dropping his napkin onto the table after wiping his mouth. He left the room and returned quickly holding a piece of paper with childish handwriting on it.

Unfolding the paper, he cleared his throat.

"Do you want me to read it to you?" Alan asked.

Shawna's hand silently crept into Jobeth's. She felt the faint squeeze of the little knobbly digits.

"I think we both need you to read it to us, Alan," Jobeth said reassuringly squeezing Shawna's hand back.

"Dear Jobeth and Alan," he began "I know you ain't gonna understand my doin' of this. You ain't the same people as me. I just tired of this world. I don't wanna be here no more. I ain't the motherin' type and I don't wanna be no one's ma. You folks will be good for the kid. Give her a home I never knew. She will have a chance in this life if you are her kin. She will be a whore if I raise her up. It's true. My ma was one and I done my share of hustling, but I ain't claimed to be no saint. Thanks for taking me in and calling me family. I know it cost you lots. Don't tell the kid about me. Let her think you was always her folks. Give her a good name. I kinda like Joy.

Tamara."

Alan folded the letter back up and grimly looked at Shawna and Jobeth. The child began to sob: the first signs of emotion since the whole incident began.

Both Jobeth and Alan went to her, comforting her, cradling her protectively in their arms. Over Shawna's blonde silky hair Jobeth looked into Alan's red-rimmed eyes.

Shawna was not alone in her suffering. Jobeth cupped Alan's unshaven face with the palm of her hand. His warmth heated her palm and she felt overcome with emotion.

"We can't stay here," Jobeth's voice trembled, barely above a whisper.

"No." Alan choked, cupping her hand to his mouth. He breathed heavily into the moist flesh, then bent down and gently kissed the top of Shawna's head. Shawna turned her hollowed, tear-streaked face up to his, her lips quivering.

"I just want to go away from that room," Shawna wept. "I keep seeing her ..."

"Shhh," Alan soothed, stroking her long soft hair. "Everything is going to be all right."

"Promise?" Shawna sniffed, rubbing her swollen blue eyes. They were so light they seemed almost transparent in color. Only a hint of sky blue circled her pupils.

"Yes, I promise. Nothing bad is going to happen to my three girls again," Alan said with determination. He meant it. He would rather die than see the women in his life hurt any more. They had all been hurt too much already in their short lives. Even Tamara's little baby. She had already experienced the loss of both her parents. It was odd, but Alan felt more like he was the baby's father than Oliver. Jobeth was definitely more of a mother than Tamara. His heart thumped thinking of the baby as his and Jobeth's. It felt so right, so very right.

"We have to sell the house, Alan. We can't raise the baby here. Everyone knows about Tamara," Jobeth said. "She would never have a normal life here. Everyone would know."

"We will."

It took awhile before the house was sold. Jobeth and Alan tried to bring things back to normal in their home for the children's sakes, but the once cozy home that had brought them so much joy and security was now cold and foreign. They could not wait to leave it and its ghosts behind.

All three agreed on naming the baby Mara-Joy. Mara after her birth mother, Tamara. They all felt since the baby would never know Tamara or the person she was, the child should have at least a piece of the name of the woman who had given her life.

When they were finally on their way again, in another little covered wagon, Jobeth wondered, as Shawna sat between her and Alan, where would their lives lead them now?

Mara-Joy cooed sitting in her arms and Jobeth gave her a gentle, loving squeeze. Alan looked at Mara-Joy and smiled as he ruffled Shawna's hair. She playfully pushed his hand away and laughed a little. That was a good sign. Shawna had not laughed in ages. With time she would heal. Jobeth was sure of it. They all would be fine, as long as they had each other.

They traveled all day until the sun began to fade behind the hills. Alan pulled up to a little church isolated in a thicket of bushes. Jobeth, startled out of her thoughts, looked up at him questioningly.

"Alan?" she asked, completely confused. She looked around. All she could see was green emptiness. There were no buildings she could make out except for the church in front of them. There were barely any trees around, just a few skinny poplars with some meager leaves clinging to them.

Alan stepped down from the wagon and bent down on one knee. Shawna covered her mouth, but could not stifle a little giggle. Jobeth suddenly felt awkward and silly. She looked around to see why Alan was kneeling before her.

Trembling Alan lifted his arms up to her, his green cat eyes wavering with emotion. Jobeth gazed at him, her hands clasped tightly around the plump baby.

"Jobeth, I know I'm not perfect and you could do better than me . . ." Alan stammered, so afraid of what she would say. He had been planning this since he sold the house. He knew they would pass this church and had made all the arrangements days before. "But . . . Oh, hell," he flustered, jumping up and running his fingers threw his hair. He turned his back away from Jobeth. This was his last chance. He could no longer put it off. Alan spun around and seized Jobeth's hand, causing her to let out a surprised yelp.

"Will you marry me?" he asked, his eyes filled with love and tears. Jobeth sat silently, mouth open. "We could be good parents . . ." he continued, not daring to stop. "Ask Shawna, she knows better than anyone." Shawna continued to cover her smile with her hands.

"Do you have anything to do with this?" Jobeth asked, unable to say anything else. She was totally taken off-guard. Never had she expected Alan to propose marriage to her.

Shawna shrugged and started to chuckle. The black under her eyes faded for a moment and light seemed to shine from her blue-gray orbs.

"Will you, Jobeth? You know I love you," Alan begged, still holding tight to her hand, he clasped it to his lips and held his breath afraid to move.

Jobeth continued to stare into Shawna's large eyes.

"I would be a fool if I said no." Jobeth smiled, feeling in her heart she was right.

"We will be one big, happy family," Shawna said, smiling faintly. "The mama and the papa and the two sisters."

Jobeth put her arm protectively around Shawna's young shoulders.

"Do you want Alan and me to be your mama and papa?" Jobeth asked, watching tears well up in Shawna's dazzling clear eyes.

"You already are my mama and papa," she said earnestly.

Jobeth kissed Shawna's warm forehead, feeling her heart would break for love of the child. She turned to Alan, her hand still held tightly in his.

"Alan, I love you so much. It would be an honor to marry such a wonderful man." Jobeth leaned over, trying not to squish the baby.

"Pass me Mara-Joy," Shawna said, reaching for the baby. The infant whined in protest, angered over losing Jobeth's attention.

"Hush now, Mara-Joy. Your mama needs to be with your papa right now," Shawna soothed, rocking the baby. She wiggled in Shawna's arms for a moment then stopped as Shawna continued to rock back and forth.

Jobeth jumped down from the wagon with Alan's help and hugged him tightly to her.

"Why are we at this church, Alan? Do you plan to get married right now?" Jobeth asked, planting a kiss on his lips.

"Yes. As of this day you will be my wife officially. No more make-believe. Marry me now, Jobeth," Alan said again, forcefully, as he got down on one knee once again. He withdrew a small gold band from his pocket, and held it out to her.

Jobeth took the ring and placed it on her finger. It fit perfectly.

"Yes, Alan . . . yes, I will marry you now."

No sooner were the words out of her mouth than Alan jumped up and swung Jobeth around in his arms.

"You have made me the happiest man alive," he grinned. Jobeth held him tightly, afraid to let go as she twirled through the air. She could not believe it. She was going to be Alan's wife.

They were married by an old reverend with milky blue eyes and flyaway white hair. He preached his sermon, his clouded eyes not seeming to notice the children who witnessed the ceremony before him. Shawna stood holding Mara-Joy in her arms, between Alan and Jobeth. Even Queenie the dog sat beside Jobeth protectively.

They were all smiles as the reverend pronounced them man and wife. Alan gently leaned over and kissed Jobeth softly on the lips. Jobeth closed her eyes, allowing the warmth of Alan's kiss to envelop her body. The ceremony was over. They were married.

They traveled for a few more hours before Alan stopped the buggy. Jobeth nervously put Shawna to sleep in the back of the wagon. The child closed her eyes quickly, sleeping deeply for the first time since Tamara's suicide. Jobeth walked over to Mara-Joy's cradle. The baby slept peacefully, sucking her fingers.

Jobeth gently touched the soft dark curls. Curls so much like her little son's hair. She pulled the blanket up around the baby's neck. She had Mara-Joy now. She was hers.

"What is the matter?" Alan whispered from the back of the wagon. Jobeth jumped, her hand fluttering to her heart. She had not heard him enter.

"I didn't see you," Jobeth said, shyly facing him. Her heart began to race.

Alan held the back flap of the wagon open and the moon's light glowed around him like a halo. Jobeth breath caught in her throat. He looked so big and handsome standing there. She loved him deeply. Her stomach began to churn. She didn't know if it was because of fear or desire.

"I'm sorry. You seem to be lost in deep thought. What were you thinking?" Alan asked, coming to sit on the bed that was now his and Jobeth's. He gazed at her as she stood staring at him. The thought of Jobeth and him together as man and wife heated him with desire. He felt ashamed and tried to hide his growing arousal by crossing his legs. He knew he would have to go slowly with Jobeth. She had been through so much already. They had the rest of their lives to become lovers. She was his wife now and that was all that mattered to him.

"Alan, I know you expect me to . . ." Jobeth turned away, embarrassed. Her fingers flew to her mouth and she began to bite her nails.

Alan stood up and went to her, gently placing his hands on her shoulders. She was shivering.

"Jobeth."

"We're married, Alan . . ." she quivered, his touch raising goose bumps all over her body. She could not face him, for fear her legs would give out from under her and she would fall flat on her face.

Jerking uncontrollably, she took a deep breath trying to relax. Her body seemed to have a mind of its own and she could not stop it from trembling.

"Jobeth, I am not Father James. I will never hurt you." His fingers gently caressed her arm, causing a shiver to run up her spine. "We have our whole lives to be together. I will wait 'till you are ready."

She turned to face him. He stood so close to her she could feel his breath on her body and the response it made.

"Thank you," she sniffed, her shivering subsiding. He tenderly kissed her forehead and went back to his bed.

"Alan, I do love you. I want to be with you as your wife, I do . . . I'm just scared."

"I love you too." He stood again and kissed her cheek. "Don't worry. Everything will be fine."

"All right," Jobeth whispered, lying down on the bed with Shawna across from Alan's. Alan went to his bunk, turning away from Jobeth. He might as well get some sleep. He was not worried about how the evening ended. As much as he wanted to sweep Jobeth into his arms and make love to her, he would wait till she was ready to be his. The important thing was that she was his bride; in time they would be together as man and wife.

Jobeth could not sleep. The sounds in the wagon told her everyone else could. Quietly she got up and went outside to clear her mind.

The cool air felt good on her face. She breathed deeply of the smells around her. She liked the fragrance of grass swaying in the wind mingled with the scent of horses. It was liberating.

She sensed someone behind her shoulder and wheeled around, alert.

Alan stood in front of her. He was dressed in just his pants, his strong naked chest rising up and down. His want for Jobeth was clearly visible. She went into his arms and he held her tightly. She could smell his special scent and kissed his neck hungrily, tasting his sweet flesh.

"Jobeth . . ." he moaned rubbing her back. She gently took his hand and moved it up her side, slowly. Shivers of fear and joy coursed through her body.

Alan sighed deeply, slipping his fingers into Jobeth's blouse. She arched her back as he released her breasts, and his warm hands encircled her soft mounds. Delicately, he bent his head and brushed his lips against an erect nipple. Currents of electricity bolted through Jobeth's body as Alan began to suck each nipple in turn.

"Are you sure you are ready?" he asked looking into her flushed face.

"Yes . . . Yes, Alan. I love you." Jobeth tangled her fingers into his sandy hair, pulling him to her waiting body.

"I love you, Jobeth . . . so much." He bent back down to her heaving bosom, feeling the texture of her with his tongue. Jobeth arched her back again, a moan escaping from her lips. Alan began to trace his hands down her tight belly. He lifted his head and kissed her hard on the mouth.

Jobeth greedily accepted his tongue.

Alan slowly removed her skirt and ran a hand between her legs, feeling her warmth. She stiffened for a moment as Alan gently laid her onto the soft grass. Little by little he began kissing her face, her eyes and her mouth. Moving down lower to her collarbone, her breast. Jobeth groaned with pleasure. She gasped when he suckled her breast and then began to kiss her belly, moving lower and lower. Her legs spread automatically as his lips explored. She had to control herself from crying out when his head went between her legs.

Never could she imagine it could be like this. She began to squirm with pleasure.

He sat up and removed his trousers, exposing his erection. It no longer scared Jobeth. She reached out and stroked his hard member, hungrily wanting him. Wanting him to consume, to fill her with a need she had never known.

He pushed her back with his smooth chest and lay on top of her, kissing her passionately. Jobeth wrapped her long lean legs around his body. Alan leaned forward and looked deeply into Jobeth's eyes as he entered her with ease.

She cried out his name as he slipped inside her. Alan sobbed as his want for Jobeth overtook him. They wrapped themselves together, their bodies becoming one. They cried together as they reached climax and lay spent, still attached, in each other's arms.

They slept for an hour then made love again, just as intensely and full of hunger. They didn't stop until the sun began to rise and the children were about to wake up. Reluctantly they dressed, kissing each other deeply, and went back to the wagon. Mara-Joy stirred.

A new day had begun.

— Chapter 16 —

Nine months to the day after Alan and Jobeth were bonded in marriage, Joanna, named after Jonah, was born. They had found a small village and made their home just outside the town. It was quiet and the people were kind.

Shawna stopped having nightmares and returned to her cheerful self. Life was good. No one could ask for more.

Two years after the birth of Joanna, Constance, named after Jobeth's mother, was born. Joanna was two, Mara-Joy was three and Shawna was twelve years old.

Late one summer afternoon, Jobeth was working hard in her garden. She loved working her hands in the soil under the sun. Constance, who was three months old, was in a sling comfortably tied to Jobeth, shaded by her mother's body. Mara-Joy and Joanna were sitting on the shady grass just beside the garden, playing with wild flowers. Shawna was at school and would not be home for another hour. The heat of the sun was pounding down on Jobeth.

Kneeling in dirt, she sat up straight, adjusted the baby and moved a strand of hair out of her face. In the distance she could see Alan and another man heading up to the house. She squinted to see who the stranger was. He seemed familiar to her but she couldn't put her finger on it.

"Mara-Joy, Joanna, come into the house. Quickly now," Jobeth said, heading toward their small home. The two little girls stood up from their tasks and began to follow their mother.

Both girls were adorable. Mara-Joy had long black curly hair with piercing blue eyes, much in contrast to her creamy complexion. Joanna, on the other hand, had long straight, sandy blonde hair with the most amazing green eyes. Her skin was a golden brown color from hours of playing in the sun. They both began to run toward Jobeth. Joanna stumbled and fell but was on her feet in no time chasing after her sister.

Inside the house Jobeth quickly cleaned herself and the children up. She didn't want whoever was with Alan to see her and the children in a state of mess.

"Jobeth?" Alan yelled from the doorway. "You will never guess who is here with me."

Jobeth couldn't help but notice Alan's voice was strained. Almost nervous.

She felt her blood turn cold. It had been over three years since any dilemmas had arisen in their lives. There was too much at stake now to deal with problems. The children just could not be uprooted. Jobeth shook her head, annoyed at herself. She always feared the worst.

"Don't be silly . . ." she mumbled, whipping Joanna's grimy face. But she couldn't help herself. The feeling of foreboding kept creeping up on her.

Joanna chimed nonsense in her small voice. Jobeth looked into the little child's tanned face. Alan's cat eyes stared back at her.

"I wasn't talking to you . . ." Jobeth said absently.

Joanna bent her eyes to the floor. Had she done something to upset her mama?

"Come along, children." Jobeth shepherded the girls into the other room where Alan stood stiffly with the foreign man.

"Pappy! Pappy!" Mara-Joy cried out when she spotted Alan. She ran full speed into his arms and he hugged her small frame close to his strong body.

"Did you bring me candy?" Mara-Joy squealed in Alan's loving arms. Joanna was jumping up and down around Alan's feet begging to be picked up and cuddled too.

"Me too, Pappy!" she said in her childish voice. Alan bent down and scooped her easily into his free arm. Both little girls, who looked so different from each other, smothered Alan with kisses. Alan laughed, delighted. His daughters were his pride and joy. He treasured them all deeply.

Jobeth cautiously looked to the dark-haired man standing, admiring Alan.

The attractive fellow looked somewhat familiar to her, but she could not quite place him.

Alan deposited the excited girls down on the floor and walked over to Jobeth. He took Constance from her arms and nuzzled her into his neck. The baby cooed, snuggled in her father's embrace.

"Jobeth, honey," he seemed skittish. "You remember Oliver, don't you?"

Jobeth's mouth dropped open. Of course--the dark hair, the handsome good looks. She glanced into his deep blue penetrating eyes. The same penetrating eyes Mara-Joy possessed. How could she not remember the man who had helped to create her dear daughter? If it had not been for Mara-Joy coming into their lives, who knows what would have happened? Alan and Jobeth might never have married and been so completely happy all these years.

She closed her mouth and glanced over at the man who unintentionally had changed their lives. Oliver looked older.

He was no longer the boy she remembered. He was much more handsome.

Jobeth blushed, unable to help the flutter of butterflies in her stomach. How could someone be so good-looking?

Out of the corner of her eye, Jobeth noticed Mara-Joy standing beside Alan, sucking on a red stick of candy. She had Tamara's fiery black hair and creamy complexion, but it was Oliver she resembled - an interesting combination of the two of them. Mara-Joy was a beauty; Just like her birth mother and father.

"Of course I remember Oliver," Jobeth said anxiously. She nervously went and embraced the man who could destroy her life. He smelled of the outdoors and horses. The combination that was very masculine and becoming. "Of course, Oliver. Excuse my rudeness when you first came in, but it has been so long." She pulled away from him and stood beside Alan who still cuddled Constance in his big arms.

"Jobeth," Oliver said in a serious voice, not in the least bit disturbed by Jobeth's behavior, "you still look as pretty as ever."

"I see you are still the same sweet talker," Jobeth smiled, trying to act normal in front of the unshaven man.

Oliver chuckled and turned to look at Mara-Joy and Joanna. Jobeth and Alan couldn't help but notice how his eyes skimmed past plain little Joanna, whose face was now smeared with red candy, and rest firmly on Mara-Joy.

"Oliver!" Jobeth nearly shouted. She didn't know what to say. She just knew he had to stop looking at her child. All eyes turned to Jobeth, including the eyes of Mara-Joy. For a moment Jobeth thought she saw anger flare in the little girl's face--almost as though she were upset that the center of attention was no longer her. Jobeth pushed the thought from her mind. How could a three year old know the difference?

"I hope you will be staying for dinner?" Jobeth asked, praying he wouldn't. She wanted him to leave, now. Never to see Mara-Joy again.

Mara-Joy scowled, her arms tightly crossed over her small chest.

"Well if it ain't--I mean isn't any bother--I would love to stay." Oliver stared at his shoes, not budging. The tension in the air was so thick you could almost see it.

"No bother at all. You are always welcome in our home. You are family," Jobeth said without emotion. Joanna began to whimper, rubbing her grimy hands into her eyes. Jobeth absently looked to her and noticed the child had wet herself. She instantly went into Mommy mode and began to peel the wet clothing off Joanna who stood sobbing. Alan placed little Constance down into her baby basket that was always left in the main room.

"Thank you, Jobeth. It means a lot to me," Oliver replied, avoiding looking at her.

Joanna's cries became louder with embarrassment over wetting herself. Alan coughed nervously, it was beginning to get hectic in the closed room and he could tell Jobeth was not happy with the turn of events. He didn't blame her for her feelings in the matter. He was not exactly jumping for joy at Oliver's arrival either.

"Why don't we go outside and clean up for dinner? Jobeth will settle the children and we can all talk at supper."

Oliver nodded and followed Alan outside.

Joanna shrieked loudly into Jobeth's ear, annoying her. Mara-Joy danced behind the two men, following them outside. She looked back at Jobeth and gave a big smile and waved.

Jobeth returned the look with warmth. Mara-Joy was so beautiful, such a gift that she and Alan had been given.

Fear began to tingle through Jobeth's veins. I wonder if Oliver has come to take Mara-Joy away! Stop it! she screamed in her mind as she went through the motions of cleaning up Joanna's mess. The little girl continued to cry and hiccup, her face a wet muddle of tears, snot and red candy. Jobeth paid no attention. Her mind was miles away. What was Oliver doing here after all this time and what did he want? There was nothing to worry about. Oliver didn't know Tamara was pregnant--let alone that she had given Jobeth and Alan the child. Oliver's child. She pushed the thought from her head. Mara-Joy was not Oliver or Tamara's child. She was Alan and hers--their daughter, and no one was going to take their child from them.

"You two went and got married," Oliver laughed later that night at the supper table. Jobeth had cooked roasted chicken with mashed potatoes, garden vegetables, stuffing and homemade bread. Oliver claimed it was the best meal he had ever eaten.

Shawna was home and she could not stop staring at the dark-haired Oliver. She was completely entranced by his dazzling good looks. Oliver seemed to relish Shawna's attention, winking whenever he could across the table when he thought no one was looking. She blushed a deep red as she tried to stifle her giggles behind her slender hand.

Jobeth knew Shawna had an instant crush on Oliver the moment she laid eyes on him. After she arrived home from school and found out Oliver was staying for dinner, Shawna ran to her room and brushed her long blonde hair till it shone like pale gold. Alan reintroduced Shawna to the devilishly handsome man, finding himself a little amused. He had never seen Shawna behave like this, her crush so plain to see. You would have to be a blind man not to notice the way the girl was beside herself with glee over Oliver's arrival.

"Alan, I remember Oliver," Shawna said with a twinkle in her eye. She remembered him all right. She remembered how handsome he was and how he had smiled at her so many years ago. Even then she had found Oliver irresistible.

"And I remember a little girl in pigtails, not much taller than my knees. This ravishing beauty before me cannot be that little girl all grown up!" Oliver said, smiling at the adolescent. He reached for her hand and gently kissed the top of it, his lips lingering on the soft flesh for just an instant.

Shawna turned crimson red, hiding her mouth with her other hand.

"It's me, Oliver. I'm not a little girl anymore." Shawna beamed, unable to contain herself.

"Well, you aren't a grown woman yet either." Jobeth piped in as she set the table for supper. Shawna bent her head, mortified. "Shawna, I need you to help with dinner please."

"Yes, Jobeth," Shawna glanced up quickly at Oliver, hoping he had paid no attention to Jobeth's outburst.

"You look like a grown woman to me," Oliver whispered softly into Shawna's ear as he followed Alan into the dinner room. She grinned from ear to ear, her face burning with fire, and ran off to help Jobeth set the table.

"Yes," Alan replied across the table from Oliver. "It has been about five years now."

Jobeth and Shawna both glanced at Alan over their plates of food. They had only been married for a little over three years, not five.

Jobeth knew immediately what Alan was doing. If Oliver knew they were married for just three years, he would figure out that Mara-Joy had been born before they were husband and wife. Jobeth bent her head so that she could face Shawna's confused look. She gave the young girl a look that told Shawna to keep quiet. Shawna obeyed, lowering her eyes and busying herself, eating her mashed potatoes and gravy. If Alan and Jobeth didn't want Oliver to know when they were married, Shawna wouldn't offer him the truth.

"You have three very beautiful daughters," Oliver announced while eyeing Mara-Joy. A cold bolt shot up Jobeth's spine as she spoon-fed Joanna some shredded chicken and potato in her highchair. Some had dribbled down Joanna's chin. Jobeth spooned it up and popped it into the child's waiting mouth. Joanna usually fed herself, getting most of the food on her, rather than into her mouth, but Jobeth had wanted dinner to go smoothly. That meant she didn't want Oliver to witness her child decorated in chicken and mashed potatoes.

"Do you think I am the most beautiful?" Mara-Joy tittered in her childish voice.

"You are very beautiful," Oliver replied warmly to the little girl, his blue eyes mirroring the child's.

What do you think of our Shawna?" Jobeth interrupted. She did not like the way Oliver stared at Mara-Joy. It was a searching look. A trying-to-place something . . . examination. Even though she didn't want to encourage Shawna's crush on the much older Oliver, it was better to distract Oliver with Shawna than to have his attention focused on Mara-Joy.

The little girl glared at Jobeth and stuck out her bottom lip in a pout.

"The last time you saw Shawna, she wasn't much older than these children," said Jobeth, feeling sick. She did not like the way Shawna was mooning over Oliver and here she was using Shawna's idolization for her own benefit.

"I remember a little frightened girl with large blue eyes hiding behind your skirts, Jobeth," Oliver turned his attention back to Shawna who would willingly worship the ground he walked on.

"You have grown into a beautiful young lady, as I have already said."

Shawna's face became flushed, once again. She was about ready to burst with delight. She could not help herself. Oliver made her stomach flutter and her heart race. She hated it and loved it all at the same time.

Mara-Joy's eyebrows furrowed together angrily. She reached for her glass of milk and let it slip from between her fingers. It hit her plate and spilled into her food. Everyone turned to Mara-Joy and her milky disaster.

"My food is all yucky!" She wailed at the top of her lungs. Large tears welled in the corners of her eyes and streamed down her face.

"I'll get you another plate, dear." Jobeth said, standing up and reaching for the ruined dish of food.

"Jobeth, sit and eat, I'll do it," Alan said getting up and retrieving the plate, careful not to spill the milk onto the table.

Shawna frowned at Mara-Joy. She was now smiling with all eyes on her. It seemed to Shawna that whenever the attention was taken off little Mara-Joy and put on someone else, the child had one of her accidents.

Alan returned with a fresh plate of food and placed it in front of Mara-Joy.

"Any sons for the future?" Oliver asked changing the subject.

"Hopefully." Alan laughed, patting Mara-Joy on the back. She grinned up at Alan as she daintily took a bit off her fork.

"I want a little brother," Mara-Joy said, as she chewed her food.

"Do you now?" Oliver bit into a hunk of meat, keeping his eyes focused on his meal.

"Well, Oliver buddy . . ." Alan sat back and pushed himself away from the table, his plate polished clean. "When do you plan to settle down and get married?"

Shawna's eyes lit up. Jobeth noticed and laughed to herself. Shawna was only twelve years old. Still a child. Much too young to think of marriage, let alone marriage to Oliver. If she remembered correctly, he was a year older than she.

Jonah had told her Oliver's age years ago when they lived in the rundown house together. That would make Oliver twenty-two years old. Nearly twice Shawna's age. Jobeth couldn't imagine Shawna thinking of marriage. She still thought of the girl as a little child.

Oliver cleared his throat. "Well that's why I'm here." He coughed again, feeling uneasy for the first time since he had arrived.

"I never thought I would run into you folks. Should have seen my face when I saw Alan working in the mill! Almost like seeing a ghost from the past." His brows furrowed with lines.

"Guess I did see a ghost." He stopped speaking and stared into space, remembering the past. He had been so alone the past four years, wanting so much to have the love of a family. When he had seen Alan earlier in the day, hope had filled him. At last familiar faces--someone who was home. But Alan and Jobeth's reception of him seemed frigid, almost as though his presence threatened them.

"Anyway," his eyes cleared, "I've been searching for Tamara for the last four years."

Jobeth and Alan looked to each other, shocked, not knowing what to do. It wasn't what they had expected Oliver to say. Looking for Tamara? He was supposed to have abandoned her.

"I love her and want to make an honest woman out of her. I'm ashamed to say I treated her badly," Oliver said, frowning. Jobeth looked to Shawna. The blonde girl was rigid, her face crestfallen. One moment, Oliver shined glorious light on her and the next, he had destroyed its fragile beginnings.

"I know it's the reason why she left me," he continued, despite the unhappy faces of the people in front of him. "I wanted to start a family." Jobeth took a huge drink from her glass of milk and eyed Oliver. The fear she had felt when first seeing Oliver was not in vain. He had come to take Mara-Joy away.

"You mean you didn't leave her?" Alan asked, amazed. He looked as though the wind had been knocked out of him; his face was a grisly grayish color.

"No, I would never leave her." Oliver stood up, searching the stunned faces around him. "She just up and left one night while I was sleeping. I swear it's the truth." He looked imploringly from one face to the other. "Have you heard from her?"

Jobeth was speechless.

Shawna sat quietly, not able to look at Oliver's frustrated face. The memory of Tamara swinging from a beam was still fresh in her mind. It was something she would never forget, just as she would never forget her sister Donna's violent murder.

"Jobeth, I think it is time the girls went to bed." Alan stood and picked Mara-Joy up in his arms. She began to wiggle in protest.

"Pappy no, I don't want to go to bed. I want to stay up." She pushed against his chest angrily.

"You just sit still till we come back, Oliver," Alan said, walking out of the room, Mara-Joy still protesting.

Jobeth stood, collecting Joanna out of her high chair. She paused. Oliver's head fell into his hands and he sat back down in his chair with a thud. Jobeth's lips tightened together. What were they going to tell him?

"Shawna, keep Oliver Company while we settle the girls?" Shawna nodded, not saying a word. Jobeth left the room abruptly. She followed Alan down the hall and into the small room with two beds waiting for their owners.

"What is wrong, Mama?" Mara-Joy asked. Jobeth's bottom lip began to tremble. She could not bear to lose her precious Mara-Joy.

"You and Pappy look scared."

"Nothing is wrong, baby," Alan, whispered into her tiny ear. He placed her on one of the beds. Shelves decorated with dolls bordered the walls. The room was painted soft pink and white. The twin beds were identical with matching pink and white quilts. Handmade toys littered both beds.

Jobeth placed Joanna on her bed and quickly tucked her in. She brushed a kiss on the child's warm forehead. Joanna grabbed her favorite teddy bear and snuggled under the covers. She felt sleepy with all the excitement of the day. Jobeth slipped over to Mara-Joy's bed and kissed her flushed cheek. Alan went to Joanna's bed and gently pulled the covers above her shoulders, kissing and hugging her good night. Jobeth could hear Joanna giggle at her father's attention and proceeded to copy Alan's actions with Mara-Joy.

The girls settled down quickly. Alan blew out the light and took Jobeth by the hand. She squeezed his fingers tightly as she followed him out towards the kitchen.

"She is our daughter," Alan choked back, knowing what he was going to do. "Tamara did not want anyone but us to raise her. She is ours now." Jobeth trembled, her mind racing. Alan stopped her in the hallway before they reached the kitchen. He held Jobeth in his arms securely. She felt his strength seep into her and her nerves began to subside a bit.

"Everything will be okay," he whispered. Jobeth nodded, believing him because she loved and trusted him.

— Chapter 17 —

"Alan?" Jobeth whispered in fear. They could not lose their daughter. Jobeth had experienced many losses in her life. Even the death of a child, but the thought of losing her precious Mara-Joy was too much to bear.

They stood holding and comforting each other in the hallway.

"She is our daughter, Jobeth. Ours, not his. We are the ones who have been raising her--caring for her. He lost his chance to be her father years ago." Alan squeezed Jobeth tight. "I'm not saying anything." his face was blank of emotion.

"Tamara never wanted us to tell. She said so herself."
Jobeth could tell Alan was trying to convince himself. "I won't lose her. I won't. Not even to Oliver." Alan said, looking away from Jobeth's eyes. Guilt was plaguing him. All he could hear in his mind were Oliver's words about how he wanted to start a family with Tamara.

"I won't lose her either. She's ours," Jobeth confirmed, taking some of the responsibility off of Alan's shoulders.

Their decision was made. They held hands as they walked down the hall way to where Oliver sat waiting.

He stood up from the table, tall and dark, when they entered the room. Shawna continued to sit still, her eyes darting between Alan and Jobeth. Her nerves felt taut and she couldn't help feeling frightened. She had made up her mind to keep quiet and listen to what Alan and Jobeth were going to say to Oliver. Shawna was the only other person besides Jobeth and Alan who knew Mara-Joy was Tamara's birth daughter. She had a sneaking feeling that Oliver might be Mara-Joy's father, remembering Tamara mentioning something about Oliver when Mara-Joy had been a baby.

"Alan? Jobeth? What do you know about Tamara?" Oliver demanded, sternly. They knew something. It showed in their odd behavior. Even Shawna seemed quiet and withdrawn when Tamara's name was mentioned.

"Oliver," Alan sat down. He scanned the cozy kitchen with its clean wooden counters and familiar warm smells. He could not bring himself to look at Oliver. "Tamara . . . There is no easy way to say this. She's dead."

"What?" Oliver choked in disbelief, clutching the table's edge for support. He was unprepared to hear the words Alan had said. Many scenarios had played out in his head as to what happened to Tamara, but he never expected Tamara to be dead.

"It's true, Oliver. I'm sorry," Jobeth murmured, unable to face the stricken Oliver. A pinched noise escaped from the back of his throat.

"No," he gagged, crumpling down into his seat.

Jobeth lowered her eyes, ashamed. The pain in Oliver's face was unbearable.

"I am sorry," Alan replied sorrowfully, remembering Tamara's gray limp body, wrapped in a white sheet, her blood staining it red.

Oliver lowered his head and cried shamelessly. Shawna, overcome with grief for Oliver and the vivid memories of Tamara, began to silently cry too.

Jobeth turned away from the sight of Oliver's bent head quivering in his arms.

Alan reached a hand under the table and squeezed Jobeth's knee for support. They had to stick together in this.

She took a deep breath and straightened her shoulders. Oliver would get over his pain of losing Tamara. They, on the other hand, would never get over losing Mara-Joy if they told Oliver the truth about the child Tamara left behind.

"What happened to her?" Oliver sobbed trying to compose himself.

Alan began to explain the grisly events that happened three years prior, omitting the fact that Tamara had a child.

Shawna sat silently listening, her eyes trained on her half-eaten food before her. She was unable to believe that Alan didn't even mention the fact that Tamara had a child with her and that child was Mara-Joy.

Oliver listened, quietly crying, saddened by his loss.

"Excuse me," Shawna whispered, standing up and leaving the room, her eyes avoiding the people around her.

Jobeth, frightened, looked toward Alan. He pointed his head in the direction of Shawna. With his eyes he told Jobeth to go to her. To silence her.

Jobeth stood up rather abruptly, excusing herself.

"Shawna still finds it hard to talk about Tamara. It was a very traumatic time for us all."

"Of course, Jobeth, go to her," Oliver sniffed, rubbing his nose on the sleeve of his shirt. Jobeth averted her eyes from Oliver. His eyes were red-rimmed and seemed to be bluer from the crying. He looked pathetic. If she looked at him too long, she would be consumed with guilt.

Quickly she went down the hall to Shawna's room. She took a deep breath before entering the room unannounced. The young girl lay on her bed sobbing.

Her blonde hair fanned around her tear-streaked face. Jobeth sat down on her bed and began to fiddle with the multicolored quilted bedspread. It was similar to Joanna's and Mara-Joy's, except theirs were pink and white, whereas Shawna's was made of several soft colors that suited her complexion and style.

The two of them had made all the quilts together for the beds, just as they had done so many things together over the years.

"Shawna," Jobeth began, unable to face the upset girl.

"Why are you and Alan lying to Oliver?" she buried her face deep into her pillow. Shawna loved Jobeth and Alan and would never want to upset them in any way. But the sight of Oliver's devastated face was too much for her to bear. How could the two people in this world who had shown nothing but compassion for others stand by and let Oliver suffer?

"Shawna," Jobeth placed a hand on her quivering back. "There are things that--"

"No, Jobeth," Shawna interrupted, sitting up, her eyes brimming red with tears. The look on her face made Jobeth shrink back in shame. "Oliver is devastated. How can you both sit there and not tell him he has a daughter? A daughter from the woman he loves."

"Stop it!"

Jobeth had never raised her voice to Shawna before and both were a little startled by the venom behind it. "She is my and Alan's child. We are the only family she has ever known." Jobeth stood up and began to pace the floor in the small, warm room, biting on her clenched fist.

"You are too young to understand. We really don't know anything about Oliver--what kind of man he is."

"That is not true, Jobeth, and you know it. I know Oliver is Mara-Joy's father and he has a right to know he has a daughter."

"He is not her father! Alan is and I am her mother." Jobeth stood with her back to Shawna, who could not believe how cold Jobeth was being. "Tamara wanted it this way. It is what Tamara wanted," Jobeth repeated, trying to persuade herself. "She didn't want Oliver to have her."

"She never expected Oliver to show up looking for her." Shawna retorted.

Jobeth swiveled around and flared at Shawna. The young girl jerked back, afraid. Never had Jobeth looked at her that way.

Jobeth strained her neck, holding back her anger.

"Shawna," she said calmly, devoid of emotion, "Alan and I have always been good to you. Have we not?" Her brows knitted together questioningly.

Shawna nodded apprehensively, unable to recognize the woman standing before her.

"We have never asked for anything in return for all we have done."

"Yes, I know that, but--"

"No one will take Mara-Joy from me. Do you understand that?"

Shawna sat in disbelief, her mouth hanging open.

"We are what's best for Mara-Joy. We are her family. You, Alan and I. We are all a family. We have all lost too much. Do you understand? I will not lose Mara-Joy." Jobeth tried to soften her voice but failed. The tightness still clung to her throat. "What kind of life could he give my Mara-Joy?"

"All right, Jobeth. I understand," Shawna mumbled barely able to speak. "I owe you everything. I won't say a word to Oliver about his daughter."

"My daughter!" Jobeth forced through clenched teeth, the veins popping angrily from her neck. "My daughter." She turned abruptly and stormed out of the room, closing the door behind her.

"Your daughter," Shawna said, staring at the closed door, tears streaming down her face. "Your daughter, Jobeth."

— Chapter 18 —

Alan, Jobeth and Oliver talked late into the night. With the threat of Mara-Joy being taken from them gone, they could relax and enjoy Oliver's company.

They spoke of what had happened in the last seven years. Oliver was saddened with the news of Jonah's death and how it had come to pass. It was hard for him to take it in all at once. Even harder to find out that Tamara and Jonah had been gone for so long without him knowing. He was happy for Jobeth and Alan. Life had blessed them with a happy marriage and three beautiful daughters and Oliver couldn't help but comment on what a beautiful person Shawna was turning into.

"She will make some man a wonderful wife," he said, sipping a cup of coffee.

Both Alan and Jobeth agreed. Jobeth smiled proudly as she gushed about Shawna's achievements, her earlier discussion with Shawna forgotten.

By the end of the evening, the three decided Oliver had no reason to continue traveling. Tamara was dead. His family was also Jobeth and Alan's. Alan would get him hired on at the mill where he worked. Oliver was humbly grateful.

When Alan and Jobeth were in their bed finally, and Oliver was asleep on their couch, Alan turned to his wife and sighed.

"Did we do the right thing, Jobeth?" he asked, cupping her naked breast beneath her gown.

"We asked him to stay," Jobeth's voice answered him in the dark.

"But is that enough?" he ran his hand up her thigh, raising her gown.

"Shhh," she whispered, kissing him lovingly on the lips.

"I love you," he reached for her in the dark, needing the comfort of her embrace to ease his troubled mind.

"I love you too, Alan." Jobeth went to him, wanting to be one with him.

The next morning, Jobeth stood by the wood stove cooking eggs for breakfast. Shawna walked into the kitchen looking as though she hadn't slept a wink all night. Joanna and Mara-Joy sat at the wooden table eating their scrambled eggs scowling, as usual, at each other.

"Shawna?" Jobeth said, stopping what she was doing and walking around baby Constance, who lay on a thick blanket on the floor.

"Yes, Jobeth," Shawna answered dully, sitting between Joanna and Mara-Joy, hoping it would stop their constant bickering.

"I would like to talk to you," Jobeth twisted her fingers. Shawna shrugged her shoulders and followed Jobeth into the living room.

"Listen, about last night--" Jobeth began.

"I won't say a word. Like you said, Jobeth, I owe you everything," Shawna said stiffly. Her nose was tipped red from crying all night.

"Oh, Shawna," Jobeth put her arm around the girl's shoulders. She was nearly as tall as Jobeth. Shawna stood rigid and unmoving.

Jobeth cleared her throat, grabbed Shawna by the shoulders and made the girl face her.

"You don't owe me anything. I was just frightened last night. I love you. You have given so much to me."

Shawna, weakened by the soothing words-- words that were familiar to her-- looked up into Jobeth's begging eyes.

"I love you too, Jobeth." Shawna hugged Jobeth furiously to her, afraid to let go of the only woman who had ever been a mother to her. She had been so frightened. The whole night she had lain awake fearing Jobeth would send her away. She knew without a doubt that Jobeth would do anything to keep Mara-Joy.

Jobeth stroked Shawna's long blonde hair and sighed. She would make it up to her for the harsh words said the night before.

"Guess what?" Jobeth asked, pulling Shawna slightly away and brushing the silky strands of hair out of the pretty girl's light blue eyes. "Oliver is going to stay with us."

"Really?" Shawna squealed, bouncing up and down, her sprits rising.

"Really. So you have nothing to feel bad about. He will have all of us as his family." Jobeth hugged Shawna to herself again. "He need never know."

Shawna frowned slightly, in Jobeth's arms.

Shouts came from the kitchen.

"Those two girls!" Jobeth pulled away from Shawna and rushed into the kitchen.

"She started it, Mama!" Mara-Joy yelled at the top of her lungs, pointing at a confused Joanna.

"Nuh-uh," Joanna said flabbergasted, clutching a strand of her hair.

"Liar!" Mara-Joy stormed, standing up and stamping her small foot close to Constance's flailing hand. Shawna entered the room and saw how close Constance was to being trampled and went and scooped her up. She held the baby protectively in her arms.

"You! Joanna pulled my hair!" Mara-Joy howled at her confused sister.

"Enough!" Jobeth shouted. "Joanna, go to your room now!"

Joanna began to cry as to why she was in trouble.

"Now!" Jobeth hollered.

Joanna slowly began to walk out of the room whimpering, her head bent low. She had done nothing wrong and she couldn't understand why Mama was punishing her. It was Mara-Joy who had pulled her hair. Why was she in trouble?

Mara-Joy watched her sister leave the room rejected. A small grin formed on her face. That sure brought Mama back into the room away from dumb old Shawna. Joanna even got punished as a bonus. Mara-Joy took a deep breath to prepare herself for a crying fit. She wanted Mama to feel sorry for her and hug her and say nice words. She was just about to let out a good wail when she spotted Shawna holding Constance in her arms, staring at Mara-Joy. Mara-Joy scowled at her, and began pouting.

Shawna ignored the look on Mara-Joy's face. She had seen the precious Mara-Joy smirking when little Joanna was punished. Shawna was beginning to think Mara-Joy was anything but a joy anymore. And Jobeth was totally oblivious to it all. Why was she so blind when it came to Mara-Joy?

A year passed in quiet harmony. Oliver didn't court anyone, which struck Jobeth as odd. Many of the town girls swooned over him, but he seemed content to be a bachelor. Oliver preferred to spend time with the family or to take long walks with Shawna. It bothered Jobeth how Oliver's eyes followed Shawna around. She was blossoming into a beautiful young woman and Oliver seemed to notice it, too much.

"He seems to spend too much time with her," Jobeth would say to Alan in bed.

"Don't worry," Alan said, snuggling her neck with his mouth. "It's not good for the baby." His hand rubbed Jobeth's small rounded belly. "Is it moving yet?"

"No, but he will." Jobeth smiled, clutching Alan's hand close to her tight, swelled tummy.

"Think it's a boy this time?" Alan asked, bending down to kiss his new baby growing inside of Jobeth. He loved seeing her pregnant with his children.

"Has to be." Jobeth murmured, wrapping her lean legs around his back. Alan gently pulled her panties down with his teeth, spreading Jobeth's legs with his head.

Jobeth groaned, arching her back. Oliver and Shawna were forgotten.

Two years passed. Jobeth gave birth to another girl whom they named Pauline, after her brother.

Shawna turned sixteen and her crush on Oliver was no longer something to ignore. Jobeth was becoming more and more concerned and complained constantly to Alan about it.

Shawna and Oliver spent all their time together.

It was almost as though they were courting and she couldn't stand the way they looked at each other.

"Jobeth stop worrying about her. It's just innocent," Alan said, hugging his wife. "She is still a child."

"Humph." Jobeth shrugged into Alan's arms. They were in bed together late at night. With four small children and Shawna and Oliver to worry about, Jobeth and Alan's only time to speak freely was late at night in bed together.

"She is no child Alan. She is a woman now. It is not proper for her to be spending all her time with a grown man. She should be courting boys her own age."

"I still see Shawna as a little girl in pig tails all of five years old." Alan mused.

"Even Mara-Joy is not five anymore dear." Jobeth gently chuckled. "Our children are growing up."

It was true. Mara-Joy was six years old: a dark, curly-haired beauty with stunning blue eyes. Joanna, a year younger, was long and lean with light brown hair and green cat eyes like her father. And according to Jobeth, Joanna was in constant trouble, trying to blame it always on her big sister, Mara-Joy.

Constance was three. A silent, blonde child with the same green eyes as Joanna. She liked to be outside studying flowers and butterflies. It was easy to see she was an intelligent child. When Constance chose to talk to people, it was always in complete, clear sentences. And then there was Pauline, a bubbly one-year-old, always full of delight and smiles for everyone.

"I guess you're right dear," Alan said, picturing his daughters' faces, including the tall pale Shawna who only vaguely resembled the little girl he had first seen, huddled close to Jobeth's skirts. His heart ached for a moment for the child Shawna had been. Could she be sixteen already?

"What's wrong, Papa? You don't like your girls growing up?" Jobeth teased, sensing Alan's thoughts.

"No, I don't," he said, turning to embrace his wife. "It makes me feel like time is going too fast and I am going to lose them all."

"You won't lose them. They're still young." Jobeth smiled, her head resting on Alan's bare chest.

"Maybe it's time to have another baby?" Alan sighed, thinking of Jobeth with child.

"Umph, maybe it's time for a boy?" Jobeth answered knowingly.

"Jobeth?" Alan sat up, "Is there something you are trying to tell me?"

"Maybe..."

Alan sat himself up on his elbow so he could look down at Jobeth lying flat on the bed. She was beautiful with her hair flowing over her shoulders. Color tinted her cheeks giving her a healthy glow. Her arms encircled his neck and she pulled him to her, her lips only inches from his ear.

"Maybe this time we will have our son, Alan. Maybe this time we will finally get our boy," she whispered softly in his ear, creating a mine field of goose bumps.

Why had Jobeth's words caused such an uneasy feeling to overtake him?

Jobeth was busy washing the supper dishes the next evening. Mara-Joy and Joanna were the only children still up. They were studying for a spelling test. Oliver and Shawna were out again, taking another long walk, much to Jobeth's dismay.

She couldn't help worrying about Shawna. This crush she had on Oliver was just not healthy. It had just grown stronger over the years, and Oliver fed on it, acting as though they were a couple. Alan tried to tell Jobeth that Oliver just liked Shawna's company, that Shawna was like a little sister to Oliver, but Jobeth thought Alan was blind. She didn't think a man paid that much attention to a young woman because he thought of her as a sister. Besides, she saw how Oliver's eyes feasted on Shawna. He was like a cat ready to pounce. Shawna was no better, flirting shamelessly in front of him. Jobeth had made up her mind.

She was going to put a stop to it tonight. It was just not right for the two to behave like this. Alan sat beside Joanna, helping her with a homework assignment. She had just started school that year and the teacher said she was an armful.

Wiping her hands on a towel, Jobeth sat down with Mara-Joy to help quiz her on her test. She was deeply engrossed in her tutoring when the door swung open.

Shawna and Oliver tumbled in flushed and out of breath.

All eyes at the table looked up at the couple. They were excited, clutching each other's arms. They were quite the pair. Oliver dark and tanned from days spent outside and Shawna blonde and pale as though she had never spent a day outdoors in her life.

"We are getting married," Oliver blurted out.

"What?" Jobeth stifled a scream as she jumped up. She looked at Shawna for answers.

Shawna ignored Jobeth's face and clutched Oliver's arm, beaming with happiness.

"I know this may come as a shock, but Shawna and I love each other." Oliver turned to Shawna and held her hand.

Jobeth felt faint. Alan came to stand behind her, grasping her shoulders tightly to support both of them. He looked as though the wind had been knocked out of him. Jobeth had been right.

"Married?" Alan directed his question to Oliver. "Are you out of your minds? She is just a child." Alan's face looked pained.

Mara-Joy looked over at Joanna and stuck her tongue out at her. She was smiling at Shawna like a silly fool. Mara-Joy wanted her mother to quiz her on the test. Who cared if stupid Shawna wanted to marry dumb old Oliver?

Joanna didn't respond to Mara-Joy. She just smiled knowingly at Shawna. This is what Shawna had dreamed of since Oliver walked back into their lives. Shawna told Joanna many times that she would love no man but Oliver. If he didn't want her as much as she knew she wanted him, she would be an old maid. She could never marry anyone but him. Joanna was happy for her. She didn't want her to be an old maid. *Maybe dreams do come true,* she thought.

"Alan," Shawna interrupted. She looked happy. It was hard to believe she had once been a frightened, haunted child. A child who clung terrified to Jobeth's skirts. Where had time gone? When did Shawna grow up before their eyes?

"I am not a child anymore." She went over to Alan and took his hand. Her other hand grasped Jobeth's. "I love you both so much." A tear ran down her cheek. Jobeth felt a tear form in the corner of her eye. "You both have done so much for me. I want you to be happy for me. You are the only parents I have ever had. If you are not happy for me, I will die."

Alan was nearly in tears. He looked at Jobeth in desperation.

"And I can't live without Oliver. I won't." Oliver came up from behind Shawna and placed his hands on her shoulders. Shawna seemed to grow with strength from his touch.

Just like Jobeth felt when Alan touched her. Jobeth bent her head. They were losing her.

"I will take good care of her," Oliver said to Alan and Jobeth's downcast faces. "I am not the man I was when we were kids. I have changed."

Jobeth nodded, knowing this was true. In the past three years since Oliver had come to live with them, he had been hardworking and dedicated to their family. The Oliver from their youth who gambled and drank and frolicked with whores was gone.

Alan moved his arms and encircled them around her shoulders.

"Oliver," Alan choked, "she is so much younger than you. We trusted you with her."

"Alan, I never planned to fall in love with her," Oliver professed to him.

Shawna beamed warmly up at Oliver and squeezed his arm. "But our feelings for each other are just as true as yours and Jobeth's."

Alan didn't respond. His best friend was taking this child of his heart from him. He and Jobeth had been so afraid those years before Oliver arrived. Afraid he would take from their family. It had never dawned on him that it would be Shawna and not Mara-Joy whom Oliver would steal.

Shawna veered her responses to Jobeth, unable to stand the look of bewilderment of Alan's face.

"Jobeth, you know I have loved Oliver since I was twelve years old, maybe even longer. I remember having a crush on him when I was five." Shawna placed a slim white hand on Jobeth's arm. She was so pale. The veins were transparent beneath the skin. "Alan loved you the moment he saw you and you were younger than I am now."

"It was not the same. We were alone." Jobeth said feebly, knowing she had already lost the battle. "You have never been alone."

"You didn't fall in love because you were alone, Jobeth. Your marriage did not grow into what it is because you were alone. It grew because the two of you are two parts of one whole. Together you are complete. Just as Oliver and I are completed when together." Shawna stood up straight, no longer needing to hold onto Jobeth's skirts for safety.

"I will make a good home for Shawna. I promise you both with all my heart," Oliver said.

"You!" Alan burst out. He had the urge to punch Oliver in the face with his fist, but stopped when he saw the look of determination and love on both their faces. His shoulders sagged knowing they were not asking his permission, just his blessing. "You better."

"I will," Oliver promised, offering his hand out to Alan, sensing the battle had been won. Alan received it and clutched the man to him, hugging him.

Shawna went to Jobeth's waiting arms and they hugged each other while crying.

"I swear, if you hurt her," Alan said, pulling away from Oliver's grasp, "you will have me to deal with."

"And me," Jobeth said, glaring over Shawna's shoulder.

At the church they attended every Sunday, Shawna and Oliver were married.

It was a small wedding with only family and very close friends attending. Jobeth held back as she watched Shawna walk down the aisle. She had never seen such a radiant, beautiful bride. Shawna glowed on Alan's arm as he walked her to Oliver.

Oliver could not take his eyes off Shawna. She looked like an angel dressed in her white wedding dress. She and Jobeth made it from the silk that they had special ordered.

Shawna's pale blonde hair was swept up into a French twist, hidden by her long flowing veil. She was a vision like Cinderella going to the ball.

Mara-Joy and Joanna trailed behind dressed in cream dresses with puffed sleeves, tossing red rose petals as they went. Flowers crowned their long flowing hair.

Jobeth could not help noticing how different the two girls were from each other. Joanna resembled Jobeth with light brown hair that hung straight down her back. Her eyes were Alan's. The strange cat-like green eyes. Mara-Joy had dark, cascading curls, so much like Tamara's, and deep ice-blue eyes, replicas of Oliver's. Her skin was soft and creamy, whereas Joanna's was tanned golden.

Jobeth smiled proudly at her daughters as she held Pauline on her lap and Constance sat quietly beside her. They looked so different, but they were both so beautiful.

As the couple said their "I do's," Jobeth knew they were in love. Shawna would be as happy with Oliver as Jobeth was with Alan.

Later that night Shawna and Oliver broke the news to Jobeth and Alan that they were moving away. Oliver had been in contact with an old friend and he had a job offer that he could not refuse.

"You are taking Shawna away from us," Jobeth sobbed, hugging Shawna tight on the couch. It had never occurred to her that Shawna would not always be living near her.

"Jobeth, we can't live in your home forever. We need to have a home of our own," Oliver explained. Alan refused to look at any of them. He only stared out the window at the new wagon Oliver had just bought.

"Can we have a ride in your new wagon?" said Mara-Joy as she bounded into Oliver's arms. She was the only child still up and awake. Jobeth released her embrace on Shawna and sat up, wiping her eyes.

"Of course," Oliver lifted Mara-Joy up into the air and into his arms where he held the little girl tightly, much to her delight. His eyes were full of emotion.

"Oliver, are you going away with Shawna?" Mara-Joy asked, snuggling into his arms. Oliver sat down on the nearest chair and placed Mara-Joy on his lap.

He looked deeply into the eyes of the child he had given life too. "Mara-Joy, honey, me and Shawna, well--" He looked awkwardly at his wife, who smiled warmly. Her heart filled with love.

"Shawna and I," Mara-Joy corrected

"Shawna and I," Oliver chuckled, glancing at Jobeth who sat stiffly beside Shawna. What he had to say was meant more for her and Alan than Mara-Joy.

"We don't want to stay in a small town. We want to live in a big city. We have stayed here because I wanted to wait until Shawna was old enough to decide to marry me and leave her family--our family. We love you all but we will still see each other. We will visit and you can visit us with your mama and pappy. Your mama and Shawna will write to each other all the time."

Jobeth felt jealous as Oliver held her darling child. He had already stolen Shawna from her. She would not let him steal Mara-Joy too.

"Do you still want a ride in the new wagon?" Oliver said, trying to break the tension in the air. Mara-Joy looked to Jobeth. Alan had turned away from the window.

"Oh Mama, Pappy, please?" she squealed in her small voice.

"Only if Oliver gives your old pa one, too," Alan exclaimed. He stood up and reached down to take Mara-Joy out of Oliver's lap. Oliver had Shawna, but Alan had Mara-Joy.

"You have a deal," Oliver laughed. They stood to leave with Mara-Joy firmly in Alan's arms.

Jobeth turned to Shawna, who was paler looking than usual.

"What is wrong, dear?" Jobeth asked, smoothing back Shawna's unbleached blonde hair from her face. Shawna had taken to wearing her hair high up in a twist, similar to Jobeth's. The young woman looked at Jobeth, frightened, her eyes large and quivering.

"Jobeth," she looked away embarrassed.

"My goodness, what's wrong?" Jobeth turned Shawna toward her. "If there is anything wrong, please tell me. I will always be here for you. Even though you are an old married woman now."

Shawna began to smile through her fears.

"I know," she said. "It's just. I'm married. You know you are married and have children . . ." Shawna blushed.

Jobeth suddenly knew what Shawna was afraid of.

"Oh, Shawna." Jobeth took the girl into her arms, just like she had when Shawna had been a little girl and frightened of the night. "I was frightened on my wedding night too, but I was in love with Alan and he loved me. Somehow it just seemed to complete our union, bonded us in a way we never had been before, as though I was not whole until we were together as man and wife." Jobeth spoke sincerely to the young bride, who listened intently, though still frightened.

"I see the same love in your eyes for Oliver. I see his love for you as strongly as I see Alan's love for me. When you make love, don't be afraid. Accept him and you will feel whole and complete in your love for each other. Tell him to go slowly and be patient with you and it will be a wondrous experience that will grow as time goes by."

"I am going to miss you so much, Jobeth," Shawna sobbed, her lips trembling.

Jobeth had settled all her fears once again, just as she always had done in the past.

"I am going to miss you, Shawna. I don't know what I will do." Jobeth cried, hugging Shawna tighter. "But," she pulled away and wiped her eyes with a other soon. We are a family and nothing will ever change that. We will write all the time. You are starting a new and exciting life. Alan and I will always be here for you. Loving you. Waiting to see you and all the beautiful children you will have. We want you to be happy, Shawna. That is all we want for you."

Shawna nodded her head, unable to speak as Jobeth buried her tear-streaked face into her sweet-smelling hair and breathed deeply. It would be a long time before she would be able to sniff Shawna's hair or touch her fair cheek. But she would see her again. They would be in constant touch with each other. It wouldn't be like the others who had left her life. Shawna would be back.

"You take care of Shawna," Alan said, standing beside the buggy. The newlyweds were already comfortably seated in the wagon ready to leave. Jobeth walked up beside Alan. She had just put Mara-Joy down to sleep after saying her good-byes to Oliver and Shawna. The child had been in good spirits to see Shawna leave. She hated the way everyone fell all over Shawna, wanting her to stay.

As far as Mara-Joy was concerned, it would be good to see her gone.

"I will," Oliver said seriously to Jobeth and Alan. "We didn't turn out so bad for a bunch of waifs, did we?"

"No, we sure didn't," Alan spoke with a laugh in his voice.

"Although," Oliver said, grasping Shawna's hand, "I think I am going to try and find out what happened to the rest of the fellas. If there is one thing I have learned, it is that we are all family. We need our family. I will find them and when I do I will let you know what has become of them. I need to know what has happened to them."

Alan nodded, his eyebrows raised. "I have always wondered too."

Oliver's eyes clouded. "We spent a lot of years together. Being a family when we were not wanted by anyone. Children comforting children." Oliver lifted his head up and smiled. Tamara's fighting spirit flashing before his eyes. They had comforted each other plenty in those days long ago. "Take care of Mara-Joy. She is very special to me. Just like Tamara, that one."

Jobeth stepped back, her hands flying to her mouth. Alan supported her arm, as they both stood stunned.

"She is lucky to have parents like you. She is so privileged in ways Tamara and I never were. I think Tamara really would have wanted that for our daughter."

"How," Alan choked taking a step back, "how did you know?"

"Alan, how could I not know? Look at Mara-Joy and look at your other children. They are combinations of you and Jobeth. Mara-Joy is a combination of Tamara and me. When I look at her, I see my eyes looking back at me, in Tamara's face," he looked at Shawna, who did not say a word. "I knew Tamara was pregnant when she left me. That is why it was so important for me to find her. She was nearly due to have the baby. You told me she came to live with you before she killed herself, but you never mentioned her being pregnant. If she had not already had the baby, it would have been impossible not to know she was pregnant. When I asked Shawna if she remembered Tamara with a baby, she would change the subject." Oliver bent his head not looking at anyone. "I guess I knew it all along. From the moment I saw Mara-Joy. Before you even told me Tamara had killed herself."

"Can you ever forgive us for not telling you?" Jobeth clutched Alan's hand in fear. "We could not lose her. She is our daughter in our heart. She brought Alan and me together–she made us a family. Without her our family would not be complete."

Oliver looked up from the reins he held tightly in his hands. How could he tell them how he had struggled trying to figure out why they would not tell him the truth about Mara-Joy? But then he knew the truth. Seeing them all together as a family through the years, he had gotten his answer.

"I am the father who helped to bring her into this world, but you and Alan are her parents. You have given her a life I was not able to. I love her. But I lost my chance to raise her when Tamara left me. I feel blessed to have seen her grow these last three years." He looked at Shawna, who was sitting firmly beside him. Her face showed her loyalty was with her husband now.

"It would be unfair to Mara-Joy if I had claimed her as my daughter. You two have always been there. You have given her the home I only dreamed of having." Oliver gazed up into the sky. The night was filled with twinkling stars. "You helped me, even though I must have been a threat to your family. You took me in and made me part of your home. You got me a job and helped me set my goals in motion for the future–a future with Shawna. And you let me have that future with her. And now I can make a life with her and the children we will have together."

"Oliver," Jobeth sighed with relief. The guilt she had felt over the past three years had suddenly been lifted from her shoulders. Oliver knew Mara-Joy was his daughter and he was not going to take her away from them. She placed her hand on his knee, genuinely feeling love for the man.

"Don't tell her about her birth parents. Let her know me as Uncle Oliver. It is the best thing I could do for her." Oliver sniffed, rubbing his nose, embarrassed over the emotion he felt.

"Thank you," Alan said quietly. "For understanding that we could not lose her. Ever."

"Send many letters, all right?" Oliver smiled, trying to brighten the mood.

Jobeth nodded, feeling suddenly light.

Looking out the open window of her bedroom, Shawna's old room, Joanna wiped a hand across her wet eyes. She had been awake the whole evening, watching from above. She was sad Shawna and Oliver were leaving, but excited for them too. Mama wouldn't let her stay awake to see them off, so she had opened the window and watched enviously as Mara-Joy got to stay up and say good-bye. She observed and listened to everything that was said below by the adults. Shocked by the information she overheard, Joanna was unable to believe or understand what it all meant. What she did know was that all was not as it seemed in her family. This realization frightened and excited her.

— Chapter 19 —

Much to Jobeth's joy, she finally gave birth to a son. They named him Alan Michael after both Alan and Jobeth's father.

With the birth of her boy, Jobeth felt a sense of peace she had not had since the death of her first born.

Oliver and Shawna kept in constant touch. Ten months after they were married, their first child Daniel was born. He was nearly two years old and Jobeth could hardly wait to see him. Her little Shawna was a mother. She had received small portraits of Daniel, but she craved to see the child in person. Shawna and Oliver were going to pay them a visit for the first time since their marriage with special news for Alan and Jobeth.

The day Shawna and Oliver were to arrive, Jobeth was busy in the kitchen cooking a special dinner that Shawna loved.

"Mama!" Joanna stormed through the kitchen as angry as could be. "You better teach that girl some manners."

Annoyed, Jobeth turned to her daughter. Joanna looked so much like Jobeth: tall and lean.

"What girl?" Jobeth asked, disturbed. Shawna and Oliver would be there any moment. She didn't need to have another confrontation with this child.

"Mara-Joy is behind the barn with that Frank Perkins' boy." Her face was all screwed up in rage. All the children were outside playing in the hot summer sun.

"What?" Jobeth yelled, glaring at her child. Quickly, she poured a pot of water from the pump in the kitchen. "Stay in here and keep an eye on the babies. They are going to wake up soon," Jobeth ordered, not looking at Joanna as she raced to the front door.

The bucket slopped water over its rim as she ran, splashing Jobeth's skirt. Joanna stood still, unable to move as she watched her mother leave, trailing water behind her.

She reached the barn in no time and could hear giggling, both male and female. Horrible thoughts coursed through her mind of what could be happening behind the barn door.

Jobeth quickened her steps in the direction of the giggles. She was just about to throw the bucket of water over the two children when she saw what was happening.

Mara-Joy and the neighbor boy, Frank, were making dandelion jewelry, putting the flower bracelets on each other's arms and heads.

Mara-Joy spotted her mother and stood up, giving her one of her winning smiles.

"Hi, Mama," she tittered, her dark curls cascading into her deep blue eyes. She absently brushed a tendril out of her eyes. "What is wrong?" she asked innocently, looking at Jobeth with her sweetest smile. "Am I not allowed to have my boyfriend over?"

"Your boyfriend?" It was as though Mara-Joy could read Jobeth's mind and knew what Jobeth had planned to do with the bucket of water.

"Yes. I am ten now. I think I am old enough to have one. What do you think?" Mara-Joy spoke while trying to put a bracelet of flowers around her wrist.

"Well, I don't think Pappy would agree with you, young lady," Jobeth looked at the beautiful young girl. The older she got, the more beautiful she became.

Her long black hair tumbled in loose curls down her back and her striking blue eyes seemed to pierce through anyone she looked at. You could not help but stare at the exquisite child.

"Why don't you ask Frank for dinner tonight? He can meet your Uncle Oliver and Shawna."

"Don't forget Daniel, Mama!" Mara-Joy squealed, clutching her hands to her flat chest.

"Never." Jobeth laughed and felt foolish. How could she have thought her precious Mara-Joy could be up to anything wrong?

"Mama?"

"Yes, my dearest?" Jobeth answered, getting ready to leave. Mara-Joy stood beside the handsome redheaded boy.

"Why do you have that pot?" Mara-Joy seemed confused, her dark brows weaving together.

"No reason, go back to playing with Frank." Jobeth turned away, embarrassed.

Mara-Joy shrugged her shoulders, and pulled Frank by the arm back to their dandelions.

"Why did you lie like that to get your sister in trouble?" Jobeth yelled furiously as she entered the house. Joanna jumped from where she stood, stirring food over the stove. Pauline was beside her, watching her big sister. She too jumped, startled by her mother's outburst. Instantly she began to whimper.

Alan-Michael began to stir on the couch where he had been sleeping.

"I wasn't lying," Joanna pouted, forcing herself not to cry. "She was in back," Joanna stalled. Her mother would never believe her now. Mara-Joy had the upper hand once again. The girl sighed dejectedly. "She was doing things she was not supposed to be doing. You told her to watch Constance and she was not doing that."

"Joanna," Jobeth shook her head and went to her crying girls, "why you make such a big deal of things, I will never know. Girls, I am sorry that I got so mad." Jobeth bent down and hugged them close to her. She was so jumpy lately.

"Where is Constance?" Jobeth asked

"She went to meet Pappy halfway," Joanna sniffed, going to the counter to get cookies.

"Joanna, we are going to be eating soon. Get out of those," Jobeth said through clenched teeth. She sat down heavily on the kitchen chair and rubbed her temples, which throbbed with pain. She felt wasted. She was twenty-eight and felt fifty." Joanna, take Pauline and Alan-Michael to meet your father, please," Jobeth said, holding her head in the palm of her hands.

"Sure Mama." Joanna obeyed, taking Pauline's hand and heading for their brother.

Alan-Michael sat miserably on the couch, half-asleep. He didn't want to go meet his father. At two years old, he didn't like many things.

Joanna forced him out the door dragging him by the arm, whining. She wasn't about to upset her mother any further.

— Chapter 20 —

"What is wrong, Jobeth?" Alan asked as he walked into the kitchen.

Jobeth had just begun to finish up last-minute chores before Oliver and Shawna arrived. She turned to him questioningly.

"The children say you are crabby." He was carrying Joanna in his arms. He placed her down gently and looked to Jobeth for answers.

Jobeth thought Joanna was too old to be carried in her father's arms. She was nine years old and quite tall for her age. She looked ridiculous, clutched to her father's neck, her long legs dangling awkwardly around his waist.

"Nothing, Alan." Jobeth turned away from him and continued to clean the counter. "I'm just edgy." She attacked the counter with a vengeance. Alan frowned at her and looked to Joanna who sat pouting on the kitchen chair.

"I made Mama mad at me," she whimpered.

Jobeth swung around and glared at Joanna. She closed her eyes tightly. The girl had a habit of making mountains out of molehills.

"Your mother is not mad at you, Joanna," Alan soothed as he bent down to her level, his hands resting on her bony knees. He scowled at Jobeth with a red angry face. In a demanding voice he asked, "Right, Jobeth?"

"No, I'm not mad at her," Jobeth said, looking away from them both. Her headache had once again returned and now she was feeling angry--angry that Alan was taking the child's side. Couldn't he see Joanna was playing on his good nature?

"Go outside and play." Jobeth said in a cool voice, her back still to them.

Joanna stared at Jobeth's straight back and felt empty. She got up and gathered the children around her. She looked at her father with a pleading face as she led Alan-Michael, Constance and Pauline outside.

"I wish you would not take your frustrations out on the children," Alan said in a furious voice. Jobeth turned to him, shocked. She couldn't believe the words coming out of Alan's mouth.

"Joanna plays you against me," Jobeth retaliated throwing down the rag she was using.

"She just wants your attention, Jobeth. You are always so harsh on her. You make her feel like she can never do anything right." Alan's face began to get red. He saw how Jobeth acted with the children. She played favorites with Mara-Joy and Alan-Michael and doted on their every move as the other three girls, especially Joanna, sat in the background starving for their mother's attention.

"That . . . that is not true Alan." Jobeth struggled to fight back tears. She hated it when Alan was irate with her. He never was unless it had to do with the children. She was about to protest more when Oliver burst through the door.

"Oliver!" Alan said, turning abruptly into the other man's broad embrace.

The men slapped each other on the back affectionately. Jobeth bounced around excitedly, looking for Shawna. She spotted her coming through the door, a baby cradled in her arms.

"Shawna!" Jobeth squealed, scrambling past the two loud men. She hugged the young woman tightly to her, nearly squishing the baby between them. "This can't be Daniel," Jobeth said, gazing into the blanket. Shawna laughed wickedly.

"No, no," she said warmly. "This is Donna. Daniel is coming out of the automobile--or trying to get out of that contraption--whatever way you want to look at it."

"You never said anything in your letters!" Jobeth said, gently taking the newborn from Shawna's arms.

"Oliver wrote that we had a surprise," Shawna giggled, moving the pink blanket so Jobeth could see her sleeping daughter. "It nearly killed me not to tell you, Jobeth. But I wanted you to be surprised."

Jobeth stared at Shawna, amazed that she had grown up right before her eyes.

"Some surprise," Oliver laughed, throwing Mara-Joy up in his arms. She had come into the house to see what the commotion was all about. Oliver had spotted her and lifted her straight into the air, overcome with emotion to see her.

"Uncle Oliver, put me down!" Mara-Joy cackled, "I am too big for this." Oliver hugged her tightly to his chest and planted a warm kiss on her cheek.

"I have missed you, my darling. I didn't think it was possible, but you have become more beautiful since I last saw you." He placed her down beside the rest of the children who waited to be tossed in the air too.

"Mommy? Mommy? Where are you?" A small voice came from the doorway.

Everyone turned to a small blond boy with pale blue-gray eyes.

"Daniel!" Everyone said in union running to greet the startled little boy.

Jobeth felt her heart swell. It was good to see Shawna again. She had missed her deeply. She looked down at the baby squirming in her arms. Her family was home and under one roof again.

After dinner and when all the children had been put down to bed, the four adults collapsed in the living room, exhausted. With Jobeth and Alan's five children and Shawna and Oliver's two, the homestead had turned into a zoo.

It took everything out of the parents to calm their excited brood down. They were still fidgeting and giggling as Jobeth and Shawna tucked the crowded children into the beds they all shared.

"Shawna and I have good news to tell you both," Oliver said, sipping some tea. He waited to continue until Jobeth settled down from serving them all.

Shawna sat glued to Oliver's arm, grinning secretly at him. Oliver reached for her hand and squeezed it tightly.

"I thought we already had the good news--your daughter, Donna," Jobeth replied, sitting down beside Alan.

Early in the evening she had apologized to him for her behavior with the children. They made up with a small peck on the lips and a hug. It would have to do for now.

"Yes, but we have more," Oliver said mysteriously. Jobeth and Alan looked confused. What more could there be?

"Well, don't keep us in suspense any longer," Alan said, holding on to Jobeth's hand. His heart was beginning to pound. He couldn't explain the odd way he was suddenly feeling.

"In two days we are going to have our first family reunion," Oliver said, nodding his head.

Shawna covered her mouth to suppress her urge to squeal.

"What?" Alan sat up straight. "We don't have any other relatives."

“Yes, that is true,” Oliver said, leaning in closer, “but aren't there three guys you two have not seen in about . . . oh . . . fourteen years?” He sat back in his seat studying the bewildered faces of the two in front of him.

Alan looked to Jobeth, his face confused. She gazed deep into his green eyes that she loved so much. She could feel his raw emotions, as though they were her own.

“I think Oliver is trying to tell us that the boys have been found,” Jobeth spoke softly to Alan's stunned face. He clutched her arm, unable to believe his ears. His face contorted with emotion. A tear began to roll down his cheek.

“Jobeth?” he asked in a shaky voice. She smiled at him and pulled him to her. “Can it be true?” Alan whispered.

She looked to Oliver and Shawna in disbelief, searching for an answer.

“It's true,” Oliver said, staring down at the floor, his own emotions flooding over him. “Our brothers are alive and coming home.”

Jobeth heard a sob fall out of her mouth.

“A miracle,” she muttered.

“They will be here in two days with their new families,” Shawna said in her sweet soft voice.

Jobeth and Alan sat back in their seats in disbelief. After all the years of wondering what had happened to them, the old gang would be together again. She looked down at her feet where Old Queenie was curled up asleep. An ancient dog now who had seen it all: Jonah, Tamara. A tear trickled down her cheek. She wiped it away absentmindedly.

Not all the family would be there.

Queenie looked up at Jobeth with her foggy dark eyes and gray muzzle and whined.

“It's all right, girl. It's all right,” Jobeth cooed, scratching the silky flap of the dog's ear.

— Chapter 21 —

The day came when Todd, Carter and Adam were to arrive with their families.

Jobeth dressed the children in their best church clothes. Shawna and Oliver had done well in the city and dressed their children in very modern attire. She liked their garments and made a mental note to make similar outfits for her children.

"I am so excited," giggled Shawna as she helped Jobeth pack the large basket they planned to bring to the picnic they were having.

Jobeth examined the beautiful woman Shawna had turned into. She had cut her long pale hair into a short bob just under her chin, making her seem years older and more sophisticated than Jobeth remembered. When Jobeth protested, Shawna had laughed and said it was modern and that Jobeth was too young to be so old-fashioned. Shawna had changed in many ways from the girl she had once been.

"I don't remember the rest of the group as well as you and the guys; but I do have vague memories of either Todd or Adam buying me one of my favorite dolls."

"That was Adam. The gang wanted you to have a normal home with the things little girls should have," Jobeth said, remembering back in time to a group of teens trying to raise a little five-year-old girl properly.

"Humph," Shawna shook her head, her bob swaying back and forth. "I do remember Jonah. He gave me an apple a day to keep the doctor away."

"Yes," Jobeth chuckled, recollecting Jonah's inviting spirit. "You used to follow Jonah around like a lost puppy. He loved you so much."

"I loved him too," Shawna said calmly. "Oliver sometimes asks me about him. If he was happy before he died."

Jobeth stopped what she was doing and looked at Shawna.

"He was one of the best people I ever met." Jobeth placed a bowl of fried chicken into a new basket.

Shawna nodded in agreement. "He is one of the finest people I was blessed to have ever known. Just like I am glad to have known you and Alan."

"Glad to know us?" Jobeth asked, spreading butter on a piece of bread. "We are just plain country folks. Nothing we do is out of the ordinary. Look at you and Oliver. You all look so glamorous and prosperous. No one would ever guess how you two started life out."

"What?" Shawna stopped her packing, giving Jobeth a stern examination. "You have the perfect family. You have beautiful children and you are happy with your husband."

"That is true . . . but I sometimes get bored," Jobeth sighed, putting down her butter knife. She wiped a strand of long brown hair out of her hazel eyes. She felt guilty for the way she spoke about her life with Alan and the children, but could not help the words that escaped her mouth.

"You should move to the city," Shawna said to Jobeth with concern. "I think you need the hustle and bustle of city life." She picked up the sandwich Jobeth had made and took a big bite out of it, trying to lighten the mood.

"What is it like?" Jobeth asked, curiosity winning her over.

"Wonderful," Shawna said as her face lit up. "Beautiful clothes, movies and sometimes you even see movie stars."

"Movie stars? You must be kidding. You have actually seen a moving picture?"

"Uh-huh. And they have the best dances." Shawna put down her sandwich and began to show Jobeth one of the dances she had learned. "Try it, Jobeth,"

Shawna laughed, tapping her toes to a song she hummed.

Jobeth tried, following Shawna's lead. She was awkward and clumsy. The two laughed, so comfortable in each other's presence that Jobeth was not embarrassed by her lack of experience.

"It is so exciting. Every day is a new adventure." Shawna composed herself, returning to her half-eaten sandwich.

"It sounds wonderful." Jobeth sighed, picking up her knife again. "But Alan loves it here. He has his work, our home. We always said we would give our children this type of life."

"What says you can't still give the children a good home in the city?" Shawna said, offended. She blushed from her outburst. Much had changed since she had become a married woman; the shy, quiet child of her youth was gone, replaced with the strong woman she was now.

"You have a life too, Jobeth. You have to be happy. If you are not happy, how do you expect your family to be happy? Besides, do Daniel and Donna look deprived?" She took Jobeth's hand encouragingly. "If I thought the city would hurt my babies do you think I would live there? You taught me how to be a good mother and to take chances."

Jobeth turned away from Shawna and looked out the window. It was fine to think of living the life Shawna did, but a different story to actually expect

Alan and the children to up and leave their home, just because Jobeth was bored with life.

"I am sorry, Shawna. I just don't know . . . but I think you might be right.

I should hint at the idea to Alan." Jobeth wiped the sweat from her brow, the seed of want had planted itself in her heart and it was going to be hard to stifle its growth now that it was rooted there. She watched a little hummingbird fly by the window and felt her own wings beginning to stretch. Could she convince Alan to move to the city with Oliver and Shawna?

"It would be so much fun. We would all be together again. Just two little mothers," Shawna chortled, putting a reassuring arm around Jobeth in the same way she had comforted her when Shawna had been a little girl.

"I miss you so dearly." Jobeth's hand reached for a strand of Shawna's blunt blond hair.

Shawna clasped her hand in return.

"Sometimes I cry at night because I miss my mama and papa so much." Shawna placed her head on Jobeth's shoulder.

"I need you and Alan. Especially you. You are my mother in every sense. You took care of me and protected me--saved me from a horrible fate. I wouldn't have the life I've lived if it weren't for you." She lowered her eyes. "The only thing I regret about marrying Oliver is that I had to move away from my family. It hurts terribly. Oliver knows it and it makes him feel bad."

"Oh, Shawna," Jobeth sighed, brushing away the tear rolling down Shawna's fair face.

Just then Oliver and Alan came storming into the kitchen.

"They're coming up the driveway!" Alan said, unable to hide his excitement.

It seemed everyone owned a car nowadays. Even Jobeth and Alan had purchased one of the automobiles.

Shawna took Donna from Oliver's arms and went to stand on the porch.

Alan and Jobeth followed, clutching each other's hands. The children ran up the steps of the porch to stand by their parents, eager to meet these strangers they had heard so much about.

Three cars followed in procession behind one another, then stopped. The doors opened and three men followed by women and children piled out of the vehicles. They looked around apprehensively. Jobeth's hands flew to her trembling mouth. A moan escaped her lips.

"They are home," she said, facing Alan. "They are finally home."

Alan nodded, trying to force back his emotions. He placed a loving arm around Jobeth's shoulders and coaxed her down the stairs to greet their long-awaited guests.

Adam, Carter and Todd had stuck together over the years. Carter and Adam eventually met two lovely girls, fell in love and married. Adam had two boys, ages twelve and seven, and his wife Caroline was pregnant again. Carter had two boys also, nine and six, and a seven-year-old daughter. Todd was engaged to a lovely young girl who was as shy as he.

They were shocked to hear about Jonah and Tamara's tragic deaths. Alan and Jobeth refrained from telling their guest that Tamara and Oliver had a child and that child was Mara-Joy. Shawna and Oliver respected Alan and Jobeth's wishes.

When all the children were asleep in the loft, the adults settled in around a roaring fire in the fireplace. It was warm and cozy in the living room and the adults felt relaxed and content with one another.

"Mara-Joy is a beauty," Carter said, sipping a steaming cup of tea. Alan and Jobeth smiled pleased. "You must be pretty proud of her, Oliver."

Jobeth grasped Alan's hand tightly causing pain to shoot up his arm. Her nails dug into his flesh, causing circles of white to surround her fingers embedded into Alan's flesh. He gently pried Jobeth's grasp from his hand and gave her a gentle squeeze. With his eyes he told Jobeth not to panic.

"Uh," Oliver said, his eyes nervously darting to a frightened Alan and Jobeth, "Mara-Joy is Alan and Jobeth's daughter."

"Oh. Sorry, I just thought she looked . . ." Carter coughed, embarrassed.

His wife put a hand on his knee and gave him a warning look. The discomfort passing between the two couples hadn't gone unnoticed. Carter's mind began to work, wondering if something had happened between Jobeth and Oliver. But there was something else--something familiar about Mara-Joy.

Something he couldn't put his finger on. Carter's wife glared at him once more. She knew he was trying to figure out the obvious. Mara-Joy was Oliver's daughter and if the two couples wanted to keep the facts secret, who was she to say anything? It was none of their business and if Carter didn't stop it, the lovely visit would end terribly--which was something Carter, Adam and Todd would regret.

"Well . . ." Jobeth cut into everyone's thoughts. She knew what was going through their minds. How could Mara-Joy be Alan's and her child when she didn't look like either of them?

All eyes turned gratefully to Jobeth. The atmosphere had become increasingly uncomfortable.

"We finally have found a place we can be together and be safe."

Alan smiled proudly at his wife and gave her hand another reassuring squeeze. Jobeth could always get out of a bad jam.

"I think we have done all right," he chuckled, helping her along.

"Yes, I never thought we would come this far," said Todd, who sat beside his fiancée, Nancy.

"Well," Adam said, lighting a fresh cigarette, "we do deserve it."

"Here, here!" Oliver cheered, raising his glass of wine. "We went through hell but we lived to tell about it. Everything worked out in the end."

"I just want you all to know that I love you and you have always been in our hearts." Jobeth choked out a sob. "If Shawna and I had not wandered into that abandoned house and found you, I don't know what would have happened to us."

Shawna looked to Jobeth with tears streaming down her face. She couldn't help the upheaval of emotion brewing in her. She reached for Jobeth's hand. Oliver then took Shawna's free hand. Jobeth held Alan's. Everyone followed suit and joined hands, creating a warm, inclusive circle.

Jobeth felt the familiar lump in her throat form. She looked around at her reunited family and could feel Jonah and Tamara's presence. She knew they were smiling down on them, happy they were finally all home.

Joanna stared down between the beams of the railing of the loft. She watched as the adults grasped hands below her.

"What do you think Carter meant, Constance?" Joanna turned to her sister who sat crouched closely beside her. All the other children slept silently behind them. Joanna and Constance, unable to sleep, had crept to the railing to watch the scene play out beneath them.

"I don't know," Constance said in earnest, brushing her soft blonde curls out of her face.

"Why would he think Oliver was Mara-Joy's father?" Joanna whispered, staring straight ahead at nothing. "And why did Mama and Pappy look so frightened?" Joanna turned her cat eyes to her mother.

Jobeth had that same look. The same look she did when Oliver and Shawna had moved away. Joanna still remembered when she listened to their departing conversation, and she had played out that night in her mind over and over again. What was this talk about a woman named Tamara and how come everyone thought Mara-Joy was Oliver's daughter and not Mama and Pappy's?

Things were starting to make Joanna wonder about her older sister; making her wonder if she was her sister at all.

— Part 2 —

AND THEIR CHILDREN SHALL LEAD THEM

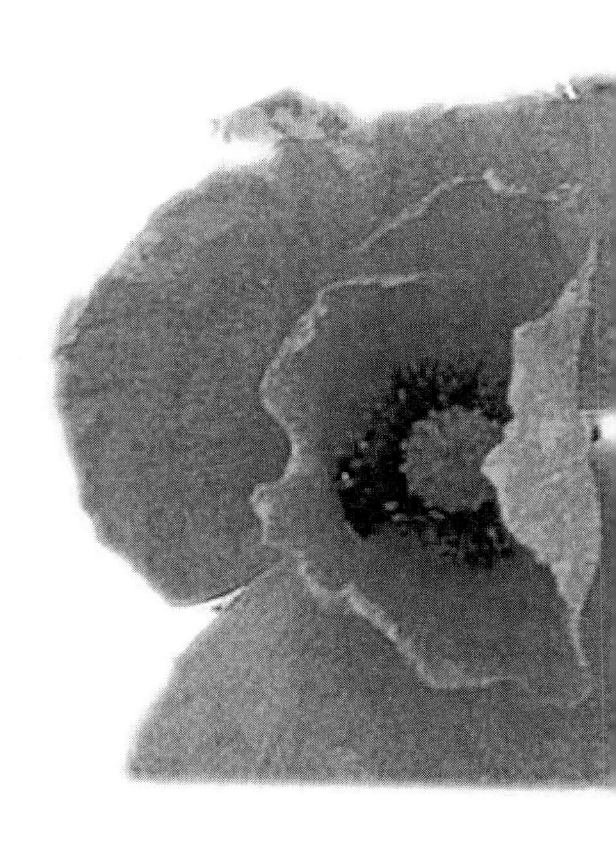

— Chapter 22 —

"But Mama, please!" Mara-Joy pleaded, stomping in the doorway of the kitchen. "I won't get into any trouble. I promise." She looked at her mother in disbelief. There was no way she was missing this party. Joanna, her sister, was sitting at the kitchen table eating breakfast with their little brother Alan-Michael and their little sister Pauline. Constance, their other sister, never ate breakfast and was already at school studying. It was what she always did.

Mama's back was turned to them all as she flipped eggs on the stove. Pappy had just left for work with Uncle Oliver, a job he claimed was not farming but was better than working in the mills, which was the job he had years ago before he moved their family to the city to live near Shawna and Oliver.

"Mara-Joy, you are only fourteen years old," said her mother. "I don't think you are old enough to go to a party with boys." Jobeth sighed, wiping her hand across her forehead. Mara-Joy was relentless with her pleadings. "Besides, you're to help Joanna with the children tonight. Your father and I are going dancing."

Jobeth looked dreamy for a moment.

The thought of dancing in her husband Alan's arms thrilled her. After fourteen years of marriage, she still tingled all over thinking of her sweet quiet Alan. She wondered what she had done to deserve such a decent man.

Jobeth looked at the red-faced Mara-Joy. Her dark black hair framed in ringlets around her perfect complexion, while her piercing blue eyes danced with frustration.

"Oh, Mama!" Mara-Joy began to cry. "It's fine and dandy if you go out and have fun. Who cares about me and what I want to do? Don't you understand how important this is to me?" She stomped her foot angrily. Life seemed so unfair. How could her mother be so insensitive to her needs? All her mother thought about was herself.

"Don't you get lippy with me, Missy, or I will swat your behind, good and hard," Jobeth held her spatula out threateningly to Mara-Joy. "Believe me, Mara-Joy, I will."

"Pooh." Mara-Joy whined. "I never get to do anything." She stuck her moist, red bottom lip out in a pout.

"Girls your age shouldn't be thinking of boys and parties anyway," Jobeth laughed suddenly. She couldn't help herself. Mara-Joy looked irresistible cute when she pouted.

"Why not, Mama?" Mara-Joy giggled. Knowing she had won. Jobeth would let her go if Mara-Joy played her cards right. "You and Pappy got married not much older than me."

"Oh you are a bold one, Mara-Joy." Jobeth swatted playfully, with the sticky egg flipper. The girl dodged her mother's laughing. "All right, you can go." Jobeth relented.

"Oh thank you, Mama!" Mara-Joy squealed, squeezing her mother's shoulders. "I love you so much. You are the best mother in the world," Mara-Joy sighed and hugged her mother tightly.

"But you are to be home by nine. And I will call to make sure you are home," Jobeth said, hugging Mara-Joy back, letting the love she felt for her daughter envelop her.

"Oh Mama, don't you trust me?" Mara-Joy angled her eyebrow wickedly at her pretty mother.

"Get to school you bad girl, before I change my mind." Jobeth gently pushed Mara-Joy from her grasp.

"Come on," Mara-Joy said to the astonished children sitting around the kitchen table. Joanna felt her face redden as she stood from the table. No matter how many times she witnessed Mara-Joy in action, it still shocked her to see Mara-Joy get her way, once again.

— Chapter 23 —

"Do you have a boyfriend, Mara-Joy?" Joanna asked mildly as she walked beside her sister.

"I have many boyfriends and always have," Mara-Joy snorted, looking forward without glancing at the slouched figure beside her.

The sky was gray and threatened rain. Pauline and Alan-Michael walked slowly behind the two older girls.

"Oh," sighed Joanna, unaware of her response, "it must be heaven . . ."

As much as she hated herself for it, Joanna envied her older sister. Mara-Joy was beautiful and had so many friends. Whereas she felt ugly and her only companions were her younger sisters, Constance and Pauline. Every time she became friends with someone, Mara-Joy would charm them away somehow.

She couldn't compete with Mara-Joy. Once someone met her, they were instantly drawn to the dark-haired enchantress like a fly to sugar. They had to know her and needed to be with her. She was a natural magnet to people and it had always been that way.

"It sure beats hell," Mara-Joy laughed, suddenly twirling around, making her dress fly high above her tiny waist, exposing her pink frilly panties. "Why?" she stopped, suddenly looking at Joanna. All the old buildings seemed to glare down on them, accusingly. It was dreary out, but Mara-Joy was happy, radiant in fact.

Joanna stood still, her eyes concentrating on the dirty surface of the pavement.

"Do you want a boyfriend, my little sister?" Mara-Joy smirked, considering her sister.

"Yes," Joanna remarked shyly. Boys had begun to be of interest to the young girl. She couldn't help herself. She wished boys would pay just half the attention to her that they did to Mara-Joy.

"Is that so?" Mara-Joy piped in, "Isn't that sweet, little Joanna wants a beau."

Joanna's head snapped up, and her eyes squinted in anger.

"Why is that so hard to believe, Mara-Joy? Is it so hard to think that maybe other people have interests that don't involve you?" Joanna belted out, unexpectedly.

Mara-Joy stood with her mouth gaping open, taken back. Joanna was always so defensive with her. Ready to attack when ever Mara-Joy opened her mouth.

"What on earth are you talking about? Joanna, I swear you are getting weirder and weirder all the time. You definitely won't be catching any men with that pissy frame of mind. And trust me, you are going to need everything you've got as it is!" Mara-Joy responded without breaking into a sweat. The little twit wasn't going to get the best of her.

Joanna felt her face flush red. She had done it again and walked right into sister's hands.

"Well, we can't all be Mama's favorite now, can we?" Joanna burst out and began to walk away coldly, leaving Mara-Joy standing alone smirking.

"Oh come on! Quit being such a baby," Mara-Joy yelled, running after Joanna. She reached out and grabbed her arm, swinging Joanna around to face her. Green angry eyes clashed with cold icy blue ones. Neither girl said a word as they surveyed each another.

Alan-Michael saw the two girls braced for combat and ran forward to stop whatever was about to happen next. History had proven to him that once Mara-Joy and Joanna started to fight, it would be very hard to stop them. His thoughts jumbled, he ran full speed ahead, collided with Joanna and fell hard on the ground like a sack of potatoes. Pauline, unaware of anything going on, walked blindly into Alan-Michael and stumbled over him. Joanna caught her in time before she fell face-first onto their shrieking brother, whose painful cries filled the air.

"See what you have done!" Mara-Joy bellowed, tossing her long curly hair out of her blazing eyes.

"Me?" Joanna thundered, holding Pauline tight to her heaving chest.

"Yes, you! If you hadn't said that horrible thing about Mama, none of this would have happened," Mara-Joy said furiously. She felt hot tears well up in her eyes, but didn't bother wiping them away.

Joanna wanted to scream. Even when she was crying she looked beautiful. More so it seemed.

Why? She screamed in her head. Why is Mara-Joy so exquisite while I am so unbecoming?

She shook her head and looked to the whimpering Alan-Michael: the boy her mother always wanted. His little knees were all scraped up, raw and bleeding.

"I'll take him home," Joanna said, lifting the burly six-year-old boy up.

"Oh no, you won't. I will," Mara-Joy stormed. She grabbed Alan-Michael's arm from Joanna, forming a tug-of-war, the child caught in the middle. "I don't want you near my baby brother. You're too much of an animal!" She gave a good yank and felt Joanna release her grip on Alan-Michael's other arm. Mara-Joy hiked the husky boy into her arms as he continued to howl in her ear. Over her shoulder she stuck out her tongue at Joanna.

Alan-Michael continued to scream heartily as Mara-Joy struggled to carry him home.

"That mindless little bitch. "Mara -Joy fumed, patting Alan-Michael's back.

Snot ran down his nose and he began to breathe heavily between wails. She placed him down on the ground and grabbed the sleeve of his sweater, wiping the mess from his nose, leaving a line of slime across his freshly cleaned sleeve.

"I can just imagine the lies she would tell Mama if she'd brought you home," Mara-Joy seethed between clenched teeth. With red-rimmed eyes Alan-Michael observed his sister. His wails turned to whimpering hiccups. He loved Mara-Joy—he adored her.

"What you going to do, Sissy?" he sniffed. His knees stung and he felt like crying again as he walked quickly beside Mara-Joy, clutching her hand obediently.

"Oh, don't you worry baby brother, I will get her for what she said," Mara-Joy said as she smiled at the small boy. His green eyes, similar to his other siblings', twinkled admiringly at her.

Joanna and Pauline stood silently together, staring after Mara-Joy and Alan-Michael. Joanna felt like screaming as she watched Mara-Joy's perfect body struggle to carry the thickset little boy. Mara-Joy's black hair cascaded over her shoulders and down her back in a luscious mane. Alan-Michael's straight, thick, brown hair flickered with every bounce of Mara-Joy's step.

How different Mara-Joy looked compared to the rest of them. Joanna, Constance, Pauline and Alan-Michael all looked similar to each other. Joanna and Alan-Michael had light brown hair, just like their mother. Constance was a pale, soft-curled blonde, just like the grandmother she was named for. Her mother said she was the image of the original Constance. Pauline had golden-flecked brown hair like their father. They all had the same strange eyes as him, a trademark from Alan their mother said, that dominated their faces. Joanna, Constance and Pauline had their mother's thin figure. Whereas Alan-Michael took after their father's stocky, strong build.

The four younger children of Alan and Jobeth had a unique look to each of them, but all resembled both of their parents a little. All of them except Mara-Joy. Mara-Joy with her black, curly hair and her penetrating blue eyes resembled none of them.

Joanna's stomach began to flip-flop as she remembered the conversation that could not help but haunt her: the conversation she overheard the night Uncle Oliver and Aunt Shawna had left after getting married, when she listened secretly by the window. She couldn't remember everything clearly, but she did remember a woman's name.

Tamara.

Tamara had a baby. A baby with Oliver. A baby Mama and Pappy felt they deserved. She also remembered a few years later how Uncle Carter had mistaken Mara-Joy for Uncle Oliver's daughter.

She felt very confused as she always did when thinking of these events.

There was something strange about her family, but Joanna was afraid to place her finger on it. If what she had pieced together was true, her whole life was a lie and her mother's behavior toward her even more of a cruel mystery.

"Joanna, let's go or we'll be late for school," Pauline interrupted, pulling on Joanna's shirt. She stood patiently waiting as Joanna was off in another world.

"Sorry, Pauline," Joanna said to her eight-year-old sister. She began walking quickly, clutching her books tightly to her chest.

"I have to find out the truth," she whispered to herself, ignoring Pauline running beside her. "If it is the last thing I do."

— Chapter 24 —

"Mama, Mama!" Mara-Joy stormed through the house with Alan-Michael in her arms. Her eyes darted from one room to the next, searching for her mother.

Alan-Michael weighed heavily in her arms and she desperately wanted to put him down, but not until her mother saw them.

"Ohh! Mama!" she screeched.

"What is it?" A terrified voice came from her mother who charged down the stairs toward Mara-Joy's cries. Jobeth's heart raced rapidly in her slender chest, every fear ran through her head. She couldn't get over her trepidation of the past. After all these years she still felt her comfortable life could be ripped away from her at any moment. Even after fourteen years of fairly uneventful bliss, Jobeth had lost too much in her life at a very young age to ever feel totally secure.

Entering the doorway Jobeth came face to face with Mara-Joy. She stopped dead in her tracks, her body numb with horror. Mara-Joy stood clutching Jobeth's only living son in her arms. Both were covered in blood. Her heart jumped and she thought she might faint. She ran to Mara-Joy and snatched Alan-Michael from the young girl's trembling arms and examined him quickly, searching for broken bones and punctured flesh. Alan-Michael cried loudly, confused by his mother's frantic behavior.

"What happened?" she asked Mara-Joy, trembling and hugging Alan-Michael close to her throbbing heart. After a thorough examination, she couldn't find anything wrong with her boy. It must be internal. Maybe he was bleeding to death from the inside!

"Oh, it was awful!" Mara-Joy cried as she wiped her nose. She reached out and caressed Alan-Michael's damp head. "Joanna was being so nasty." She paused for dramatic effect and continued when Jobeth's full attention was focused on her.

"Mama, that girl was saying horrible things about you. Saying you don't love her. When I told her to stop her ridiculous talk, she turned on me and knocked baby Mikey onto the ground. Just look at his poor knees!" She pointed to Alan-Michael's bloody knees. It was becoming all too apparent to Jobeth that this was the sum source of blood covering her two children.

"They are scraped raw." Mara-Joy began to sob. "And she said such mean, horrible things about you Mama." Mara-Joy continued as she followed her mother into the washroom. Jobeth, relieved to know that Alan-Michael's injuries were superficial, began to clean his wounds.

Alan-Michael continued to cry, his cuts stinging painfully as his mother rinsed them with disinfectant.

"Now, now, my sweet. It's over with," Jobeth cooed to her son. She reached for a damp face cloth resting on the rim of the sink and began to clean Alan-Michael's tear-streaked face.

"But to hurt poor baby Mikey!" Mara-Joy continued, lifting her swollen face to her mother. Her blue eyes were puffy from crying, causing her eyes to stand out even more brightly from her flushed face.

"It's just so terrible to take her anger out on him. He is just a baby after all." Mara-Joy patted Alan-Michael's shoulder. He shivered and let out a slobbery sigh.

"It's all right Mara-Joy; I'll have a talk with Joanna when she comes home. Stop crying dear." Jobeth got up from doctoring Alan-Michael's knee. It seemed his wounds were a lot less serious than Mara-Joy believed. Jobeth looked at her forlorn daughter and walked out of the washroom, only to return shortly with a fresh dress for Mara-Joy.

"But Mama, it hurts me to hear her say that you don't love her like the rest of us," Mara-Joy whined, taking the clean outfit and walking into the hallway to dress. It was a narrow hall, but she wanted to be near enough to speak to her mother. The room she shared with Joanna was down the corridor and she would have to yell at the top of her lungs for Jobeth to hear her.

"Well, I don't understand that girl. She knows that isn't the truth." Jobeth shook her head, helping Alan-Michael to change into clean clothes. Joanna was a constant thorn in her side. The girl seemed to always be at odds with everyone. Jobeth didn't know what to do with her anymore.

"I will write a note for you and baby Michael. After you have finished dressing, the both of you can return to school."

"All right Mama, but if this keeps up I don't know what I will do."

Mara-Joy zipped up her dress. She walked back into the washroom and looked into the mirror, frowning at her puffy eyes. She turned the cold tap on and splashed water onto her face.

Jobeth placed a comforting hand on Mara-Joy's back.

"Don't worry, Mara-Joy. It won't happen again," Jobeth said, smiling into the mirror. It hurt Jobeth to see Mara-Joy so upset.

Anger filled her. Joanna was starting to really push it. Her behavior was getting out of control. This jealousy towards her sister had to come to an end. She pulled free the hair trapped in Mara-Joy's collar, letting the curls tumble down her shoulders.

"Now get to school. I will deal with your sister later."
Mara-Joy smiled brightly into the mirror, her sapphire eyes sparkling.

"I love you, Mama." She turned and wrapped her arms around Jobeth's waist.

"Oh my darling, I love you too," Jobeth sighed, hugging Mara-Joy back.

"Me too!" Alan-Michael interrupted, sitting on the toilet. He jumped off, his knees forgotten, and ran over to Jobeth, seizing her leg in a bear hug. Jobeth bent down and untangled the child from her leg, lifting him up into her arms.

"Yes, you too." She planted a kiss on his warm cheek. "You too, my precious little boy." Mara-Joy grinned, leaning over Jobeth's shoulder to peck a kiss on his other cheek, causing the boy to burst into giggles.

— Chapter 25 —

"I hope Mrs. Wood won't be mad because we're late, Michael." Mara-Joy smiled as she leisurely walked beside her little brother. The boy kicked a bent can into the empty street grumpily. He had no reason to cry. The crisis was over and no one cared if he cried any more.

"She better not or I'll get Pappy's gun and shoot her dead," snarled Alan-Michael. His scrapes kept stinging and if Mara-Joy didn't slow down he was going to fall again and split his knees open once more.

"Oh!" snickered Mara-Joy as she threw back her head with amusement, her hand flying up to her nose. "That would solve all our problems, little brother. It sure would. If only you could." She grabbed her brother's hand and started to run, dragging a cranky, stumbling Alan-Michael behind her.

His mind tried to digest Mara-Joy's words, but he was lost in his murky thoughts. The only thing that came through clearly was the crisp tones of her voice saying, "That would solve all our problems."

They reached the schoolhouse in a short time and strutted into the classroom. Mrs. Wood, a recent widow after a thirty-year marriage to a kind but loveless man, turned from her lesson to stare at the two late children. She was fifty-eight years old and had been a teacher for nearly twenty-five years. She had seen many kinds of children in her time, but none were as rotten as the two who had just ambled in.

"Why are you late?" the elderly woman hissed, her eyes bulging.

Unconsciously, she pushed her bifocals up her nose and placed a strand of white hair behind her ear.

"I have a note," Mara-Joy said, dismissively handing the slip of paper. "My mother wrote it. If you, and I doubt you will, have a problem with it, talk to her." Mara-Joy smiled wickedly into the stern eyes of her teacher. She turned to her seat and sat down with the rest of the children.

That girl, Mrs. Olga Wood steamed. She is just a horror. She and her brother.

How was it that they were so terrible and the three other children such sweet young girls? Mrs. Wood sighed. It didn't really matter. She didn't care to think about Mara-Joy or her siblings. All Olga Wood wanted was to finish the day and go home. She was a sad woman, lonely for human contact other than the children she taught. *Maybe I will call Mary and see if her offer to live with her is still open,* Olga Woods thought. Mary was Olga's daughter. She was a teacher in the next county. Anything would be better than teaching these brats. Mrs. Wood shook her head and turned back to the blackboard to finish her lesson.

Joanna watched Mara-Joy intently. She felt herself heat up with anger.

Alan-Michael sat down at his desk in the corner away from the other students.

Mrs. Wood had put him there only a week ago. His desk would be placed there permanently until he could play nicely with the other children. Alan-Michael was prone to viciously attacking children smaller than him.

"How could Mr. Wood have ever climbed into bed with that old wrinkled bat?" Mara-Joy whispered into Joanna's ear as she sat down next to her. "Maybe that's what killed him." Mara-Joy chuckled as she took her books out and placed them on her desk. Joanna pretended not to hear her.

"Oh, by the way little sister, you are in deep shit."

"Shut up, Mara-Joy. I am sick of your voice," Joanna spit out. A strong urge to slap Mara-Joy's perfect heart-shaped face overcame her.

Mara-Joy gasped, her mouth hung open in shock. Joanna was becoming a little too sassy for her own good.

"You just like to bury yourself deeper don't you, little twit sister?" Mara-Joy hissed, crouching close to Joanna's beat red face. Mara-Joy's lip curled into a sneer and she huffed, content with herself. "Haven't you realized yet that you can't clash swords with me because I will crush you?" Mara-Joy sat up straight and satisfied, surveying her shapely manicured nails. "Kinda like a bug." she smiled to herself.

"I could be like you and just weasel my way out of trouble," Joanna whispered, looking blankly at the chalkboard. Mara-Joy turned abruptly to Joanna's pale, stone profile. She folded her arms tightly across her large breasts.

Like everything about Mara-Joy, her body had seasoned into a perfect figure eight. Joanna, on the other hand, was lean with breasts only starting to bud, and hips just beginning to curve.

Joanna turned gently to look at Mara-Joy's surprised face. "Just like you did when you had Frank Parkins in the back of the barn when you were ten. You were showing him your breasts and letting him touch them. I would never have lied for you if Shawna and Oliver hadn't shown up."

"Listen, Joanna!" Mara-Joy stifled trying not to yell. She grabbed Joanna's arm and began to squeeze it tightly, digging her nails into Joanna's soft skin. "You don't make threats to me. Who do you think Mama is going to believe? You or me? You think about that before you start threatening me. Remember--you are notorious for trying to get me in trouble."

Joanna tugged on her arm trying to break free of Mara-Joy's painful grasp. She could see small droplets of blood escape between the tightly gripped fingers.

Mara-Joy abruptly released her clutch on Joanna's arm, causing her to lose her balance and teeter backwards on her chair. Mara-Joy sneered as Joanna flapped her arms aimlessly, struggling to regain her balance.

"Quiet!" hollered Mrs. Wood, "You two girls, if you cannot stop bickering and disturbing the rest of us, you can stay after class."

"I'm sorry, Mrs. Wood," Mara-Joy said in a clear voice as she stood up straight from her seat. All eyes turned to see what she was going to do next.

Even Mrs. Wood held her breath dreading the worst. She was in no mood for this smart-mouthed little deviant today.

"My sister is bothering me. Can I be moved? PLEASE?" Mara-Joy exhaled heavily, her chest swelling.

Joanna rubbed her arm. It ached where Mara-Joy had grasped it.

"Yes. Yes. Anything to finish up the day without any more distractions," Mrs. Wood huffed, her hands flying in the air irritably. "Go sit beside Pauline--Constance, you sit with Joanna."

Mara-Joy scooped up her books and sauntered over to Pauline who had just realized the lesson was disrupted. She had been daydreaming about running in a field of wildflowers when she felt Constance stand up and walk toward Joanna. She wrinkled her forehead, confused, when Mara-Joy flopped into Constance's empty seat. Mara-Joy didn't bother looking at her youngest sister. She just glared at Joanna who was speaking softly to Constance.

Why did Joanna always get the best of her?

"I will get her one day," Joanna scowled. Her fist clenched tightly under the desk.

"Take it easy," Constance's calm, soothing voice penetrated Joanna's thick aura of anger. A firm hand patted Joanna's shoulder. "She is not worth getting angry over."

"She just gets to me," Joanna spat through clenched teeth.

"There is nothing you can do about it now, so why let her see you frustrated and mad? It's a losing battle, Joanna."

Joanna nodded in agreement and surrendered back to her studies, wishing she could do something to hurt Mara-Joy as she had hurt her.

"Mama, Pappy, I am leaving for the party." Mara-Joy hollered that night, as she walked out the front door of her home.

"All right, dear. Remember, home by nine." Jobeth answered from her and Alan's bedroom.

"Right," Mara-Joy said, rolling her eyes while straightening her blouse.

"You better," Alan grumbled from behind Jobeth.

"I will, Pappy," Mara-Joy chirped.

She opened the door quickly and left before her father could say more. He was not as easy to persuade as her mother was.

"Jobeth, I really don't agree with you permitting Mara-Joy going to parties." Alan said, sitting on their bed and fumbling with his tie.

Jobeth was situated at the vanity, clipping her pearl earrings on. She smiled at his reflection in the mirror. Her earring secure, she stood and went to him on the bed. Crawling up behind him, Jobeth wrapped her arms around his shoulders and began to fix his tie, watching him in the mirror as she manipulated the silky material.

"Alan, it is 1920. Times are changing." Jobeth kissed his ear, lovingly. He smelled clean and fresh from his bath. Jobeth could not help herself from warming up with desire for him.

"Times changing, bah. She is just fourteen," Alan grumbled, not liking his girls growing up so fast.

Jobeth quickly interrupted.

"It seemed like we were adults when we were fourteen. I fell in love with you." She caressed his ear with her finger, stroking the lobe up and down gently.

"You weren't fourteen when we married and neither was I. Besides," Alan turned to face his wife as he put his arms around her still tiny waist, "we had to be adults. We weren't as lucky as Mara-Joy. We weren't able to be children."

Jobeth smiled down on Alan and ran her fingers through his hair. He closed his eyes and thrust back his head, moaning.

"I want to make love to you, Jobeth," he groaned, lifting his face and nuzzling it between her breasts.

"Oh Alan, the children--and we have to get to the dance." Jobeth shuddered, wanting him just as urgently. He had a way of doing that to her, causing her to want him at any time. "Besides, Shawna and Oliver are waiting," she giggled as

Alan undid her blouse and released her plump breasts into his waiting hands. He growled hungrily as he gazed at the mounds of flesh, kissing them as Jobeth shivered with delight.

"We have plenty of time and the children won't hear anything they have not heard before." Alan's muffled voice came from between Jobeth's breasts.

She breathed deeply as she removed her blouse and lay back on the bed.

Alan leaned over her and kissed her warmly on the mouth.

"I love you, Jobeth," Alan whispered as her removed Jobeth's skirt with the skill of a man who has done it many times.

"I love you too, my darling," Jobeth exhaled, reaching out for him.

— Chapter 26 —

"Mara-Joy, you are finally here!" the red-haired girl standing in the door way shrieked. Mara-Joy smiled wickedly up at her friend, Loran.

"Of course I'm here. More importantly, is he here?" she asked, coolly walking into the house.

"Everyone is here," Loran giggled, unable to control her excitement. She straightened her sleeveless yellow dress unconsciously. She was an attractive girl with deep auburn hair and gray, oval eyes.

Mara-Joy looked spectacular. Her lush black hair hung in coils around her shoulders. She wore a slim fitting dress of royal blue that shaped her figure perfectly. The blue in her dress accentuated her eyes, making them jump out of her creamy colored face.

Loran had spent all her money that day on a new perm, hoping to capture some of the waves Mara-Joy had naturally inherited. She'd been pleased with the red curls and before Mara-Joy's arrival, she had been the center of the boys' attention. Loran had hoped that tonight she would be the envy of all girls. But she knew at once when she saw Mara-Joy that the spotlight would be on her friend and off her.

"Well--my, my, Lore, you look quite striking," Mara-Joy said as she surveyed her friend. She removed her hat and shawl and deposited them in the girl's waiting arms.

"As always, you outdid yourself," Loran sighed, taking Mara-Joy's apparel and placing them in the closet with the other guests' coats.

"Please! I just threw this outfit on," Mara-Joy said, looking herself over in the hallway mirror. Satisfied with herself, she turned to Loran.

"Well, is he here?" she demanded, her hands resting on her tiny waist. "Is Chad here?"

"Oh, yes. He's here and he has been asking for you," Loran giggled.

"Wonderful. Wonderful," Mara-Joy smiled with contentment. "Let us retreat to the party. My fans await me." Mara-Joy was shining as she encircled Loran's arm in hers.

"You are a tease, Mara-Joy," Loran laughed, squeezing Mara-Joy's arm and heading for the cellar door. Al Jolsen's music flooded up the stairs along with the smell of cigarette smoke.

Mara-Joy flushed with excitement. Loran's parents were sitting in the kitchen having their own little party. Mara-Joy waved as they went down the stairs and the adults returned her wave with a big smile.

"Pleasant child, that Mara-Joy," commented Loran's mother. She took a drink from her glass of whiskey and lit a cigarette.

"Yes, yes indeed," replied Loran's father as he observed Mara-Joy's young body wiggle down the cellar stairs. He could feel himself stiffen under the table and placed his hand down to cover it. If his wife saw what their daughter's friend did to him, there would be no end to the yelling. Mara-Joy wouldn't be able to come and play with Loran anymore and he would no longer get to see that luscious body parade around his home. He thought to himself what it would be like to screw his daughter's young friend. It would be nothing like those damn whores he picked up. He could imagine her perky breasts, ripe in his hands. Just the thought made him groan out loud.

"Something wrong, dear?" Sarah, Loran's mother, queried.

"Nothing, dear," Loran's father, Harve murmured. He couldn't stop the throbbing in his pants. "Let's go upstairs, Sarah."

Surprised, Sarah looked at her husband; her cigarette seemed to be suspended in mid air as it hung from her gaping mouth. Not often did Harve want to make love to her. She didn't even bother asking for it anymore. That was okay. She had her best friend, Sue, and Sue's husband. The three of them had reckless times. Sarah didn't need her husband to fulfill her hungers when Sue and Bill were all to glad to do so. But his request took her by surprise, so she nodded and followed her overweight husband up the stairs.

Down in the cellar the air was thick with smoke and loud music. A tinge of air now and then reeked of alcohol. Mara-Joy spotted some friends and went to sit with them as Loran went and locked the door. Mara-Joy was pleased. She didn't want Mr. Smith, Loran's father, down there. She enjoyed the way he looked at her, but she was not interested in an obese man for a lover. She wanted Chad, and she was going to have him.

She looked around the room brimming with people. Most of the faces were familiar: friends from school and people from around town. She couldn't spot Chad anywhere.

"Hey, Mara-Joy," a deep voice declared behind her. She pivoted around with a bewitching smile spreading across her face.

There he was--Chad.

He was leaning against a wall, smoking a cigarette with one hand and holding a jug of whisky in his other.

"Hello, Chad," Mara-Joy said coyly. Her friends beside her started to giggle and whisper to each other. Chad pretended not to notice the twittering girls and stood perusing Mara-Joy, looking very charming.

Chad was the best-looking boy she knew, except for her Uncle Oliver.

Every girl was crazy about him, including Mara-Joy. He was seventeen with dark-brown hair that curled appealingly over his forehead. His blue-green eyes sparkled with life and laughter in conflict with his long straight, sharply angled face. He was the most debonair chap around.

The music turned to a waltz and people got up to dance.

"Would you like to dance?" Chad smiled, stubbing his cigarette out in a nearby ashtray. He reached his hand out invitingly.

"I would be honored," Mara-Joy replied in a husky voice. Chad placed the jug of whisky down on a table and took Mara-Joy's delicate hand in his. He led her to the middle of the room and took her into his strong arms.

They danced together until eight o'clock, paying attention only to each other. Chad then led Mara-Joy up the stairs and out into the yard. Loran's parents were nowhere insight.

"Wait, Chad," Mara-Joy stalled outside the house. A wind blew cold against her. "My shawl and hat."

"Be back in a minute," Chad gallantly disappeared into the house only to return shortly with her shawl and hat.

"My lady," he exclaimed, bending and relinquishing her garments. Mara-Joy placed the hat on her head.

"Would you help me put my shawl on?" she asked in her sexiest voice. He placed the delicate material over her pretty shoulders. It draped like silk gauze, hugging her body perfectly. Taking his hand, Mara-Joy raised her heavy lidded eyes up into his.

Chad's heart skipped a beat. Her steel eyes pierced his soul.

They walked to the bushes where benches scattered. They sat down on the farthest bench from the house, far from peeping eyes

"So, Mara-Joy," Chad said, nervously twiddling with her fingers encased in is hand. He couldn't look at her, only her slender hands and well-shaped nails. She was made so perfectly. No girl he knew was made like her.

"Yes Chad?" Mara-Joy said innocently to him, searching his face.

"When do you have to be home?" he asked, wondering if Mara-Joy knew he was trying to decide how to kiss her. He felt awkward, which was unlike him. It was easy at the clubs, the girls expected you to maul them to death. But what was Mara-Joy expecting? He didn't want to rush her and then ruin his chances of making her his girl.

She leaned over and whispered into Chad's ear, warm and hot, "Kiss me, Chad." He swiveled toward her, leaned over and kissed Mara-Joy gently on the lips. She exhaled as Chad kissed her again.

"Oh Chad, you are so wonderful," she gasped as his lips began working down her neck. "Kiss me hard on the lips." Chad obeyed but opened his mouth over hers. Willingly, she opened her mouth in response, taking his tongue hungrily. "Oh Chad, you make me tingle inside." Mara-Joy mewled, squirming beneath his heaving body. This was no lie. She couldn't seem to get close enough to him. "I think I love you Chad."

"I love you, Mara-Joy," Chad whispered, huskily into her neck. He no longer felt afraid of what Mara-Joy wanted or didn't want. His hands went behind her back and started to unbutton her blouse. He leaned down on the bench with Mara-Joy beneath him. He breathed into her ear, unable to control his body.

She reached out pulling him closer to her, kissing him passionately. Never had she wanted something so badly. The feelings flooding her body were new and exciting.

There was no turning back. She didn't want to. This was her destiny. She reached down between their crushing bodies. Chad's eyes darted up, confused as she undid his pants, releasing his pent-up excitement.

Minutes past and all that could be heard was heavy breathing and the creaking of the bench as the two young people meshed together into one. Chad pulled a panting Mara-Joy tightly to his bare chest as they reached climax at the same time falling exhausted and spent into each others arms.

— Chapter 27 —

"Mama!" Mara-Joy called out merrily at the door. "I'm leaving now."

Joanna, who was doing her homework with her two younger sisters at the kitchen table, looked up at Mara-Joy and wondered why she was so happy lately. It must be because of that boy, Chad. All Mara-Joy talked about lately was Chad, Chad, Chad. Joanna shook her head. What on earth did he see in Mara-Joy? Then again, Joanna was always surprised at how her sister seemed to draw people around her. It was like she was a magnet and everyone else, metal. For the life of her, she would never understand people's attraction to Mara-Joy.

She was beautiful, yes, but couldn't anyone see past her looks and into her soul? Couldn't they see how ugly Mara-Joy really was?

Apparently not. Joanna absently shook her head and dove back into her schoolwork.

"Another date with Chad, dear?" Jobeth asked, walking into the kitchen.

"Make sure you are home by ten. Your father will be home with Oliver by ten thirty, so be on time or he will have both our hides. You know how he disapproves of you dating this young." Jobeth leaned over and kissed Mara-Joy on her rosy cheek. "Luv you."

"Me too, Mama." Mara-Joy beamed and flushed with excitement. Nothing was going to spoil her mood tonight. She was flying high on life and had no plans of coming down. "I better go. Chad is waiting." She grinned, pecking Jobeth one more time on the cheek.

"Bye dear, don't be late." Jobeth stepped away from the door. Mara-Joy nodded as she waved a hand behind her and ran down the patio stairs, into the waiting car.

Jobeth watched her daughter hop in and drive away. She closed the door, slowly feeling worried that maybe Alan was right and it was time to tell Mara-Joy to start dating other boys and not just this Chad fellow. What did they know about him anyway? They knew he came from a good family, but that was it. Mara-Joy had barely introduced him. Well, if she intended to keep seeing this boy, he would have to be properly introduced to Jobeth and Alan.

She turned to the girls sitting and staring at her from the kitchen table. Joanna was frowning disapprovingly at her once again. Jobeth turned away and went upstairs to get ready for Alan.

This would have to wait until later.

Joanna went back to her schoolwork, baffled. As much as she tried to get it out of her head, she couldn't recall her mother ever saying she loved her.

"Hi babe," Chad said to Mara-Joy when she hopped into the car. She looked really pretty tonight. Her hair was curly as always and hung nicely on her shoulders. She was wearing a blue dress: one of the new styles that hung loosely to her knees. A beaded white necklace dangled low between her breasts.

Chad leaned over to kiss Mara-Joy on her red, lipsticked lips. She turned her head away, leaving him with a mouthful of hair. He pulled back, astonished.

"What's wrong?" he asked, gripping the steering wheel and looking out the front window. The sky had already turned a bluish black and stars were beginning to shine dimly through. His mood was good. He had the prettiest girl in town on his arm and she seemed to be quite happy with him. Every time they were together she could barely take her hands off him. The night of the party, when they first made love, was just the beginning of their passionate affair. Every night they were together in the past two months ended with them grasping at each other's bodies and inhaling each other's souls.

What could possibly be wrong?

"Drive to the point. We have to talk," Mara-Joy said sternly, but with confidence, not bothering to look at his stressed face.

Mara-Joy smiled to herself thinking of the secret she was about to share. Her news would get her what she wanted: Chad.

"Sure, babe. Anything you say." He was confused, but drove out of the driveway and toward the point, asking no questions.

He stopped the car when they reached the clearing nestled in the bushes overlooking the town. He turned to face Mara-Joy who was smiling. Relief began to lift the heavy feeling off his chest. Maybe she wanted to make love again. It would not be the first time she had initiated it.

"What did you want to talk about?" he teased, his hand reaching out for her breast. This was more like the Mara-Joy he had come to know.

"First, kiss me, you fiend." She reached out and pulled him to her, kissing him greedily like a starved animal to a bone.

Chad pulled away, pressing his pulsing lips together. "You had nothing to tell me. You just wanted to come up here for some loving." He smiled wickedly.

"You do know me." She lowered her eyes and began to unbutton her blouse.

Chad reached over and helped to release her perky breasts. Dark nipples pointed out at him.

A deep grumbling noise erupted from his throat. He lowered his head and sucked up a nipple into his mouth.

Mara-Joy let out a squeal, holding tightly to his head. She wiggled out of her dress and began to work on Chad's bulging pants. With his pants off she swung over his throbbing member and mounted him. Chad reached out and grabbed her thighs, rocking her back and forth in heated desire.

A half hour later, Chad sat back in his seat inhaling deep of his cigarette. Beads of sweat rolled down his forehead. Mara-Joy was buttoning up her dress, completely satisfied after their quick ordeal.

"Chad?" she asked as she adjusted her dress around her waist.

"Yah, babe?" he asked as he smoked, feeling gratified. He could lie in her arms for hours. Every time he was with her, he felt like a million sticks of dynamite had exploded in his body.

"I do need to talk to you," she leaned forward so she was situated closer to his face.

"About what? He opened his one eye and focused through the twirling smoke.

"Well," Mara-Joy said calmly as she placed her white gloves on her lap, "I wanted to talk about our wedding." She looked immaculate, no one would be able to tell that moments before she had been thrashing against Chad's thighs like an animal in heat.

"Our wedding!?" Chad choked, the smoke from his cigarette sliding down the wrong pipe. He ran his fingers roughly through his hair and inhaled deeply of his cigarette. He rested his head back against the seat and began to chuckle to himself. He thought he loved Mara-Joy. Or maybe he just desired her. One or the other, it was not enough to marry her. He liked what they had. Just thinking about it made him want her again, even as she sat there glaring across at him.

"Well, Chad darling," Mara-Joy said, screwing up her lips in a matter-of-fact way, "I want to get married. And we have to."

Chad's eyes flew opened, confused. If she thought they had to get married because of what they had done together, she was sadly mistaken. No one had forced her to take her clothes off. In fact, she had been the one to initiate everything in the first place. He lifted his head slowly from its resting place.

"What do you mean?" he asked as he sat up straight looking at Mara-Joy for answers.

"I am going to have your baby."

"What?" Chad choked. He had not been prepared for the words that escaped Mara-Joy's lips. He shook his head, trying to erase her words form his brain. He clasped his hands over his ears and leaned against the steering wheel.

It had to be a joke. This couldn't be happening.

But it could. They had never been careful. Not once. And they had been together intimately countless times over the last couple of months.

What was he going to do? Mara-Joy came from a good family. He would be ruined in town.

He sat up and looked out the front window into the night sky. He took a deep drag from his nearly burnt-out cigarette and exhaled.

"I have heard of these places," he began, formulating a plan, "these places where doctors can get it out." He glanced quickly at Mara-Joy out of the corner of his eye. She was staring at him, her lips pursed tightly. "No one would ever know." A cold sweat broke out on his brow; the car suddenly felt like a small cage slowly crushing him.

"No," Mara-Joy spoke firmly. She continued to look at Chad, her eyes never leaving his crestfallen face. A grin of malice began to slip over her face as she spoke, very composed. "I want our child."

"No, Mara-Joy. I can't get married. I won't." He shook his head furiously. He remembered his brother saying how some girls would do anything to get a guy to marry them. Why had he not listened to his brother? He was so stupid to not see this coming. What girl would give herself freely? He had been an idiot.

"You will," Mara-Joy said unruffled, "Yes, you will marry me, Chad, and we will have our child. No doctor is going 'to get it out' as you say."

Chad looked at her. She seemed so cool, so sure of herself. A chill went up his spine. He was soaked in the image of her sitting there glaring at him, defying him to continue. What did he know of this girl, anyway? What had he gotten himself into?

"You see, Chad, if you don't marry me, I will be forced to tell everyone you raped me and forced me to keep seeing you or you would kill me. I will say you used me every time we were together and I was so frightened of you that I kept quiet. Kept quiet, that is, until now." She smiled, pleased with herself.

"Imagine my horror when I discovered I was pregnant with your bastard child." She leaned over toward Chad like a pouncing black cat and wrinkled her eyebrows. "Poor me. Ruined by a monster. The people in this town will tear you up for raping and impregnating a fourteen-year-old virgin. Not just any virgin either. A daughter of one of the town's most respected families. It would be such a tragedy." She looked deeply into Chad's frightened eyes.

"You wouldn't get away with it. No one would believe you." Chad stuttered, his future flashing before his eyes. Hate started to bubble up inside of him. This girl sitting beside him was not the girl he thought he knew. The girl he had held in his arms in the heat of passion had felt warm and inviting. The person in front of him was cold and conniving.

"Oh, wouldn't I Chad? My father and his friends would believe me. Have you ever met my father and his friends? They are very protective of me. They would kill anyone who would hurt me--especially someone who defiled their little girl."

Chad remembered Mara-Joy's big burley father and the men he was always with: Mara-Joy's uncles. Important men in the town. Men who were known to be protective over each other's children.

"They would move heaven and earth to see you pay for what you have done to me. Your reputation would be destroyed, ruined, finished." She sat back in her seat and looked out her side of the window, letting her words sink in.

"The authorities don't take kindly to men who rape a fourteen-year-old girl and get her in a mothering way."

"You lie," Chad whispered while his head slumped on his chest.

"No, I tell the truth." She pivoted to look at the collapsed form beside her. "So, what is it going to be, Chad? Your life or marriage to me?"

"It seems you have already decided that for me," Chad said softly, his eyes becoming unfocused as he stared mindlessly at the leathery steering wheel.

"That is not true. You always have a choice, Chad. It's just a matter of what the smart choice is to make? That, my dear, is for you to decide." She leaned over and clasped his chin firmly between her palms. Her elbows dug painfully into his thighs as their eyes locked. "I have just laid out your choices."

Chad had made his choice. They were going to be married and it would be very soon.

He drove her home not saying a word. Ghostly gray trees whizzed by the side window as he tried to grasp how he had gotten himself into this mess. For all he knew, Mara-Joy could be lying about the baby. She didn't seem to have a problem with lying to people.

"Chad," Mara-Joy said, stepping out of the car and straightening the dress he had so easily and willingly pulled off her earlier, "tomorrow we will tell our families about the wedding."

She leaned over to kiss him but he turned his head mutely away from her pursing red lips.

"You will have to learn that I always get what I want." She rotated away and then swerved back again as though forgetting something, her purse thumped like a prison ball against the side of the car.

"By the way, don't get any ideas about running, either. The authorities will find you. My parents will make sure of that. Running away will only prove I was telling the truth." She bent down and blew him a kiss through the window, turned and left. Her heels clicked merrily down the path leading to her house.

The lights were on and Chad knew that behind the whitish-gray door, Mara-Joy's mother would be waiting as always.

“Everything is going as planned,” Mara-Joy said out, loud happily trying to contain herself from skipping down the pathway. “We will be one big happy family, Chad, you will see!” She laughed as her heels clicked up the front steps and up into the house.

— Chapter 28 —

Chad sat silently on the couch not saying a word, with a look of utter terror on his face as Mara-Joy exclaimed happily how much Chad and she were in love.

Alan sat still, breathing hard as he watched the scene unfold before him. Jobeth was oblivious to what Mara-Joy had planned to spring on them. Her mouth dropped open when Mara-Joy announced that she and Chad planned to marry, and marry as soon as possible.

"What do you mean as soon as possible?" Alan asked through clenched teeth as he gripped the arm of his chair.

"Well, Pappy, Chad and I feel there is no reason to wait. We are in love and want to share our lives together as man and wife, now," Mara-Joy said, coming to kneel beside Alan's lap.

"What exactly does that mean, Mara-Joy? When do you plan to spend your lives together as man and wife?" Alan asked, looking into Mara-Joy's face.

His heart was breaking and he wanted to kill the little son-of-a-bitch sitting stunned on his couch. He wasn't a stupid man and he knew what was going on, even if Jobeth would never believe it.

"Well, Pappy, I want to be married next week," Mara-Joy beamed.

"No!" Jobeth stood up, flinging her hands into the air, "Alan!" she pleaded helplessly, unable to say anything else.

"Yes, Mama!" Mara-Joy announced, standing up to confront her mother. "I love him and he loves me. We need to be together."

Chad sat silently, not saying a word, as the scene played out in front of him.

Alan watched the boy who had taken his daughter and shook his head, his fears confirmed. Mara-Joy would have to marry this weak, decrepit creature. She would have no choice. Her bed was made and now she would have to lie in it with this man Alan could never respect. How could he respect Chad? This man had robbed his daughter of her innocence?

"Alan, are you going to just stand there or are you going to talk some sense into your daughter?" Jobeth demanded, her mind in an uproar. Everything was falling apart and she didn't know how to stop it.

Alan observed his wife of fourteen years and his heart swelled for her and her blindness towards their daughter, her baby. The baby so like the one she had lost long ago. He understood her fixation with Mara-Joy, even her refusal to see what was going on in front of her very eyes. And he didn't have the heart to break the portrait Jobeth held of Mara-Joy.

"Okay, Mara-Joy," Alan said, not looking at the two women gaping at him. "You will be married by the end of next week."

Mara-Joy squealed and ran to Alan and clasped him tightly around the neck.

"Thank you, Pappy! Thank you! I love you so much for understanding!" She gushed into his ear.

He hugged Mara-Joy back with little strength. How could he tell this child of his heart that she had kicked him in the stomach with her actions? How could he tell her when she seemed so utterly happy?

"Alan, you are not serious!" Jobeth barked, trembling all over. She couldn't believe her ears. The words she was hearing couldn't be from the man she had lived with all these years?

"Jobeth, I am very serious. Mara-Joy will marry next week and we will stand beside her and help her as we always do," Alan said sadly but sternly, his eyes not wavering from Jobeth's stunned gaze. Mara-Joy clutched his arm tightly.

She was radiant beside him.

"Alan? You are joking?" Jobeth's hands flew to her throat. It constricted tightly, making her feel like she was choking. Her fingers wrapped forcefully around her neck in an attempt to anchor her to the reality playing out in front of her.

He shook his head.

"Alan?" Jobeth begged, knowing his mind was set and nothing she could say would change it. Why he had agreed to let Mara-Joy marry was beyond her.

"I have had enough excitement for today," Alan declared, releasing Mara-Joy's grip and walking from the room, leaving an astonished Jobeth behind. "If you will excuse me, I need to go and rest for a while."

Jobeth went to follow him, but Alan turned and said, "Alone."

Taken aback, Jobeth watched Alan walk out of the room and wondered why on earth he would let Mara-Joy get married when it was so easy to see it was the last thing in the world he wanted?

Chad's parents were overwhelmed that their son was getting married. They believed in early weddings and thought it was time for Chad to settle down. He was seventeen and a bit of a wild one. They had been worried his ways would land him in trouble and if marrying would settle him down, they were all for it.

Besides, they liked Mara-Joy. She was charming and came from a good family. Their son had made a good choice in their opinion and it didn't matter that the young couple insisted on marrying so soon.

"Look happy, Chad," Mara-Joy sang, standing in a white lace wedding dress that clung perfectly to her body. Alan had walked her down the aisle, handed her over to Chad with tears in his eyes and a pain in his heart. He kissed her flushed cheek, told her how much he loved her, that she was beautiful and that he would always be there for her if she needed him. Mara-Joy, overcome with emotion, squeezed her father lovingly before going to stand by the somber Chad.

"We don't want our guests to think we are not a happy couple," she giggled, beside herself with jubilation.

She was going to be Chad's wife and the mother of his child. Her heart fluttered with happiness as she pressed her hand on her flat stomach. She couldn't yet feel the child growing inside of her, but she would with time. Her life, like her belly, was expanding forward.

"We are not a happy couple, Mara-Joy," Chad sneered, barely able to hold back his contempt. He stood stiffly in his best suit, unable to believe what was transpiring. He was going through with it. He was marrying Mara-Joy.

"Oh, yes, we are Chad. At least I am and you better be if you know what's good for you."

He looked away from Mara-Joy's radiant face. How did he get from Loran's garden bench to here?

Mara-Joy clutched his arm happily, excitement radiating from her every pore. Chad felt like turning and running from the church.

To hell with Mara-Joy. To hell with her threats. Who would believe her now?

He looked at the girl by his side and thought of how many times he had held her naked in his arms. How good it felt when she touched him. He looked around the crowded church packed with his beaming parents and his cheering friends and family. Everyone was happy for them except for him.

Mara-Joy responded to the minister as he asked her to recite her vows and Chad couldn't help noticing how beautiful she looked in her wedding dress. She truly was a magnificent bride. At that moment he knew he didn't have the guts to abandon her at the altar. When it came for him to repeat his vows that would seal his life forever together with Mara-Joy, he did so without Mara-Joy pushing him.

After the wedding there was a dance held by Jobeth and Alan. Mara-Joy, always the entertainer, cherished the gala affair.

Chad stood off to the side watching his wife go from person to person laughing and chatting, the mistress of the ball. She was in her element. He felt numb.

"What on earth possessed you to marry her?" a voice interrupted his dark thoughts.

He turned to face a tall girl with light brown hair, pulled up and off her long, slender face. Another girl with soft blonde hair and the same slender face stood beside the defiant one. They looked similar to each other, but different. The blonde had satiny curls, whereas the brunette had smooth hair. But both were owners of identical cat-like green eyes. They were definitely related to each other. Most likely sisters. The blonde blushed deeply when the other spoke.

"Are you stupid? Can't you speak? That would explain this senseless display." The girl waved her hand around the room disgusted. No one seemed to pay any notice, except the shorter, fairer girl.

"Joanna, stop it. You will make a scene." The blonde reached for the other's arm to settle her down.

Joanna glared with distaste as she scrutinized Chad. She pulled her arm away from her sister rather forcefully and tried to compose herself.

"I will never understand how come no one sees through her. You all fall like stupefied animals at her feet. What makes you so mesmerized by her?" Joanna stuck out her chin, defiantly. "It can't all be her looks. Is it that superficial? Can it be that pathetic?" She shook her head in repulsion, turned and walked away. The young blonde girl was left standing embarrassed in front of Chad.

"I am sorry, Chad. Please forgive my sister." She reached out her hand in introduction. Chad took it, amused by Joanna's outburst. It was the first entertaining thing that had happened all day.

Of course she was right. It was that pathetic. He had been entranced by Mara-Joy's beauty just like a spooked deer in the middle of the road. And like a deer in the road he had been hit with a terrible blow.

"My name is Constance," she said shyly offering her hand.

Chad leaned forward from the wall he had been leaning on and shook it.

"Who's your friend?" he asked, speaking for the first time.

"That was Joanna. You must excuse her behavior. She and Mara-Joy have always been at odds with one another."

"Why is that?" he watched Joanna glare at him from across the hall. She sipped a glass of soda pop and turned away, irritated, to a small girl who also resembled her.

"Chalk it up to sibling rivalry, and the fact that Mara-Joy has a tendency to always be the one to win." Constance shrugged her shoulders and looked to where Chad was staring. "Excuse me. I am going to go join my sisters." She started to go but changed her mind and turned to face him again.

"By the way, welcome to the family," A crimson red color washed over her face as she averted her eyes and walked away, quickly lost in the crowd.

"Family?" Chad said out loud, recalling Mara-Joy had siblings.

"Sisters?" He felt confused.

Joanna and Constance were the last people he would think would be Mara-Joy's sisters.

"Well," Mara-Joy said, late that night, coming out of the washroom of the little cabin Chad's parents had given them, "let our honeymoon begin." She giggled and flopped onto the bed next to Chad. She was dressed in a sexy white nightie that stopped just shy of her knees

"Go to hell, Mara-Joy," Chad said crossly, grabbing his pillow and heading for the couch. He kept his eyes from resting on the milky white folds of her cleavage, or the way her dark curls cascaded down her shoulders.

Mara-Joy bounced off the bed, pouting.

"You will do as I say, Chad Willis. You won't ruin my honeymoon. Oh no."

She rolled onto the bed and started to laugh. Chad looked at her in disbelief, and headed to the couch.

Mara-Joy crept out of bed later that night and went to the living room. Her new husband lay fast asleep curled up in an old quilt. She sat down beside his sleeping form and tapped him on the shoulder.

"Chad? Chad darling?" she whimpered. "Please wake up, my love." Chad rolled over, drowsy from sleep and looked up into Mara-Joy's blue eyes that were slowly filling up with tears. For a moment he forgot about the wedding and the baby. All he could think about was how beautiful Mara-Joy looked in her white nightie.

Joanna's words began to echo through his mind. *Is it that superficial? Can it be that pathetic?*

"What do you want, Mara-Joy? I am trying to sleep." He turned his back to her, mad at himself for the stirrings of desire coming over him.

"Oh, Chad darling, please don't be mad at me. I love you." Mara-Joy whined in a little girl voice. Tears rolled down her cheeks. She let them. She had learned a long time ago to never wipe tears away.

"Love?" Chad sat up brutally, nearly elbowing Mara-Joy off the couch. "You don't know the meaning of the word love."

"Oh Chad, I do because I love you." She started to cry harder, surprising even herself at how easily the tears fell. Her hand flew up to her nose to prevent it from running.

He felt himself soften as he witnessed Mara-Joy falling apart, but then pushed it away. She had tricked him into getting married.

"Go to bed, Mara-Joy. You got what you wanted." He lay back down facing the back of the couch, leaving Mara-Joy to stare at his back.

"Oh Chad, don't hold this against me," she sobbed. "You can't blame me. Can you?" She started to cry harder, making little heaving noises with her breath. "Hold me Chad. Hold me like you used too."

Blame you? Of course I blame you!" he hollered, sitting up again. The urge to strike her possessed him.

"Chad, please listen," she reached for his arm but he pulled away, repulsed.

Refusing to be put out, Mara-Joy continued, "I was so scared. I couldn't go home pregnant. It would be scandalous. My poor parents would be devastated."

She looked up at him, trying to place where she stood with him. His jaw was tense but he was listening. "You don't know what it's like at home," she paused for dramatic effect.

"I am the eldest of five children. My parents look to me to be an example to the younger children. What would this do to them? My sister, Joanna,"

Chad's eyebrows shot up upon hearing Joanna's name--the spunky little kid had guts.

"She is only a year younger than me. What message would I be sending her if I came home pregnant?" Tears streamed freely from Mara-Joy's eyes. She took a deep breath. "My sister and I already have such a strained relationship. This would have torn us apart. How could they ever look at me with respect?" She stopped to put a hand to her quivering mouth and let out a sob.

Chad's jaw began to slacken. He hadn't really thought what would have happened to Mara-Joy if they hadn't married. She would have been disgraced. Ruined for life. She was telling the truth about the strained relationship with her sister, Joanna.

"We could have solved the problem, Mara-Joy," Chad said in a voice that was beginning to soften. Although he still refused to look at Mara-Joy, he found himself being drawn into her web.

"How, Chad?" Mara-Joy's eyes were glazed and red-rimmed. Her face was wet from the tears she shed. "By killing it?" She shook her head. Her eyes closed tight. "I couldn't kill your child. Besides, it is illegal and some women have died doing it."

Chad looked up into Mara-Joy's heartbroken eyes. The blue of her irises shone brilliantly against the red from crying. His stomach began to churn as his heart beat quicker.

God, she was beautiful. The more she spoke, the more he felt selfish. How could he have asked her to risk her life? Just so he wouldn't have to marry her? Was he not just as responsible for her being pregnant? Had he not held her shuddering in his arms?

"Please forgive me. I only hurt you the way I did because I was desperate and I felt it was the only thing I could do. We could be happy. The three of us..." Mara-Joy burst into uncontrollable tears. She covered her eyes with her hands, overcome with how much she truly wanted everything she said she wanted. She loved Chad and the child she carried.

Chad looked at Mara-Joy and yielded. They were his responsibility now: Mara-Joy and the baby. Sitting there defeated before him, she seemed more like the old Mara-Joy, the one he cared for. The one he enjoyed holding. Without even thinking he put his arms around her shaking form.

"Mara-Joy," he whispered, holding her quivering body tightly. She went to him willingly, hungry for his embrace. "Stop crying Babe." He cradled her head to his chest.

"Oh Chad, I've made a mess of your life. How can you ever forgive me?" She buried her head deep into his smooth skin and breathed deeply of his scent. "I love you so much."

"Maybe I'll have a better view on marriage after the baby is born," Chad said, caressing her curly hair.

Mara-Joy lifted her head up to face him, her nightie falling open. Chad could see the swelling mounds of her breasts and for the first time noticed that they seemed larger than before.

"Chad, you are so wonderful. You forgive me then?"

"Yes, I do." He smiled in spite of himself. His body was heating up with desire as he held Mara-Joy in his arms.

"Oh Chad, I love you." Mara-Joy bounced up happily, kissing him on the lips. "It hurt me to threaten you like I did." She pressed her warm lips on his, shoving her tongue roughly inside his mouth. Chad leaned back and moaned.

"Let's stop talking about it, all right?" He grasped her head in the palms of his hands, kissing her feverishly, sucking in her breath, her lips. He wanted her. He wanted her badly. She had control over him--over his body. All that she had done to him was washed away with the need to have her. To consume her.

"Whatever you say, darling," Mara-Joy sniffed, lifting her negligee over her pointy breasts, Chad lunged for them hungrily, everything else forgotten.

The next morning Mara-Joy lay awake, naked beside her sleeping husband. She smiled contentedly to herself. Chad had finally fallen asleep after hours of fervent lovemaking. It had been better than ever before. More heat and more emotion than either had ever felt. Thinking about it she felt a warm surge flow over her from the tip of her toes up to her ears. She giggled thinking about it as she stretched out her legs lavishly.

"I told you, my darling. My honeymoon would not be ruined." She laughed and rolled over to kiss Chad's naked back.

— Chapter 29 —

Married life still did not sit right on Chad's shoulders, but what was he about to do? He knew he desired Mara-Joy, but he was not sure that was enough to last him through a lifetime.

When his friends went out to parties and picked up girls, he longed to be with them instead of enduring the responsibilities of marriage and the baby that would eventually be born.

Mara-Joy had not lied about being pregnant. No one could tell when they saw the slim girl always dressed in the latest fashions, but when she was naked, he could see that a tiny bulge had taken over her flat stomach.

As much as Chad wanted to get excited about the baby, he couldn't. The more Mara-Joy looked pregnant, the more trapped he felt.

It was a beautiful day. The sun was shining forth new life, which springtime always seemed to bring. Chad was at his father's grocery store where he now worked full time. With time, he would run the store for his father alongside his older brother, Neil junior. This made Neil senior, very happy. He had always dreamed of his two sons running the store, the family business, together since the boys were little. And his dreams were nearly crushed when the boys showed no interest in the grocery business he had worked so hard to make a success. Neil had wanted to become a soldier until he was denied enlistment because of his bad eyesight. And Chad, well, Chad was an entirely different story. Who knew what Chad wanted to do with his life? What Neil Senior did know was that with Chad marrying Mara-Joy, the boy was forced to support a family; and since Chad had no skills to speak of, he had no choice but to work at the family grocery store.

It was a good living, an honest living.

Chad hated every moment of it.

He watched his old friends drive by as he stacked canned goods and longed to be with them, carefree. They came into Willis' Grocers once in a while to visit their old friend, but the visits were becoming less frequent.

Chad was a married man. They were still single, wanting to do things like partying and courting girls. Chad just wasn't fun anymore. His friends' abandonment hurt him, but how could he blame them? If one of them were in his situation, he'd probably do the same thing. Everything was different now and it always would be.

"Oh Mama, I am so happy," Mara-Joy beamed, sipping her tea with pure delight. She was sitting at the kitchen table of her mother's house, surrounded by her female family, which consisted of Jobeth, Shawna, Constance, Pauline and Joanna.

Jobeth couldn't help smiling at Mara-Joy. Since the wedding she had bloomed and continued to glow with happiness. What reservations she'd felt over Mara-Joy marrying Chad were beginning to fade. Anything that made Mara-Joy this happy couldn't be all bad.

"I am so glad for you, darling."

She is a woman now, Jobeth thought to herself. How time flies. It seems that only yesterday Alan and I were blessed with our little bundle of Joy. What would have happened if we had not been given Mara-Joy? We might never have married and been so deeply happy all these years.

She smiled to herself thinking of that morning, of Alan's sweet caresses and felt a blush rise up her neck. We still act like newlyweds. Imagine! We've been married for fourteen years and he still makes me feel as if we wed yesterday. She smiled inwardly and her heart warmed as she looked at Mara-Joy. If her daughter could be half as happy with her husband as Jobeth was with Alan, then Mara-Joy's life would be full.

"Thank you, Mother, I am feeling quite glad myself, if I do say so," Mara-Joy conveyed, smoothing down her conservative light blue dress over her rounding belly. It was a pale blue that made the color of her eyes stand out against her creamy white skin.

"Look at us three old married women. What more could we want than this?" Mara-Joy sighed to her mother and Shawna as she relaxed deeper into her chair.

Joanna rolled her eyes at Constance, who stifled back a laugh behind her hand.

Mara-Joy noticed her sisters laughing at her expense but brushed it off. She was a married woman and soon she was going to be the mother of Chad's child. They were just impudent little girls compared to her. What did it matter what these two fools thought of her? Their trivial lives were pathetic compared to the life she had planned for herself and Chad.

She lifted her cup of tea to her lips, suddenly feeling a little queasy. She'd felt little pains in her abdomen earlier that morning and made a mental note to talk to the doctor the following day. She sipped the warm liquid, letting it slide down her throat, hoping it would ease the increasing discomfort that seemed to suddenly come over her.

Jobeth noticed that Mara-Joy suddenly became very pale.

Those girls, she thought, *are going to hear it from me.* She glared at Joanna and Constance, relaying her feelings clearly.

Feeling guilty that their mother had caught them, Joanna and Constance sulked in their chairs, ashamed.

Mara-Joy watched the scene play out in front of her but couldn't enjoy it. She was feeling increasingly ill. The night before she had felt the same churning in her stomach. If she had thought about it, she would have realized that it was a feeling which had been going on for a week, getting stronger and stronger every day.

A sharp pain pierced through her lower abdomen.

"Aaah!" Mara-Joy squealed in agony as she grasped the small orb of her stomach protectively. Everyone in the little kitchen twirled toward the ghostly white girl.

"Mara-Joy!" Jobeth jumped up and knocked over her chair. She rushed over to Mara-Joy who was beginning to tremble with pain.

"Mama. My God, something is wrong!" Mara-Joy squeezed out, knocking her steaming tea to the floor. She stared numbly at the fluid quickly running down through the planks in the hardwood floor and seized her stomach as another sharp pain slashed through her. She looked up into her mother's frightened face and clutched her hand tightly. Everything began to go black and then there was nothing. Just the faint sounds of Jobeth calling out her name.

"Doctor, what is wrong with my daughter?" Jobeth asked as she waited impatiently in the doorway of Mara-Joy's old bedroom. She had been standing there waiting since the small, bald man arrived shortly after Mara-Joy fainted.

Shawna tried to comfort her, but Jobeth wasn't going to be well until the doctor told her that Mara-Joy was going to be all right.

"She is going to be fine, Mrs. Benson," the plump doctor said, rubbing his creased forehead. He bolted all the way there after the second oldest daughter had arrived to summon him. He felt beat after what he had just faced. He wiped his forehead with a hanky and turned back to the frantic woman beside him.

"I am sorry, but she lost the baby," he said. The younger woman with the pale blonde hair stood and swiftly put her arm around the astonished Mrs. Benson. He hadn't even seen the pale woman sitting in a chair close by. By the way she held onto the shocked mother, it was plain to see the two women were very close to each other.

"Baby?" Jobeth spit out. A lump started to form in her throat. She clutched Shawna's hand tightly. "We didn't know she was with child." Jobeth seemed stunned. She was speaking more to Shawna than to the doctor. He stood uncomfortably before the two women. Shawna looked at the doctor for answers.

"Doctor?" she asked in a soft, confused voice.

He shook his head.

"I am sorry. It sometimes happens," he replied to the pale woman.

Shawna nodded and held tightly to Jobeth.

"Can I see her?" Jobeth stood up straight and pulled herself together. She had to be strong for Mara-Joy. If anyone knew what Mara-Joy would be feeling right now, it was Jobeth. Although it had been a long time since she had lost her little son, the pain was still there, like a dull ache. It had taken a long time to fill the emptiness in her heart from losing that child. With each child she had, the pain lessened, starting when she had been given the opportunity to raise Mara-Joy as her own. She finally had a son to replace the one who had been born too soon when Alan-Michael was born.

"Yes, but don't upset her. She needs comfort now," he said. "She has lost a lot of blood and she needs to build up her strength."

Jobeth nodded and wiped away the fresh tears. Shawna went back to the chair in the hall to sit and wait as Jobeth entered the bedroom.

"Doctor?" Joanna stopped the short, heavy man as he was opening the front door to leave. She had been waiting patiently for the doctor ever since he had told her mother about Mara-Joy's miscarriage. Something was forming in her mind and the doctor's answer would give her the truth she already believed.

Constance, who had been waiting with her sister, came to stand beside Joanna.

He turned to the two girls standing before him. Now these two looked like sisters, he thought to himself. Not like the goddess in the room upstairs. He flushed when he thought of the poor creature he had just left. My God! He thought. The poor girl had just delivered a dead fetus and nearly died in the process. He recalled the enormous anguish the young woman expressed as he broke the horrible news that her pregnancy had ended.

"Yes, yes." He shuddered, feeling sorrow for the devastated creature upstairs.

The older girl's eyes quizzed him. He could feel her reading his thoughts and he wanted desperately to leave this house.

"How far along was my sister?" Joanna asked, her hands resting on her hips.

There was no point in beating around the bush, the doctor was obviously uncomfortable and would flee without giving her the information she needed if she pussyfooted around.

He looked at the girl who could be only twelve or thirteen and shuddered again. He must be becoming a pervert or something. The youngster before him was no raving beauty like her sister upstairs, but there was something about her too. He looked at the girl about two years younger standing behind the other.

He sighed relieved. She was a child still. He felt nothing.

"Doctor?" Joanna started to become annoyed. What was it with men that they had a hard time looking at her face? Was she that dull that they couldn't give her the decency of answering her questions.

"Three months, possibly four." He placed his hat on his head. "Funny she didn't say anything." He looked again at the older girl and felt his loins pull. "Well, good-bye girls." He flushed and ran out of the house as fast as he could, hoping he would never lay eyes on either sister again.

"Why that..." Constance whispered. "No wonder they got married so suddenly." She turned to Joanna, who was deep in thought with a smile spreading over her face. Constance smiled too. "Shall we tell Mama?" She beamed, her hands clutched together.

"Of course not, silly." Joanna simpered at her younger sister. "Mama would be blind if she didn't figure it out for herself by now. Besides, she will forgive her darling Mara-Joy in an instant. No, we have to be patient, but we will get her. We have to get her. This is just more fuel for the fire. We have to be smart about this, Constance. Mara-Joy has always been one step ahead of us. We have to think like her. Be one step ahead of her."

Constance looked at Joanna as she squeezed Constance's hand tightly, a smile spreading across her face.

"Let's go out to the shed. I have some ideas to toss around to you and I don't want anyone interrupting us."

Constance nodded eagerly and followed Joanna outside into the bright sunshine.

"We have to get all the information we can against her first. Then we damage her with something that is really significant to her and her alone,"

Joanna remarked, sitting on a stack of wood. They were in the shed just out back from their residence. Constance was fiddling with some hay she sat on, looking anxiously at Joanna. She seemed to be thinking again, rolling Joanna's words around in her head.

The shed was small and damp and although the girls were sitting across the room from each other, their knees were nearly touching.

"What would really hurt her?" Joanna tapped her cheek with her index finger.

"I know," Constance squealed, jumping to her feet and tripping on a piece of wood. She stumbled right onto Joanna's legs.

"Oh, this is brilliant. This is too brilliant!"

She quickly jumped up and brushed the straw off her shorts.

Joanna sat looking at Constance, egging her on with a huge smile, ignoring the pain in her legs caused by her clumsy sister.

"But you will have to do it because you are the oldest," Constance said more to herself than to Joanna. Plans were already formulating in her mind and she no longer took notice of Joanna waiting impatiently for her to reply.

"Well, what?" Joanna squealed, jumping up and shaking Constance out of her thoughts.

She looked at Joanna with a wicked smile creeping swiftly across her face.

Joanna felt like hitting Constance for not telling her. The suspense was killing her. If Constance had an idea, then it would work. She was the smartest in the family. But what did Joanna's age have to do with her sister's schemes?

"What's Mara-Joy the most proud of? Or, should I say, who is she the most proud of?" Constance asked coyly, resting her hands on Joanna's legs. She leaned forward egging Joanna on, pressing all her weight down on her legs. Joanna stood wide-eyed, unable to answer.

"Chad, of course," Constance said matter-of-factly, standing and taking straw out of her blonde curls. Joanna stared opened-mouth, confused.

"Chad? What could I do to take Chad away from Mara-Joy?" Joanna thought back to the young man. He had seemed lost on his wedding night. Oblivious to the whole affair.

"Become Chad's lover." Constance avoided Joanna's astounded face and continued. "You see how she brags about her marriage. We have just found out that her marriage is a sham. They obviously got married because she was pregnant. What better way to ruin Mara-Joy than to expose her marriage for the joke that it is? Steal Chad away from her. Become his mistress."

Joanna looked wide-eyed at Constance, unable to believe what she heard. Her mouth suddenly felt dry and pasty.

"His lover? Me?"

"You can do it, Joanna. With time." Constance paused. "You're too young right now. You will have to be at least fifteen or sixteen. Then you will have developed pretty much into the woman you will be. You will have to get to know him. Be friendly to him. That will be hard since your first meeting was a disaster."

Joanna blushed, remembering her outburst.

Constance continued, "But it could work. There is no baby anymore, and if that was the reason they were married," she shrugged, "then getting married was a waste."

"I don't know if I could do it, Constance. It's so…extreme." Joanna twisted her fingers painfully. "To be his lover? I don't even care for him that much."

"Well, that is the only thing that would hurt Mara-Joy, Joanna. Think about it. There is nothing else you could do to hurt her."

Joanna lowered her eyes. How badly did she want to get back at Mara-joy?

Constance reached out and touched her arm.

"Listen, Joanna. You don't have to make up your mind right now. There is time. You never know, maybe Chad is a decent person. Just because he married Mara-Joy doesn't mean he is totally ruined. He is cute."

Joanna smiled. He was kind of cute.

"All right, I will do it."

Constance clapped her hands and hugged Joanna tightly.

Joanna stood silently taking in her sister's plan, as Constance droned on. She felt weird, unreal, like she had just made a pact with the devil and there was no turning back.

"Mama, Mama," Mara-Joy sobbed sincerely from her little bed. The cheery bedroom decorated in pink and blue seemed too buoyant for the events that had taken place within its walls.

Jobeth stood at the doorway, wanting to seize her daughter and sweep her away to some time in the future. The tears she had hoped not to shed in front of Mara-Joy were again welling up.

"My baby is dead." Mara-Joy looked to her mother. "Dead, Mama, dead," she cried, reaching out for Jobeth. Jobeth, the mother hen that she was, ran to the aid of her daughter and fell at the foot of Mara-Joy's childhood bed.

"Why didn't you tell me, dear?" Jobeth sobbed while she looked at Mara-Joy's stricken face. Mara-Joy sat up and new tears slid down her already streaked face.

"I didn't know, Mama." Mara-Joy lied reaching for her mother's hand. "I didn't know that Chad's child was growing in my womb." She started to wail, her heart truly breaking.

"Now, now," Jobeth said, cuddling the weeping girl. She placed her arms around Mara-Joy's shivering shoulders and held her damp head to her breasts. "There will be others babies," she cooed, rocking back and forth.

Mara-Joy sat straight up and looked at her mother, holding back real tears of sorrow.

"No, Mama, there will be no babies," she cried. "The doctor said if I do--" she stopped, seeing the look of horror on her mother's face.

"Go on, dear," Jobeth whispered her eyes downcast, not wanting to hear that her baby would never be holding her own in her arms.

"If I did," Mara-Joy sobbed, "it could kill me next time." She looked into her mother's eyes and with all her heart asked, "Oh Mama, what am I going to tell Chad?" Mara-Joy looked at the blue ceiling, the images of the child she was to have bursting like frail bubbles before her eyes. "He so wanted children of his own. He was hoping I would get pregnant right away. Now he'll never have a son, and I'll never have a daughter."

"Mara-Joy," Jobeth said, seizing Mara-Joy by the shoulders and hugging her tightly. "I don't know what to say, my darling, this is just so unfair."

"Mama, my heart is breaking. How do I make it stop? I can't handle the pain, Mama. Please make it stop," Mara-Joy implored, pounding her weak fist against her thighs.

"I can't, Mara-Joy. I can't," Jobeth sobbed, hugging her tightly. And she couldn't. For once in Mara-Joy's life, Jobeth couldn't fix what was ailing her. And for the first time in Mara-Joy's life, she couldn't get what she wanted, and the one thing she secretly wanted most was a baby.

— Chapter 30 —

There was a small farewell a few days later for the little babe that never was.

It wasn't truly a funeral since there was no baby to bury, but a small ceremony to say goodbye to what might have been. Mara-Joy wore a black dress with a matching black veil fashionably covering her face so no one could see the expression that blanketed it.

Jobeth had insisted that Alan get a wheelchair for Mara-Joy to sit in. She didn't want her child to strain herself. They had nearly lost her through the whole ordeal as it was. Jobeth wasn't having Mara-Joy overdoing it.

Chad stood beside the tiny headstone and wept real tears for the child he had never really wanted. He had tried to fantasize about playing ball with a son or showing his friends how beautiful his daughter was. He really believed that when the child was born, he would have begun to feel good about the marriage he felt forced into. The child was supposed to do that. It was supposed to take away that feeling of being an animal trapped in a snare. Or at least the baby was supposed to make his bondage bearable. But, then again, it was the baby that had put him in this prison in the first place.

And now the baby was dead and he was in a pit he didn't know how to get out of. He looked over at Mara-Joy who sat stiffly in her wheelchair. Her mother was next to her holding tightly to her hand, hovering like a bobcat ready to pounce. Mara-Joy had not exaggerated when she said her parents would hunt him down and make him pay for getting her pregnant. The way her mother hovered over her sent chills down Chad's spine. What was it that made him shudder when he thought about how possessive his mother-in-law was over his wife? He couldn't help but think it was destructive in some way.

He shook himself briefly and looked again at Mara-Joy's somber form. She wouldn't talk to him. He had received the message about the miscarriage shortly after it had happened.

Jobeth sent Alan from work to the grocery store to deliver what Chad considered his life sentence.

He looked up into the gray sky as clouds began to form quickly. Soon they would drop their tears on all of them.

In his mind Chad screamed repeatedly, *Why me? Why has this happened to me?*

Then it dawned on him.

There was nothing holding him to Mara-Joy anymore.

There was no baby.

Mara-Joy couldn't threaten him anymore. It was obvious she had wanted to marry him. No one would believe he raped her now. He could do it. He would have to wait awhile. Get his plans together.

His heart began to beat. Could it be over? Could the hell that he had brought into his life finally come to an end?

He would have to leave town, of course. He would never be accepted after abandoning Mara-Joy.

Chad shook his head. It didn't matter. He'd be glad to see the last of this hellhole town. Good riddance to bad rubbish. It would be great to start fresh in another town. Away from his father's damn grocery store and away from the responsibilities of being a husband to Mara-Joy.

As the plan formulated in his mind, Chad knew he could do it. He could be young and carefree once again.

A hand tapped him on the back of his shoulder, crashing him back to reality.

He turned to the assailant.

Mara-Joy stood before him. She looked weak and tired. Dark circles etched her torrid blue eyes. Jobeth stood a short distance behind her, her tissue twisting nervously in her hands. Mara-Joy had insisted on walking over to Chad instead of using her wheelchair, causing Jobeth great amounts of anguish. By the look on her daughter's face, the walk had been an immense burden.

"Take me home, Chad," Mara-Joy looked coolly into Chad's wooden face.

He looked down at the ground, unable to look into Mara-Joy's enchanting blue devil eyes, feeling she could see into the very core of his soul.

"I want to go to our home."

Chad's head shot up nervously. He began to break into a cold sweat. Mara-Joy reached out and grasped Chad's arm with surprising strength.

"Chad, please!"

He nodded idiotically and took her arm in his, obediently. Mara-Joy smiled up at him wickedly.

"That's a good husband," Mara-Joy purred. Chad began to tremble. Where had he seen her smile like that before?

They drove in silence as Chad turned into the driveway of their home. He stopped the car and was about to open the door to help get Mara-Joy out when she reached across and placed her hand gently on his lap, very close to his privates. He felt her fingers lightly brush against him and was ashamed at how he responded.

Mara-Joy chuckled.

"Chad darling, you are such a walking hormone."

Blood surfaced on his face and he pushed Mara-Joy's hand away, disgusted with himself. She leaned back in her seat and laughed maliciously, her hands cupping her jacket snugly around her neck. The black veil half covering her eyes couldn't shield the menace behind it.

"Cut it out, Mara-Joy, let's just get into the house and I will make you some hot tea," Chad shifted uneasily in his seat and opened the door again.

Something was frighteningly familiar with this scene.

"That is a wonderful idea," Mara-Joy simpered as she unbuttoned her coat.

Chad tried not to look as she expertly unfastened the snaps on the front of her black dress.

"Mara-Joy?" He swallowed the lump forming in his throat, and uncomfortably shifted in his seat.

A perky breast popped free from her bra. It was big and swollen from the pregnancy. Chad swallowed hard unable to sustain his growing arousal. He hated himself for wanting her so much, when moments ago they had stood at their unborn child's grave.

"Touch me," Mara-Joy ordered as she caressed herself. "Touch me."

He reached out and grabbed her eagerly, diving into her warm, waiting breasts. He nuzzled them shamefully, unable to control himself, feeling himself heat up with want.

Mara-Joy cried out in delight, clutching his head to her tightly.

"Oh, you are mine," she mewled, "you will always be mine, Chad." She pushed his back against the seat, her chest naked and heaving in front of him. "Do you want me?" she asked, straddling him. She pinched her nipples hard, tossing back her head in a frenzy.

Chad encircled her waist, his mouth sucking up her body. She pushed him away, reaching down between his legs.

"Do you want me?" she cooed again as she rubbed between his legs. Chad reached up and grabbed a bobbing breast. Again she pushed him away. She sat back in her seat, Chad's hands reaching for her. Slowly, she bent her head down between his legs. She breathed hot air on the protruding member buried under his pants.

Chad shuddered, unable to contain himself. He was going to have her, miscarriage or not.

Mara-Joy unzipped his pants, letting his member jump free from its confinement. She pressed the tip of her lips to the smooth tissue. Chad looked down, anticipating Mara-Joy's next move. She looked up, her eyes glinting with mischief. The dark circles were still there under her eyes, but there was something else too. Something that frightened and excited him at the same time.

"Do you want me?" Mara-Joy said, almost pleading, her lips caressing him, her tongue flickering.

"Yes, yes," he snarled, forcing her head down onto him. He closed his eyes and leaned back, letting the pleasure envelop him.

As he succumbed to wave after wave of Mara-Joy gratifying him late into the night, he felt each nail hammered deep into his own coffin.

Lying awake naked in bed with Mara-Joy sleeping deeply on his chest, he realized where he had seen Mara-Joy smile like that before. It had been on their wedding day. When she married him, it had been for life, and she would do anything to keep him hers, forever.

— Chapter 31 —

Pauline stood outside of the shed waiting to be invited inside by her sisters.

She twisted her light-brown hair streaked with gold around her finger. Gingerly, she put the ends into her mouth and sucked. She liked to suck on her hair even if mean old Mara-Joy would yell at her and say she was disgusting. That just made Pauline want to suck on her hair more. She would have thought Mara-Joy would be nice to her, considering she couldn't have any little kids of her own on account of the "miscarriage" that happened two years ago and wasn't allowed to be mentioned. But that didn't matter. Mara-Joy continued to be mean to Pauline. She would always find something to hit her for. Whether it was for slurping her milk or dragging her feet, which Pauline did all the time when Mara-Joy came over to the house. She liked getting Mara-Joy angry. The only problem was that whenever she got Mara-Joy angry, Mama got furious and would start declaring that Mara-Joy should not be made upset in her own home.

Her own home?

Pauline thought she lived with Chad in their home. Mara-Joy only came over to get Alan-Michael and take him on special trips to the zoo and movies. She never took Pauline on these special outings. She never even asked if Pauline wanted to go. Maybe it was because Alan-Michael was younger and it made Mara-Joy feel like she had a child to care for. Alan-Michael was only two years younger than she. Not that much younger. Besides ten years old wasn't all that grown up.

Pauline sighed. It didn't really bother her that Mara-Joy neglected to take her anywhere. What bothered her was that Mama never told Mara-Joy to include Pauline as well as Alan-Michael on these outings. Mama insisted Joanna and Constance take Alan-Michael with them whenever they took Pauline out.

Why didn't Mama uphold the same rules with Mara-Joy?

It didn't matter. Joanna and Constance liked taking Pauline places, and not Mikey.

When Joanna and Constance found Pauline in their secret hiding place, they weren't angry with their little sister. They let the shed be her special place too.

Pauline kicked a few stones with the toe of her shoe. The pebbles flew up and made a pinging noise as they hit the side of the shed. Joanna and Constance both turned around from their crouched positions, startled. Relief spread across their faces when they realized it was only Pauline.

"What are you doing lurking over there? Come on, get out of the shadows and sit with us," Joanna waved Pauline over.

Pauline smiled, releasing the sticky strand of hair from her mouth. She clumsily ran over to her sisters who sat huddled together like conspirators, and she crouched between the two girls. All three looked alike except for a slight difference in hair color. Joanna's long hair was light brown and poker straight, very much like their mother's. Constance's hair was a wavy blonde that fell to just below her chin. Pauline's was kind of a mix between the two. It was brown with lots of gold highlights sprinkled throughout her shoulder length hair. It was not wavy like Constance's, but not as straight as Joanna's either.

All three had their father's eyes: large, slanting green eyes. All the girls had tan complexions, as did their brother Alan-Michael, who, unlike the girls, had inherited their father's looks. The only one who was fair skinned was Mara-Joy.

She didn't resemble any of them, not even Alan-Michael, who looked a little like his other sisters.

Joanna turned to Constance, bent on continuing her conversation where she left off.

"How can I get him to notice me?" Joanna asked, firmly pressing her lips together, strained. At fifteen, nearly sixteen, Joanna had transformed from a plain, gangly girl into a strikingly pretty one. She was tall and lean with an attractive oval face. She had grace and elegance that were appealing, but not threatening, to the opposite sex.

"I have it all planned out," said Constance as she waved her hands into the air, a habit she employed when wanting to explain herself. Pauline lifted her hands, mimicking Constance.

Joanna gently, but kindly stopped Pauline's waving hands and observed Constance's animated face.

"Well, don't keep me in the dark. Tell me. How can I get Chad to notice me?" Her eyes twinkled. The time had finally come. It was the opportunity to get back at Mara-Joy for all her years of torment, to teach her a lesson and give her a dose of her own medicine.

"Mara-Joy comes over every Friday to take Alan-Michael out to God knows where. When she comes back, she always stays and visits with Mama and Pappy. When Mara-Joy leaves with Alan-Michael, tell Ma and Pa you have a date." She looked at both Pauline and Joanna, making sure she had their full attention.

"Go over to Chad's. He will be there," she said before Joanna could interrupt.

"He works over the bills on Friday. You know, trying to figure out some way to pay for the stuff Mara-Joy buys."

Joanna began to get excited. It did make sense. Mara-Joy and Chad enjoyed the same routine every Friday for months. She couldn't remember the last time it had not been so.

"But what if she comes home before I have left?" Joanna stuttered, trying to find a hitch in Constance's plan. The prospect of actually proceeding with their plans they had schemed up two years prior both excited and frightened her.

"I'll call when she leaves home," Constance said matter-of-factly.

"You are so smart, Connie," Joanna squealed, grabbing hold of Pauline and hugging her. Pauline had stopped listening to the two girls and proceeded to daydream. When Joanna clutched her, squealing in delight, she then squealed back in tune, caught up in the excitement.

Constance shrugged but laughed. She loved Joanna dearly and only she had permission to call her Connie. Everyone else, including Pauline, called her Constance. Connie was a term of endearment meant only for Joanna. Constance firmly believed that the name Connie did not evoke an image of intelligence. She knew Joanna thought she was smart, but to everyone else she had to prove her mind worked. With a no-nonsense name like Constance, people had to see that she was more than just a girl, but an astute person.

"Then it is set." Constance beamed, crossing her arms across her swelling chest. Her plan was foolproof.

"I suppose it is." Joanna covered her mouth with her hands, not knowing what to do. She didn't know if she should burst out laughing or throw up.

"You can do it, sis. I have faith in you," Constance said, reaching out and placing her hand gently on Joanna's knee.

Joanna smiled weakly, placing her hands on top of Constance's. They felt warm and smooth, familiar and safe, and at that moment she needed to feel safe. What they planned to do was uncharted territory to them. There would be no turning back after she succeeded in her plan.

"I hope so, Constance, and I hope I know what I am getting myself into."

That Friday, Mara-Joy began her usual ritual of preparing herself to take her brother to the movies. They enjoyed going to the silent films, particularly the comedies. The world was moving fast. She had even heard rumors of "talkies."

How she dreamed of becoming a movie star. She just knew she could do it if given the chance. She had the looks and the talent. She admired herself in the vanity mirror and pretended to be surprised by Charlie Chaplin.

Chad stood by the bedroom door watching his wife's performance. He shook his head, wondering again what was on her mind.

"Can't you stay home tonight for once?" Chad asked. Mara-Joy turned around venomously. She didn't like to be snuck up on. Chad had a way of suddenly being there when she least expected. If there was one thing Mara-Joy didn't like, it was to be startled. She had to be in control.

Always.

She scowled at Chad and turned back to the mirror. Picking up a brush, she began to brush her hair. She had it set that day, so the tight curls were somewhat tamed for the moment.

"You know how important my brother is to me." She brushed harder into her black locks, glaring at Chad's reflection in the mirror.

"What about me? Am I not important to you?" Chad asked. He had aged a lot in the two years since his marriage to Mara-Joy. He didn't look his nearly twenty years.

They fought constantly. Mara-Joy was always demanding something of him and cruelly making him do it for her. The mask was off. He knew who Mara-Joy was now. Anytime he threatened to leave her, she held some kind of blackmail over his head, saying he beat her--or worse--raped her when she refused to make love to him. He felt weak and like not much of a man because he stayed. When she wanted him, he went to her like a dog in heat.

He couldn't seem to help himself. She knew how to make him fall to her feet.

This alone made Chad loathe himself. Every time he climaxed in her arms, he hated himself more for being so weak.

"Have you forgotten that I will never have a child of my own?" She didn't turn to Chad but continued to glare at him through the mirror.

Chad turned away from her ice-cold stare, unable to stomach looking at her. It was almost as though she blamed him for her failure to have children. As if it were his fault she had lost the baby and couldn't get pregnant again.

"Do you not realize that he is the closest thing I will ever have to a son?" She turned around forcing Chad to look at her. "Are you so selfish as to deny me the only mothering experience I shall ever have? You know how close my brother is to me. You can see me any time. I am your wife."

Chad pulled away from her stinging words.

"Go," he said, turning his back to his wife.

Heading toward the front door, Joanna called back to her parents in the other room. Jobeth didn't look up from her knitting. She wanted to finish the matching sweaters she was making for Mara-Joy and Alan-Michael. Alan looked up from his newspaper. He had never been a strikingly handsome man, but time had given him a debonair look. Many women found him nice to look at and envied Jobeth's married status.

"Where are you going, love?" he asked, smiling up at his daughter.

Joanna smiled back feeling a tinge of guilt for what she was about to embark on. She loved her father dearly. He was a good man and was kind and loving to all his children.

"Out with friends, Pa," Joanna said nervously. At least it wasn't lying, really.

If she kept telling herself that, she would eventually believe it. Then the guilt of lying to her father would hopefully fade.

"Well, are you too old to give your father a kiss good-bye?" Joanna went over and planted a dry kiss on Alan's whiskery cheek. She went to leave and thought twice about it, turning and giving her Pa a hug too. Alan warmly patted her back, gently kissing the top of her forehead.

"Be in by nine," he said, rearranging his paper again.

"Oh, Pa!" Joanna implored, and gave him a frown that melted his heart.

Only Alan's children and Jobeth could make him do as they pleased. Everyone else listened to Alan Benson. But when it came to his family, he was all heart and couldn't turn any of them down. He thought of the childhood he had, alone and unloved by his parents.

Life with Jobeth had changed all that. With Jobeth they had formed the family Alan had always dreamed of.

"Ten, please? It is Saturday tomorrow," Joanna requested.

"Ten, no later," Alan said firmly.

"Thank you," Joanna squealed and kissed Alan once more on the cheek, before running out the door.

Alan looked at his paper and chuckled to himself. His children were leading lives so different from his own childhood.

"Alan, that girl has you wrapped around her baby finger. Ten o'clock indeed!" Jobeth tried to look upset with her husband, but she wasn't really. She enjoyed watching Alan dote on his children. He was a good father and she loved him dearly. She went back to her knitting, faking disapproval.

"Oh why not, darling? Mara-Joy was out 'till ten many nights when she was younger than Joanna. Besides, this is the first time I have ever heard Joanna mention a friend. Other than Constance and Pauline she never mentions any other children," Alan sighed, "It's nice that our daughters are close, but it is also nice to see them interact with the outside world."

"Mara-Joy and Alan-Michael have always been popular, unlike our other girls. I just hope Joanna won't be naive and get mixed up in trouble. She is not sophisticated with the outside world like Mara-Joy is," Jobeth said, busily attacking her yarn. Alan rolled his eyes at his wife.

"What?" Jobeth asked, looking up from her work.

"She is not a moron, Jobeth. Joanna is just as sophisticated as Mara-Joy. She is just not as flamboyant."

"Well, whatever," Jobeth said, placing her knitting down and going to her husband. "I went to see Shawna today. I just cannot believe that little girl of hers. She is the spitting image of her mama when she was six." She sat down beside Alan.

"Yes dear, she is." Alan placed his arm around Jobeth's shoulders.

She snuggled into his familiar, safe embrace.

"You are going to miss them terribly when they leave."

Jobeth wiped away a tear already forming in the corner of her eye. She would never forgive Oliver for taking Shawna away again. Why did he have to move to the country?

Was it not he who insisted they move to the city?

"I will." Jobeth wiped away the tear and leaned into Alan more for support. "She is like a daughter to me. I just find it hard to believe sometimes that she is all grown up with a family of her own." Jobeth frowned and looked up into her husband's face. He had aged, he looked thirty-nine instead of thirty-three, but then she had aged too and she was only thirty-one. Life had been hard for them and although they still looked quite good, their faces sometimes showed the weary roads they had traveled. They didn't look hard or rough, but they had never really been young.

"At least Alan-Michael is still young." She grinned, erasing the signs of time in her eyes.

"Do I get the feeling you want another baby, Jobeth?" Alan asked, placing his hand on her belly. Even after giving birth to five children, Jobeth's stomach was still flat and smooth.

"Oh, Alan!" Jobeth laughed and clutched his hand to her. "I only wish Mara-Joy could have given us a granddaughter who resembles her. It seems so unfair to her." She sighed heavily.

"We do have three other daughters and a son who will all give us grandchildren one day." Alan could not believe how much he loved Jobeth.

After all their years together, he loved her more with each passing day. She was more beautiful to him that day then she was the day before. He still wondered how he had been so lucky to have her as his own, his wife, and the mother of his children.

His forever.

"I need to hold you, my love," Alan whispered into Jobeth's ear as he held her tightly.

She felt a shiver run up her spine and tucked her head under Alan's chin.

"Let's go to bed, Jobeth," he said huskily. She reached up and kissed Alan tenderly on the lips.

"Lead the way, my darling," she whispered into his lips. "I will always follow."

— Chapter 32 —

The patio to Mara-Joy and Chad's house was lit up with small wooden garden torches. Mara-Joy was a fine decorator and had to have quality things. Needless to say, the outside of her home was as richly assembled as the inside.

Cherry wood wicker furniture with deep emerald green cushions furnished the terrace. A half empty wine glass sat on the little wicker table with a dirty ashtray beside it.

Joanna stood surrounded by her sister's things. Everything reeked of Mara-Joy.

She swallowed hard, her heart pounding a mile a minute.

What was she thinking? Did she really think she could pull this off? Joanna shook her head. It had all seemed fine and dandy at the time. Take away the one thing that could hurt Mara-Joy: her husband. But now she felt ridiculous.

Shaking, she sat down on one of the wicker chairs. It creaked noisily under her weight. She reached across the table and took the wine glass, gulping down most of the liquid. Leaning back against the chair, she closed her eyes and let the wine slide down her throat and relax her.

Faint memories of long ago filtered through her head.

Memories of Oliver and Shawna sitting outside their old house, talking with her parents about Mara-Joy. Talking as though Oliver were . . . as though Mara-Joy wasn't . . .

Joanna sat up and opened her eyes. She sipped the wine that remained in the glass, enjoying its fragrance. She looked at the fairly full ashtray and began to rummage through the butts, searching for a salvageable smoke.

"I didn't know you smoked," a deep voice said behind her. Joanna jumped with a gasp. Her sooty finger flew to her chest, smudging her cream-colored dress.

"Chad . . ." she stammered, trying to contain her embarrassment.

He was leaning against the side of the house. He stood in the undershirt and slacks he wore at the grocery store. His hair was ruffled, as though he had been running his fingers through it.

"Yes, my dear sister-in-law?" he smiled, looking down at the slim girl. She reminded him of a fawn lost in the woods. He took a smoke out from behind his ear and handed it regally to Joanna.

"For you. It wouldn't be very gentlemanly of me to let you smoke Mara-Joy's butts."

"Thanks," Joanna could barely speak. Her words wouldn't come out. She reached out and took the cigarette.

Cautiously, she put it into her mouth and searched in vain for a light. She stopped when Chad leaned over with a lit match.

"Thanks, again," she said, puffing deeply. She tried not to inhale for fear of choking.

Chad looked at her, amused, and lit up a cigarette for himself as he sat down in the chair across from Joanna's.

He inhaled deeply and looked across at the girl. She looked green and ready to spill her cookies at any moment. This one did make him laugh. Every time he saw her he couldn't help but remember their conversation at his wedding.

She'd seen right through the facade and had hit the nail on the head when she blasted him that night. Then he had been too stunned to appreciate the ball of fire she was. He was too jolted by the fact that he had just made the biggest mistake of his life.

"Enjoying that cigarette?" he smirked, trying to hide his smile behind a puff of smoke.

Joanna turned crimson red, and crushed the cigarette out into the ashtray.

"I...I have had enough." She sat up straight in defiance. She wasn't going to let him laugh at her. She was no longer a little child and he wasn't going to treat her like one. She had been a fool to think she could entice Chad. He thought she was nothing more than a joke.

"Well, have you had enough wine too or would you like some more?" He leaned forward and grinned at Joanna.

She did not know if he was serious or teasing her still. Her mind whirled and she felt a little sick from the cigarette.

"As a matter of fact, Chad, I would like some more wine." She sat up straight. It irked her how he patronized her. "But unlike my sister, I prefer white to red. So if you could be so kind, I would love a glass of white."

Chad's raised his eyebrows in mild surprise.

"Well, Miss Joanna, you are in luck." He stood up and snubbed out his smoke. "Much like yourself, I too prefer white to red." He stood up tall and sleek and disappeared into the house leaving her alone.

Joanna breathed deeply of the warm evening air. It was nice outside and she felt safe, semi-hidden in the darkness.

Chad returned swiftly carrying a bottle and two wine glasses. He placed the glasses in front of Joanna and proceeded to fill them to the brim with wine.

"Cheers," he said, lifting his glass to Joanna.

She lifted hers and raised it to Chad, taking a sip. He sat down in the seat next to her and sighed.

"Nice night," he said to no one in particular.

"Yes," Joanna said, looking around uncomfortably. Now that she was finally there with Chad, she didn't know what to say to him.

"So what brings you over to this neck of the woods? It can't be to see your darling sister. I know how fond you are of her," Chad said, sipping more of his wine. He was beginning to relax and was enjoying Joanna's interruption. He knew he should send the kid home. Mara-Joy would freak out if she knew Joanna was here alone with him. But he was lonely. He never saw his friends anymore and Mara-Joy was always off doing something or another.

Besides, Joanna was refreshing compared to Mara-Joy. She was soft where Mara-Joy was rough. Joanna was like a dove, where Mara-Joy was a hawk.

The two sisters are really not alike at all come to think of it, he thought.

Joanna was slim and graceful with straight golden brown hair. Mara-Joy was slender, but she had voluptuous curves and arches, and her hair--that black mane of wild hair that encased her creamy skin. You would have thought the hair was enough of an attraction for one person, but she had those eyes. The eyes that ate into his soul. Never had he seen eyes like hers before.

He shook his head.

That was not true.

There was her uncle, or something. What was his name? Oliver.

That was it: Oliver. He was somehow related to Mara-Joy's clan. Married her aunt, or something.

Come to think of it, Mara-Joy really looked like this Oliver fellow.

Chad grimaced. He didn't like where his thoughts were going. Mara-Joy's mother seemed very in love with her husband. Chad couldn't picture her being unfaithful to him. There must be some story there. But what? How come it never had occurred to him before?

"Chad?" Joanna interrupted.

Chad looked up, chasing his thoughts away. He would have to investigate the matter later. Suddenly, wanting to know about this Oliver fellow seemed important.

"Umph," he said, raising his glass to his moist lips.

"I said I was just walking by and thought I would stop in and say 'hi'," Joanna answered. It was obvious Chad had been somewhere else and had not heard her.

"What's that?" he asked confused. "Oh right, why you're here." He sat up straight and concentrated on Joanna's company. He didn't want to come across as rude. Joanna struck him as the sensitive type.

"What were you doing walking over here?" he grinned, knowing there was no one around his neighborhood that Joanna would know. They were very isolated.

Joanna stood up abruptly, nearly spilling the wine she clutched in her hand.

Surprised, Chad stood up too.

"Well... pardon me for being friendly," Joanna stammered, feeling like an idiot. Chad stood mockingly in front of her.

"I will not pester you any longer, Mr. So-Important-I-Can't-Have-Company... Guy." Joanna blushed. She even sounded mentally disturbed.

Chad began to chuckle. "Sit down, Joanna. You have your feathers all ruffled for nothing. Whatever your reasons for being here, I'm glad. It's nice to get company, especially someone as lovely as you."

Joanna's head snapped up in response.

He thought she was lovely?

She looked at him standing and smiling mischievously at her. Something deep inside told her she should run. She was in way over her head. Her heart began to pitter-patter again. She had never noticed how handsome Chad was. She'd never really looked at him at all before. He had only been her brother-in-law and a means to get back at Mara-Joy. Never once had she thought of him as a personality behind his name.

She took a big gulp of her wine and sat down. There was no turning back, she was on a mission.

"Oh, my gosh!" Joanna stood up looking frantically around. She and Chad had polished off the bottle of wine plus another as they sat talking quietly together. "I didn't notice the time. I have to get home." She stumbled slightly, feeling tipsy from the wine.

Chad reached out and grasped Joanna's arm to support her.

"I think you are drunk," Chad replied, holding the intoxicated girl up straight.

"No . . ." Joanna cooed as she wobbled in his arms. "Just a little tipsy." The truth was that she was not used to drinking great quantities and was indeed drunk.

"Don't worry. I'll drive you home," Chad said, placing his hand on her shoulder. He felt her tremble under his touch. "Are you cold?" The night air outside had started to chill over the past couple of hours while they sat talking and drinking wine.

"No." Joanna beamed up at him, eyes glazed with liquor.

His hands felt warm on her shoulders, and he gave her a gentle squeeze in response.

Mara-Joy was coming out the front door of her parent's house when Chad's car pulled up. Surprised, she stopped in her tracks. This was odd. Didn't Chad know she had taken her car? He made the trip for nothing.

Oh well, she thought. It was sweet, if not too bright. She might give in and let the boy touch her tonight. She wrapped her fur coat snugly around her neck.

Oh how she loved mink.

Yes, she would definitely let him into her bed tonight. She was in high sprits and felt a little dramatic. She began to walk toward Chad's car, not noticing Joanna sitting in the front seat.

"Thanks for the ride," Joanna said, reaching for the car handle to let herself out, "and the evening." She reddened, unable to stop herself.

"Joanna?" Chad called, grabbing her free hand. She stopped and looked into his green eyes. She couldn't help her breath suddenly speeding up. What was wrong with her?

"Yes?" she nervously replied, taking small quick breaths, holding tightly to the handle of the door.

Chad shook his head.

"Never mind. See you kid."

"Can I come again next Friday?" Joanna blurted out, not believing her nerve.

Chad dropped her hand, his face paling as he looked past Joanna and outside the window. Joanna turned toward the object of his attention.

Mara-Joy opened the door to the car abruptly, nearly taking Joanna with her.

The cool air breezed in, causing both of its passengers to shiver. Mara-Joy glared down accusingly at the two.

"Yes," Chad sputtered, "yes that would be good."

Joanna, overcome with sudden panic, stepped out of the car and almost collided with Mara-Joy.

"Mara-Joy," she said, standing tall. She was at least two inches taller than her older sister.

"Joanna," Mara-Joy smirked, taking out a silver pack from her purse and lighting up one of her long cigarettes. She liked to smoke them on long filters. They made her feel glamorous.

"What are you doing with my husband?" She asked, blowing smoke directly into Joanna's face.

Joanna coughed and moved out of the direction of the assailing smoke.

"Oh Mara-Joy, thank goodness for your husband." Joanna leaned towards the open car door. "You really are my hero tonight, Chad."

Chad looked guardedly at the two girls. Mara-Joy did not know what was going on and stood there tapping her foot, smoking like a master.

"You see..." Joanna stood back up and met Mara-Joy's distrustful face. Chad leaned forward, wanting to hear what she was about to say.

"Oh boy, the shit is going to hit the fan," he hissed under his breath, his heart pounding. He was a little confused at his own reaction. What was he afraid of? They had done nothing wrong. Why didn't it feel that way?

"You must promise not to tell Ma and Pa, first." Joanna grabbed her sister's fur-clad arm, begging

Mara-Joy, who pulled away, annoyed. Something didn't seem right.

"I'll do no such thing!" Mara-Joy said, outraged. "Joanna, you tell me this instant what is going on. Why is my husband your hero?"

"Well, it's like this. A couple of girls and I were going out to a local dance. Or so I thought. It turns out that they were actually going to a dance club."

Mara-Joy's head shot up. She knew this nightclub. She frequently went, sometimes accompanied with Chad, but more often with a girl friend. It was much more fun pretending to be single and flirting with all the men.

"Well, you could just imagine my surprise when we arrived. Here I thought I was going to a church dance, and I wind up in a liquor-soaked joint." Joanna sighed, letting her dilemma sink in.

Chad had to force himself not to laugh. This kid was a pistol.

"Anyway, I couldn't call Ma or Pa and you weren't home, so I called Chad to come pick me up. He was the only one I could think of." Joanna looked innocently at Mara-Joy, her eyes slightly lowered. "He is kind of like a brother now."

Mara-Joy looked with disbelief at Joanna. "Humph. How is it you smell like booze? I think, little sister, you left out some parts of your story." She crushed out her cigarette with the heel of her black pumps. "Surprising, I didn't think you had it in you."

Joanna halted. What did she mean? Did Mara-Joy see through her lie?

"You've never struck me as the party girl type."

"Ah . . ." Joanna shifted, getting ready to leave. "You would be surprised what type of girl I am."

And with that she pushed past Mara-Joy and walked stiffly toward the house.

Mara-Joy watched Joanna walk away. She chuckled to herself.

"I don't know what that one is up too, but I'm sure it's quite dull," she said, resting her arm on the open door of the car.

"I think you could be wrong," Chad said, staring out the front window and watching Joanna open the door and disappear inside the house.

What type of girl was she really? He had never paid attention to the kid before this evening and now he couldn't get her out of his mind. Thoughts of the "date" he had made with her for the following Friday flooded his mind.

What was he doing? This was definitely not a smart move--planning to spend an evening with his wife's little sister. What was he thinking?

“What is that supposed to mean?” Mara-Joy vocalized, disrupting his thoughts.

“Nothing.” He turned to the steering wheel and began to start up the car. “Let’s just go home, it’s late.”

Mara-Joy lowered her eyelids and tightened her lips.

“What are you thinking, dear husband? Hmm?”

“What are you talking about, Mara-Joy?”

“You know what I mean. You know exactly what I mean.” She pushed her head into the cab of the car, coming face to face with Chad.

Disgust crinkled his face. He could barely stand to look at Mara-Joy anymore.

“I wouldn’t go and do anything you would regret husband. It would really be in your best interest if you kept that in mind.”

“Go to hell, Mara-Joy,” he spat in her face.

“Oooh, feisty are you?” She reached over and grabbed between his legs. Chad recoiled and tried to push her hand away. “I like it when you are feisty.” She held on tightly, Chad’s hands unable to pry Mara-Joy’s away without hurting himself. “Just remember my warning.” She released him and crawled back out of the car.

Chad leaned over and grabbed the handle of the passenger’s door.

“I’m quite through doing things I regret, my dear wife! I have a lifetime full already!”

Mara-Joy continued to walk toward her car, as though she had never heard Chad’s words. Her mink snuggle was tucked around her neck.

Chad walked into his bedroom, and there like a pouncing bobcat laid Mara-Joy naked in bed. She rolled over facing him and touched herself.

Chad, disgusted, felt himself harden.

“What took you so long, lover?”

“I stopped for a drink. What are you doing?”

“What does it look like I’m doing?” A hand cupped her breast. “I’m waiting for you.”

Weak, he went to her. Falling into her arms he took her, roughly, with venom.

Mara-Joy cried out in delight, riding Chad like the obedient animal he was.

Later, after they had finished and lay breathless and sweaty, Mara-Joy smiled smugly to herself. Chad was hers as always, as he always would be.

Chad was smiling, too. But not for the same reasons Mara-Joy was.

He was thinking of someone else. Someone who looked like a fawn and had the grace of a dove.

— Chapter 33 —

"So what happened?" Constance squealed, bouncing on her bed.

Joanna put her finger to her lips to silence the excited Constance. She slowly and quietly shut the door to their bedroom, taking care to see if her parents were around.

The blond waves bobbed on Constance's forehead as she suppressed another outburst. She and Pauline had been waiting impatiently for hours for Joanna to return.

Joanna flung herself down on her bed and buried her face into her pillow, moaning.

Constance, aggravated, jumped onto Joanna and turned her over.

"Joanna, I swear, don't you keep me in suspense any longer." She squeezed her nose and pulled away from Joanna's face.

"Phew. You smell like a brewery." She waved her hand in front of her nose.

"You are lucky Ma and Pa went to bed early."

Joanna sat up feeling a little woozy.

"They don't know I'm late?"

Constance shook her head.

"They didn't even stay awake for Mara-Joy to bring home Alan-Michael. I thought I was going to die when Mara-Joy showed up and you still weren't home."

"Yes, well we bumped into each other outside." Joanna flung her hair behind her shoulder, feeling sluggish and giddy. "She was as charming as ever."

They both laughed.

"Ugh." The room was spinning. Joanna had to lie back down. "I drank way too much wine."

"Wine?" Constance cocked an eyebrow questioningly.

"Yes, wine. And it was delicious," Joanna grinned, feeling mischievous. "I smoked too, but it made me feel sick. I don't think I'll be much of a smoker."

"That's good. Mara-Joy smokes and you don't want to be like her."

"True."

Pauline, who had been silently falling asleep when Joanna crept into their room, wormed onto the bed with the other two girls.

"Joanna, are you and Chad lovers yet?"

Constance and Joanna both snorted with laughter onto each other's shoulders.

Pauline looked wide-eyed at the two, with a sagging lip. Constance had spent the evening trying to explain what lovers were and what they did. Pauline didn't think she liked the idea of Joanna becoming lovers with Chad.

"No. Not yet," Joanna wore a dreamy expression on her face. The look was not lost on Constance.

"Joanna, I hope you don't go and fall in love with him." She stood up, straightening her gown, frowning. "He is married to Mara-Joy, and nothing can change that."

"I know that!" Joanna crossed her arms angrily over her chest. "I just had a good time, that's all. Can't I have fun with him at the same time as proceeding with our plan?"

"Have fun all you want, although I find that hard to believe. You have always thought Chad was weak. A walking puppet, obeying Mara-Joy's every command."

"Alright Constance, you've made your point. I haven't changed my opinion of the guy. I still think he's whipped."

"A little? Besides, one day you will find your own husband and he'll have a spine in his back."

Joanna chortled,

"A spine, huh."

"Yes." Constance sat back down near the head of the bed and gazed at Joanna. "A wonderful man who won't bow down to you but stand beside you equally. Like Pa. If you expect more from Chad, you'll only be cheating yourself."

"Point taken, Connie." Joanna reached out and hugged her sister, hoping she could follow her sound advice.

The days dragged for Joanna as she waited for Friday to come. She couldn't concentrate in school and felt scatterbrained and nervous. All she could think of was Chad.

Finally Friday came. With the same lie she used before, Joanna was able to leave the house without much trouble. Jobeth was a little suspicious of her daughter. Joanna was not the type of girl to go out much. She shrugged it off as paranoia. The girl was entitled to have friends. She just wasn't used to seeing Joanna so social. Now if she were Mara-Joy or even Alan-Michael, she wouldn't have batted an eye. Both were very popular and always on the go with friends. It was good that Joanna was finally starting to be more like her other siblings. Jobeth just hoped the other two girls would follow suit.

Walking out of the house, Joanna nearly bumped into Mara-Joy.

As always, she was wearing her mink and looked very sophisticated in the latest style, with her hair freshly set from the hairstylist. It shined a glossy black.

Joanna stood back, feeling frumpy. She had spent an hour in front of the mirror trying to make herself look desirable. Constance had set her hair and brushed it into an attractive wave, which had pleased her very much until she saw Mara-Joy. As always, Joanna felt plain beside her sister.

How could two sisters be so totally different?

Memories began to surface again. Memories of the night she and Constance sat listening in on the adults talking downstairs.

The night of the reunion.

They didn't know she had heard them confuse Mara-Joy for Oliver's...

"Well, Joanna." Mara-Joy appraised Joanna up and down. She blushed, her memories quickly fading away. Why did she always have a bad feeling in the pit of her stomach whenever these memories surfaced? She couldn't even remember them fully.

"You clean up fairly nicely when you want to." Mara-Joy opened her gold cigarette case and took out a cigarette. It had been a gift from Chad the past

Christmas. "Where are you off to tonight? I hope your wayward friends don't lead you down the wrong road again this Friday." She inhaled and artfully blew smoke from her painted lips.

"Don't worry, Mara-Joy, I wouldn't do anything you would do." Joanna turned to leave.

"That won't leave you much fun now, will it little sister?"

Joanna could here her cackling behind her. Her heart started to pound. She actually felt a little guilty.

"Knock 'em dead, sister," Mara-Joy hooted, still laughing behind her.

Chad was outside waiting for Joanna when she arrived. There was a bottle of wine already chilling on the little wicker coffee table with two empty wine glasses.

She took the bus and he had watched as she arrived stepping down off the bus steps. Chad held his breath as she began walking towards him. She was lovely. She wore a simple light coat that shaped her lean figure and she had done something different with her hair. He liked it. In fact, he liked everything about Joanna's appearance.

Joanna smiled warmly when she spotted him and waved. Chad grinned back and raised a hand, which held a smoke. He couldn't help himself. He was glad to see her.

"Good evening, sir," Joanna chimed. She noticed the wine and the glasses.

"Oh, what is this, are you going to try and get me drunk again?" she teased, lifting up the bottle and examining it. "A girl could get herself into trouble that way."

"She could, could she?" Chad came up behind her. She was flirting with him. What was this girl up too? Whatever it was, he couldn't help liking it, even though he knew he shouldn't.

"Yes." Joanna could feel Chad's presence behind her. "Why don't you pour us a glass?" she asked without turning around.

Chad reached around her and grabbed for the bottle. His hand went over top of hers and he left it resting there, still holding the bottle.

"You're cold." His voice had become husky. Her head was inches from Chad's face and he could smell her scented hair. She leaned back, her back almost touching his chest. His hand still held hers.

"Maybe you should warm me up?" Joanna felt his hand squeeze hers tighter.

She turned around, coming face-to-face with Chad. His eyes twinkled with uncertainty as she looked into his hazel eyes.

"Joanna?" Chad still had his hand on hers, the bottle clutched between the two.

"I mean why don't we go inside tonight, instead of staying out here?" Joanna released her hold on the bottle, her hand burning from Chad's touch.

"I was thinking the same thing." Chad coughed, grasping the cool bottle with both hands.

"Of course you were," Joanna said gracefully.

Comfortably seated inside, Joanna sipped her wine slowly, careful not to get intoxicated. The wine tasted good and seemed to give her the courage she needed to begin her seduction.

He watched her closely, admiring her long, slender face and graceful neck. Her skin had a healthy color to it, as though she had been in the sun and had tanned slightly. It was golden and had warmth to it.

"How is it that you and Mara-Joy look so different?" he asked, still staring at her. Joanna glanced at him beside her and relaxed into the couch, closing her eyes.

"Are you saying you don't like the way I look?" She smiled, very well aware of his eyes on her. "I definitely like your looks."

Joanna felt him move closer to her.

"It's just that you two are so different both inside and out. It's like you didn't come from the same factory or something."

Joanna's eyes fluttered open. Her heart started to race and she felt panicky.

Why was she feeling trepidation?

She sat up and gulped down the remainder of her wine.

"Don't be silly, Chad. Many siblings don't resemble each other. My grandparents are all dead so I don't know what they looked like, but I am sure there is some deceased relative that my sister resembles." She reached for the bottle. Chad got to it first and refilled her glass. She sipped back a healthy amount.

"That's true, she does look a lot like your Uncle," Chad said as he refilled his glass. He hadn't thought Joanna would be so sensitive about the subject.

"You know, Chad, I really don't feel like talking about my family right now," Joanna said, turning the conversation around. The mood had changed and she was beginning to feel uneasy, as if she wanted to run away. "Let's talk of more pleasant things, shall we?"

"Like what?" he asked, closing in on her. "What would you like to talk about, Joanna?" He slid his hand onto her knee, gently caressing her leg.

Joanna eyed him cautiously.

"What are you doing, brother-in-law?" she asked, eyeing him over her glass. Heat rushed to her face. This was too easy.

"I don't really know." Chad said pulling back. "All I know is I haven't been able to get you out of my mind since you were here last." He stood up and walked around the spacious living room, wine glass in hand. "I am very attracted to you and that is dangerous." He looked at her still face. "You are very beautiful." Chad turned away and looked at a picture of him and Mara-Joy on their wedding day.

"I made the biggest mistake of my life that day," he said, more to himself than to her. "Remember how you told me off?" He chuckled and took a drink from his glass. "The sad part is you were right, partly. I was a slave to her beauty. It really was that simple, but it was more."

"The pregnancy?"

Chad turned around, surprised.

"Yes. The pregnancy. The child who never was. The beginning of my nightmare." He drained his glass and poured another drink. "You never think of the repercussions of adolescent lust. All I thought was that I was sleeping with the most popular girl in our group. She was mine when every one else wanted her. She was like a trophy. But I was a fool."

"How is that?" Joanna asked quietly, not enjoying what she heard. Her hands held her wine glass tightly, anchoring her in place.

"Mara-Joy is no one's trophy. You are her trophy. Her toy. Her puppet to do her bidding." Chad's face had turned a deep red. His glass was empty again. He reached for the bottle but it was empty. Joanna stood up and reached out her hand to him.

"I feel so trapped with her and I don't know how I can escape." Chad's voice was choked full of emotion, his face becoming a purplish red. "I can't even stand to look at her."

Joanna remained quiet standing before Chad's turned back. She had no idea how tortured Chad's life had become. Feeling pity for him, she embraced his defeated frame.

He easily fell into her arms and began to sob. He was larger than Joanna, so she had to grip him firmly with her slim arms. His solid frame shook uncontrollably.

They remained like that for a while: neither talking, just holding each other.

Finally Chad pulled gently away from Joanna's embrace.

"I'm so sorry," he said, embarrassed, wiping his eyes. His brown hair had fallen playfully onto his forehead. Joanna warmly smoothed the hair back out of the way.

Chad took her hand that touched his hair and kissed the underside of her palm.

Electricity skyrocketed through her body.

"You should stay away from me, Joanna." Chad said into her hand.

"Why is that?" she whispered, her legs turning to liquid under his hot breath.

"I am your sister's husband," he said as he raised his lips to her wrist," and I have been known to be unfaithful to her."

"What are you suggesting?" Warmth flooded her veins.

"I have no love for my wife, but I feel a great need to be near you." He lifted his head and looked into Joanna's fevered face. "If you stay, I can't promise you anything."

"Do I need promises?" She ached to be in his arms.

"You deserve promises."

"Do you want me to go?

"You are just a kid. I can't do this to you." He grabbed her shoulder roughly.

He wanted her, but how could he?

Joanna savagely flung herself into his arms embracing him with a passionate kiss. Chad's arms encircled her waist, snugly holding her in place. They melted into each other, starved for one another.

Joanna unlocked her lips from his, panting.

"I am not a kid."

"No, you are not," he said, embracing her once again.

Chad drove Joanna home, but this time he dropped her off a block from her house. They lingered, kissing one another for a few moments, until Joanna had to pull away.

"Will I see you next Friday?" Chad asked, feeling desperate. They had spent the evening kissing, talking and touching. Never had he felt such desire. But it was not just because he was so attracted to Joanna physically; he enjoyed her company as well. They had laughed a lot that evening and talked about many things they had in common.

"Yes," Joanna smiled through the open window at him. "But I have to go before my parents kill me."

"I will be counting the days."

Joanna blew him a kiss and ran off.

Fridays became a regular event. Each Friday Joanna rushed into Chad's waiting arms and found it harder and harder to pull away from him. Constance was becoming concerned for her sister. She didn't think Joanna realized it, but Joanna was falling in love with Chad.

Constance was wrong. Joanna knew she was in love with Chad. And when she admitted it to herself, she knew she had to end her relationship with him. Love had never been part of the plan. In fact, she wished she had never started the plan in the first place. It had been stupid. Mara-Joy was the one who was supposed to be broken-hearted, not her.

Mara-Joy didn't even know what was going on. All she knew was that her husband seemed cheerful lately, and she was too self-centered to think it could be Joanna who put a smile on her husband's face.

Chad opened the front door smiling broadly.

Joanna stood in the rain sobbing. His face crumbled as he quickly scooped her into his arms.

"What is wrong, darling?" he soothed, kissing her damp forehead. Joanna clutched his shirt, not wanting to let go of him.

"This has got to stop, Chad," she cried harder.

"What? No, no it doesn't. Please don't say that." Chad began to panic.

He couldn't stand to lose Joanna. She was the only light in a life filled with darkness.

"But it does," she said, looking up at him with a tear-streaked face. "I thought I could handle this. I thought I was in control of things. But I'm not."

"Joanna, I don't understand," he said, cupping her face with his hands.

Instantly, Joanna tilted her head so that he would caress her cheek with his hand. This brought about fresh tears.

She had to do this. It couldn't go on any longer. Her heart was breaking.

"Understand? Chad, what is there not to understand? I can't be yours. You can't be mine." She buried her face in his shirt.

"But I am yours."

Joanna pulled away and walked into the living room.

"Look around you, Chad." She opened her arms and waved them around the room. Everywhere you looked were signs of Mara-Joy's presence. The house was decorated in her taste. Her things were everywhere and her picture adorned every wall. In several of those pictures, she was with Chad.

"You are not mine, you are hers!" Joanna sobbed, pulling away from his embrace. She felt her heart breaking with sorrow. How did she get herself into this mess? How could she have walked blindly into this nightmare? A nightmare she had purposely created.

Chad walked over to Joanna's distraught frame and tried to embrace her once again, but Joanna fought him.

"No, Chad, please." She tried to wiggle out of his hold, but she became weak. It was too hard for her. The need for him was winning over her sense of logic.

"Listen!" He forcefully grabbed her shoulders, shaking her to attention. Tears fell from his eyes, freely and without shame. The thought of losing Joanna terrified him.

"I don't love Mara-Joy, but I do love you!" He forced his lips hard onto her eager ones, his tongue probed for hers, tasting the warmth of her mouth. She sobbed as he bent and kissed her eyes. "Don't cry, my little one, don't cry. I will always be here for you, always." His hands scaled the side of her body until they reached her erect breasts.

Within moments he held them naked in his hands, caressing each as though it were a rare gem.

Joanna arched her back, her body responding to Chad all on its own. She couldn't go back now, it was too late.

"Make love to me Chad." She grabbed his head to her, their bodies rising back and forth with each touch. "Make love to me, please? Give me one night to remember you by, to dream about when I am alone. If I can't have you forever, let me have you now."

Chad lifted her up and carried her to the fireplace. Gently he laid her down and artfully removed her clothing.

"You are so beautiful," he sighed, gazing down on Joanna. She lay naked in the firelight. Long and graceful, sweet and innocent, her hair fanned out behind her. Chad bent down into her waiting arms and they melted together.

They were like two pieces of the same puzzle finally connected, finally back together.

"I can never have enough of you," Chad said through clenched teeth as he held her in his arms, wanting desperately to be one with her. Even though they were physically joined, he felt it was not enough. He pushed himself deeper and deeper inside of her.

Joanna let out a cry of glory as she pushed Chad's buttocks harder with her legs.

"I love you! Damn it! I love you!" he announced as he climaxed.

Joanna withered as bolt after bolt of her own satisfaction released.

"I love you too," she panted, unable to contain her emotions.

"Don't go away, Joanna. Please continue to see me." Chad raised himself up on his elbows so he could see her warm body beneath him. "I can't live without you."

There were tears in his eyes as he spoke every truthful word.

"I won't," she said, reaching out for him again. "Only death will keep me from you."

— Chapter 34 –

Once they had a taste of each other, Joanna and Chad couldn't have enough.

They met whenever they could, not settle for just Friday nights. And they met everywhere, taking little care to avoid getting caught.

It was obvious to anyone who saw them that they were in love. Their eyes were always locked in a dreamy expression, oblivious to anyone around them. Only a fool couldn't see what was going on.

Constance gave up warning Joanna. She knew her sister was head over heels, and although she didn't approve of Joanna's love affair with Chad, she couldn't stop it. Their romance lasted for a year.

Summer came and Mara-Joy and her redheaded friend Loran sat across from one another at their favorite restaurant, where they lunched together every Wednesday.

"What is it, Loran?" Mara-Joy said, annoyed with her friend as she picked at her salad. She pushed it aside, disgusted. "We should really eat somewhere else; this place is turning into a dump."

Loran laughed nervously and lit a cigarette. She offered one to Mara-Joy who took it willingly, lighting up.

She inhaled from her cigarette, squinting her eyes at Loran. They had somehow managed to stay friends, although Mara-Joy didn't particularly care for Loran much as a person. She was flighty and tended to get on Mara-Joy's nerves but somehow Mara-Joy felt obligated to her.

"What's up? You have been chomping at the bit all afternoon to tell me something. Spill it before you burst," Mara-Joy demanded, inhaling deeply. She shouldn't be so hard on Loran, but the girl made it so easy to do so.

Loran was jittery. She wanted to tell Mara-Joy she knew about Chad and Joanna. She wanted to hurt the self-righteous bitch, but she couldn't help but be afraid of the black-haired devil.

"I've been hearing things, Mara-Joy," Loran puffed on her cigarette, shaking. She steadied herself, not wanting Mara-Joy to notice how frightened she was.

Mara-Joy noticed and was slightly amused. Could she have actually figured out Mara-Joy was having an affair with Loran's boyfriend?

No. They were discreet, as she was with all her friends' husbands and boyfriends.

It was a game with Mara-Joy. She enjoyed taking her friends' men to bed.

They always went willingly into her arms and begged her constantly for more.

Once she became tired of them, she dumped them, knowing it was she they desired when they went back to their wives with their tails between their legs.

Some had been a nuisance, wanting to leave his wife or girlfriend for her. But she wasn't interested in the weak rascals. She had no intentions of leaving Chad. Chad was the man she married, even if he didn't perform like he should anymore.

It was a mystery. She had always been able to lure Chad into her bed, but now he would have nothing to do with her. He actually avoided her as much as possible. Everything she did to try and entice him ended up in failure. It had been a long time since they had been together as man and wife and it was beginning to really upset her.

"I have heard some things about Chad." Loran paused, getting herself ready to spill the news about Joanna and Chad. She wanted to hurt Chad for dumping her a year ago, when she had been one of Chad's lovers. That was until Joanna entered the picture. He dumped Loran without a word of explanation and the humility of it enraged her. He walked around town with that girl as though he didn't care if they were caught. He had never done that with Loran.

Never.

"What are you trying to say, Lore?" Mara-Joy didn't look impressed as she sucked back on her cigarette.

"He's been seen with your sister Joanna a lot lately. Actually for some time."

Loran took a deep breath. The words were out. She quickly shoved a fork-full of salad into her mouth.

Mara-Joy looked shocked. Joanna and Chad? It couldn't be true. Or could it?

"Are you trying to say that my husband and sister are sleeping with each other?" Mara-Joy laughed, composing herself. She wouldn't let Loran know how much the news had affected her.

"Well..." Loran felt embarrassed as she swallowed her lettuce whole. Maybe she was wrong, but it didn't seem likely. Besides, Loran of all people knew Chad was not faithful to Mara-Joy. If he could cheat on Mara-Joy with her best friend, why couldn't he do so with her sister too?

"Lore, Joanna is Chad's sister-in-law. They have a right to see each other."

Mara-Joy laughed again, tossing back her dark hair casually. "That doesn't mean they are lovers. They're family for Christ's sake."

"It's just that people are talking, Mar . . ." Loran looked around eyeing the other occupants of the restaurant.

"Oh . . ." Mara-Joy leaned over the table. Their eyes locked; Mara-Joy's were ice blue and cold. Corruption lurked behind her orbs. "People talk a lot, don't they Loran? They talk all the time about all sorts of people. People like . . ."

She shrugged her shoulders.

Loran sat back in her chair blushing. She knew the look in Mara-Joy's eyes.

"Take for example . . . your parents. Why just the other day, I heard those same people talk about your mother again."

"Stop it, Mara-Joy." Loran was aware what people said about her mother. She didn't need to hear it from Mara-Joy. "All right, you're right. Chad is not seeing Joanna."

"Well, to believe people who talk about my husband, Loran, really! These are the same people who call your mother a--how do I put this kindly? A pussy licker." Mara-Joy relished making Loran suffer. Loran sat open-mouthed, stunned, and unable to say a word.

"And your father!" Mara-Joy leaned back, admiring her long painted nails, not carrying if her voice was heard by anyone else in the restaurant. "They say he's a child molester."

"My father is not a child molester." Loran looked at her half-eaten plate of food, ruined. Why had she foolishly thought she could somehow knock Mara-Joy off her high horse? Hadn't she learned after all these years that she was no match for Mara-Joy?

"Well, people say he has been going to Millie's place, and we all know Millie runs a whorehouse. They say he only wants the sweetest and youngest of the lot. Pays big bucks I hear."

"Stop it!" Loran erupted, grasping the table hard. "I was only being a friend and telling you what I heard. I'd think you would want to clear up all the rumors, Mara-Joy." She lit another cigarette and tried not to look at Mara-Joy's cold eyes.

"I know, I know you were just trying to be a good friend," Mara-Joy said sarcastically. She could see through Loran so easily. She was an easy target. Too easy. It wasn't even fun. "Let's forget we ever had this conversation." Mara-Joy reached across the table and placed a comforting hand on Loran's shaking one.

"All right?" Mara-Joy soothed.

Loran nodded, not saying anything.

"Chad adores me, Loran. He would never make love to anyone but me," Mara-Joy said sincerely.

Loran's face bobbed up to Mara-Joy's anticipating eyes. Visions of Chad's naked body covering hers filtered into her mind.

"Of course he wouldn't," Loran smiled forgivingly, looking Mara-Joy straight in the face.

Joanna lay on her little bed in the room she shared with Constance and Pauline. She wiped away the tears that fell freely down her cheeks.

It finally was really over. They had gone too far this time.

Earlier that day she had taken a bus to another town. Under a false name, with a cheap wedding band on her finger, she had gone to a doctor to confirm her fears.

She was pregnant.

"Oh Chad!" she cried out loud. There was no fear of being heard. The entire family was out of the house for a change.

"What am I going to do? We were fools to love each other and now this!" she sobbed into her pillow.

"Joanna!"

Joanna bolted up straight, startled by the sound of the voice outside her door.

It was Mara-Joy and she sounded furious.

"Joanna!" Mara-Joy pounded on the door. "You let me in this instant!"

"Go away!" Joanna sobbed. She couldn't take facing Mara-Joy at that moment. She was the reason Chad and Joanna would never be together.

Mara-Joy threw open the door. Her hands rested on her tiny waist, legs braced apart. Mara-Joy looked like a volcano ready to erupt. Her black hair frizzed madly around her face and her steel eyes burned with hate.

"Get out of here!" Joanna screamed hysterically, waving at the door. "Get out of here!"

"Not until you tell me the truth, you hussy!" Mara-Joy heaved, ready to pounce on the crumbled form on the bed. "Are you sleeping with my husband?"

"Leave me alone!" Joanna screamed, unable to deal with Mara-Joy on top of everything else. The world as she knew it was coming apart. Everything was crashing down around her. "Get out of my room, you bitch!"

Mara-Joy jumped back, her face had gone crimson in anger. Never had she felt such rage.

"You call me a bitch? You don't even have the decency to sit there and lie about it, do you?" Mara-Joy was no longer yelling, but the venom in her voice was much more poisonous.

"You filthy slut. How can you call yourself a sister?"

"You are not my sister!" Joanna hurled out unintentionally. She covered her mouth, shocked by what she was saying. The memories started flooding her mind. Oliver telling her parents to take care of his little girl. The constant confusions over Oliver's resemblance to Mara-Joy. How Mara-Joy was the only child out of five who didn't take after anyone in the family. Except, that is, Oliver. And Oliver mentioning Mara-Joy's name. How some woman would have liked it--what was her name?

Tamara.

She killed herself and left her daughter to be raised by Alan and Jobeth.

Mara-Joy, the child who brought her parents together. They must have married so they could give Mara-Joy a proper home.

It all made sense now. Why had she not seen it before?
Mara-Joy was not Joanna's sister. Not even Joanna wanted to believe that.

"Stop it, Joanna." Mara-Joy stormed. "That is not even funny to joke about. You may hate me all you want, but I will always be your sister."

"No, you are not," Joanna said soberly. She stared off into space, the web of lies unraveling. "You are not my sister or Constance's sister or Pauline's sister, not even Alan-Michael's sister." Joanna wiped hair away from her wet face. "You are no one's sister. You were born a bastard. Your real mother killed herself and left you with Ma and Pa to take care of. I heard them all--I heard them all talk." She began to laugh, beside herself with emotion.

"You are nuts. You don't know what you heard." Mara-Joy was no longer yelling. She was too stunned for words.

"Oh, but I do know. I heard them talking to your real father." A tear rolled down Joanna's cheek and she looked at Mara-Joy's ghostly white face. She felt sick to her stomach as she continued. There was no going back now. It was too late to take back her excruciating words.

"He told Ma and Pa not to tell you about him, that it was better if you knew him like the rest of us knew him."

"Stop it!" Mara-Joy covered her ears with her hands and stomped her foot. "I don't want to hear any more of your lies!"

"And you know how we saw him, Mara-Joy? We saw him as our uncle."

"No! Please don't!" Mara-Joy begged, agony escaping her throat from deep within her very soul.

"Uncle Oliver."

"It's not true!" Mara-Joy wailed, running to strike Joanna. "Why are you being so cruel?"

Joanna held back Mara-Joy's hands, as she tried in vain to strike her.

"It is true." Joanna yelled, full of fury for all the times Jobeth had paid more attention to Mara-Joy than her. Her mother loved another woman's child more than she loved Joanna, her real child.

"Ask them, Mara-Joy. Ask my mother and father to show you your mother's suicide letter." Joanna couldn't believe the words that flew from her mouth.

Suddenly everything she had ever overheard her parents say was crystal clear in her memory.

"This isn't true. You are just trying to hurt me." Mara-Joy collapsed on the bed beside Joanna and whimpered quietly, her head hanging low, overcome with grief.

Joanna had never seen Mara-Joy so destroyed, not even when she lost the baby.

"Get out of here," Joanna said softly, devoid of emotion. "Get out of my room and my life and stay out. You have ruined enough lives."

Mara-Joy wiped real tears away from her eyes. She didn't want Joanna to see her crying.

"I'll find out the truth." Mara-Joy stood up straight and glared down at the crumbled form beside her. Joanna looked as bad as Mara-Joy felt. Both their faces were red and wet, and their eyes were puffy from crying.

"I'll find out from our parents! Do you hear me? Our parents!"

Mara-Joy's sudden outburst caused Joanna to jump. She began to feel cold at the very root of her being.

"And then my main goal in life will be to pay you back for the pain you have caused me--if you thought your life was ruined now, just wait, dear sister! When I am through with you, Joanna, you will wish you were dead!"

And she was gone like a ball of blazing fire.

A frigid finger traced up Joanna's spine, causing her skin to break into a minefield of goose bumps. She believed Mara-Joy. She believed every word she said.

"It wasn't supposed to be like this!" she screamed into her pillow. "It wasn't supposed to be like this!"

Mortified, she sat up.

Mara-Joy was probably headed home to confront Chad. Joanna jumped out of bed and headed to the kitchen. She had to tell Chad that she had destroyed his wife's life.

Chad answered shortly after Joanna dialed his number. In a shaky voice she said his name.

"Joanna, what is wrong?" Chad asked, concerned. She sounded frantic.

"I need to see you right away, now."

"Joanna, what is wrong? Tell me." Chad said, getting worried.

"I can't on the phone. I'm leaving now." She proceeded to tell him where to meet her.

Within ten minutes he was dressed and in the car.

Joanna was already waiting when he pulled up to the little park.

Jumping out of the car he ran to her and embraced her tightly in his arms. She was crying hard, and it didn't seem like she could stop.

"Hon?" He caressed her hair. "Sweet Joanna, what is wrong?" "Mara-Joy knows about us," Joanna blurted out through her tears. There was no point beating around the bush.

"What?" First panic, then relief flooded Chad. If Mara-Joy knew, maybe she would give him a divorce and he could be with Joanna properly, like it should be.

"I said terrible things to her, Chad." Joanna continued telling him the details of what had transpired between the two sisters. She explained how all the things she had overheard as a child suddenly surfaced, and how she had blurted them out to an unsuspecting Mara-Joy.

"I am a monster for what I have done. I thought I would enjoy the day I obliterate my sis—obliterate Mara-Joy. All I feel is ashamed." Joanna rubbed her raw face against Chad's shirt.

"Everything will turn out all right. You will see." Chad cradled the woman he loved in his arms, not caring who saw them.

Joanna frowned.

"That isn't the only thing, Chad."

"What else could there be?"

"I don't know how to tell you this but," she pulled away from him, not daring to look at his reaction, "I'm pregnant."

Chad's mouth dropped. Joanna faced him.

"I am going to have your baby."

His hands ran through his brown hair and he stared down at his feet.

"Oh God," he whispered.

"Chad?" Joanna began to sob. Could he really hate her for ruining his life? Did he think he was having a repeat performance from yet another Benson sister? Mara-Joy didn't need to worry about ruining Joanna's life. The look in Chad's eyes had done it.

"A baby?" he asked in disbelief. "My child?"

"Chad, I won't force you to do anything, don't worry. I'll leave you and your life forever. You will never have to worry about me again." Joanna sobbed her face a crumbled mess.

"My God, what are you saying, Joanna?" He pulled her back to him and gripped her arms tightly. "Don't you remember me telling you that I loved you? You and only you! I want to be with you. I want you to be my wife."

"How?" Joanna yelled pulling away from him. It was all pointless.

"We are leaving," he reached for her arm and started for the car.

"Leaving?" Joanna was confused. "Where?"

"I don't know where, all I do know is that I want to divorce Mara-Joy and marry you. You are the only woman I have ever wanted to marry. I never loved or wanted Mara-Joy as a wife."

"But where will we go, Chad? By now Mara-Joy has probably told my parents what I said and did to her, and once they find out about the baby . . ."

They were nearly back at the car. Joanna stopped in her tracks, causing Chad to come to a sudden stop.

"Get in the car," Chad said, taking control.

"But, Chad–"

"Do you trust me?" he asked, turning and meeting Joanna full in the face.

"Always," she replied, a ripple of emotion running through her body.

"Then trust that as long as we are together, everything will be all right. We are leaving now and we are not coming back."

Joanna nodded soberly and followed Chad into the car.

— Chapter 35 —

"I won't believe it," Alan said, running his hands roughly through his graying hair. His back was facing Jobeth who held Mara-Joy in her arms, hugging her tight to her breast.

"Believe it, Alan," Jobeth snapped, "Joanna has stolen our daughter's husband."

Alan looked to his wife, unable to close his ears to the poisonous venom in her voice.

Mara-Joy sat up from her mother's embrace, her face streaked with tears.

"Papa?" Mara-Joy didn't want to ask the question eating at her heart, but she had to.

Jobeth, as though feeling Mara-Joy's apprehension, placed a protective arm around her shoulder.

"Yes, what is it, Mara-Joy?" Alan asked, unable to handle what was happening to his family.

His precious Joanna? Could it be true? Could she have really done this to Mara-Joy? He felt instant anger for the boy, Chad. He must have seduced Joanna, just as he had done to Mara-Joy years before. Joanna was still such a child, still innocent to the world. But he liked her that way. He wanted his children to be blind to the world and how cruel it could be. Hadn't he and Jobeth been through enough of the ugliness of the world? Wasn't it enough that their children could be spared?

He gazed at Mara-Joy's appearance. She was shattered. He knew his daughter was no angel but was tough and seasoned. His heart felt like breaking, seeing her so destroyed. It took a lot to knock Mara-Joy down and he found it hard to believe that what Joanna and Chad had done could do it all alone.

"She said some things . . ." Mara-Joy raised her courage. She had to know the truth. Too many of the horrible things Joanna said made her think. Mara-Joy looked at her father. He was the only one who would be truthful with her. Her mother would never say anything to hurt her. Jobeth was always there to protect Mara-Joy, even if it meant hiding the truth from her.

Mara-Joy took a deep breath. There was no point in postponing the inevitable.

"Mara-Joy, forget it," Jobeth piped in, grabbing hold of her arm.

"Mama, stop," Mara-Joy chided, pulling away while still looking at her father. Her eyes begged him for honesty. "Papa, please, I need to know the truth. The things Joanna said, they make sense, and that is what frightens me."

Her hands flew to her face, unable to bear the truth.

Alan went to his daughter and pulled her up into his arms. Holding firmly to her, he asked what could possibly be eating her up so.

"Joanna said I am not your daughter," she blurted out.

She had said it. It was out. The silence that followed was suffocating.

Mara-Joy held her breath, but from the look on Alan's face, as it crumbled in resignation, she knew. It was true. It was all true. The two people she had loved all her life as her parents were, in fact, not even related to her.

"Mara-Joy, we should have told you, you had a right to know."

"Alan!" Jobeth stood up in protest.

"Jobeth, no, we should have been honest from the beginning." Tears were in his eyes. Jobeth shrank away from him; a look of horror was plastered on her pale face. Alan averted his eyes from the ravaged woman. He would lie no more to Mara-Joy.

"Alan, please!" Jobeth implored, reaching out and grabbing his arm. He pulled his arm away, ignoring his wife, something he had never done before.

Mara-Joy stood still as a statue, bawling like a baby as she listened to the man she had always known as her father.

"You were not born of your mother and me."

"No, it can't be true." Mara-Joy sobbed, her hands covering her ears.

"I should have known this day would come. It was wrong of your mother and me to keep this secret from you. But, you see, we did it because you are our daughter." He brought Mara-Joy into his embrace and held her trembling body protectively close to his chest. "You are our daughter as much as the other children are our children. I know it was wrong, but we didn't need to be reminded that we didn't create you, because in our hearts you were ours and ours alone."

"Pappy? Who?" Mara-Joy looked up into Alan's watery gaze. Her blue eyes stood out, wet and red-rimmed, on her pale face. Alan clutched her tighter, not wanting to lose Mara-Joy.

"I am so sorry, my darling. I guess your mother and I were just afraid of losing you. You were such an instrument of love in our lives. If it wasn't for the love we felt for you and the desire to give you a loving and nurturing home, your mother," he looked at the shattered Jobeth who sat lifelessly, not looking at the two, "and I might never have been. The day you entered our lives, our future was sealed and it has been the life we had always dreamed of."

Alan grasped Mara-Joy's head between his strong big hands.

"Do you understand that, Mara-Joy? You may not be our child of blood and bone, but you are the child of our hearts. You are the reason our family came to be. You are us."

Mara-Joy nodded, feeling warm and secure in Alan's arms. He was the only man she could never trick or desire to deceive. He was the only man she knew that loved her with pure abandonment. It was a love that was simple and pure, a love that a father has for a dearly cherished daughter. She had always felt it from both her parents and she felt it still—stronger than ever.

"Papa, who are the people . . ." It was hard for her to ask. She could feel her mother's anxiety behind her, but she had to know. "Who are my birth parents?"

"They were both good friends of ours," Alan began. It was time to air out the closet. He thought of Tamara. Mara-Joy was so like her in sprit. Sometimes when he looked at Mara-Joy from behind when she rambled on, bent out of shape about something, her black curly hair so like Tamara's flaming down her back, he couldn't believe how much she resembled Tamara. But as soon as she turned around, it was Oliver that dominated Mara-Joy's features.

"Tamara," he began. Jobeth sat defeated, her head clasped in her hands. There was no point in fighting Alan anymore. He was determined to tell

Mara-Joy the truth. All she had done to keep the secret of Mara-Joy's paternity was in vain. Her precious Mara-Joy stood silently listening as Alan began the long story of how she came to be. He left out nothing. Mara-Joy was a grown woman who wanted answers and Alan was there to give them. He told her how Tamara's life had been and how she was as a person. He knew so much more than Jobeth. Jobeth had only known Tamara briefly whereas Alan had known her long before he had even known Jobeth. He laughed with Mara-Joy when recalling her birthmother's spunk.

And he told her about Oliver.

Leaving nothing out, he told her how Oliver had stood back to let Alan and Jobeth raise Mara-Joy. He explained in kind words how Oliver had never abandoned her; he just didn't want to take her from the only home she had known.

"He knew how important you were and still are to us. That is all that mattered. You were our daughter, not his anymore," Alan said.

They all sat around the kitchen table drinking coffee. It had been hours since they began talking. The three were exhausted from the exertion of raw emotion. Alan looked at the time on his watch. The other children were staying away, hiding in their rooms, trying to avoid notice. It was obvious that the three in the kitchen shouldn't be interrupted.

Alan wondered when Joanna would be home and another explosion would take place. He had to get to the bottom of this mess. He loved Joanna but was greatly disappointed in her at the moment.

"I hope you can forgive us for keeping this from you." Jobeth reached across the table and held onto Mara-Joy's hand.

"I could never hate either of you." Mara-Joy felt the ball of emotion choke her again. She inhaled deeply, feeling lighter from the conversation, but there was still the matter of Joanna to deal with. At least she had Alan and Jobeth on her side.

"I need you both so much now that it looks like I have been betrayed by my own sister with my husband."

Jobeth stiffened.

"We are here for you, Mara-Joy. We are always here for you."

Alan sat back in his chair. A cold shiver went up his spine. He watched as Jobeth soothed Mara-Joy, who had broken into fresh tears once again.

He would be there for Mara-Joy to comfort her and help her heal her wounds from this ordeal, but he wouldn't choose between her and Joanna. He would not abandon one daughter for the other. Not even for Jobeth.

Alan received a letter a month after Joanna disappeared. It was addressed to him only. His heart pounded as he ripped open the envelope. He'd been sick with worry since Joanna ran off with Chad. He stood outside in front of the mailbox and sighed with relief as he stared down at the familiar handwriting from his daughter. Trembling, he read the words his daughter left for him.

Dear Papa,

I am sorry for the pain and trouble I have caused. To know I have disappointed you will be my cross to bear in life. I cannot excuse what I have done, but I also cannot deny my love for Chad any longer. Papa, I know we should never have let this happen, but it did. We love each other. Please, if you cannot understand, could you at least find it in your hearts to one day forgive me. I know Mama never will. Tell Constance and Pauline I love them and when I am settled I will write and tell you how I am doing. Please forgive me, Papa. I said some awful things to Mara-Joy that I wish I hadn't. For everything that has happened, she is still my sister and I should never have said the things I did. I regret it terribly.

Love, your daughter, Joanna

P.S.

Tell Mama I love her and I am sorry. I know it will not be enough for what I have done to her daughter, but still, please tell her for me.

Alan folded the letter and walked slowly back into the house. Jobeth was doing the dishes at the sink. Her back straightened stiffly as he spoke.

"I got a letter from Joanna," he said, clutching the paper in his hand.

Jobeth dropped the glass she was washing into the soapy water. Her hand froze in mid air.

Joanna was safe.

Her shoulders sagged with relief. The weight of worrying and wondering what happened to her child was finally lifted. Alan came up from behind and placed his hands on her slumped shoulders, sensing his wife's relief.

"She says she loves you," he said, circling her waist with his arms. Jobeth relaxed into the folds of his chest. She'd been so sick with worry. Not just for Mara-Joy, who was a mental basket case after all that had happened, but for Joanna too. She had been gone for a month without word. Jobeth had no idea what had happened to her.

"She says she is sorry and wants us to forgive her."

Jobeth stiffened.

Forgiveness was something altogether different.

She thought of Mara-Joy visiting with Oliver and Shawna, trying to figure out who she was now that the secret of her heredity was out. Her daughter was with Oliver and Mara-Joy wanted answers that only he could give her. It wasn't fair. Mara-Joy was her child. So what if Oliver contributed to bringing her into this world? It was Jobeth and Alan who had raised her. Suddenly she felt angry. This wouldn't be happening if Joanna had kept her mouth shut and if she hadn't stolen Mara-Joy's husband away. Mara-Joy would be home with her, not with Oliver, confused and wanting to figure out who she was now that she knew he was her father.

"I don't want to hear that name in my presence again," Jobeth said coolly, her back becoming ridged.

"She is still our child, Jobeth." Alan pulled away, still staring at his wife's back.

Jobeth abruptly turned around with a look that frightened Alan.

"After what she has done to this family? She wants forgiveness after destroying everything? Now that she has gotten what she wanted with no regard for the people she hurt? No, I can't forgive that." Jobeth said with steel in her words.

Alan walked away without saying a word. There was no arguing with Jobeth at the moment. Yes, what Joanna did was terribly wrong, but she was still their daughter. Jobeth needed time to forgive, and with time she would forgive if

Not forget.
He hoped.

Mara-Joy lay alone in her bed, screaming into her pillow, her rage bubbling over. Beside her lay the crumpled divorce papers Chad's lawyer had sent her. The words were burnt into her mind. Chad wanted a divorce so he could make a life with Joanna and their unborn child.

Unborn child! She lay back on her bed clutching her heart, her mouth open in a silent scream. Tears streamed down her face without stop. Joanna was having Chad's baby—the baby she was supposed to have. Joanna, her sister, had taken everything that meant anything to Mara-Joy. Chad, his children and her parents. Basically, Joanna had taken her identity. She rolled over and grabbed a Kleenex on the end table.

She blew her red tender nose and tossed the soiled tissue, not caring where it fell. There were many such tissues littering the floor, one more would make no difference.

Betrayed by her own sister.

Mara-Joy began to laugh through her tears. Her sister? What a joke. Joanna wasn't her sister after all. The family she thought was hers, wasn't. She was Oliver's daughter.

Oliver and a dead prostitute's.

A heavy weight descended down on her, crushing the living spirit out of her.

How would she live through this? She thought back to her stay with Oliver and Shawna.

She had visited them several months earlier, wanting answers. Oliver and Shawna prepared for her arrival and opened their doors with loving arms.

Oliver tried to explain why he stood aside and kept quiet about Mara-Joy's true heritage, but all Mara-Joy could see was his daughter with Shawna seated happily on his lap.

The daughter he didn't abandon.

Mara-Joy sniffed and sat up rubbing away the tears in her eyes. Anger fuelled her once again. Images of a woman with the same black hair as her filled her mind.

What was her mother like?

Oliver said he loved her, but why would her birth mother leave him? It didn't make any sense if they loved each other so much. Mara-Joy leaned over the bed once again and opened the drawer of the end table. She rummaged around until she found her cigarette case. She opened it up and took out one of her long cigarettes and quickly lit it.

Breathing deeply, she wrestled with all that had happened. She wasn't Alan and Jobeth's daughter, but the bastard child of a prostitute who killed herself rather than raise Mara-Joy.

And Joanna had stolen Chad out from under her eyes. Joanna was going to have Chad's child—the child Mara-Joy would never have. Tears threatened to surface again but Mara-Joy sucked deeply from her cigarette. She wouldn't be defeated. Someway, somehow she would live through this. Joanna wouldn't get the best of her. She stood up and looked at her reflection in the mirror of her vanity. Her blue eyes were puffy and red-rimmed.

Oliver's eyes. She shook her head pushing back her black kinky hair. She may look like Oliver and Tamara's child, but she was Alan and Jobeth's daughter. They were the only people who hadn't betrayed her.

She reached for a tube of lipstick and sat down at the vanity. Putting her cigarette in a nearby ashtray, she began to apply the red color to her full lips. Just the motion of applying her makeup made her feel stronger.

Forget about Oliver, he was no one to her. She had her parents and nothing was going to change that, not even the truth about her birth. He had his own family and she had hers. His children were not her siblings. Constance, Pauline and Alan-Michael were. Even Joanna. Her lips trembled thinking again of Joanna pregnant with Chad's child.

Yes, even Joanna, as much as she hated her, Joanna was her sister, which made what she had done to Mara-Joy even more despicable. Mara-Joy was no saint but she wouldn't have hurt Joanna the way she had been hurt.

She put the lipstick down, took a drag of her cigarette and searched her reflection. She would make Joanna hurt the way she had made Mara-Joy hurt.

How she would do it was another question yet unanswered.

— Chapter 36 —

"I am so frightened, Chad," Joanna said, sitting in the front seat twisting her hands in her lap. Chad looked over at her as he drove and smiled.

They were finally doing it. They were going home.

"Don't be, honey." He patted her lap and looked back at the road. The car was loaded down with their belongings.

The two children in the back of the car were busily counting the unfortunate dead animals that had been struck by the oncoming traffic.

"Besides, Mara-Joy can't still be mad after all these years. My God, we were never happily married together anyway."

"Chad, don't you remember my sister at all?" Joanna's eyebrows rose in amusement. "You can guarantee she is still royally peeved. Besides, it's not her

I'm worried about. It's Ma and Pa and the other girls." Joanna placed her hand on Chad's lap. It was warm and familiar.

After more than seven years together she still felt as though they were falling in love for the first time.

"I left so abruptly. Without a word to anyone. My poor parents, they must have been devastated. They didn't even know about you Chad."

"They loved you before, they will love you again." He reached for her hand on his lap. "Did I ever tell you how much I love you?"

"Yes." She smiled softly, placing her head on his shoulder. It had all been worth it. Loving Chad meant loosing her family but she had gained so much in return.

"But I never get tired of hearing it." Joanna beamed out the window as she watched the trees zoom by, blending into one green blurb.

"I love you, Mommy and Daddy!" Jena's musical voice sung from behind them. The blonde-haired seven year old sat up closer so she could see her parents better, her green eyes twinkling.

"Me too! Me too!" Five-year-old Charles pushed his sister out of the way, wanting to be the center of attention. His brown hair so like his father's was tasseled on his smooth forehead. Joanna looked at her two children, amazed. She still couldn't believe these two beauties were made from their love.

"Charlie, stop it!" Jena shoved back, "Mommy, tell him to quit pushing me!"

Joanna reached over the seat and put a gentle hand on her young son's arm.

Charles sat back and crossed his arms angrily across his chest.

"At least I have this family," Joanna replied smiling warmly at the boy's resemblance to his father.

"You will have your other family too," Chad reassured, not taking his eyes off the road.

They reached Chad's parent's house and were greeted with hugs and kisses.

Alexandria and Neil Willis were ecstatic to have their son and his family home with them. They loved the children and were beside themselves with happiness knowing that they would be able to take part in their lives as they continued to grow up.

"Well, look at her!" Alex huffed in disbelief, standing in the open doorway.

She placed her hands on her round hips and chuckled. Jena, not being a shy girl, was tugging her own suitcase up the stairs of her grandparents' house.

Elbowing her thin husband in the ribs, Alex said with pride, "Neil can you believe this little one?"

"Hello, Grandmother," Jena said through strained teeth as she carried her suitcase diligently up each step. "It's me, Jena."

"I see that," Alex replied, her large chest puffed out like a hen. She too was not shy and she could see herself in her granddaughter. "Neil, have you ever seen such green eyes! Who does she look like?"

"My mommy tells me I look like my aunt Constance," Jena said with pride as she reached the top of the steps. "She said when I was born I had a tuft of blond hair on my head and so she said to Daddy, 'That is my sister's hair.' And that is why my middle name is Constance after my aunt, who I never met before, but I look like her." Jena sighed and caught her breath.

"My, your aunt must be beautiful." Alex laughed. She knew who Constance was and Jena was right. She did look like her.

"I don't know if she is or not because I have never met her. Mommy moved away with Daddy and has never seen her since."

Joanna came up behind Jena and smiled down on her standing solemnly, clutching her suitcase.

"All right, motor mouth, let's get inside before you talk your grandmother's ear off," Joanna said, easing Jena on.

"Well, Jena, the name is appropriate." Alex said. "I too was named after a relative. My grandmother. 'Granny,' as I called her. It would please me very much if you and your brother would call me 'Granny'." Charles had just come up the stairs followed by Chad.

"What is your real name, Granny?" Jena asked, her sea green eyes dancing.

The plump woman already adored her granddaughter. It amused her how spunky Jena was. She reminded Alex of herself. She had never been one to keep a closed lip either.

"Alexandria." Alex smiled

"I like the name Alexandria. I'm going to name my daughter after you, Granny."

"Oh my, aren't you just precious. Neil have you ever seen such a child?" Alex said, clutching her chest tightly.

Short and balding, Neil just smiled back at his wife. He was a quiet man, not prone to many words, but this child made him want to laugh. Alex had surely met her match.

"She is a pistol, Alex. And look at our grandson—he is the spitting image of his father," Neil said while patting Charles on the head. Charles looked up at his grandfather with delight written all over his face. He liked when people told him he looked like his dad. It made him feel like a man.

Joanna had a warm feeling envelop her entire body. Chad's family was so warm and inviting. She watched her family as they talked with the older Willises. Chad stood proudly beside his children, a hand on either shoulder. They were the apples of his eye.

His prized possessions. She chuckled to herself.

After all these years she still felt like her love for Chad was just a dream. Never had she been loved so wholly and completely. And the children were such a blessing, two precious gifts she was able to give to the man she loved.

How Chad loved the children! It was a shame to think that he had almost lost his chance at fatherhood.

Joanna pushed those thoughts out of her head. Chad was not Mara-Joy's husband anymore and hadn't been for a long time. He was her husband and the father of her children.

That was a fact.

The image of her parents' faces invaded her consciousness.

Her love for Chad had made her lose her parents, the children's grandparents.

A ball formed in the back of Joanna's throat, thick as molasses.

Could her parents ever forgive her?

It had been so long since she devastated their lives with her actions. Could they forgive her not only for loving Chad, but also for revealing their secret about Mara-Joy? She rung her hands together nervously and averted her eyes from the people on the porch.

Joanna was wrapped in guilt. How could she have ever told Mara-Joy about her parentage? It hadn't been her place to do so and it was something she would never forgive herself for doing. As much as she knew for certain that Mara-Joy was not her biological sister, she also knew Mara-Joy was her sister in her heart.

Joanna had long ago forgiven Mara-Joy for the way she had treated her all her life. She only wondered if Mara-Joy could forgive her for taking Chad away and revealing her dark past.

Mara-Joy's final words to Joanna filled her mind and a cold shiver ran up her spine. Deep inside of her soul, Joanna knew Mara-Joy wouldn't forgive her for what she had done. It had been too raw and too painful. She had wanted to hurt Mara-Joy terribly and she did, and it was too late to take it back now.

The next morning, dressed in a light yellow spring dress that enhanced the green of her eyes, Joanna stood on the front porch looking sweet and elegant.

"Wish me luck," she said to her husband, who stood in front of the door admiring her.

"Are you sure you don't want me to come with you?"

"No, it's best that I go alone," Joanna replied. "I don't want to add insult to injury. Let me face them alone first and see if I am accepted before I bring you and the children to them."

Chad nodded, leaning over and giving Joanna a lingering kiss.

"If you need me, I'm here," he said, touching her light brown hair. It was shoulder length now and set in a soft wave going away from her face.

"I know," she said, touching the hand on her hair, "you always are."

"You don't owe anyone for your happiness, Joanna."

She nodded, holding back tears, knowing that it wasn't completely true.

She owed Mara-Joy.

"You don't have to do this, Joanna," Chad called behind her. Joanna looked over her shoulder back at the house. He stood anxiously in the opened door.

The children suddenly appeared behind his legs. They waved frantically at their mother and called out their good-byes.

"Yes, I do," she said firmly and blew her family a kiss.

It was a short drive to Constance's house. Alexandria had informed Joanna with as much information about her family as she could. Constance was now married and lived with her husband and two-year-old son only a few blocks from Chad's parents.

Joanna pulled into the driveway, stopped the car and took another deep gulp for courage.

Would Constance understand?

She got out of the car and pushed her skirt down flat on her legs. She'd taken great care that morning in choosing her clothes and hoped she had done herself justice. Constance knew Joanna was coming because Joanna had called the night of their arrival. She was excited to hear her older sisters' voice. She told Joanna that she had received all her letters and wanted to write her back, but couldn't understand why Joanna wouldn't leave a forwarding address.

They made plans to meet the next morning, which brought Joanna before the front door of Constance's little white house. Her heart pounded as she procrastinated. Part of her wanted to flee from the scene at once, but she had run away for the last time. She didn't want to run anymore.

Joanna held her breath and knocked firmly on the white door, her legs jumping and anxiously wanting to bolt.

A small boy with light brown hair and brown eyes answered. Joanna inspected the boy briefly. Although his face was shaped the same as Constance's, that was it. The boy must take after his father.

"Hello," Joanna bent down to face Constance's son, her nephew, for the first time. "Is your mother home?"

Suddenly a medium-sized woman of slender build appeared behind the child.

"Patrick, go and play dear," the woman said, looking down at Joanna.

Joanna's heart stopped.

Constance hadn't changed much. She was still blonde with soft curls that framed her face. Her green eyes were the same, just like Joanna's. Joanna stretched back up and the two stood still staring at each other, soaking in the changes the years had placed on them.

Joanna was taller and slimmer than Constance. When the boy, Patrick, went back into the house, it was plain to see that Constance was very much pregnant. Despite these differences, they still looked very much alike.

Sisters.

"Joanna!" Constance cried, knocked out of her shock. She embraced a startled Joanna in her loving arms.

"Connie!" Joanna hugged back overcome with emotion. She had always missed Constance, but didn't know just how much she missed her until that moment.

"It is so good to hear that name again." Constance pulled back and wiped tears away from her eyes. She admired Joanna's appearance. "You look absolutely beautiful."

"I didn't even recognize the woman in front of me at first." Joanna held a tissue to her red nose.

"Oh come in, come in!" Constance grabbed Joanna's arm and lead her into the warm living room of the cozy home. "Joanna." Constance hugged her again. "I have missed you so much. I don't understand why you wouldn't let me get in touch with you."

Joanna pressed her lips tightly together and sat down on the light blue couch. She motioned Constance to sit beside her and Constance sat down heavily, her bulging tummy pushed forward.

"I was afraid," Joanna began, her hand fluttering to her mouth, which had begun to quiver secretly behind the shield. "I was afraid to face you. You had warned me not to fall in love with Chad, but I couldn't help myself—we couldn't help each other." Joanna dabbed her eyes with the hanky she retrieved from her purse.

"I don't regret my decision to be with Chad. We are so happy with the Children," Joanna replied, trying to excuse her behavior.

"But, Joanna, you wouldn't let me write you. Why?" Constance felt all the old hurt surface. She needed answers for those years filled with tears over Joanna's rejection of her. It was bad enough that Constance felt responsible for setting the plans in motion that would destroy her family.

"Don't you understand? If I didn't speak to you, you could not snub me. I could handle rejection from Ma and Pa and even the other kids, but I couldn't handle it from you, Connie. If you would have nothing to do with me, I would have been lost. It was my way of protecting myself."

Constance shook her head in disbelief.

"Joanna, you should have known I would forgive you for anything. We have wasted years because you were mistakenly afraid."

"I realize that now. It's one of the reasons we came back home. We couldn't run and hide any longer from the past." Joanna placed her smooth palm on her sister's tight stomach. "I am here now. I won't run anymore."

Constance fixed her hand firmly on Joanna's.

"Good. I need someone around to share the important aspects of my life."

Just then the baby inside her gave a strong kick, causing their hands to jump up.

"It looks like I came home just in time. This little one is going to be a handful," Joanna said in awe of the child growing inside Constance.

Constance laughed. "If the child is anything like his big brother, I will need all the help I can get."

And as though hearing his mother talking about him, Patrick entered the living room. He stood shyly in front of the two women on the couch, a wet pinky finger twisting in his mouth.

"He must take after his father," Joanna observed. The brown-haired child continued to stare blankly, almost dim-witted.

Oh no. Joanna thought. Was the child slow? She thought of Pauline, the youngest of her sisters. Although she was always a sweet girl, she had sometimes seemed a little on the slow side. Could Constance, who was so intelligent and so smart, have a child who was more like her younger and less astute sister, Pauline?

"Yes, he is the spitting image of George." Constance tried to stand up, but fell back into the sofa. Joanna leapt to her feet and assisted in lugging Constance's bulk up off the couch.

"You are already here for me." Constance puffed and arched her back painfully. "I tell you, the end of pregnancy is a prison term for women. If it weren't for the outcome, I doubt any one of us would have been born." She gently took Patrick's fingers out of his mouth.

"This is Auntie Joanna, Patrick. She is Mommy's sister who used to live far away." Patrick nodded. "Do you remember me talking to you about her?" She smoothed back his soft wavy hair. His head moved back and forth in acknowledgement.

"Hello, Patrick," Joanna extended a cheerful hand to the boy. He accepted Joanna's offer with his own small hand. "I'll be seeing a lot of you and your Mommy from now on and I have two children who would love to get to know their cousin. Would you like to meet them?"

"Do you have a boy?" he asked in a clear, bird-like voice. Animation suddenly illuminated his eyes. Joanna instantly realized that what she had taken for slowness was in fact, boredom. What would a two-year-old boy find interesting in two women reminiscing? Patrick was not slow; comprehension danced in his eyes and voiced itself in his clear, perfect speech.

"Yes, I have a boy. His name is Charles and he is five years old." Joanna felt pride rise in her voice when speaking her son's name. This was right. Her son should know her sister's child. They should play together and be friends. She had been a fool to stay away so long.

"We play cars and build things with my blocks." Patrick stood twisting his wet fingers, trying not to shove them back into his mouth.

"My goodness, Patrick, you are quite the talker," Joanna was flabbergasted. Her earlier diagnosis of her nephew was apparently totally without merit. The two year old was a genius.

"Patrick, you will meet your cousins soon, but for now it is time for Mama and Aunt Joanna to have some adult time alone. Please play quietly in your room. I'll be in shortly with a snack." Constance scooted the small child out.

"Now," she said, returning to Joanna, breathing slightly harder, "I have to make a call to our little sister."

"Pauline?" Joanna stood up, frightened, her hands clenched tightly.

"Yes, Pauline. She would never forgive me if I didn't call and tell her you are here. I am not the only one who missed you all these years."

"She was still a child when I last saw her last." Joanna felt emotions welling up again and tried in vain to fight them back.

"She isn't a child anymore," Constance said, going to the phone.

"I have missed so much. Your marriage, your son's birth, our sister growing up." Joanna felt over whelmed. "How can I face her after what I have done?"

Constance stood before Joanna, the phone handle cradled back in the receiver. "You will face her. This is a happy day. You have returned to us. Stop worrying about the past. You will be around for all the rest of the children and marriages." Constance touched Joanna's shoulder strongly. "There is still so much time left for all of us to share."

“Connie, you haven’t changed.” Joanna sniffled, conjuring up some courage. “I’m glad for that.”

“Wait till you see Pauline.” Constance went back to the phone and began to dial. “She is quite the beauty. She outdoes us all, I’m afraid to say. She still lives at home with the folks. And, can you believe this, she dates George’s brother. We really hope that works out.”

“How are the folks?” Joanna asked softly, the words barely leaving her mouth. She couldn’t look at Constance. She focused her attention on her hands twisting the tissue she held to bits.

“They are fine.” Constance replied in a far off voice.

“Do they ask about me?” Joanna held her breath.

Constance hung up the phone again. Wrenching her lips, she wrestled with her own thoughts.

“Listen, Joanna. I am not going to sugarcoat things for you. I am glad you are home again and I know Pauline will be happy but–”

“Ma and Pa are not glad is what you are trying to say.” Joanna fought back the physical pain she felt deep in her chest. She closed her eyes and tried to compose herself.

What did she expect?

“They all became very close after you told Mara-Joy about her parentage.”

Guilt flooded Joanna. The look on Mara-Joy’s face that day would haunt her, forever.

“Even though she knows Ma and Pa aren’t her biological parents, they got real close. Closer than before, if that was ever possible.” Constance paused and then decided to continue. “You really knocked Mara-Joy for a loop. A big loop.”

“I will never forgive myself for the things I said to her.” Joanna said, unable to look Constance in the face.

“Well, she has never forgiven you for taking Chad from her.”

“He was never really hers.”

Constance’s left eyebrow rose in disagreement.

“She doesn’t feel the same way, I am afraid.” She paused, deciding whether or not to continue. “She’s been married twice since you’ve been gone.”

Joanna’s head snapped up surprised. Maybe Mara-Joy had moved on.

“She is still with her third husband. He has two girls from a previous marriage, which is good for her since she—“

Constance stopped and blushed a deep red.

Joanna didn’t need to be told that Mara-Joy could have no children of her own. She was very much aware of that bit of information.

“He is very rich and much older than she is, but she seems happy, finally.”

“That is good to hear,” Joanna piped up. “I want her to be happy, Connie. Even though I have always had a rivalry with Mara-Joy, I still love her in my own way.”

“I understand,” Constance said knowingly. She too felt the same emotional ties to Mara-Joy. They had been raised together, lived together, had lives that intertwined. And Constance had witnessed Mara-Joy’s honest pain when Joanna and Chad ran off together. Pain that she had helped to create by putting the idea of stealing Chad away from Mara-Joy into Joanna’s head. If she hadn’t convinced Joanna to be Chad’s lover, Joanna would never have fallen in love with Chad. And Constance would never have had to live with the knowledge that she had started the chain of events that followed afterwards.

"I wish I could take back all the pain I have caused her," Joanna said, eyes downcast. "But I don't regret my life with Chad. He is my world and we have been so happy. I know he was my sister's husband, but it was in name only, Constance. It was in name only."

Constance nodded. Her own guilty heart torturing her.

"We all have said and done things we regret Joanna. You're not alone in your regrets over past deeds."

"But she is my sister--and what I did to her--"

"I know. I know."

"Well, I better get the coffee going. We have a lot of catching up to do," Constance said, rummaging through the cupboards in the kitchen, her belly getting in the way.

"Here, let me help you." Joanna gently pushed Constance into a chair. "Now tell me where the coffee is."

Constance laughed, rubbing her swollen belly and motioned to the top shelf.

"You should have heard Pauline squeal when I told her you were here." Constance sat back, pressing her strained spine on the padded chair cover.

Finding what she had been searching for, Joanna began mechanically making the coffee.

"I can't wait to see her," she replied, filling the coffee pot with water from the sink. "She won't be the same Pauline I last saw."

"Oh, she's still the same old Pauline. Sweet and loving in a childlike way." Constance pressed her hand to her back grimacing.

"Tell me you didn't have these horrific backaches when you were expecting?"

"I am afraid to tell you, little sister, that I did. Twice." Joanna said over her shoulder, smiling.

"Uhgh. Must be a family curse. We should warn Pauline."

"Warn Pauline about what family curse?" asked a feminine voice from the kitchen door.

Both Joanna and Constance turned toward the direction of their disruption.

There stood a tall, gorgeous brunette with the most outrageous golden streaks in her hair. She was lean and sleek with startling green eyes. Her hair was pulled modestly back from her oval, tanned face in a ponytail. She was dressed in a white button-up shirt that was un tucked casually over her slim tan pants. She absolutely took Joanna's breath away.

This little sister who had been lost somewhere in the shuffle of their lives was by far the rarest gem of the four sisters, for she exuded beauty and elegance, grace and style. And she did all this while being totally unaware of herself. All you had to do was look into the young woman's face to see all the sweet innocence welled up inside. Pauline was rare. She was beautiful both inside and out.

"Pauline, my God!" Joanna was speechless.

Tears welled up in Pauline's large eyes. Her lips began to tremble and she dashed headfirst into Joanna, circling her with a fierce grip of love.

"Joanna, we have missed you so much!" Pauline cried wholeheartedly into Joanna's chest. Joanna returned her embrace, overcome with the emotional outburst Pauline so openly and freely displayed.

"Look at you," Joanna said, composing herself, pulling Pauline in front of her and giving her a thorough inspection. "You are a beautiful young woman."

Pauline blushed innocently. Joanna couldn't help but notice that this was new information for the exquisite Pauline. She smiled. The child was totally oblivious to her splendor.

"Well, I'll always be your baby sister," Pauline giggled.

"Yes," Joanna said, hugging Pauline tightly to her again. Pauline felt wholesome and Joanna breathed deep of her scent, burying herself into her soft-smelling shoulder.

"Joanna?" A deep voice from the doorway caused Joanna to open her eyes, heart pounding. The voice was one she had dreamed of hearing again, but thought she never would. She turned slowly around from Pauline, afraid her ears had deceived her.

Standing beside Constance stood a graying-haired man with the most beautiful green eyes. The same green eyes she had.

"Papa!" Joanna stood frozen to the spot. Pauline stepped aside, leaving Joanna alone to face their father.

"Oh Pappy!" she cried, forgetting her fears and running into her father's waiting arms. Alan hugged her tightly to his broad chest, a hoarse sob escaping from deep beneath the barrel of flesh.

"Joanna," he sobbed, clutching his daughter tightly to him. She felt unreal as he held her tighter and kissed her wet cheeks, afraid she would suddenly disappear. "I have missed you, girl."

"Oh Pappy, I have missed you so much. I have missed everyone terribly," Joanna proclaimed staring, unbelieving, into his green watery eyes.

"How could you have stayed away from us all these years?" he asked, cradling her head in his large hands. Joanna kissed each palm and held them to her cheek.

"I'm sorry, Pappy. I was afraid." Joanna turned to Constance and Pauline. Their arms were intertwined together, holding each other for emotional support. "I was afraid you all hated me for what I had done."

"Hate my own daughter--my flesh and blood?" Alan turned Joanna's face up to his. "I could never hate you no matter what you did." He brushed away the fresh tears streaming down Joanna's face. She looked up at him, swelling with pride. There was so much love in his heart. How could she have not trusted it?

"Are you still with–are you still married?" Alan asked, sitting at the kitchen table surrounded by his three daughters. He couldn't bring himself to say Chad's name. As much as he made Joanna happy, he had broken Mara-Joy's heart. And as far as Alan was concerned, Chad had stolen two of his daughters from him and was instrumental in tearing his family apart.

"Yes, Pa, I'm still married to Chad and we have two beautiful children: Jena and Charles." Joanna searched her father's eyes. She could see the struggle behind them. "Chad and I are very happy together, Pa."

Alan, lips tightly pressed together, ran his hands through his graying hair and looked into his coffee mug. "Where are these beautiful grandchildren?" he replied, trying to change the subject away from Chad.

"They're with their father at his parents' house," Joanna replied, making it clear that Chad was a permanent part of her life and if Alan was going to accept her, he was going to have to accept Chad as well. “I can’t wait for you to see them. You will be so proud.” She took a deep breath and took a sip of her coffee. “Pa, we are here to stay. We have moved back home.”

Alan’s head shot up. He was stunned. “What?” He had put on some weight and he fell seated onto one of the kitchen chairs.

“Pappy, I can live with Mara-Joy’s hate and--” she paused building her courage, “and Mama’s, but I can’t stay away from the rest of you any longer. I can’t run away anymore.”

“They don’t hate you, Joanna,” Alan said softly. “It’s just that you hurt them so badly.”

“I understand, Pa, and I wish I could take their hurt away,” Joanna continued. “There is nothing I would like more than to heal all the wounds I have caused. But understand this: I am here to stay whether they can forgive me or not. I won’t lose you all again. Not even if it means hurting them once again.”

Alan nodded in acknowledgement. He thought of Jobeth and Mara-Joy. Even Alan-Michael. It was not going to be easy for Joanna. She didn’t know just how much she had hurt them with her actions.

— Chapter 37 —

"Are you going to tell Mom about Joanna?" Pauline asked Alan later that night as they stood outside their home in the dark. The entrance light shone down on them.

Alan rubbed the top of his thinning hair, contemplating his next move.

"It's not going to be easy," he replied honestly to Pauline.

"No. I'm glad it's you and not me." Pauline smiled weakly. She leaned over and kissed Alan's tired face. He grinned sheepishly and rubbed Pauline's lean back.

"You go on to bed. I'll deal with your mother."

Pauline obeyed and went straight to her room. She shut the door slightly so she could hear her parents in the next room. Sitting down with her legs folded beneath her, she pressed her ear to the door and held her breath.

Alan placed his hat on the rack and walked into the living room where Jobeth sat quietly, listening to the radio and reading a book.

"Hello, darling," she said as he walked into the room. She sat her book aside as Alan leaned down to kiss her.

"Jobeth," he said seriously after kissing her on the cheek,. Jobeth was a stubborn woman, but it had always been one of the many things he loved about her.

"What is it, Alan? You look odd," she said, starting to stand. Alan placed a reassuring hand on her shoulder. "Is it one of the children? Are they all right?"

"Joanna is back," he blurted out, finding no other way to say it.

He watched Jobeth's face for any sign of emotion.

At first Jobeth's face lightened, the faint creases in her forehead slackened, but just as quickly her face hardened.

She stood up abruptly.

"I don't want that name mentioned in my house," Jobeth hissed, looking around to see if Alan-Michael was near. He couldn't hear the name of Joanna without a slew of vile words spewing from his mouth.

"Jobeth!" Alan beseeched, confronting her. Although he expected her reaction to be mixed with some confused emotions, Alan thought that deep in Jobeth's heart she'd be glad to hear Joanna was back.

"Alan," Jobeth glared menacingly, "I mean it."

"She has two children, Jobeth. Our grandchildren."

For a brief moment Jobeth's face softened, but then chilled, causing the soft crow's feet in the corners of her eyes to look harsh. The torment behind her hazel eyes was evident. She wanted to be happy, but the hurt and anger were still too strong to let go of.

Jobeth thought of Mara-Joy and the child she should have had with Chad—the child that had cost Mara-Joy the ability to ever have children of her own. She thought of Mara-Joy's tribulation over wanting children of her own and how she had to suffice with other women's children. Like the stepdaughters she shared with her new husband.

"Those children were supposed to be Mara-Joy's children, not Joanna's," Jobeth spat, refusing to look at her husband, the injustices evident in her voice.

“Think about what you are saying, Jobeth,” Alan remarked, shaking his head in disbelief. “As hard as it was for her, Mara-Joy has come through all this. She is happily married again and has a life of her own. We have to stop all this nonsense, Jobeth. Our family needs to be reunited once again. We have other children besides Mara-Joy and Alan-Michael. I think it’s time we put the past behind us and moved forward as a family.”

Jobeth stood open-mouthed and unable to avoid staring at Alan. They had rarely fought in there nearly twenty-five years of marriage. And she had rarely seen Alan so disappointed in her.

“I know I have other children, Alan. I’ve always been quite aware of them,” she said rather nastily. She regretted her tone of voice the moment she heard the words fly out of her mouth. It sounded cold and cruel. She pulled back, the front of her hand covering her mouth as though trying to stop any more nasty words from coming out.

“Really?” Alan exploded. All the sentiments he had toward the way Jobeth treated the other girls seemed to be frothing to the surface. Unable to stop the volcano inside of him, he erupted.

“I’m ashamed to admit that I have sat back and watched you play favorites with our children. I didn’t want to believe that the woman I loved could love her children so unequally. You have always preferred Mara-Joy and Alan-Michael to the others. And Joanna,” he said as he ran his finger’s roughly through his sparse hair, “my God, you’ve been the roughest on her. You never let up on how she wasn’t like Mara-Joy. You put the rivalry between them Jobeth, and I helped by sitting back and allowing you to do it. If I had been a better father, I would have put a stop to you and the way you were with those children.”

“I have always loved my children!” Jobeth countered, unable to believe her ears. She clenched her fists tightly to her sides, ready for battle. “How dare you say I loved them differently! It’s just that my love for Mara-Joy is the reason you and I are together. She brought us together! She did Alan! If that child hadn’t needed parents, who knows if we would ever have ended up together.”

“We loved each other before there ever was a Mara-Joy, Jobeth. We would have ended up together eventually. It was meant to be,” Alan said, softening.

He couldn’t stand the anguish in Jobeth’s voice.

“You don’t know that, Alan. You don’t know that for sure.” Tears sprang to her eyes. “Don’t you remember those times when everything seemed to be taken from me? From us? My baby boy and Jonah . . .” Jobeth hadn’t spoken of either in years and saying their names brought their faces fresh to her mind.

Jobeth rubbed her nose with the back of her hand, trying to erase the memories of those long dead.

“Did you forget them, Alan? Because I didn’t.” Her eyes were red-rimmed and full of misery. “When I look at our son, I see the baby boy I lost. I see his tiny body gasping in vain for air as he slowly died in my arms. When Alan-Michael was born, it was like I had him back again, but alive and healthy. And then I see the man who helped me deliver him. And I remember how that man, Jonah, helped me to love again. And Mara-Joy, oh, Mara-Joy. Every time I look at her, I see the child who set me free to love you. I didn’t feel I deserved to love, but Mara-Joy’s presence in our lives forced me to make choices I was too afraid to make. Can’t you see?” She implored, begging Alan to see her side.

"Can't you see our children have brought me to where I am? Alan-Michael is the baby I lost and Mara-Joy is the baby I found that brought me finally to you."

"Jobeth, I'm so sorry that you're still haunted by all this pain, but that is still no excuse. Joanna is your child as well and she needs you too. Think about making up with your daughter, Jobeth," he said rather coldly, "before it is too late and you wish that you had."

He turned and stomped out of the room.

Jobeth fell back onto the couch like she'd been socked in the stomach. She closed her eyes, listening to Alan's progress up the stairs to their bedroom. Her throat tightened and her eyes began to water.

"Joanna," she whispered, "Joanna."

"I can't believe the nerve!"

Mara-Joy stormed around the kitchen in Jobeth's house. She was livid.

Jobeth and Alan-Michael sat at the kitchen table, caught in the cyclone of Mara-Joy's wrath.

Her hair swung freely in tight curls down her back.

Jobeth thought of how much Mara-Joy resembled Tamara when she was angry. She had the same feisty spirit.

"Settle down, Mara-Joy," Jobeth said, feeling slightly annoyed. She glanced at Alan-Michael out of the corner of her eye. He was completely frightened by Mara-Joy's outburst. They had become quite frequent since Joanna and Chad's return. "You are frightening your brother." Jobeth said dully.

Alan-Michael straightened in his chair.

"No… she's… not," he stuttered, his lips flapping pathetically. Alan-Michael, now sixteen, was a handsome boy with light brown hair and hazel eyes like his mother. In fact, out of all of Alan and Jobeth's birth children, Alan-Michael was the one who looked slightly different from the rest. He didn't have his father's distinct eyes or his mother's long, oval face that his other siblings inherited. He had his father's broad face and his mother's eyes but this didn't make him less attractive than the others, just different.

"But, Mama!" Mara-Joy hollered, throwing her hands up into the air. "She stole the only man I truly loved away from me! I hate her! I hate her! I hate her! Don't you hate her?" Mara-Joy slammed her fist down on the table, making both Jobeth and Alan-Michael jump.

These outbursts were also becoming more and more violent each time.

"That is enough, Mara-Joy!" Jobeth stood up, shaking. Alan-Michael slunk back in his chair, paralyzed. He'd never heard his mother raise her voice to Mara-Joy.

Stunned, Mara-Joy stepped back, speechless. She was just as shocked by her mother's outcry.

"Of course I don't hate my own daughter. I have never hated Joanna. She is my daughter just like you are my daughter and I could hate her no more than I could hate you, Mara-Joy." Jobeth's chest rose up and down in anger. Something was breaking inside her, letting go like a damn finally released.

"And the man you love should be the husband you are married to now, not the one you married so many years ago when you were still a child."

"But, Mama," Mara-Joy sobbed in a quiet voice, "she hurt us all so badly!"

She plunked down dejectedly in the nearest kitchen chair.

"What Joanna did was wrong, very wrong. But that was so long ago. You two are sisters. It is time the two of you made up. This family has been torn apart long enough," Jobeth said with resignation, resting her forehead in the palm of her hand.

In the weeks since Joanna returned, her thoughts had been occupied with what Alan had said. His words were ringing true. Maybe she had favored these two children more. In fact, if she was really true to herself, she knew she had. For whatever reasons, she had done it. She now needed to fix the mistakes of the past before it was too late.

"Enough is enough, Mara-Joy." Jobeth's eyes shot to her son who sat totally mesmerized by what was going on. "Look how you've turned your own brother against his sister. He barely even remembers her and he has a horrible hatred for her."

"It isn't Mara-Joy who makes me hate her, Ma," Alan -Michael said calmly. "I dislike her for my own reasons. I don't take kindly to tramps stealing respectful women's husbands away, especially when that respectful women is my sister. Besides Ma, have you forgotten how she flung Mara-Joy's adoption into her face? That was just cruel. You know, she seduces Mara-Joy's husband, gets pregnant with his bastard brat and then screams out a mound of filth at Mara-Joy. And we are supposed to forgive and forget?" Alan-Michael stood up and put his arm protectively around Mara-Joy's quivering shoulders. He was already taller than her and she seemed small and defenseless in his arms.

"It seems Alan-Michael and I are the only ones who are not blinded to Joanna's schemes," Mara-Joy said defensively to her mother. She crossed her arms defiantly.

Jobeth stood staring at them, feeling the hate steaming off of their very essences.

"I realize your sister has made a lot of mistakes in her life, but that doesn't change the fact that she is still your sister. Whether you like it or not that isn't going to change." She turned and left the room, unable to face their anger anymore.

"You are blind, Mother, blind! And I can't believe you're turning against me!" Mara-Joy followed after Jobeth. Alan-Michael grabbed her arm, holding her firmly back.

"Mara-Joy, I just want my family to be whole again," Jobeth said tiredly, not bothering to turn to the steely eyes that accused her. "And, like it or not, that includes Joanna."

Jobeth opened the front door, leaving the house and her two flabbergasted children behind. The fresh air hit her like a liberating breeze.

"Did you see that?" Mara-Joy swung around to face Alan-Michael.

"I saw it, but I don't believe it," Alan-Michael said, shaking his head in disbelief.

"Bitch! Bitch! Bitch! She has even turned our mother against us. Our mother!" She curved away from Alan-Michael's stocky sixteen-year-old body.

"What do you say to that little brother? Isn't that a fine how-do-you-do?"

"She is really an evil little devil," Alan-Michael articulated, while placing a sheltering arm back around his sister. She snuggled into his thick chest, letting his warmth protect her.

"It is so true, Mikey. So very true. You are the only one who understands the pain and agony Joanna has caused me. The rest have just forgotten." She wrapped her arms around his waist.

Alan-Michael felt himself become stronger under Mara-Joy's grasp.

"I would love to see Joanna's brains in a puddle on the floor. I would love to see her squirm in pain as I watch her die," he sneered with passion.

Mara-Joy looked up and smiled into Alan-Michael's darkened face. He had always had a dark side but the older he got, the more it had grown, twisting and developing into something possibly unnatural. She'd noticed it when he was small. First in his cruelty to animals and then to other children. Mara-Joy had pushed it aside, choosing to ignore it. He was hers. Her Mikey. Always there to defend her at any cost. So what if sometimes he was a little too weird?

"Oh, Mikey, you do love me, don't you?" she asked sweetly, her head pressed firmly to his heaving chest.

"You know I love you more than anyone," he choked full of emotion, hugging her tighter.

"Wouldn't it be great if Joanna were dead? Wouldn't it be great if something happened to her, an accident or something?" Mara-Joy sniffed, closing her eyes and feeling safe in Alan-Michael's love.

Alan-Michael became confused. Was Mara-Joy serious? It was so hard to know when she was serious.

"Then Ma and Pa would be ours again and I would have Chad back with me where he belongs."

"What are you saying, sis?" Alan-Michael asked, looking at his sister with total confusion. "You aren't saying we should have her killed, are you?"

"Oh, I don't know," Mara-Joy sobbed meekly, shoving her head under Alan-Michael's chin. "I just know her children should be mine and Chad's children. Not hers!" She sighed and pulled away from Alan-Michael's warm embrace.

Mara-Joy flopped down on the nearest kitchen chair. "She ruined me, Mikey. Having an affair with my husband and running off with him. Carrying his illegitimate children." She placed her head down on the table, letting the cool surface calm her skin. "They left me alone and abandoned. The humiliation I suffered by my own sister's hand!" She raised her head to Alan-Michael's frustrated face. A red, angry ball had developed on her forehead.

Alan-Michael was listening intently to every word Mara-Joy said and she smiled wickedly to herself.

"You know, Mikey, she never did pay any attention to you."

Alan-Michael's brows furrowed together, trying to remember his childhood with Joanna.

"She hates you just as much as she hates me. Why, I bet she is cooking up some way to hurt you next." Mara-Joy jumped up dramatically and grabbed Alan-Michael by the shoulders.

"We have to stop her before she gets me! You have to stop her before she gets us!"

“I won’t let her hurt you again!” Alan-Michael sobbed. Mara-Joy took his large head and cradled it to her chest. Her perfumed body made his nose tingle and he felt himself harden when Mara-Joy rubbed her thigh against him. He hugged his sister tighter, burying his face deeper into her fragrant breast.

“There, there,” she cooed, rubbing the boy’s back. She was beaming sinfully, quite amused at how anger aroused her brother. She rubbed her thigh harder on Alan-Michael’s erection. He groaned, embarrassed, between his sobbing.

“She better not try and hurt me, right Mikey?”

Alan-Michael muttered louder as he held Mara-Joy tighter to him. He was entranced by her, obsessed with her. He always needed more of Mara-Joy.

Always.

She pulled away from the confused, aroused boy. Alan-Michael stood drunkenly before her, hands reaching out in vain. She placed a silky hand on his trembling shoulder.

“You have to stop her, Mikey, before she hurts me more.” Alan-Michael yearned to be in Mara-Joy’s arms again.

“You love me, Mikey? You do?” she pouted. He nodded eagerly like a trained dog. “I’ve always loved you the most in this world, Mikey. The most. Please stop her!” Mara-Joy fell to the ground and clutched Alan-Michael around the waist, panting heavily on his erect member that lay squashed and ready to pounce out of its tight confinement.

“I will,” Alan-Michael said venomously while clutching Mara-Joy’s head tight to him. “I will.”

Mara-Joy looked up at her brother. His eyes were screwed shut with intoxication. She grinned to herself and gave him one more hug around his waist, pressing her lips close to his bulging appendage before standing up. She straightened her dress and looked at the helpless blob of a boy in front of her.

“Thank you, Mikey,” she breathed into his ear, her hand firmly pressed against his chest where it lingered for a moment. She then wheeled and left hastily, aware of what she had done to her own brother.

As soon as the door shut behind Mara-Joy, Alan-Michael shamefully ran upstairs to his room and stripped his soiled underpants off.

As he stood in the bathroom scrubbing his tainted underwear, he bellowed with torment and shame, “She’s my sister! She’s my sister!”

— Chapter 38 —

Jobeth stood on the front porch of Chad's parent's house. She was excited and frightened for more than one reason.

One, she was going to see her daughter after so many years and two, she was afraid Joanna wouldn't want to see a mother who had cast her aside so easily.

She took a deep breath and knocked on the door. The wind rustled the few grays in her hair and her hand flew up to tuck the loose strands back into their proper places.

Alex answered the door, surprised to see Jobeth standing before her. The women were around the same age but looked quite different from each other.

Alex was round and stern looking, whereas Jobeth was lean and soft. It was funny how looks could be deceiving. It had been the stern looking woman who'd taken Joanna under her wing and nurtured her burdened soul, and the soft woman who had cast her out of the nest so coldly.

"Hello, Mrs. Benson," Alex said matter-of-factly. She didn't know Jobeth Benson, but she did see how her rejection of her daughter tortured Joanna day in and day out. Alex had never had daughters. Only Neil junior and Chad had blessed their home, but if she had been fortunate to have a daughter of her own, she knew she would never have been able to abandon her child, no matter what they had done.

"Good day, Mrs. Willis." Jobeth stood up tall and straight in front of Chad's mother. One thing Jobeth despised was people looking down on her. She'd been looked down on as a young girl. She wouldn't be looked down on now or ever.

Alexandria Willis began to frown. Jobeth looked ready for a fight the way she adjusted her back so rigidly. She couldn't help remembering a few years back when Joanna and Chad had first run off together. Jobeth came pounding on their door, demanding that they tell her where Chad and Joanna had taken off to. When they refused, Jobeth had been furious. She'd accused Chad of ruining the Benson family and said that Mara-Joy would never be the same after the cruelty their son had inflicted on their family.

Thinking about that night more than seven years ago, Alex became very angry. What did this woman want now? Was she ready to cause another scene?

I won't let her do it, Alex thought. I'll be a mother to that sweet girl. I won't allow this woman to hurt Joanna anymore. She frowned defensively at Jobeth.

Jobeth noticed Alex frowning at her and felt a twinge of guilt. She too remembered the last encounter they had and was not proud of herself.

"Could I please speak to my daughter?" Jobeth said steadfastly. She needed to speak to Joanna. She realized how much she had treated her differently throughout her life and maybe Constance and Pauline too. She couldn't remember doing anything special for her natural daughters' lives as she had always done for Mara-Joy and Alan-Michael. She had favored her eldest and youngest children and now she had to make it up to the rest of her offspring before it was too late. If it wasn't already.

"She's not here," Alex said, crossing her arms over her plump breast. "She's with Chad and the children." She watched to see if Chad's name made Jobeth flinch. When it didn't, she felt a little relieved and figured she might as well tell Jobeth where they were.

"Your husband and two other daughters are with them. They are having a picnic down by the lake," Alex continued, hoping she wasn't making a mistake.

"Thank you." Jobeth smiled warmly. Alex nodded and watched Jobeth quickly run down the front porch stairs.

"I hope it's not too late for you, Jobeth," Alex said, shaking her head. "I hope you aren't going to continue spending time ignoring your daughter. If you do, you will miss out on the lovely woman you've created, a daughter much sweeter and kinder than that one you have revered all these years." Alex gave a soft kind of smile as she watched Jobeth disappear.

Joanna sat peacefully on a rock by the stream. She watched as her beautiful daughter, Jena, ran toward her calling out her name.

A warm feeling washed over Joanna as Jena stopped in front of her with a big pout protruding from rose petal lips.

How I love this child, she thought. This child truly represents the strong parts of myself.

Jena rested her tiny hands on her straight waist and pinched up her oval face in concern. Her wavy blond hair framed her expression, making her look more like a beautiful cherub than a child of seven.

"Mommy, please don't look gloomy," Jena's wee voice implored. She turned to her grandfather who was sitting on a blanket in the sand.

Joanna smiled at her father as he admired them from afar.

"I'm just fine, Jena," she said, noticing her father was listening to them. "Go play with the other children."

Jena looked from her mother to her grandfather, searching for help. When she saw that her pleas fell on deaf ears, she ran off toward her father and brother. They were playing in the water, laughing and having a good time. Jena glanced back for a moment at Joanna and waved. Joanna waved back vigorously so that Jena wouldn't worry about her but would have some fun. It must have worked because the little girl jumped into the water where Chad scooped her up into his arms. She giggled wildly as he tossed her up in the air and dropped her softly into the waiting water. Charles tugged at Chad's swimming trunks, eager for his father to repeat the same process with him.

"Papa?" Pauline called, walking toward Alan. Alan turned and admired his youngest daughter as she plunked herself down on the blanket beside him. She was a beauty of a girl. Her hair was pulled back in her favorite style, a ponytail, and as usual she was dressed in shorts and a casual button-up shirt with tennis shoes on her stocking-less feet. It amazed him how she could dress so plainly and look so elegant, without being aware of it. Out of all his children, it was only Pauline he could honestly say this about. All his daughters were beauties, but only Pauline was totally unaware of it. Maybe that was the reason she was the loveliest. That and her total innocence toward the world.

He sighed as he watched the young woman sit down beside him.

"All my children are growing up," he said, placing his hand on Pauline's face.

She clutched his hand with her own and rubbed her cheek with it.

"What's wrong, Dad?" Pauline asked, sensing her father's mood. Alan released his hold on her hand and turned toward Constance, who was picking apples with her family near the creek. Her baby was just about due and she was heavily weighed down with the burden of the child.

"Oh," he said reflectively, "I wish your mother and the rest of the family were here enjoying this glorious day with us." He looked at Pauline's worried face.

Pauline felt uneasy about her father. He was thirty-nine years old, but sometimes he looked much older and this frightened her. She was afraid for him all the time. She loved him dearly and couldn't stand the thought of anything happening to him.

"Dad, I wish that too," Pauline said, giving his hand a squeeze. "But Mara-Joy—"

"Now it is not Mara-Joy's fault," Alan grumbled. "Constance and you are always blaming Mara-Joy for everything. You have to realize that your mother is the one who makes her own decisions in life. She always has and always will. She will have to take responsibility for her own actions. Good or bad."

"Well," Pauline rolled her eyes in jest, "I suppose so, Pop. Anyway, I didn't come over here to argue about Mom, I came to tell you I have to go. Pascal is waiting for me." She leaned over and kissed Alan warmly on the cheek. He reached up and held her face to his, feeling the heat that was created from his daughter flow onto him. He closed his eyes and silently prayed for his younger daughter. Pauline cupped his hand and closed her eyes. She was so innocent. Alan was afraid she would be eaten up in the big, bad world. All he wanted to do was protect her.

Pauline felt tears she couldn't explain form in the corner of her eyes and a lump was developing in her throat, choking her. Quickly she kissed her father again and stood up, dusting the sand off of her legs.

"Is this Pascal treating you right?" Alan shielded his eyes from the glaring sun beating down on him as he looked up into Pauline's face.

"Yes, Dad," Pauline said, walking away. "Of course."

Alan bit his bottom lip hesitantly. He liked George, Constance's husband, well enough; but there was something about his brother, Pascal, that he just didn't trust.

Pauline trotted away wiping tears from her eyes. Alan wished he could be everywhere with his children protecting them, but he couldn't. He also couldn't force them to stay at home with him any longer, either.

Jobeth stood in the hedges watching Pauline and Alan. She wondered what was wrong with her youngest daughter as she left in tears. She shook her head.

Pauline wasn't a little girl anymore. She was a grown woman. Jobeth jiggled her head, not wanting to believe Pauline had grown from a child into a woman without her ever recognizing it.

Jobeth hadn't noticed Joanna standing up after spotting her mother hiding in the bushes. She didn't even notice the look Joanna gave her: a look of complete and utter joy.

"Mama!" Joanna cried out with all her heart. Alan pivoted from his spot. He could see Joanna running toward his wife, who was standing behind a bush.

Jobeth, hearing Joanna, twirled towards her and ran straight into her waiting arms. They hugged each other tightly, holding on like two drowning people.

Alan nodded to himself with approval, a tear rolling down his cheek. He knew Jobeth wouldn't let him down. She never had. She never would. She couldn't abandon their daughter any more than he could.

"Mama," Joanna cried on her mother's breast. "You do love me?"

"Of course, my darling, I always have. I always have." Jobeth held Joanna close, enjoying the feeling of her once again in her arms. She didn't notice Jena running toward them. Alan stood up and went to stand beside Chad who had come out of the water with Charles after hearing Joanna cry out. They stood silently together watching their wives embrace one another.

Constance and George stood watching too. Constance smiled to herself and turned back to face her husband and son, encouraging them to continue picking apples.

This was Joanna's moment.

"Oh darling, I have been so foolish. Will you ever be able to forgive me?"

Jobeth lifted Joanna's tear-streaked face to her own.

"There is nothing to forgive," Joanna sobbed. "I have you back and that is all that matters."

"There is so much to forgive and I plan to try to make up for the wrong I have done to this family. It's this family that means everything to me. Your father,"

Jobeth glanced at Alan, who stood proudly looking on, and smiled, "and you children have always been my life. Always."

Jena, who was confused by what was happening, looked up at the woman her mother was hugging. She tugged on her skirt, wanting to find out who she was and why she was causing her mommy to cry.

Jobeth, startled by the child, looked down unconsciously and lost her breath.

The child was the spitting image of her long dead brother Pauli. Her hand flew to her mouth in astonishment. Her throat tightened. Memories, long since forgotten, flooded her mind. She never forgot Pauli, but had put his memory away to protect herself from old pain. Just like she had done with all the ones she had loved and lost.

"Ma? What is wrong?" Joanna asked, frightened. Her heart skipped a beat as she reached to grab Jena. Jobeth was a ghostly white. Was Jena a reminder of what she had done to hurt the family? Did she still feel that Joanna's children should be Mara-Joy's?

"Pauli." Jobeth whispered bending down to Jena. "Do you remember me and your father telling you about your names, Joanna?"

"I don't understand, Ma," Joanna said, confused, her heart racing. She held on to Jena's arm defensively. Could her mother turn on her once again, now that she was face to face with the child she had with Chad?

Jobeth touched the little girl's face and the soft down of her blond hair. Still looking at Jena, Jobeth continued.

"Mara-Joy was named after Tamara, her birth mother, whom you children never knew about. Joy was a nickname Shawna had picked out for her when she was just a little baby. It was very appropriate because she brought us such joy at a time when we didn't have a lot of it." Jobeth paused remembering the past vividly as though it were yesterday.

"We had a wonderful friend whom we loved dearly named Jonah."

Joanna nodded, familiar with the story. She had known how Mara-Joy had received the name Joy, but hadn't realized that she also carried her birth mother's name.

"Jonah was one of the sweetest people anyone could ever have known. It nearly killed your father, Shawna and me when he was killed. The pain was unbearable. But," she brightened up, "we persevered and later had a daughter--you." Jobeth beamed at Joanna. "You were our first natural child and it only seemed right that we name you after Jonah. He meant so much to all of us that I needed to feel his spirit near me and so I honored him by naming my child after him, twice."

Joanna was confused. Twice?

"That is another story I will tell another time. It will all make sense, I hope, in the end."

"And so you became Joanna. Then Constance came, and we named her after my mother, whom I loved dearly. I will tell you many stories about what a wonderful woman she was. When Pauline was born was born I really thought she was a boy," Jobeth chuckled. "I'll be honest-really thought all you girls were going to be boys. I wanted a son to name after your father and mine. So when I had another girl, I named her after my little brother, who died after falling out of a tree. His name was Paul, but I called him Pauli. He was a fun, mischievous boy my parents and I adored."

"That's the name you said to Jena," Joanna whispered, hugging Jena to her side, everything falling into place.

"Yes, it is," Jobeth said to the silent child. The little girl stood transfixed by her grandmother's words." My little brother has been reborn in this child's face. I swear," Jobeth said, more to herself than to those around her.

— Chapter 39 —

"Where have you been?" The ugly man hollered from the car. Pauline walked quickly and got in. She lit a cigarette from her purse and inhaled deeply.

"I told you, Pascal. I was with some of the family." She offered her opened package of smokes to the fuming man. He didn't take the peace offering, but continued to glare.

Pauline took another cigarette and lit it for the black-haired fellow. He took it roughly and smiled as he took a drag from the filter.

Pascal was, in short terms, a slimy little creep. But he was a popular, slimy little creep. He was the envy of all his friends. Every guy he knew wished they were him.

And the reason? It was not his good looks. He was five feet six inches tall with a thick build. His dark hair was slicked away from his pitted face with a large amount of Brylcream. He had sadistic gray eyes that centered in on his long beak of a nose. Pascal was not attractive. But he had one thing going for him: Pauline.

For some unfathomable reason, Pauline loved him. She not only loved Pascal, she adored him. And because she did, every male comrade he knew envied Pascal.

All of his friends would give their right arm to date the exquisite Pauline. She had the beauty of a goddess and the soul of an angel. She doted on Pascal without question or reason, in such a simplistic way that all the boys couldn't help but compare their girlfriends with her, which in turn made Pauline less popular with the girls. They despised her. They couldn't stand her splendor, her devotion, her seeming lack of awareness of how she affected people.

What everyone did know was how much Pauline worshipped Pascal. And because jealousy makes many people do crazy things, many silly girls spent the night in Pascal's bed not because they found him attractive or particularly likable, but because he was Pauline's boyfriend. And if they couldn't be Pauline, they could take the one person who meant something from her.

So Pascal's friends had many reasons to envy him. He had the most enchanting sweetheart on his arm and the pick of many women in his berth.

Pauline was totally unaware of it all.

Pascal put the car in gear and drove off at full speed, squealing the tires behind him. Pauline held onto the dashboard, her heart in her mouth. She hated the way Pascal drove but didn't dare tell him how she felt. She was afraid to anger him, which was quite an easy thing to do. She hated when people were angry with her, especially when it was Pascal.

Pascal drove for some time before Pauline noticed the car pull off onto a road headed toward a cliff. This was a favored place couples were known make out.

She glanced nervously toward the persistent driver. Anxiously she chewed on her nails--something she did whenever she was fearful.

It was getting harder and harder to stall Pascal. He was increasingly demanding when it came to being intimate. Pauline didn't know how she was going to delay him much longer.

Pascal pulled onto the cliff and turned off the engine. He had picked a secluded area away from any traffic that might happen to come by.

"Come here," he demanded, pulling Pauline close to him. She shivered in Pascal's arms. He leaned down on Pauline and started to kiss her roughly. She responded with little passion. His hand grabbed her right breast coarsely. As though hit by a bolt of lightening, she pulled sharply away.

"Pascal?" She lit up another cigarette, nervously. "When are we going to get married?" She avoided looking at the twenty-year-old man slouched hostilely beside her.

"Would you get off my back?" he sneered, pulling Pauline to him once again. She lifted her lit smoke up out of the way of his face and tried to pull back from him, unsuccessfully.

"I don't want to do these things before we are married." She yanked back, unable to break free of Pascal's tight grip. "I want to be your wife and feel our baby inside me." Pauline trembled.

"You damn well will!" Pascal laughed wickedly as he continued to caress Pauline's breast again.

"But when? You said when I turned eighteen we would get married. I'm eighteen and we aren't married yet," she said pathetically. She took another drag of her cigarette, hoping it would fend Pascal off.

Pauline might have been the girl every guy wanted, but she was the last to know it. Totally unaware of herself, she was a very lonely young woman.

Never one to have many friends, Pauline spent most of her time with her sisters, Constance and Joanna. When Joanna had run off with Chad, only Constance was left. It hadn't been long after Joanna left that Constance met and fell in love with George, leaving Pauline alone. Being the youngest daughter of four girls, Pauline was the last to get attention from anyone. And since she had never been an overly imaginative child or particularly intelligent, she fell short of consideration, an undemanding offspring lost in the shuffle of ever-requiring siblings.

But Pauline did have needs. She wanted and needed to feel love.
When Constance married George, Pauline was thrilled when George's younger brother, Pascal, asked her to dance.

They spent the evening together talking and dancing. Pauline had been on cloud nine. Never had anyone paid so much attention to her and only her. Pascal seemed enthralled in her every word, just as she was with him. It didn't take long for Pauline to fall madly in love. All it took was a little attention and Pauline was a girl who craved attention. It didn't matter how Pascal looked, it only mattered that he had been the first to show interest in her.

In the beginning he had been charming. He couldn't fathom how such a beautiful girl like Pauline would ever be interested in him. He'd never been popular with girls, so he too was captivated by the romance he shared with her. Then outside attention started. The moment Pascal was linked to Pauline, his reputation grew. Suddenly he was the man to be seen with. Girls flocked to him like flies. He was The Man and he loved it. He was too blown up with self-importance to realize that his sudden fame was credited to Pauline and not to his unbecoming personality. But it didn't matter. By that point Pascal's true self had surfaced and Pauline was already too entangled in his web to do anything about it. She was too afraid of going against Pascal for fear of losing him and being alone again. At least with Pascal, there was someone in her life and that seemed to make putting up with the cruel behavior worth it.

"Don't pressure me Pauline or else I will end it all together," Pascal threatened while nuzzling on Pauline's breast.

Fear gripped her for two reasons: for the fact that he handled her clothed body so obscenely and for the possibility of losing him.

Pascal noticed Pauline's frightened expression. Threatening their relationship always worked to shut her up. He leered at Pauline's frightened face.

"Hey, I would never leave you." He had a wicked look in his icy gray eyes.

Pauline seemed to shrivel up inside. Why did he make her feel so small? Was this the way she was supposed to feel with the man she loved?

"Do you mean it?" she barely squeaked out, her back pressed firmly against the door of the car. Pascal began to kiss her neck hungrily.

"Of course, baby," he said, sucking in her essence. He had to admit he did desire Pauline, even if he found her a bit tiresome. It would be so much easier to dump her off at home and drop by one of his many stand-by girls. They always seemed ready to romp turbulently into his grasp. But they were easy to sack. Pauline was a challenge and a virgin. There was a strong appeal to being a girl's first. The first to break ground, so to speak.

Yes, that was enough of a reason to stay plastered to Pauline's stiff body. He did plan on marrying her, eventually. He would be crazy not to. Every guy he knew wanted Pauline and that was power too. He would be the first and only man to possess her.

"Oh, Pascal!" Pauline cried, relieved, hugging him to her.

"Unless--" he interrupted, digging his fingers into her arms painfully, "you don't give me what I want."

She pulled away, knowing all to well what he wanted.

"I told you I don't want to do that until our honeymoon," Pauline sobbed. Did she really even want to do it then? She snubbed out her cigarette that had burned down to the butt in the car ashtray.

"You know what happened to Mara-Joy and Joanna. I don't want that! I want it to happen like it did with Constance--like it's supposed to happen."

She pulled away from Pascal and began to chew on her ruined nails, gazing out the front window.

"Christ, Pauline!" Pascal flopped back in his seat, slamming his hands on the steering wheel. Pauline began to turn white as a ghost, terrorized. "Constance was no damn virgin when she married George. Do you honestly think my brother would buy the cow without tasting the milk first? Damn it, Pauline, you are more stupid than I thought."

Pauline winced as his words stung her. He always seemed disappointed in her. She never pleased anyone.

"Listen, if you really loved me, you would want to share yourself with me. Show me that you love me," Pascal's voice softened, but his gray eyes remained cold.

Something inside Pauline tightened with fear. Who was this man claiming his love for her? She turned away and glanced out the window. A tear fell down her cheek and she quickly brushed it away with her fingertips. She didn't want Pascal to see her cry. He would just ridicule her more.

"Hey," Pascal confided. A warm hand was placed on Pauline's tense shoulder.

She involuntarily shivered hoping that there was something of the old Pascal she had first met in that touch. She turned and looked into his gleaming face. He looked calmer.

"We'll be married by Christmas if you let me make love to you," he cooed, slowly caressing her shoulders. Pauline began to weaken to his touch, melting like snow under his warm hands.

"You promise? By Christmas I will be your wife?" She closed her eyes. Everything would be all right after they were married. He would be the same Pascal she had first met, sweet and caring. Things would be different when she was his wife. She knew it. It had to be so.

Pascal kissed Pauline's neck as he began to unbutton her blouse. She lay stiff and unmoving and began to sob, unable to control herself. She didn't know how to stop him. She wanted to wait until they were married, but she didn't want to lose him by refusing his persistent urges.

He released a shuddering breast and gasped. This was the farthest he had ever gotten with Pauline before. Flustered, Pauline continued to cry louder in utter trauma. She didn't want to do this. Her embarrassment screamed red in her face and she closed her eyes tight against her humiliation.

"That's my girl." Pascal cupped her breasts aggressively between his palms, admiring the silky feel of them between his fingers. He bent down and inhaled their milky scent. "By Christmas, darling, we will be married."

Pauline didn't feel better for his promise. She just felt more scandalized and continued to clamor louder.

"Stop your crying! For the love of Jude, Pauline, you sure know how to ruin a mood." Pascal sat up. His face was flushed with excitement. He jumped into the back seat and pulled Pauline roughly back with him.

"You are hurting me!" Pauline whined, trying to sit up and cover her naked front. Pascal's hands were all over her, quickly undoing her skirt and the rest of her blouse.

He grabbed Pauline's wrists and swung her onto her back, pressing her firmly onto the back seat. Savagely he began to kiss her face, her shoulders and her bare chest. His one hand held her wrists pinned above her head, while his other hand worked on removing his own clothing.

Unclothed from the waist down he began to remove Pauline's panties.

"Pascal, please no!" Pauline cried out as he pressed firmly on top of her. She could feel his ridged excitement steadily approaching and couldn't stand it.

"Listen, Pauline!" Pascal forced himself to speak through clenched teeth as he grabbed her by the bare shoulders, lifting her up to face him. Her head sagged back, weakly, as she cried out louder. "If you love me, you will do this."

He dropped her abruptly and without feeling. She landed with a thump, banging the back of her head violently on the door handle.

Pascal chuckled, unable to compose himself. The sight of Pauline breasts jiggling as she landed on the car door was too much for his thrilled mind to contend with. He had to have her and he had to have her now.

"You say you love me, but how do I know it is true?" he breathed lustfully into Pauline's blanched face. "You want me to marry you but you give me nothing in return. Do you love me, Pauline? Do you? Because I feel you need to show me to make me believe it's true."

"Please don't make me do this, Pascal," she cried unable to move, she was so frightened. She felt bruised and defeated, both mentally and physically.

"Do you love me?" He demanded again, forcefully, pressing his aroused weight on her.

"Yesss!" she wailed, body shaking with emotion. "I do love you."

"Good, then you will do this," Pascal said directly, leaning down onto Pauline's exposed body, crushing her with all his mass. She bit firmly on her lip and closed her eyes tight, praying for it to be over, quickly.

At least they would be married by Christmas.

— Chapter 40 —

"Bye, babe," Pascal waved after Pauline as she hopped out of the car and ran up the stairs to her house. "Call yah later," he said, humming the wedding song to himself. He smiled and put the car in gear.

Pauline didn't stop to respond to him. She couldn't stomach to look at Pascal at that moment. All she wanted to do was run and hide away in her room for the rest of her life.

What Pascal had done to her was horrifying. She couldn't stand the thought of it happening again, and would never understand how anyone could enjoy what she had just done.

Pauline reached the front door and paused with her hand on the doorknob. Taking a deep breath, she straightened out her clothing and adjusted her ponytail. Strands of her golden hair had come loose in disarray around her pallid complexion. She self-consciously stuffed the loose strands back into the bundle of hair secured in the back of her head.

She must look normal.

Turning the knob of the door hesitantly, she walked into the warm kitchen of her parents' house. The smell of coffee filtered through her nostrils as she looked around the large room in disbelief.

There, sitting at the table with Jobeth and Alan, were Chad and Joanna.

They were plainly in a deep discussion, looking as though they always sat together and had coffee as a family. As if the last seven years had never happened and Joanna had never run away and been abandoned by her family.

"Close your mouth, Pauline, before you catch some flies," Joanna chuckled, lifting her mug of coffee to her ruby lips.

"I...I don't understand . . . " Pauline said, mystified. She didn't move a muscle. What was going to happen next in this crazy day? Would Mara-Joy and Alan-Michael show up and ask to play cards with them all?

"Sit down, Pauline. You look terrible." Jobeth stood up and pulled out a chair for her daughter to sit down. She went to the counter and got a cup of coffee. Placing it in front of the colorless girl, she sat back down in her own chair and looked at the astounded creature, sternly.

"What on earth has happened to you?" Jobeth asked, the palm of her hand holding up her chin. She looked across at her daughter, concerned.

"Nothing." Pauline lowered her eyes and began to sip her hot beverage.

"You look a fright," Jobeth continued eyeing her child suspiciously.

Pauline turned to Joanna and smiled warmly, trying to avoid her mother's intense scrutiny. Something had transpired between mother and daughter and she wanted to wash away the memory of Pascal on top of her and focus on the matter at hand. Besides, if her mother interrogated her further, Pauline was afraid she would break down and expose the horrible truth about what had happened that evening.

"What is going on here?" she asked, forcing a surprised smile. "Ma and I made up." Joanna placed a warm hand over Pauline's cool trembling one. Unconsciously, Pauline pulled away, not wanting anyone to touch her.

Joanna paused, slightly put off by Pauline's behavior, but when she looked into her young sister's eyes she could see how happy she was for Joanna, and something else, something she couldn't read.

"That is the most wonderful news I could hope to hear," Pauline said in all honesty. She looked to Alan, who sat beaming with pride across the table from her.

"Yes, it is. Yes, it is," he said, shaking his head in disbelief. "Your mother and sister are back on the right track with each other."

"I am so glad," Pauline said, standing up painfully. The full impact of what had happened earlier was starting to course miserably through her. She just wanted to have a hot bath and curl up in bed alone. "But if you don't mind," she looked around at the people staring at her, avoiding Jobeth's eyes, "I think I'll head off to bed. I don't seem to be feeling all that great."

"What is it, dear?" Alan asked, about to stand up. Pauline raised her hand to stop him.

"It's nothing, Dad. I'm just a little under the weather. Please excuse my bad behavior. Just be assured that this is the best news I could have heard. Continue catching up. It has been a long time and you need this time alone. Enjoy."

Pauline then stood and walked out the door. They could hear her ascending the stairs to the washroom. Soon after, the sound of water running came from behind the closed door.

"I should see what is wrong with her." Jobeth said, standing. Joanna reached out a restraining hand and placed it on Jobeth's arm.

"Ma, I think she just wants to be left alone," Joanna said. There was something in the way Pauline looked that spoke to every inch of Joanna's marrow, saying, "Let her be for the moment."

"Leave her alone?" Jobeth sputtered. "I have left that girl alone one too many times. I think maybe it is time I stepped in and found out what is going on in my children's lives."

"I'm not disagreeing with you, Ma. It's just . . . something tells me Pauline isn't ready for a confrontation just yet." Joanna listened to the sounds of the shower running and felt certain that something had happened to her little sister. But what?

Alan cleared his throat.

"I hope it has nothing to do with that rascal," he said with bitterness in his voice.

Joanna looked to her father whose face showed the distaste he felt for Pascal. He wasn't one to voice his opinion when it came to his children. He was one who always let them make their own choices in life, good or bad.

"You mean Constance's brother-in-law? George's brother?" she asked, a little surprised.

"The very one," Alan spat out. "I don't like the devil. Not one bit. The thought of my sweet Pauline with that troll of a man sickens me." He took a deep gulp from his mug and slammed the cup down onto the wooden table, causing both Joanna and Jobeth to jump.

"Pauline talks quite highly of him, Pa," Joanna said, trying to defend her sister's choice in a mate. Apparently much had changed in the time she had been away. Alan was not a man to say such things about other people. He was the type of man who liked almost everyone. Then again, he hadn't liked Chad once either, but he had had good reason.

"Pauline, bless her angelic soul," Alan sighed, "is not always the quickest draw."

"Alan!" Jobeth reached out and gently slapped his arm. "How could you say such a thing?"

"It's true, Jobeth, and you know it," he looked from Jobeth to Joanna to Chad. "Don't get me wrong, she is the sweetest girl . . . a special child . . ." He looked to Joanna, apologetically. "I have never played favorites with you children. I love you all equally, but Pauline is the one child out of all of you who has never asked for anything. Never demanded anything of us, and has gone unnoticed the most."

"Pa--" Joanna began, ashamed. She had demanded her mother's attention and when she didn't get it, she turned their lives upside down. Even though she and Chad were deeply in love with each other, it had all begun because Joanna wanted to hurt Mara-Joy for all the affection she got from their mother.

"No, listen, Joanna. It's time I said my piece. Mara-Joy has always been a large focus in this family and now you know the reasons why. She brought your mother and me together when we wanted to be together but were afraid. You came along and you were our first birth child. There was always a rivalry between you and Mara-Joy since the day you were born. I saw it right away when the two of you were little girls and it was not always one-sided. I have to say a lot of it was two-sided. You two girls were always trying to hurt one another and it was exhausting on the rest of the family. Your mother defended Mara-Joy and I defended you.

"When Constance was born, she was our third child and also a girl, but not just any girl, she was a genius. So smart was that child, she could have been anything." Alan looked a little misty-eyed as he thought of Constance.

"She is something, Alan," Jobeth said. Joanna could feel that this was a conversation Jobeth and Alan often had.

"She's not what she could have been. She wasted all that talent, all that brain--" Alan's neck began to turn red under his collar. He twisted his head trying to compose himself.

She is a wife and mother. There is no shame in that." Jobeth said softly, her eyes lovingly caressing Alan's temper.

"But she could have been more."

"Could have, should have. We have a beautiful grandson and another grandchild on the way." Jobeth touched Alan's arm. He nodded and placed a hand on hers, giving it a light squeeze.

"No point in looking at what could have been," he said.

"That's right." Jobeth replied, proud of how Alan kept his disappointment at bay.

"Anyway," Alan said, looking back to Joanna and Chad. "When we had our fourth child and she too was a girl, well," Alan smiled to himself, "I could have had a dozen girls and it wouldn't have bothered me. All you children were such a blessing. Never in my wildest dreams as a child did I imagine having Jobeth as a wife and wonderful children of my own. My childhood was so terrible; I just wanted my children to have all the joys in life I had been deprived of."

"You did do that, Papa," Joanna said, full of emotion. How she loved this big strong man sitting across from her. He was the first man she had ever loved and she would always love him. "You were the best father a girl could ask for."

"Well, I don't know about that. When Pauline was born, you other children were so," he tried to think of the right words to express himself with, "full of piss and vinegar."

Joanna and Chad suppressed chuckles.

"That much is very true," Jobeth said, standing up and fetching the coffee pot. "The three of you were quite the handful. We weren't prepared for it one bit. Our only experience with girls was Shawna and she was so grateful for a normal childhood she never gave us any trouble. So we were unprepared for you girls." Jobeth couldn't help but laugh quietly to herself, remembering her years with Shawna and later with the other children.

"Yes. You and Mara-Joy were always up to something." Alan continued, "Usually trying to demolish each other someway or another. Constance was always busy studying things . . . everything. We always had to help her out of messes she'd somehow gotten herself into while exploring. But Pauline, we never had any problems with her. She just went with the flow, trying not to get in the way. She was mild-mannered and easy-going.

"It took nothing to please her, because she expected nothing in the first place. She knew all the attention was needed on her older sisters and she didn't care. How could she, she didn't even realize she was supposed to be jealous of the three of you. When Alan-Michael was born, she lost the position of being the baby of the family. She was the second-to-last child in a household filled with all girls except one, the child born after her.

"Even this, having a baby brother after so many girls, didn't seem to faze Pauline. She was too innocent and tender-hearted to get filled up with jealousy over any of you children."

Joanna cleared her throat and shifted her eyes uncomfortably.

"What are you trying to say, Pa?"

Alan looked at his daughter and shook his head.

"Any one of us would have felt left out if we were her, but she didn't. Why is that?"

"I don't know," Joanna responded, feeling a little guilty. She hadn't realized how self-absorbed she was growing up. How her and Mara-Joy's bickering had affected everyone in the house beside herself.

"I do," Alan announced, placing his hands firmly on the table. "She is a rare and pure creature. She isn't jealous or envious because she doesn't know how to be. She only knows how to love--and love she does, openly and honestly. She wasn't envious of you children because she loved all of you and to be jealous would have been to be negative towards the ones she cared for. She doesn't know how to do that. She can't do that. I love Pauline, but she has the mind of an innocent child and she always will. I'm afraid that naiveté will be fully exploited by that cad Pascal."

"How so, Pa?" Joanna asked, feeling slightly ashamed. She didn't have the same abandonment of self that Pauline did.

"I'm afraid she'll respond to that bastard from her heart because her mind doesn't know any better."

— Chapter 41 —

Gone were the old days when a baby was born in its parents' home. Erica, Constance's new daughter, was born in a hospital while her father and the rest of the family lingered anxiously in a waiting room.

Joanna sat with Pauline, playing cards. Chad stayed home with the children. They had just purchased a nice home by the lake, close to Chad's parents, and he was busy setting up the house for them.

Jobeth sat with Alan, lounging and idly talking.

George sat quietly alone, biting his nails, worrying about Constance and the baby. Little Patrick played with toy cars solemnly by his father's feet.

No one noticed the storm moving toward them.

No one saw the dark-haired inferno charging forward, followed by her young companion.

"Well, well," Mara-Joy announced, standing with hands on her hips. She was dressed in a blood-red dress that accentuated her curvy figure. A black mink coat was draped casually over her shoulders. She inhaled from the cigarette in her hand.

"Is this a private party or can any family member join?" she queried rather smugly.

Alan-Michael slouched beside her. When she began to speak, he straightened his shoulders proudly. She was such a woman of substance. Every time he was near her, he felt empowered.

"Mara-Joy." Jobeth stood up, smiled and went to her daughter. She hugged her, kissing Mara-Joy's cool cheek. "I am so glad you are here. You too, Mikey."

Joanna and Pauline put down her cards as they both looked to Mara-Joy and Alan-Michael.

Joanna hadn't seen Mara-Joy since that eventful day seven years before.

She hadn't changed much. She was still beautiful, if not a little older looking, and very distinguished. By the looks of her attire, Mara-Joy was doing extremely well for herself.

Unconsciously, Joanna looked down at her simple dress. She couldn't help but feel dowdy in front of the glamorous Mara-Joy. Ashamed at herself for feeling that way, she sat up straight.

This envy she had for Mara-Joy had to stop. It was the reason the two had torn their family apart for the last seven years and more. She wasn't going to have it anymore. Especially when they were all here for Constance and her new baby.

Joanna could feel Mara-Joy's eyes glaring at her and looked her straight in the eyes. She had forgotten how blue Mara-Joy's eyes were and shivered involuntarily.

"Well, look who is here, Alan-Michael," Mara-Joy said, eyes blazing with hate. "If it isn't our traitor sister come back from the dead."

Alan-Michael began to laugh like a weasel. Mara-Joy cracked him up--the things she would come up with.

Joanna stood up, her hands clutched tightly to her side.

"Mara-Joy," she said, "it's good to see you."

"Hmph!" Mara-Joy said, turning away. "Where is my husband?" She swung venomously back around to Joanna. "I mean 'ex-husband' since you stole him from me."

Joanna pulled back as though she had been physically struck. It was plain to see by Mara-Joy's reaction that she was still very angry. Seven years hadn't dampened her resentment.

"That will be enough, Mara-Joy!" Alan stood up and went to his eldest daughter. He stood defensively between Joanna and Mara-Joy, feeling the heat of bitterness between them.

"We are here for Constance and the child she is having right now. You two will have to settle your differences another time. It won't be here while I am waiting for my grandchild to be born." Alan was red with fury. "I won't have this wonderful day ruined by the two of you and this continually senseless bickering."

"Mama?" Mara-Joy wheeled to Jobeth for help, her black mink nearly falling from her shoulders.

Jobeth stood firmly beside Alan.

"I agree with your father. This is a day for Constance. The two of you will have to deal with each other another time. It will not be today," she said dryly.

"This family has gone nuts!" Mara-Joy said, throwing her arms into the air.

"Come and sit with me while we wait," Jobeth said, taking Mara-Joy's mink clad arm. "The doctor said that it shouldn't be much longer."

Mara-Joy followed Jobeth to the waiting seats and plunked herself down beside her mother.

"I am here on behalf of my sister's child," Mara-Joy replied, taking out a decorated box from a bag she carried. It was beautifully wrapped with an elaborate gold bow on the top.

She looked over toward Joanna who was sitting back down with Pauline. They were eyeing Mara-Joy and Jobeth with caution.

"I have always been here for Constance's children. I am their auntie. Since I have been robbed of any children of my own, I have always tried to be the doting aunt." Mara-Joy dabbed the corner of her eye with a silk hanky from her black beaded purse.

Jobeth patted Mara-Joy's knee comfortingly.

"You have always been a wonderful aunt to Patrick."

Joanna watched Mara-Joy's performance and cringed.

She hadn't changed. Not at all. A shiver ran up her spine as she recalled the last words Mara-Joy had said to her all those years ago.

Revenge. She promised to make Joanna pay.

Joanna suddenly felt afraid and she couldn't understand why.

"Larry!" Mara-Joy howled from her bedroom later that night.

Constance had given birth to her daughter, Erica. Mara-Joy had seen mother and child and deposited her gift. She left, taking Alan-Michael with her. As usual, he clung to her like a leech. She disposed of him at his home after sobbing on his youthful shoulder about how unfair it was that Joanna had turned the family against her. The nerve Joanna had, showing up at the birth of Constance's child. Was it not enough that she had stolen her husband and bore the children that should have been hers? She had to go and flaunt herself in front of Mara-Joy too?

Alan-Michael had been sympathetic as always. How could he not? He was so obsessed with her he couldn't breathe without her permission.

Mara-Joy had shaken uncontrollably in Alan-Michael's arms, clutching him tightly around his muscular waist, her face buried in his lean chest. For a boy of sixteen, he was built quite nicely. Mara-Joy felt very secure in his strong young arms. Too secure for a sister to be in her juvenile brother's presence. She seemed unable to control herself around him.

It was so easy to get him going. To stir his teenage arousals. All she had to do was lean on him a certain way or brush up against him and he would tremble under her touch. Sometimes all it took was a breath on him as she fed him words of hatred about Joanna.

It was too easy. And yet she didn't stop herself from doing it even though she knew she should. Alan-Michael was her brother, but the thought of the young girls who eyed him whenever they were out together made Mara-Joy more feverish in her seduction of him, brother or not. She loved the fact that he adored her, his sister, over any other green, adolescent girl.

When she left him earlier, breathless and hot, she had felt a little over-heated herself. She wouldn't do anything morally wrong, in her opinion, with Alan-Michael. She only teased him with her movements and words, enticing him.

It worked. She felt her effect on him as she pressed up against his body to hug Alan-Michael good-bye that evening.

"Good night, dear brother," she had said breathlessly into his ear as she pressed her full weight against him. "Thank you for being the only one I can trust in this family . . . this world." She pulled back from his embrace.

Alan-Michael was flushed with emotion. Mara-Joy wasn't aware just how much she affected him. Each time he was near her, he had to restrain himself from tearing her clothes off and forcefully plunging himself into her. It was starting to scare him. He didn't know how much longer he could control himself. Alan-Michael had taken to bedding girls who looked like Mara-Joy. Girls who easily came to him. He had that attraction with women. He was handsome and looked older than he was. The problem was once they were with Alan-Michael, they wanted to run away.

He was a brute and used them roughly and savagely. When he was done, he would lie in their arms crying like a baby, begging for forgiveness.

The women he bedded didn't know the demons Alan-Michael struggled with. The shame that dug at his heart. How could he tell them that when he lay with them he thought of Mara-Joy? What would they think if they knew? They would be appalled and disgusted. What kind of man, even a boy about to be a man, could lust for his own sister?

"I will always be there for you, Mara-Joy," Alan-Michael said huskily into her black curly hair.

Mara-Joy looked straight through Alan-Michael with her piercing blue eyes.

"You will, won't you?" she whispered, a little shaken by just how devoted Alan-Michael was to her. It surprised even her on occasion.

"Always and forever."

"Good night, Alan-Michael," Mara-Joy brushed a kiss onto his hot cheek. "I'll call you tomorrow."

He nodded and walked toward the house. Mara-Joy felt aroused with power and pressed on the gas, hurrying to get home.

"Larry!" Mara-Joy yelled once again from the bedroom.

Larry, Mara-Joy's older and slightly rounded, definitely balding husband, bustled quickly into the bedroom.

He gasped. Mara-Joy lay sprawled across their marital bed, naked.

"Yes, my love?" his voice quivered. He was a powerful businessman who was jelly in his wife's beautiful hands. She looked fantastic, arranged on the bed, exotic and enticing.

"Are Ann and Bobby-Jo out?" she purred, touching her breast slightly.

Larry swallowed hard, his mouth watering in anticipation.

"No . . . I mean, yes." This was the reason he left his wife of eighteen years. This creature stretched out like a lioness on the bed, waiting for him. He wasn't crazy. Larry knew a ravishing creature such as Mara-Joy didn't marry a man like him for his looks. It was for his money. He knew it and he didn't care. He looked upon Mara-Joy with unconstrained desire. How else could a man like him have the pleasure of a woman like her without a very deep wallet? He was just glad he had a substantial purse, because it had left him a winner. The prize was the naked goddess waiting for him on the bed.

"Good," Mara-Joy cooed as she crawled across the bed. She reached out and pulled the plump man to the edge. "Will they be back soon?" she asked, undoing his pants slowly and with skill, her long red nails slightly raking against his groin.

"No," Larry choked, touching the top of Mara-Joy's curly head. His heart began to race as her fingers curled inside his zipper. He closed his eyes and rolled his round head back on his shoulders. He would do anything for her, risk anything for this exquisite animal. For that was what she had to be, an animal. She'd been able to make him do things he would never have thought he could have done for anyone.

The men who worked for Larry feared him. His enemies cowered from his sight. He was no wimp, but the mere bat of her blue eyes unglued Larry to the very core of his being.

"Make love to me, Larry," Mara-Joy mumbled, lying back on the bed, legs spread vulgarly out.

Larry pounced on her like a cat on a mouse, quickly discarding his clothing in his wake.

"Mara-Joy! Mara-Joy!" he cried out as he grunted on top of her naked form.

Mara-Joy wrapped her legs around his broad waist and bit into Larry's neck savagely.

"Harder, you fool!" she shrieked out pushing herself onto him. The events of the evening had been too much for Mara-Joy. The power she held over Alan-Michael's body saturated her, filling her with sexual desire that needed to be unleashed. It didn't matter with whom. That had never been an issue with Mara-Joy. All that mattered was that she was desired over anyone and that those who yearned for her would do anything to have her.

This had always been Mara-Joy's aphrodisiac and there had always been plenty of men to comply. Such men like Larry who lay withering underneath her thrashing body.

Most of the time he repulsed Mara-Joy. He was fat and not very attractive. But she knew he would do anything to touch her; and that, cradled with the fact that he was one of the richest men in town, was enough for her to scream out in pure delight when she coupled with him.

They fought furiously, pounding on each other like wild beasts, until they were both spent with satisfaction and lay breathless and sweaty next to one another, gasping deeply.

Larry pinched Mara-Joy's nipple between his fingers, wondering if he could muster another round with her.

Mara-Joy, agitated, pushed his hand away from her body. She raised herself onto her elbow and glared down at Larry. His naked stomach protruded out like an extended balloon. She squinted at the sight.

"Why can't I get pregnant? I want a baby! It is just unfair. I should be able to have a child of my own too," she cried out, suddenly without warning.

Larry placed a hand on her bare arm and rubbed gently to calm Mara-Joy. He knew the anguish she felt. It was the one thing Mara-Joy couldn't hide about herself: the desire to have a child of her own. Larry had offered adoption as a solution. He would do anything to keep Mara-Joy happy in her marriage to him. But she had refused. She wanted a child that grew in her. A child she could birth, not another woman's child.

Larry had been surprised at Mara-Joy's reaction to adoption, since she had been forthright with the fact that she had been adopted. Her only response to the situation was that her parents were extraordinary people and would accept any child thrust upon them. She, on the other hand, was not that type of person.

Larry had to concur. Mara-Joy never warmed to his own daughters, Ann and Bobby-Jo. Fortunately, the teenage girls lived with their mother, and weren't regularly exposed to Mara-Joy and how they annoyed her. On the other hand, they were teenagers, maybe what Mara-Joy needed was a baby who hadn't already been exposed to other parents.

"We could adopt," Larry braved, trying to console his young wife. He couldn't careless if he had another child. Ann and Bobby-Jo were plenty for him. They were nice girls--he loved them but let their mother raise them. Even when their mother and he had been married, that had been her sole job. He believed that the part of parenting rested with the women of the family. The men did the providing and the women the nurturing. So if Mara-Joy wanted a baby, he would provide for the child as he did with his other children. He had the money--that was not a problem. He would do it if it made Mara-Joy happy.

It was not that he did this begrudgingly. He really didn't know any different way to do things. This had been the way he had been raised and the way every person he knew had been raised. It was a fact of life to Larry that was quite comfortable for him.

"I don't want to adopt," Mara-Joy said, sitting up and pulling on her silk nightgown. Her tousled hair stood up on end and she flattened it down with the palms of her hand.

"Don't you want a child that is yours and mine, Larry? Not Ann and Bobby-Jo, they are not mine. But a child that is ours. A son perhaps, one who could one day follow in your footsteps?" Mara-Joy leaned over the mound of flesh and looked into Larry's brown eyes. Her blue orbs seemed to look deep into Larry's soul.

"Wouldn't that be nice, Larry? A little Lawrence Junior."

"That would be nice," Larry said breathlessly. Suddenly he was wondering why he had never thought of having a son of his own before. Was he crazy? It would be wonderful to have a son with Mara-Joy to follow in his old man's footsteps and one day take over the business. Ann and Bobby-Jo were girls. He had always assumed their future husbands would join his side in business. But a son! That would be different. It would be a child of his flesh and blood. His seed. His creation with Mara-Joy.

"That would be very nice, my dear," he said, suddenly wanting it more than ever.

"Well, you have connections. We have money." Mara-Joy smiled as her finger circled the hair on his flabby chest. "You could make it happen, baby. You could do this for me," she said demurely as though it were all Larry's idea.

"I could make some calls, my dear," Larry said, basking in Mara-Joy's attention. "In the morning I'll be right on it."

"Larry, you are so wonderful." Mara-Joy jumped on top of the startled Larry, who grasped her firmly in his arms.

She kissed him passionately on the lips stirring Larry up again."

You will do this for me, Larry? You promise to do this for me?" she asked, removing her slinky nightie, exposing her perky, full breasts.

Larry grabbed one hungrily.

"I promise. I will do it. Anything."

Joanna stood up from the vanity table and put down her brush. Chad sat in bed, reading, and looked up when his wife sat down beside him, pulling up the blankets.

"Busy day?" Chad asked, closing the book he held. He placed it on the nightstand and turned his attention to Joanna.

She looked preoccupied with something.

"Umph," she mumbled, not really paying attention to him.

"At least we're all moved in now," Chad said, trying to rouse his wife's attention.

"What's that?" Joanna asked, absently turning to Chad's handsome face.

"Where are you?" Chad asked sitting up. "You seem a mile away."

"I suppose I am," Joanna said, sitting up straight too. "Do you ever feel like we were wrong for what we did to Mara-Joy? Selfish?

Chad wrinkled his forehead.

"What is this all about Joanna? Did something happen today at the hospital?"

"Yes. I saw her. Mara-Joy." She lowered her head, letting her hair fall into her face. She didn't know it, but this was a habit she inherited from her mother, when she felt like hiding from the world.

"Oh brother, what did she say?" Chad asked, rolling his eyes. He could just imagine what his darling ex-wife had to say. He hadn't seen Mara-Joy in years, but could visualize what had taken place between her and Joanna.

"She is definitely still bitter about everything that has happened," Joanna said, tucking her hair behind her ears. "She blames me for her inability to have children."

"That is ridiculous," Chad steamed. "How could she blame you? She can't have children because of what the miscarriage did to her."

"What did it do to her, Chad?" Joanna turned to her husband, "I have never been clear on that. How is it that she has a miscarriage and can never have children?"

"Joanna, why does it matter?" Chad asked, "It just brings up the past. A past I would like to forget."

"Why, because it hurts?" she asked, grimacing.

"Yes, it hurts." Chad looked at Joanna face turning crimson. "Why are you doing this?"

"I need to know Chad. We have never really discussed this before. We have never discussed your marriage to Mara-Joy," Joanna said, quietly. It had been a subject she had avoided because it hurt her too much to talk about it.

"Why do you need to know?" he demanded, tight-lipped.

"I need to feel like I am not to blame for Mara-Joy's marriage ending. I need to know that there was no marriage before I entered the picture," Joanna begged, "Do you understand what I am saying, Chad? I need to know that I didn't steal you away from my sister."

"That is something you will never have to worry about, Joanna," Chad sighed, resigned that he would have to discuss this painful part of his life. He lay back in bed searching the ceiling for answers.

"Mara-Joy and I were married in name only," he said, blocking out the images of he and Mara-Joy entangled in a naked frenzy of lovemaking. "We married because she was pregnant. End of story."

Chad turned away, not wanting Joanna to see more in his eyes. He loved Joanna and didn't need to hurt her with all the facts of his life with Mara-Joy. She didn't need to know how Mara-Joy had controlled him with her sexual powers of persuasion. She didn't need to know how he caved under Mara-Joy time and time again, just because she let him touch her. Chad couldn't handle Joanna knowing what kind of a coward he had been living with Mara-Joy. How he bent to her every whim. It would kill her.

He closed his eyes, ashamed. After all these years he still felt disgusted over his behavior.

"Did you leave her because I was pregnant with Jena and you knew Mara-Joy could never give you children?" Joanna had always wondered this but had been afraid to ask. She and Chad had been so happy over the years she didn't wanted to think about the possibility that she could have been the cause of Mara-Joy and Chad's divorce.

"What? *No*!" Chad reached out from the bed and grabbed Joanna by the arms, pulling her and clutching her to his chest. "You crazy fool," he said, kissing her forehead. It felt cool and smooth.

"Don't you know how much I love you, you little nut? Mara-Joy and I were headed for divorce no matter what would have happened between you and me. I didn't love her," Chad said truthfully. He may have lusted after her, but he knew he had never loved Mara-Joy. He never really liked her. He snuggled Joanna tightly to him, loving the feel of her in his arms.

"I fell in love with you, Joanna. I needed to be with you. Jena and Charles were just extra bonuses thrown into the bargain. If you never had children, I still would have loved you and been with you."

"What if I never had shown up on your doorstep that one night? What then? Would you still be married to Mara-Joy?" Joanna asked bravely, cradled in Chad's arm.

"Joanna, I can't say what would have happened, but I know one thing. I was unhappily married to her and that was before you came and changed my life, making it worth living again."

"I can't help but feel that I deserve some of Mara-Joy's fury against me. I did take what was technically hers."

Chad lifted Joanna's face to his and looked into her eyes, the same eyes as his daughter's.

"You listen to me. I was never hers to take, do you understand? I was never hers." He touched Joanna lightly on the chest above her heart. "I was yours the moment I saw you at the wedding and you told me off. Remember that? You were just a kid and you had me already figured out," he chuckled.

Joanna smiled in spite of herself as she rested her head on his chest, listening to his rich laughter rumbling from deep inside.

"What is this all about anyway, Joanna?"

"It's just what she said to me today. She feels so strongly that I am to blame for your failed marriage and the lack of children you had together. Honestly, I did try to destroy her at one time Chad. The plan was to steal you from her," Joanna confided.

"Joanna," Chad tried to stop her from saying anymore, "it's water under the bridge now. You can't torture yourself with this nonsense anymore."

"I suppose you are right. She has gone on with her life."

"That's right," Chad said. "She has re-married. A fat cat, so I hear, and we have never been happier. All's well that ends well, etc., etc."

"You never did answer me," Joanna said, lying down in bed and fluffing her pillow.

"Answer you what?" Chad asked, arranging his own pillows.

"How is it that Mara-Joy can't have any more children?"

Chad thought for a moment before answering.

"I'm not sure about all the medical lingo," he said, remembering back to that dark time. "I just know that the baby was growing in the fallopian tube, the end of it or something."

"And?" Joanna asked, encouraging Chad to continue.

"It, the baby, caused the fallopian tube to burst, killing the baby and nearly killing her. She got some kind of infection." He paused, remembering how he and Mara-Joy had made love only days after the miscarriage had taken place. Could that have caused the infection? They had been told to abstain from any intercourse for at least six weeks.

He brushed the thought from his mind, refusing to accept responsibility.

"The infection caused some sort of blockage in the remaining fallopian tube. The doctor said it was pretty much entirely closed."

"Causing her never to be able to conceive a child," Joanna finished.

"That's right," Chad said, resting his head on the pillow. "He did say it was possible with the small opening, but he wasn't very optimistic. Besides the chance of the baby implanting in the remaining tube was too great of a risk."

He closed his eyes, wanting to erase the memories of how devastated Mara-Joy had truly been. "Is that it? Do you want anymore morbid information?"

"No," Joanna said softly, feeling pity for Mara-Joy. What had happened to her could easily have happened to Joanna or any woman. Joanna cherished her two children so dearly and couldn't picture life without them.

"Good. Besides, maybe it was a blessing in disguise. Think about it, Joanna. What kind of mother would Mara-Joy be?" Chad shivered, beside himself. He couldn't picture the woman he used to be married to being the mother of any child.

"Well, I guess we'll never know now, will we?" Joanna said, turning off the reading lamp on her bedside table. She lay still, eyes wide open, thinking about Mara-Joy and the child she would never have.

— Chapter 42 —

Pauline sat in the coffee shop, waiting for Pascal to arrive. Months had past since the night they had consummated their union. Now her worst fears had come.

She was pregnant and not married.

She sipped her coffee, lost in her own thoughts.

What had she done? What was she going to do now?

Christmas had come and gone and she still didn't have Pascal's ring on her finger. She didn't doubt he would marry her. She had come to realize that he would. He just liked to use that as leverage over her head, so she would perform his carnal acts with him.

The question was, did she still want to marry Pascal?

And the answer was that she wasn't so sure anymore. Over the last few months Pauline had seen a different side of Pascal, not that she hadn't seen this side for some time. It was just that for the first time she was allowing herself to realize that maybe this Pascal she was witnessing was the real one.

Pauline sighed and looked out the coffee shop window, wishing she had someone to talk to about this. But she didn't. Who would understand her trepidation over her relationship with Pascal?

Pascal was not blind to what was going on with Pauline. He was starting to notice her ambivalence toward him. When Pascal threatened to leave Pauline, she didn't seem to react the way she used to and this bothered him.

He had always taken comfort in the knowledge that Pauline adored him. This had been his power, his control over her. If her feelings for him changed, then he would be powerless and life as he knew it would end. He was no fool.

He knew that the only reason he was getting attention from other women was because he was Pauline's choice for a mate.

What Pauline didn't know was Pascal had been trying to get her pregnant. He wanted to get her pregnant so that she would be helpless again. He needed her to want him as her husband once more. He could sense that he might have pushed Pauline too far and her feelings were changing. If she were pregnant, she would have to beg him to marry her. Pascal would, of course. He wasn't going to risk losing his hold on her. Not now, not ever. In fact, he wanted to marry her soon, before Pauline got cold feet and ran. She would be his and he would never have to worry about it again.

Pauline stared blankly out the window, lost in thought. A thudding on the windowpane brought her back to reality with a jolt. She adjusted her eyes to the figure outside waving at her.

It was Mara-Joy and she looked surprisingly happy.

Pauline waved back, glad to see her older sister in such good spirits. Mara-Joy disappeared and reappeared inside the coffee shop.

The eyes of every man in the place turned toward the fur-clad woman as she breezed her way toward the delicate girl sitting alone in the corner.

"Pauline, darling!" Mara-Joy called out loudly. "Fancy meeting you here!"

Mara-Joy sat down in the seat across from Pauline, bringing with her the buoyant fragrance of her perfume. She lit up a cigarette and inhaled deeply before continuing to speak.

"Why do you look so glum?" Mara-Joy asked, blowing smoke out of her red painted lips. She began to shrug out of her black mink coat, intent to stay for a while.

Pauline looked around nervously, hoping Pascal wouldn't show up early.

She'd arrived beforehand to have time to think before facing him with her news. He didn't like Mara-Joy. He felt clumsy and awkward around her, and he hated to feel that way around anyone. So he wouldn't be happy if he arrived and saw Pauline having coffee with her sister.

"Do I?" Pauline whispered, trying to hide her emotions. Mara-Joy scrutinized her. She didn't miss a thing. Pauline was distressed about something and she intended to find out just what it was.

"Listen, Pauline, whatever it is, it can't be so bad. I know we have never been terribly close, but I am your sister and if I can help, I will." Mara-Joy inhaled, blowing smoke out of her mouth. It was an art the way she did it.

Pauline, mortified at herself, began to cry uncontrollably. Mara-Joy tensed and reached across the table grabbing onto the young woman's hand.

"There, there, Pauline. Is it all that bad?" Mara-Joy said trying to comfort her. She felt foolish with this outward display of emotion coming from Pauline. Constance and Joanna had always hidden their emotions, not unlike Mara-Joy herself. The three older sisters were similar in some ways. But here sat Pauline, the youngest of the lot, sobbing her heart out. Mara-Joy didn't know what to do. She was stunned.

"Is it that boy you've been seeing?" Mara-Joy said with a tone to her voice.

"Constance's brother-in-law?" she asked with distaste. Like Alan, she didn't care for the little weasel. Pauline was much too attractive to be with such a homely fellow with a bad attitude. Besides, Mara-Joy thought, he doesn't even have any money to compensate for his bad looks.

Pauline nodded, blowing her nose into the tissue Mara-Joy handed to her.

"Well, what has the little bastard done now?" Mara-Joy offered Pauline a smoke. Pauline shook her head and sat up straight. She was miserable and wanted to tell someone why. Mara-Joy was the first person that seemed to want to know what was going on in Pauline's life.

"I don't think I want to see him anymore," she said, trying to compose herself now that the words were finally spoken out loud.

Mara-Joy looked at Pauline in disbelief. This is why she sat there sobbing like a broken faucet? She wanted to break it off with that little troll?

"Well, break it off then," Mara-Joy said, stubbing out her cigarette in the tin ashtray. She motioned to a waitress to bring her a cup of coffee. "How awful is that, Pauline?"

Pauline began to cry again. Mara-Joy didn't know she was pregnant on top of it all. She didn't know that Pascal was not the sort of man you just broke it off with. It was just not that simple and she said so.

"How is it not so simple?" Mara-Joy asked before sipping the coffee the waitress had brought to her. She shooed the blonde girl away with her hand when she lingered, wanting to know if they needed anything more. Pauline blushed. She knew the waitress and was embarrassed by how Mara-Joy dismissed her like a servant.

"It's complicated," Pauline spoke softly, twirling her spoon in her cooling cup of coffee. How could she tell Mara-Joy the truth? It was too awful.

"Well, it seems to me you would be doing yourself a favor getting rid of that baggage. You know Pa can't stand the guy." Mara-Joy commented, looking around casually. The coffee shop was not a place she frequented. It amused her. She preferred restaurants of quality to the dinginess of a coffee shop. She would have passed by the shop completely if she hadn't noticed Pauline sitting inside stewing alone.

Pauline's head shot up. Her face crumpled with emotion.

"Dad doesn't like Pascal? Since when?" she asked, surprised. If she'd known this, she would never have started seeing Pascal in the first place. There was one thing about Pauline; she never went against her parents' wishes. Too many times they had been hurt by their children's decisions. Pauline didn't want to be one of them.

"Since always, Pauline. I thought you knew that," Mara-Joy said, surprised. Why was it that Pauline always seemed to be clueless to matters that were obvious to everyone else?

"No one can stand Pascal. He is beneath you and our family. I'm surprised you ever gave the creep the time of day." Mara-Joy said matter-of-factly.

"I never knew." Pauline said, dazed. "I always thought everyone approved."

Mara-Joy shrugged her shoulders.

"Well, maybe Constance at first. And that husband of hers. But the rest off us are still wondering what on earth you are doing with him." Mara-Joy looked up and was startled by the expression on Pauline's face.

"What?" she asked, "You can't be surprised by this information, can you? The guy has nothing to offer you. He is nasty to look at and has the personality of a slug. He gives me the creeps just thinking about him," Mara-Joy said, shivering for effect.

"You are much too good for the likes of that guy; I don't care if he is Constance's brother-in-law." She sipped her coffee again, totally unaware of the effects of her words on Pauline.

"You really think so?" Pauline asked, astonished. Mara-Joy had never shown such interest in her before. Let alone compliment her.

Mara-Joy rolled her eyes. Pauline was so eager to please and so easily pleased.

The kid would be eaten up by the likes of Pascal.

"Pauline, you could have any fellow you wanted. You are drop dead gorgeous!" Mara-Joy eyed Pauline as she flushed crimson red. "Much to my dismay," she added cocking her eyebrow. Pauline smiled shyly, drawing her shoulders inward.

"And," Mara-Joy paused, sighing deeply, "if you ever tell anyone I said this, I will kill you," she threatened bending in closer. "You are sweet. Men like that quality in a woman. Especially when they want a woman to share their life with."

"Mara-Joy--".

Mara-Joy raised her hand to silence Pauline.

"I'm not finished. What I am trying to say is, why waste your life on the likes of Pascal when you could have the pick of the litter?" Mara-Joy waved her hand around the coffee shop. "I happen to know that you are a much desired woman in your peer group. So much so that your little boyfriend gets more attention than he deserves simply by virtue of your acquaintance."

Pauline sat silently stunned. Every word stuck in her brain like a fly caught in a web. The only problem was now she was certain she didn't want to be with Pascal. How was she going to get out of the relationship, now that she was pregnant with his child?

"Anyway," Mara-Joy stood up, "I have to get back to Larry. We are having a little celebration tonight," Mara-Joy looked as though she were glowing. It was the first time Pauline noticed. Mara-Joy actually seemed ecstatic.

"What are you celebrating?" Pauline asked curiously. She couldn't remember ever seeing Mara-Joy so happy before.

Mara-Joy looked around as though not wanting anyone to hear. She bent down her expensively set head to Pauline's pony tailed one.

"Can you keep a secret?" Mara-Joy whispered, barely able to contain herself.

Pauline nodded, touched by Mara-Joy's outreach of affection.

"Larry and I have been seeing a doctor," she said with a glint in her eye.

"What kind of doctor?" Pauline asked, confused. Mara-Joy didn't look sick.

"A baby doctor," Mara-Joy looked around again. "You have to promise not to say one word." She pointed a long finger painted deep red into Pauline's face. "I mean it."

"I won't, I promise," Pauline said with sincerity, pulling slightly away from the accusing finger.

"I am going to have a baby!" Mara-Joy could barely contain her excitement. She covered her mouth with her heavily jeweled hand.

"Mara-Joy--But I thought?" Pauline was stunned to say the least. Her mouth gaped open in shock.

"I know! I know! But this doctor has been working with us for months and," she stopped to take a deep breath, clasping her hands to her heaving chest, "a miracle has happened."

Pauline had never seen Mara-Joy so happy. She couldn't help but feel a surge of delight for her. She stood up and hugged Mara-Joy tightly to her.

"This is the most wonderful news, Mara-Joy. I am so happy for you and Larry. The family will be so delighted!" Pauline hugged Mara-Joy warmly, smelling her airy perfume. It felt good to share Mara-Joy's news. It felt right.

Mara-Joy pulled away, composing herself, jerking her mink high around her neck.

"Yes, well, you promised not to say a word," she said, unable to contain her pleasure, the blue of her eyes radiating with life.

"I promise. Mom is going to have a fit when she hears. Mara-Joy, she is going to be beside herself," Pauline said, feeling a little weird. Her mother wasn't going to feel so happy finding out Pauline was also pregnant.

"I know, I know," Mara-Joy beamed, clutching Pauline's arm. "But I just want to wait a little–you know, 'till I am sure everything will be all right."

Mara-Joy's face darkened. The memory of her last pregnancy was always fresh in her mind.

Pauline picked up on her emotions.

"Everything will be fine," she said, placing a warm hand on Mara-Joy's. "Tell Larry I said 'hi and congratulations'. You deserve this."

Mara-Joy brightened up and lifted her head regally.

"I will, and I suggest you prepare yourself," she said, looking toward the door where Pascal had just entered, "to dispose of certain garbage." She deposited a twenty on the table. "For the coffee," she said and waved her fingers at Pauline as she brushed passed Pascal without saying a word.

"What was that all about?" he asked, sitting down in Mara-Joy's seat.

"Nothing." Pauline smiled. There was something to be said about Mara-Joy. She didn't pull any punches. She let you know exactly what she wanted you to know.

Pascal leaned over the table, already bored with the conversation and looked at Pauline. She looked good, even though her eyes were a little bloodshot.

"You look good, babe. Let's blow this place. I need to feel the wind at my back." Without a response from Pauline, he stood up, expecting her to follow him.

Pauline huffed and stood up, placing the change from the twenty into her pocket. She left the waitress a hefty tip, hoping it would make up for the abuse from Mara-Joy, and followed after Pascal.

"Do I need some loving tonight," Pascal said, loudly hammering his steering wheel with his closed fist.

Pauline sat huddled in the corner of the passenger's seat. A shiver ran up her spine. She was not going to comply this time. No matter what.

"No, Pascal. I need to talk to you," she said barely above a whisper.

"What?" he asked, scrunching his face in disbelief at her. "What are you talking about? You do as I say, right, babe?" He turned his attention back to the road. He made a sharp right turn into a bushy, secluded area. There were no streetlights here and the only illumination available was from the car's front lights. He continued to drive.

Pauline had no idea where he was driving, but assumed that he was taking her to a place where they could be alone and undisturbed.

"No, Pascal, I can't do this anymore," Pauline shook her head, summoning all her courage.

"Pauline, listen. I don't need your shit tonight okay. Let's just get to our destination, have a little fun and then if you're lucky--" He looked over at the frail form huddled in her seat. She had taken down her ponytail and her hair was hanging loose, hiding her face from his view. She never wore her hair down. He didn't like it. Pauline was an attractive girl. Hiding her face behind her hair was unbecoming of her. He pushed the hair out of her face. Pauline pulled back instinctively.

"What's with your hair?" he demanded gruffly. "I don't like it like that. Put it up."

Pauline obeyed, taking an elastic hair band from her purse and pulling her hair back in its customary ponytail.

Pascal observed her and smiled.

"That's better," he said, pulling into a clearing of dense bushes. He stopped the car and turned off the engine. He leaned over and pulled Pauline to him.

She jerked back stiffly from Pascal's embrace.

"What the hell is the matter?" he said angrily.
"Pascal, I don't want this anymore." She swallowed, feeling afraid.
"Listen, if this is about not being married yet, well don't sweat it." Pascal swelled up with pride. "That is the surprise, baby. I want us to get married. I was planning on asking you tonight."
Pauline sat with her mouth open. This would solve her problems regarding the pregnancy, but she didn't want to marry Pascal anymore.
"And you can make it as big as you want." Pascal grinned sure of himself. "In fact, you should make it the biggest wedding of the year--hell, the century."
"I don't want to marry you," Pauline spoke the words before she realized they were out of her mouth.
Pascal looked at her, amazed. His hand shot out in front of him striking Pauline firmly across the face. She flew against the door, banging her head hard on the window.
She hunched in the corner of her seat, frightened.
"You don't want to what?" he asked venomously. Fear rippled through him. He wasn't about to lose his little gold mine.
"Pascal, please," Pauline begged, clutching her throbbing head. "I just can't do this anymore."
"I just can't do this anymore," Pascal mimicked in a cruel voice. "Well isn't that a little too bad now." He reached out and grabbed her arm roughly. Pauline tried to pull away but his grip was too firm.
"Since when do you make the decisions in this relationship, Pauline?" He glared down at her wickedly. "I am speaking to you, woman!"
"You are hurting me, Pascal. Stop, please!" Pauline was terrified. Pascal looked manic and completely out of control.
"You don't know what hurt is, but it looks like you're going to find out."
Pascal pulled Pauline closer and a fist flashed as everything went black.
Several hours later, he dumped her in front of her house.
Both Pauline's eyes where black and her left arm hung limply in her right hand. She knew it was broken. But that was not all that was broken.
After beating her senseless, Pascal had raped Pauline continuously until she was unconscious. She awoke as he hastily pushed her battered body from the car.
"Babe," Pascal said as Pauline stumbled up the stairs. She turned to him unable to see clearly out of her swollen eyes. "Remember. You met up with some hooligans. I never saw you tonight," Pascal said very calmly.
Pauline turned away, numb with pain, both physical and emotional.
"I mean it, Pauline. Hey," he continued sounding uplifted, "we will announce our engagement afterwards."
Pauline continued up the stairs, not bothering to respond.
Pascal smiled to himself. This would work out well. He would look like a big man, announcing that he would marry Pauline after her attack. He pressed on the accelerator and drove off, not bothering to look back to see if Pauline had made it safely inside.
As soon as the car spun away, Pauline fell to the ground in front of her door.
What would she do? She had no one to turn to for help. The one thing she did know was that she wasn't going to marry Pascal and she didn't want to have his

child. Life with him would only get worse. Once they were married, her life would turn into more of a nightmare than it already was.

Her thoughts turned to Mara-Joy.

She had money. Maybe Pauline could borrow some and go away for a while.

If she left without Pascal knowing where she was, she could heal and deal with this pregnancy one way or another.

She stood up. If she told Mara-Joy the truth, maybe she could help Pauline. One thing was for sure, she couldn't face her parents.

Pauline held her injured arm. She looked a mess. She couldn't lie and protect Pascal from what he had done to her, and she couldn't face telling her parents the truth. There was no one who could help her except Mara-Joy.

Mara-Joy came down her staircase, pulling a silk robe around her protectively.

She was half asleep when Larry woke her, telling her Pauline was there. He had warned Mara-Joy that something had happened, but she was not prepared for what she saw standing in the doorway.

Pauline looked terrible and about to collapse. She had taken a cab over, using the money Mara-Joy left at the café.

"Larry, get her on the sofa!" Mara-Joy ordered. He obeyed and carried the sagging Pauline into the living room as Mara-Joy followed behind, frantic.

"What the hell has happened to you?" Mara-Joy stood with her hands on her hips, staring down at the battered form of Pauline.

"I need your help." Pauline mumbled through swollen lips. She could barely see Mara-Joy's stunned face through her black eyes.

"Larry, call Dr. Avery," Mara-Joy ordered, needing to take control of the situation. She was totally unprepared for Pauline's unexpected visit.

"No!" Pauline protested. Mara-Joy pivoted to Pauline.

"Larry, make the call!" she said sternly ignoring her little sister.

Larry, obeying his wife, left the room to call his personal doctor. Whatever happened to Pauline, Mara-Joy had decided to keep it secret, for now.

Once Larry was safely out of the room Mara-Joy bent down to her beaten sister. She looked at the pounded face and felt her anger rising. Never had she felt this type of anger. Not even after Joanna and Chad had run off together.

"Who did this to you, or do I need to ask?" she inquired coolly, gently smoothing the matted hair from Pauline's bloody face.

"Mara-Joy, I need your help," Pauline sobbed trying to lift her head. She winced in pain as she moved her broken arm.

Mara-Joy eyed the ruined arm and cocked her eyebrow, her mind racing.

"You need my help, do you?" she said through lips pressed firmly together.

"Yes, I need to borrow some money and I need your word that you won't tell Mom and Dad about this," Pauline sputtered through cracked lips.

"You expect me to help you when you haven't even told me what has happened?" Mara-Joy stood up and walked around the spacious living room, richly decorated in the newest fashions.

"Please, Mara-Joy, I have nowhere else to turn," Pauline begged, trying hard not to cry. Mara-Joy was her only hope. Without her, Pauline didn't know what she would do.

"Don't beg, Pauline, it is very unbecoming," Mara-Joy turned abruptly back to her crumpled sibling. "Did that boyfriend of yours do this?" she demanded, full of hate for the man.

Pauline, weakened from the nights events, nodded, defeated.

"I thought so," Mara-Joy went to the fireplace mantle and retrieved a cigarette from the pack that rested there. She lit the white stick and breathed in.

"How did it happen?" she asked, feeling chilled to the bone.

"I told him I didn't want to marry him," Pauline cried weakly, looking like a broken doll.

"So he beat you," Mara-Joy said, disgusted, her arms firmly crossed against her chest.

Pauline breathed in ragged breaths that rattled in her lungs.

"Monster!" Mara-Joy said under her breath. She turned her attention to Pauline, resigned.

"Well Pascal has made a very grave mistake."

Pauline's swollen eyes looked up beseechingly to Mara-Joy. She didn't resemble the pretty girl Mara-Joy had spoken to only hours before.

"He should have never messed with my sister. To mess with you was to mess with me," she inhaled, her arms still pressed against her chest. "And everyone knows not to mess with me."

Mara-Joy was very efficient. Dr. Avery arrived and mended the broken Pauline as best he could.

With a bit of Larry's money stuffed in his pocket, he agreed to keep quiet about the whole affair. Arrangements were made for Pauline to go to a hospital in another town where no one knew her. There, she could heal from her injuries without being recognized.

With great trepidation Pauline revealed the whole story to Mara-Joy, including the most imminent problem: her pregnancy.

Mara-Joy arranged it so Pauline would no longer have that burden to carry. There was no way Pauline was going to be forced into marrying Pascal. At the hospital where Pauline would stay, they would take care of that problem along with the broken arm and bruises.

Pauline, grateful to have the responsibility taken from her shoulders, fell back into the seat of the car, exhausted and eased of her burdens. She sat snugly wrapped in a thick blanket in the back seat.

Larry sat in the front seat with the doctor. Mara-Joy had insisted he go with Pauline to settle her into the hospital safely. Mara-Joy stood outside the car looking in. She clutched her robe tightly to her bosom. She hadn't any time to change in all the excitement.

"Now listen, kid," Mara-Joy said, lighting another cigarette, "Don't worry about the folks. I'll take care of it."

"I don't know how to thank you." Pauline said, eyes welling with tears.

Mara-Joy brushed her comments aside and, feeling ill at ease, shushed Pauline up.

"What are sisters for?" she said casually, dismissing the tenderness in Pauline's voice.

"What about Pascal?" Pauline trembled thinking about how mad he was going to be when he found out Pauline had disappeared.

Mara-Joy glared down on Pauline and in a very cool and steady voice, she said, "He is never going to be a problem again for you, Pauline. Right, Larry?" Mara-Joy grinned wickedly at her husband in the front seat, as she inhaled deeply from her cigarette.

Larry turned his heavy bulk around, his eyes and nose visible over his shoulder.

"That's right, Mar. He ain't going to be a problem anymore." He laughed deep in his chest.

Mara-Joy tried to contain her own laughter and turned back to Pauline in the back seat, tossing her cigarette behind her.

"Leave everything to Larry and me. I'll be up tomorrow to visit with you and see that you are all settled in." Mara-Joy reached a hand inside of the car and placed in on Pauline's shoulders.

"You are not going to ruin your life over this man," she said. "Everything will work out fine. Trust me."

Pauline nodded sleepily. The drugs Dr. Avery had given her were starting to work. She lazily closed her eyes, feeling safe and secure. Mara-Joy was going to fix everything. Pauline was going to be all right and, thankfully, free of Pascal.

— Chapter 43 —

Alan-Michael is with Mara-Joy, laughing. He is dreaming, and everywhere he looks, blood covers everything. He looks down on Mara-Joy as she laughs hysterically, arms stretched out. She is dripping with blood from head to toe.

Alan-Michael looks down at his own body. He is naked and blanketed in blood also. A knife is clasped in his right hand. Blood drips lazily from the pointed tip of the razor sharp edge.

"Mara-Joy," he says dreamily. She veers from him in slow motion, hair flowing out behind her. A blood-soaked hand motions him to follow.

He does. It feels like he is floating. Floating on a wave of red. He can hear her tinkling laugh through his deep breathing as she gets farther and farther away from him.

Alan-Michael hurries his pace, bent on catching up to her. He turns a scarlet-drenched corner and stops dead in his tracks.

She stands still above a blood-sodden mass.

He moves slowly to her, his heart racing as he floats toward his goal with each step.

She smiles at him and giggles, looking down at the bloody pulp at her feet.

Alan-Michael gazes down at what Mara-Joy is concentrating on.

Joanna lies in a heap of blood and gore. Her eyes are blank and staring. The life has gone from them. Her tongue rolls from her mouth grotesquely. A large gaping wound pumps blood slowly from her neck.

His head snaps back up to Mara-Joy.

She is naked, blood sprinkled all over her exposed torso.

"You've done it, Alan-Michael. I told you, you could do it," she says in a faraway voice. Her hands lift from beside her hips and extend out toward him. She pulls his nude body to her, undisturbed by the corpse of Joanna lying between them.

"You did it, my love," she says, leaning in and kissing his wet lips. Drops begin to fall onto their locked faces. Suddenly rain begins to pour on top of their naked bodies.

Alan-Michael opens his eyes to the sudden rain falling inside the blood-drenched room.

It is not rain. It is blood.

Joanna's blood.

Mara-Joy tilts back her head and raises her arms high, squealing with delight. Drops of blood race down her naked form, leaving red streaks.

Alan-Michael lifts his head to the downpour of blood and laughs out loud too.

"Alan-Michael, Mikey," Mara-Joy says softly, pulling his head down to her waiting lips. "I am yours." She plunges her cool wet tongue into his mouth, hungrily searching for his waiting one. She finds it and sucks on it thirstily.

He grasps her shoulders tightly, pulling her small frame onto his. His desire prods her with full force. She tosses back her head and moans, grasping his stiff shaft. He groans with heated passion, pulling her down to the bloody floor.

He is on top of her in a flash. Mara-Joy squirms like a wild beast beneath him, blood sloshing under her back.

"Now, Mikey, now!" she gasps, forcefully guiding him into her. "Now!" She arches her back, displaying her jutting breasts soaked with blood.

He pounces on her forcefully, pounding on her harder and harder. She cries out, cackling, raking her painted fingers down his bloody back.

His pleasure is mounting higher and higher. His desire building stronger and stronger. He feels his buttocks tighten in anticipation of his climax.

Something wet and slimy wraps firmly around his ankle. He ignores it and continues to enjoy himself on the withering creature, wailing beneath him.

Mara-Joy calls out his name, gripping her hands firmly on his pumping rump.

His head falls back, purely enthralled in his work at hand. Eyes closed, he feels something moist and sticky touching his face gently. He opens his eyes, not wanting to miss seeing Mara-Joy bloom. He looks down to see her startled face, gazing past him. Her hands clasped to her mouth. She looks green with fright.

"Mara-Joy?" he says, confused with her behavior.

She points behind him and begins to scream. Alan-Michael turns around, sensing the sickly-sweet smell of putrid waste.

To his horror, Joanna is crouched behind him, her body arched perfectly to his. Blood oozes from the open gape in her neck. Her vacant green eyes stare blankly out at him. Deep from within her extended mouth, her voice bubbles through.

"Why brother? Why?" the inhuman voice filters out.

Alan-Michael sat straight up in bed, heart pounding in his throat. He was soaking wet with his own perspiration.

"It was just a dream," he panted, half relieved. He looked at the clock on the bed stand. It was three thirteen in the morning. He lay back down on his damp pillow, dropping his head gently into the soft folds of feathers.

It had been such a vivid dream. So life-like. He closed his eyes and visualized how Mara-Joy had looked in the dream. His lips couldn't help curving into an evil smile, his last memory of Joanna already forgotten.

— Chapter 44 —

Mara-Joy took a deep breath before entering her parents' home. She had called them early that morning to tell them that Pauline had spent the night at her house.

Confused, Jobeth and Alan accepted the fact, as odd as it seemed. Mara-Joy and Pauline had never been close, but if they were starting to form a bond, Jobeth and Alan were all for it. They wanted all their children to get along with each other and maybe this was a step in the right direction.

Mara-Joy snubbed out her cigarette on her boot and straightened up, her hand briefly resting on her flat abdomen. Her heart fluttered like a bird in a cage and she smiled in spite of herself.

Larry had really come through with his promises about speaking to a doctor.

The problem was rectified almost immediately. A trip to the specialist had led to some painful procedures. She recalled the discomfort she'd felt.

Apparently the doctor had been able to fix the problem. She was now free to get pregnant, and with Larry's help, that is exactly what she did.

She was beside herself with happiness. At long last she would have what she always dreamed of having: a child of her own.

Larry couldn't believe the change in his wife. She was so grateful for the money he spent getting her the best doctors that she doted on him like never before. When she found out she was pregnant, it was like Christmas day had arrived. She was even friendly to Ann and Bobby-Jo. If having a child made Mara-Joy that happy, Larry figured she could have as many children as she wanted.

Mara-Joy cleared her throat and opened the front door. She entered the kitchen and instantly saw Alan-Michael seated at the kitchen table eating his morning cereal.

"Hello, little brother," she chirped, dropping her purse on the table and shrugging off her mink coat. "It's a beautiful day. You should go outside and get some fresh air. You look a little peckish."

Alan-Michael looked up from his bowl of cereal and stared at Mara-Joy, open-mouthed. He had not expected to see her so early in the morning, with his dream still so vivid in his memory.

"What are you doing here?" he asked, mouth gaping.

Mara-Joy plunked down in the kitchen chair closest to him. She removed a cigarette package from her purse, retrieving a long, white, tobacco-filled cylinder. Snapping the case shut, she lit up her smoke as she squinted her eyes mysteriously at Alan-Michael.

"I came to see our parents, if that is all right," she said, grinning through the smoke. "What on earth is eating you?"

"Nothing. I just didn't sleep well last night," Alan-Michael murmured, spooning up his cereal. He stuffed a heaping spoon into his mouth and munched loudly.

"Alan-Michael, please," Mara-Joy scrunched up her face, repulsed. "Mouth shut." Her stomach churned.

He complied, wiping milk from his mouth with the back of his hand.

"You seem in a good mood. What's up with you?" he asked, still chomping on his food.

"Can't a girl be happy on such a wonderful day?" Mara-Joy breathed.

"What happened? Did Joanna drop dead or something?" Alan-Michael laughed into his bowl of cornflakes.

Mara-Joy was taken off guard. It was in her behavior to make faulty comments about Joanna's life or lack of it, but it all seemed frivolous now that she was going to have the baby.

Everything seemed different now that she would have her own child. She didn't really want Chad back, if she thought about it. He had no real money to speak of. He definitely had no power. Larry, on the other hand, had both. He had money to give Mara-Joy a child of her own. He had money and power to set Pauline up in a private hospital room, with no questions asked from the staff. Pauline's life wouldn't be destroyed because of the power Larry possessed. She wouldn't have to marry Pascal because she was pregnant, that problem was probably already disposed of. And no back street butcher would perform her abortion. Oh no! Only the best doctor would treat Pauline. Larry would make sure of it. Pauline would never have to worry about that little troll, again. Larry had taken care of him with just a few phone calls. Mara-Joy was certain Pascal would disappear, never to bother Pauline again. That was the kind of power Larry wielded.

When Mara-Joy thought about it, it was kind of a blessing in disguise to be rid of Chad. He'd always been wimpy and never able to give her the lifestyle she needed to have. If she was true to herself, she realized she would have eventually left Chad on her own accord.

She shrugged her shoulders and puffed on her cigarette.

"For once, Joanna has nothing to do with my mood," Mara-Joy said, enlightened. She might not want Chad any longer, but it was going to take a lot more to forgive Joanna for what she had done to her.

"Well, what is it?" Alan-Michael asked, raising one broad eyebrow, starting to feel uneasy. Mara-Joy was acting in a way he wasn't familiar with and it frightened him.

"Never mind, nosey," Mara-Joy teased. "Are the folks up?" she asked, looking to the door that went to the rest of the house.

Alan-Michael nodded, not enjoying being left out of Mara-Joy's secret. She always included him. Why was it different now?

"Why did Pauline stay at your house?" Alan-Michael asked rather nastily.

Mara-Joy's blue eyes shifted back to the red-faced adolescent.

"My, my, Mikey. If I didn't know better, I would say that you are behaving like a jealous little boy," Mara-Joy smiled wickedly. She loved to toy with him.

It was so easy. He was such simple prey. Putty in her hands.

Alan-Michael pushed himself angrily away from the table and stood up, disgusted.

"I am not jealous!" he tried to contain his voice from yelling. "It's just that you're acting weird, like you're up to something and you don't want to share it with me."

Mara-Joy rolled her crystal blue eyes.

"Sit down, Alan-Michael, before you hurt yourself," she said.

He continued to stand, his chest moving up and down furiously.

"Oh, for crying out loud," Mara-Joy sighed, crushing out her cigarette in the ashtray. "You are worse than a baby. I'm up to nothing. Now sit down and relax. You are starting to bother me."

Alan-Michael sat down slowly, his breathing shallow. His face felt hot and clammy.

"You haven't been planning things without me, have you?" he asked, hands firmly gripping the wooden table.

"What things? Honestly, Alan-Michael, I don't know what you are talking about," Mara-Joy replied with exasperation. He was becoming increasingly paranoid and demanding. Mara-Joy didn't like it and it was starting to get on her nerves. It had been fun conspiring with him against Joanna all these years. She had no one except him to vent to about her pain and anguish over Joanna running off with Chad. But Alan-Michael was pushing too much now. He was obsessed with Mara-Joy and with pleasing her. It was starting to feel boring.

"You know . . . things about Joanna," Alan-Michael's eyes roamed the room, fearful of eavesdroppers.

"There is nothing I can do about Joanna." Mara-Joy sighed, tired of the whole matter. "We might as well get used to it and move on with our lives."

"Good idea," Jobeth's voice said from the doorway. Both Alan-Michael and Mara-Joy were startled.

Jobeth stood smiling on her two favorite children.

"That is just the thing I have been praying for," she said. "It would please me immensely for you and Alan-Michael to bury the hatchet with Joanna."

"Oh, Mama, don't be thanking any lucky stars yet," Mara-Joy said, standing up and smoothing out her navy-blue dress.

Alan-Michael couldn't believe his ears. This was not the Mara-Joy he knew and loved. He sat with his mouth open, appalled. Had she just given up hope? Had Joanna won and Mara-Joy lost? He shook his head in disbelief.

"I am going upstairs," he said to the two women. They nodded, not really paying attention.

"I'll see you later Mikey," Mara-Joy said, not bothering to look at his large form leaving the room. He bumped into Alan as he ascended the stairs.

"Good morning son," Alan said cheerfully, slapping Alan-Michael's back. It made a solid thudding sound.

"Yah, morning," Alan-Michael said distractedly as he continued on to his room.

Everything seemed unreal. Could he have heard Mara-Joy right?

He collapsed on his bed and closed his eyes. His mind was jumbled with questions.

Had Mara-Joy said she forgave Joanna?

No. She told Jobeth not to count her lucky stars.

Alan-Michael sat up in bed and smiled, dementedly. Mara-Joy hadn't said she forgave Joanna, she just felt there was nothing she could do about her.

Nothing Mara-Joy could do about her, but maybe something Alan-Michael could do.

He wondered what Mara-Joy would do if he took care of her Joanna problem for good. Images of his dream from the night before filtered through his head and he moaned out loud. He pressed a hand firmly onto his growing crotch.

He would do anything for her. Anything.

"Where is Pauline?" Alan asked, entering the small kitchen. Mara-Joy and Jobeth were seated together at the table, each sipping a coffee.

Alan went to the coffee pot and poured himself a cup. He sat down next to Mara-Joy and looked at her questioningly.

"Well, that is why I am here," Mara-Joy said, glancing between Jobeth and Alan. "I have something to say on behalf of Pauline to both of you and I am not sure how you two are going to take it."

This doesn't sound good, Mara-Joy," Jobeth replied. "What is going on?"

"Well, it's like this," Mara-Joy said, mustering up her best poker face. "Pauline has been unhappy here for some time."

"What?" both Alan and Jobeth remarked in union.

Mara-Joy raised her hand in protest.

"Now, now she doesn't mean here with the two of you," Alan and Jobeth relaxed and listened patiently.

"She has been unhappy with her life here. I mean her life with that boy Pascal." Mara-Joy looked to Alan, knowing his feelings toward Pauline's boyfriend.

"And now that she is finished with school, she wants to do more with herself than become a wife and mother." She paused, always conscious of the reaction of her parents.

"Pauline wants something different than the rest of us. She wants to be a career girl." There, she said it, now she sat back and waited to see if Alan and Jobeth bought it.

They sat silent for a moment.

"Wha . . . What kind of career girl does she hope to be?" Jobeth asked, not sure what to say. This seemed sudden. Pauline had never expressed any desire to have a job before.

"Well, she isn't sure herself, Ma," Mara-Joy continued.

"How is she going to be a career girl if she doesn't even know what it is she wants to do?" Alan interrupted.

"That is where I come into the picture," Mara-Joy took a deep breath and decided to light another cigarette. "A few weeks ago Pauline came to my house, devastated. Pascal had asked her to marry him and she didn't know how to say 'no' to him."

Alan and Jobeth nodded. Except for the part of Pauline going to Mara-Joy's house, this was easy to believe. They had both felt it was just a matter of time before Pauline told them she was going to marry Pascal.

"Imagine my surprise seeing Pauline standing outside my door crying," Mara-Joy continued, sensing their trepidation.

"At first I thought, why did she come to me? Why not Constance or even Joanna?"

She took a puff of her cigarette letting each sentence soak into her parents' minds.

"But then I realized why she couldn't go to them. They are happy being just wives and Pascal is Constance's brother-in-law. It made sense. I am the only one she could go to. I know the hard reality of life. I know what it is like to be in a bad marriage."

Jobeth looked surprise. She never heard Mara-Joy say her marriage to Chad had been bad before.

"So, naturally, I was the most logical choice for her to come to for help," Mara-Joy said, swinging her cigarette as she talked. "I brought her into the house and calmed her down. Finally, she told me how she felt about Pascal, that she didn't love him and she definitely did not want to marry him. She then confided to me how she wanted to do more with her life, become more than just a wife,"

Mara-Joy examined her parents' faces. They were both pale, unable to digest all she was saying. But they were listening intently.

"I got to thinking to myself," Mara-Joy resumed, "'how can I help Pauline? I don't want her marrying Pascal. I don't really like the fellow much. I think Pauline deserves better than him.'"

"Here, here!" Alan piped in. Jobeth suppressed a laugh. She had to admit she felt relieved that Pauline didn't want to spend the rest of her life with that particular young man either.

Mara-Joy rolled her tongue around her mouth triumphantly. She'd won them over to her side. She knew her parents would agree to anything she said now.

"So I asked her, 'What do you want to do with your life?' And do you know what she said?" Mara-Joy asked, leaning in closer to her parents.

"No," Jobeth said dully, "And I'm afraid to ask."

"She said she wanted to go to college," Mara-Joy slammed her hand down onto the table.

"College?" Alan said in disbelief. "She's not the type of girl to go to college."

Jobeth blinked her eyes and pursed her lips at Alan.

"What type of girl goes to college, Alan?" Jobeth asked, a little annoyed.

"Come on, Jobeth, Pauline is sweet but we both know she hasn't got what it takes to go to college."

"Why is that? Pauline is just as smart as the next girl," Jobeth defended her daughter. Everyone took Pauline's naiveté for stupidity and she did not like it. Not one bit. Just because Pauline was innocent didn't make her brainless.

"I love her dearly too, Jobeth, but Pauline is not as smart as the average girl."

Well, I beg to differ with you, Alan. I think Pauline would do just fine in college," Jobeth stated and sipped her coffee, effectively ending the conversation.

"Mama, I have to agree with you. Sorry, Papa," Mara-Joy said. "That is why Larry and I have decided to send Pauline to school."

"What?" Jobeth and Alan asked in unison once again.

"The three of us--Larry, Pauline and I--discussed it last night and we feel that Pauline would be best off in college. There is a good one that Larry knows of and he made all the arrangements. It is already done. Pauline will be enrolled in the next session come next month." Mara-Joy paused, letting the information sink in.

"Who said you could do this?" Jobeth asked, stiffly clutching her steaming mug.

“Pauline did, Mama.” Mara-Joy replied. “I also have to tell you that Larry has already taken Pauline to the school. We felt it best that she leave town as soon as possible, so that Pascal couldn’t influence her to stay.”

“Mara-Joy,” Alan said, running his hand through his hair. “I don’t understand why you did this behind our backs.”

“Listen to your attitude, Pa. You don’t think Pauline can do it. She knows you love her but she doesn’t need to hear you say she is only smart enough to be a wife. Why wouldn’t she keep it from you?” Mara-Joy asked, looking at the bewildered Alan.

This was going too smoothly. Everything was falling into place, easily.

Alan felt ashamed. She was right. He would have discouraged Pauline.

“Now what do we do?” Jobeth asked in a daze. Another child had run from her with hidden secrets.

Mara-Joy looked at her mother and felt a small amount of pity for her. She didn’t know that Pauline was in a hospital recovering from a beating and preparing for an abortion. She didn’t know that everything had taken place only a few hours ago, not weeks like Mara-Joy had made it seem. What could Mara-Joy do but hide the real truth from them? It was what Pauline wanted.

“You don’t need to do anything, Ma. It’s already done.”

— Chapter 45 —

Pauline recovered quickly, hidden away in the private hospital. Mara-Joy came to visit often, harassing the staff to no end. She always seemed to have something to complain about to the nurses who took care of Pauline.

Mara-Joy's behavior embarrassed Pauline, but she felt she had no right to judge her sister after Mara-Joy had helped save Pauline's life.

With her pregnancy no longer an issue and Pascal far behind her, Pauline began to wonder about her own life and what she would do with it. She voiced these questions late one afternoon, two weeks into her stay at the hospital.

"What do you mean what are you going to do?" Mara-Joy asked, startled, lighting her usual smoke.

She sat down in a chair beside Pauline's bed. Her eyes were almost normal again, the traces of the black bruises finally fading.

Pauline held her heavily plastered arm to her chest.

"I feel like I've been given a new start in life," Pauline said, wrinkling her nose at the smoke. "I want to do something special with my life."

"Well, sister, you can do as I told the folks and go to school." Mara-Joy said, not bothering to fan the smoke away from Pauline, who seemed to attract it like a magnet.

"Hmm. That is a good idea but I think I have something else in mind," Pauline said, looking out the window and smiling to herself.

What Mara-Joy didn't know was Pauline had met a woman about seven years her senior shortly after her arrival at the hospital.

It had been right after the abortion.

Pauline had rested in her room a couple of days after the procedure and couldn't seem to stop crying. She knew she made the right choice in not going through with the pregnancy, but she couldn't stop herself from crying. Tears fell freely from her eyes like a leaky faucet. She blew her nose roughly into a tissue and decided to go for a walk around the hospital corridor. Anything was better than lying in bed feeling sorry for herself.

She walked aimlessly through the sterile halls, not paying much attention to the occupants that filled it. Her mind was a million miles away. Pauline's eyes focused on nothing and no one, so she didn't see the tall, slim woman coming toward her. Not, that is, until she collided headlong into her.

Both women fell back from each other, but didn't fall. Pauline grasped her chest with her one good arm, her cast raised in self-defence.

"Hold on there, stranger, no need to strike," the woman said in a deep voice.

Pauline looked at her assailant. She seemed none the worse for their collision.

The woman was a bit taller than Pauline, who was tall herself at nearly five feet seven inches. She had sandy blonde hair that hung in a bob, casually in loose curls around her ears. Freckles sprinkled the bridge of her nose and her fair skin had an unusual shade of soft brown, achieved by spending much of her time outdoors.

"You seem to be lost in thought," she declared, raising her hand in offering to Pauline. "Name's Eleanor Wimsbey."

Pauline stood still staring at the freckled hand jutting toward her. She must look a mess. Her bruises were out in full, decorating her face with a multitude of black and blue. She walked stiffly, still aching in every part of her body.

"Pauline . . . Benson," she said slowly, offering Eleanor her good hand.

Eleanor grasped it warmly and pumped Pauline's cool hand up and down.

Her grip was firm and friendly.

"Pleased to meet you, Pauline." She let go of Pauline's hand and looked into the blackened eyes.

"Sorry I didn't see you coming, I was deep in thought."

Eleanor shook her head in disgust, causing her bob to bounce to and fro.

"You must forgive me. I am not use to being inside, watching my every step."

"Oh," Pauline whispered, noticing Eleanor was dressed in tan slacks and a matching button-up top. Pauline had never really seen a woman wear pants before, except for herself. She had read about it in one of her magazines, but she had never met anyone brave enough to actually wear them. Pauline couldn't help but wonder what kind of woman Eleanor was.

"Well, sorry to have startled you," Eleanor said, taking leave. "Good to have met you, Pauline Benson."

Pauline watched Eleanor begin to leave. Her shoulders were hunched protectively around her broken body. Something inside her was compelled to call out to the slim older woman.

"Why is that?" Pauline blurted out. She jumped a little, startled by her outburst. Her voice didn't sound like her own.

Eleanor pivoted back to the battered figure.

"I beg your pardon?" Eleanor asked, confused.

"I mean . . . that is," Pauline cast her eyes to the floor. "Why are you not used to the indoors and watching your step?"

Eleanor began to laugh to herself.

"That's because I am an anthropologist. I study different primitive cultures. I am used to wide open spaces," she said, raising her hands up high. "I prefer the sky above me rather than these roofs." She laughed.

"That sounds terribly interesting," Pauline said shyly, looking up into Eleanor's light gray eyes. She had to admit to herself she wasn't sure what an anthropologist was.

"Oh, but it is," Eleanor said, her mind already far away from her current position. "It is fascinating work. The different places and people. Whenever I come back, I am heartsick to return to the wilds." She looked at Pauline, somewhat embarrassed.

"I apologize for my enthusiasm. I just love my job."

Pauline couldn't help but smile. She'd never met a woman like Eleanor before and wanted to get to know her more.

"I would love to hear about it," Pauline said, summoning all her courage. For the first time in days, she wasn't thinking about what Pascal had done to her.

"You would?" Eleanor said, startled. "That would be lovely." She pulled out a piece of paper and a pencil from a rumpled tan bag she had slung over her shoulder. Pauline marveled on how she was capable of finding anything in the jumble of papers that looked ready to burst from the satchel.

"I have to go and meet with a friend," she looked up, smiling warmly. "He's a doctor I work with. He gets his funding from an uncle who works here as a doctor." She looked up from the paper she had begun to write on.

"I've just thought of a great idea. Why don't you join us for lunch in the cafeteria? Frederick loves to discuss our work and he is such a dear."

"Oh . . . I don't know..." Pauline said, shaking her head. A strand of her gold-highlighted hair fell into her bruised face. She brushed it away. "I'm such a fright."

"Nonsense. You look fine," Eleanor said, gently squeezing Pauline's good arm.

"Besides, what is there better to do around this place than to eat and converse?" she asked, smiling. There was something about the beaten young woman that attracted Eleanor. She could tell she had been terribly abused by someone and she seemed as shy as a mouse. The fact that she had spoken out to Eleanor made her want to know Pauline more.

"I insist," Eleanor said softly.

"All right then," Pauline said, encouraged. "I'll be there."

Eleanor gave Pauline a time to meet her and her colleague, Frederick. Pauline promised to meet them and went back to her room to change.

Later that afternoon, after showering and freshening up as much as was possible, she pulled back her hair from her face into her comfortable ponytail. She could do nothing about the bruises that littered her body, so she chose to pretend they were not there. Eleanor had not seemed to pay much attention to the obvious marks. Why should Pauline?

Eleanor spotted Pauline coming into the cafeteria and waved her over.

Pauline walked slowly toward her, forcing one foot in front of the other, her heart racing a little in her thin chest.

"Pauline, I am so glad you made it," Eleanor said, standing up and pulling out a chair for her. Pauline sat down and looked bashfully at the gentleman already sitting at the table.

"Pauline Benson, I would like to introduce you to Dr. Frederick Jefferson Kane," Eleanor said, palm out toward the young man seated between them.

"Pleased to meet you," Pauline said, just above a whisper. She liked the way Frederick looked. He had auburn hair that hung a little too long over his forehead and into his chocolate brown eyes that were soft and friendly. He smiled timidly at the frail girl.

"The pleasure is mine," he said in a gentle voice, picking up a pair of spectacles beside his plate. He polished them quickly and placed the round, wire-rimmed glasses onto his straight long nose.

"I was just telling Frederick how you are interested in learning about our work," Eleanor said, lifting her napkin up and unfolding it on her lap. She had taken the liberty of ordering Pauline some lunch. "Wasn't I, Frederick?"

"Yes," he said, then sipped some water. "It is quite an interesting life we lead," he said, coming out of his shell. Frederick was a shy man, but would open up with ease when talking about his work. "We travel all around the world. Eleanor does her studies and I dole out my medical skills to people who would otherwise not have the luxury of modern medicine."

Pauline smiled to herself as Eleanor and Frederick continued to talk about their work. It was easy to see that the two worked wonderfully together and were good friends. Pauline could not help but be pulled into their warm circle and slowly she began to ask questions that were quickly answered, often in unison, by Eleanor and Frederick.

By the end of their lunch, everyone seemed to be sorry that it had come to an end.

"Pauline, I can't tell you how much I enjoyed our lunch together," Eleanor said, sad to see it end.

"I have to agree with Elle," Frederick responded. "We have work here at the hospital for the next couple of weeks. Would you do us the honor and join us again?"

Pauline swallowed, unable to believe what she was hearing. Could she join them? All she wanted to do was sit and talk with these new friends she had met.

They were fascinating and wonderful. She'd never met people so interesting with such adventurous lives. She nodded eagerly, her shyness fading quickly away.

The three met every other day or so. Pauline was transfixed by the way Eleanor and Frederick lived their lives: traveling around the world, living in huts with half-naked people whose lives were so different from her own. She listened to how Frederick had turned a breech baby around in its mother's stomach to free it from certain death, all the while the entire female population of the community stood by watching. It seemed unreal to the inexperienced Pauline.

The more she listened to Eleanor and Frederick, the more she wanted to lead their type of life. She eventually opened up to her new friends and explained how she had ended up at the private hospital. She held nothing back, knowing that Eleanor and Frederick were not the type of individuals to judge.

Pauline marveled on how fate had brought them all together feeling certain it was not just coincidence that brought Eleanor and Frederick to her.

The day Mara-Joy had come to visit with Pauline, bent on convincing Pauline to go to college, Pauline had sat with both Frederick and Eleanor for the entire morning in a conversation that would change her life.

"I want to go with you," Pauline said. She was basically healed both mentally and physically, except for the cast on her arm.

Eleanor and Frederick looked at Pauline with little surprise. They had become quite fond of her as well and hoped she would want to join them. The two had discussed it together a few nights before, coming to the conclusion that, if Pauline wanted, Eleanor could use Pauline as an assistant.

They knew Pauline was not educated as an anthropologist, but she could learn through the guidance of both Eleanor and Frederick. It seemed like an easy conclusion. Pauline had already left her old life behind. She had no desire to return. She was a perfect candidate for the job.

"It is not always easy," Eleanor warned. The three sat in one of the many ready rooms supplied by the hospital for its occupants. Eleanor sat with Pauline on the couch with Frederick sitting to their left in a plush chair. He sat quietly, letting Eleanor do the talking. She was better with words than he was.

"I am aware of that," Pauline said, in her own defense.

"You won't have the comforts of modern life," Frederick said, motioning his hand around the expensive hospital.

"I have never been a slave to modern technology," Pauline smiled, knowing they knew who had foot the bill for her stay at the pricey private hospital.

Frederick grinned. Pauline's face was finally starting to reveal itself to the outside world, now that the bruises were nearly gone. He was surprised at what a lovely creature Pauline was, both inside and out.

"Pauline, are you sure this is the life you want to choose for yourself?" Eleanor asked, holding Pauline's hand in hers. "You will be far away from the people you love and so removed from the way you are used to living. Life is different out there."

"All my life I have been an outsider to those I love," Pauline said without becoming emotional. It was just a fact. A fact she was capable of facing without any animosity toward anyone.

"For the first time I feel like I am doing something that feels right . . . that fits." Pauline bent her head down and tucked a loose strand of her ponytail behind her ear. She sat up straight, courage running through her spine.

"You and Frederick are the first people I have ever felt truly comfortable around. I can be myself with you. I know this is what I am supposed to do. I want to do it with the two of you, but," she looked to both her friends, "if I have to, I will find another way."

Eleanor gazed at Frederick and blinked her eyes in acknowledgement. It was all they needed to hear. Pauline would join them.

So Pauline sat on her hospital bed swallowing hard as Mara-Joy blew smoke in her face, telling Pauline to go to college.

"Mara-Joy, I don't know how I am going to ever thank you for what you have done for me. You don't even know exactly how much you have done," Pauline said, swinging her legs over the bed. She slipped into some hospital slippers and stood up, standing a few inches taller than her big sister.

"Well, you can thank me by doing something with your life, like going to school," Mara-Joy said, fanning her cigarette-clad hand through the air.

Pauline couldn't help but laugh at Mara-Joy's antics. If anything, she was persistent.

"I do plan on doing something with my life, but it isn't going to college."

Pauline pulled out a chair for Mara-Joy. "Sit down and please put out that cigarette. It can't possibly be good for the baby," she said, steering Mara-Joy into the chair.

Mara-Joy sat open-mouthed.

"Since when did you become an expert in obstetrics? ...And I am not putting this out because you said so. If Dr. Avery doesn't have a problem with my smoking, than neither should you." Mara-Joy said as she stubbed out her cigarette and crossed her legs smugly.

"Mara-Joy, I need your help once more," Pauline said, continuing to ignore her sister's insults.

"Figures," Mara-Joy steamed. "You help someone once and they keep coming back for more. Well, you might as well spill the beans. What is it?" she asked, wrapping her stole around her neck protectively.

Pauline took a deep breath and blurted her plans out to the flabbergasted Mara-Joy. She told Mara-Joy her plans to leave with Eleanor and Frederick for Africa in two days and how she planned on becoming Eleanor's apprentice.

She explained how her life had been changed and that she knew this was her calling in life, ending the story with how if it weren't for Mara-Joy, she would never have found herself.

Mara-Joy sat back, stunned and unable to speak. For the first time in a very long time, she was speechless. This was something she hadn't been expecting.

Suddenly she began to laugh. At first, it was a choked laugh in the back of her throat, then a full-out, deep belly laugh that hurt her sides.

Pauline didn't know what to make of Mara-Joy's reaction to the news and just stood back from the cackling madwoman.

Mara-Joy's laughing finally subsided and she wiped her wet eyes with a hanky from the pocket of her fur coat.

"This is just great," she laughed anew. "How on earth am I going to break this to the family?"

And she began to laugh hysterically again.

— Chapter 46 —

Alan-Michael sat slumped in Mara-Joy's living room chair, sipping his rye and ginger ale. The ice made clinking sounds in his glass. He was feeling warm and fuzzy from the alcohol and his eyes began to droop.

"Wakey, wakey, Mikey!" Mara-Joy's shrill voice startled Alan-Michael out of his coma.

"Christ, do you have to be so loud?" he asked, raising his glass to his forehead. It felt cool on his damp brow.

Mara-Joy smirked and sat down on the sofa, lounging back and lighting a smoke. She was wearing a silk black robe with oriental geisha girls dancing around the hem. It clung to her figure perfectly, tracing out the small bulge just beginning to emerge from her mid-section.

Alan-Michael averted his eyes from her growing belly to hide his revulsion.

He didn't share in the rest of his family's joy over Mara-Joy's pregnancy. In fact, the very thought of her with child nauseated him.

"Now, brother, is that the way you talk to a pregnant woman?" Mara-Joy teased, tossing her high-heeled slippers off her feet and onto the floor.

"Must you always talk about your condition?" Alan-Michael demanded nastily.

"No. If it bothers you we can talk about something else. What would you like to talk about, Mikey? School?" she said, sarcastically, "Girls?"

Alan-Michael glared at Mara-Joy. "Stop it," he said, downing the rest of his drink and standing to make himself a fresh glass. He didn't like it when Mara-Joy teased him. Especially after just having a terrible evening.

Alan-Michael had been out on a date with a young girl who slightly resembled Mara-Joy. "Slightly" meaning that she had dark hair. That is where the similarities ended. He wined and dined the young woman and she was charmed by his good looks and manners. That was until he it was time to take her home.

He'd stopped at a make-out location and proceeded with the usual kissing and petting that went with a good date; but then he became increasingly forceful and demanding, nearly raping the poor young girl, who fled from the car, crying. Alan-Michael, driving slowly beside the frightened girl as she walked, tried to persuade her to get back into the car. She refused, claiming Alan-Michael was sick and she never wanted to see him again.

What Alan-Michael didn't understand was that the girl had even more reason to be afraid of him than he was aware of. While he was forcing himself on the terrified girl, he called out Mara-Joy's name, saying he had done it, he had killed her.

Confused and scared, the girl had maneuvered herself out of the car and ran from Alan-Michael, spooked.

His eyes had terrified her most. They were glazed and fixed, not focused on anything in reality. They were the eyes of the insane and she knew if she valued anything normal, she must flee from Alan-Michael and never have anything to do with him again.

She told him as much while he followed her in his car.

Angry and humiliated, not understanding the bitch's' attitude, he came to the one place he always felt drawn too, Mara-Joy's.

Mara-Joy, not surprised to see him, filled him with booze as she played records from her favorite singer, Al Jolson.

"Toot, toot, tootsy, good-bye," Mara-Joy sang along, wiggling her toes.

Alan-Michael rubbed his temples, his headache pounding behind his eyes. He gulped down his drink and refreshed it once more.

"Please, Mara-Joy, do we have to listen to that music?" he whined, sitting back down in his chair with a thud.

"As I recall, it was you who came to my house," Mara-Joy said joyfully. She loved to torment him.

"Ha. Ha. Very funny." Alan-Michael melted back into the chair and slurped his drink. The strong bitter taste burnt his throat and he felt himself relax.

"Ma got a letter the other day from Pauline," Mara-Joy said, sitting up. It had been two months since Pauline left for Africa.

"I know," Alan-Michael said dully.

"Can you believe it, our Pauline off in Africa living with a bunch of barbarians!" Mara-Joy said with pride as she took a drag of her cigarette.

"They are called 'pygmies' and they are not barbarians. They are hunters and gathers, or so Pauline writes," Alan-Michael said, bored, his fingers massaging his temples.

"Well, whatever they are, it is very interesting. Pauline seems to have found a good calling in life," Mara-Joy said, smiling to herself. "I can't help but feel responsible for helping her life change."

"For crying out loud Mara-Joy, you sent her to school and she took off with the first weirdoes she met, leaving you high and dry to explain it all to Ma and Pa," Alan-Michael said jealously.

What was wrong with Mara-Joy? Since when had she taken such an interest in that idiot's life? Pauline had always been an imbecile and Mara-Joy had once thought so too.

"You are just being a jealous green-eyed monster, Alan-Michael, and I won't let you ruin my good mood," Mara-Joy replied and swung her feet onto the ground.

"Jealous of what? Of being an idiot?" Alan-Michael asked, sitting up.

"Yes," Mara-Joy said, standing up and touching her bud of a tummy affectionately. "That idiot is doing more with her life than any of us. It is that idiot who will accomplish more than you or I could have dreamed of having achieved."

"You have got to be kidding," Alan-Michael snapped waspishly, draining his once more. He was beginning to feel considerably drunk. "You mean to tell me that you honestly think that no-brain Pauline--"

"Stop! I am tired of hearing your resentful words," Mara-Joy said, raising her hand .

"Fine. Since you are so fond of what our sisters are up to these days, I thought you would like to hear the latest news on your favorite sister." Alan-Michael smirked, sensing he had Mara-Joy's attention.

"What favorite sister?" Mara-Joy asked, strained, settling back on the couch and lying down.

"Oh you know the one," Alan-Michael said going over to Mara-Joy. He sat down beside her and placed a cold hand down onto her firm round belly. Mara-

Joy tensed and let out a gasp. Her hands went protectively over Alan-Michael's strong hold.

"Remember the sister?" Alan-Michael said, slowly rotating his hand around on her stomach. Mara-Joy felt herself become rigid.

"Stop, Alan-Michael," she said through clenched teeth.

"You know the sister I'm talking about. The sister who stole your husband right from under your nose."

"Alan-Michael, stop it, I mean it," she said, trying to pry his hands from her tummy. He held on firmly, her attempts futile.

"The sister who bore your husband's bastard children when you couldn't even carry one to term." Alan-Michael was dazed, his eyes glassy. A humming had begun deep inside his ear and he could hear nothing over the sound of it.

"Seems our fertile sister is full of baby again," he continued. Mara-Joy's head shot up, surprised. Heat raced to her face.

"I wonder whose baby it is." Alan-Michael droned on. "Maybe she is preparing to give Larry a son, in case something should happen again to yours. Joanna is always ready to supply your husbands with the children you can't have."

Mara-Joy struck Alan-Michael forcefully across the face. His head flew sideways easily in his muddled state. A red handprint began to surface on his pale skin. Alan-Michael raised his hand off of her stomach and placed it to his hot cheek.

"How dare you!" Mara-Joy said, scrambling up and advancing on Alan-Michael like a madwoman. He sat unmoving, clutching his stinging face. "How dare you spew that filth in my house! You have some nerve!"

"What hurts you more, Mara-Joy," he asked, rolling his glass casually in his free hand, "the thought that Joanna is once again pregnant with your husband's bastard, or that she might have another child where you will be left with none?"

"Get out!" Mara-Joy said, protectively draping a hand across her belly. "Get out of here and never come back. You are no longer welcome in my home, Alan-Michael."

Startled, Alan-Michael looked numbly at Mara-Joy. He had intended to get her riled up but not to get himself thrown out, exiled from her presence. He had only wanted to get her blood boiling about Joanna.

"Come on, Mara-Joy, you don't mean it," he pleaded, tilting his glass to his lips. She grabbed the glass from his hands, banging his teeth in the process.

"I do mean it, Alan-Michael. You don't make fun at the expense of my baby!" she snarled, her voice getting louder. She was shaking, she was so angry.

"You don't come into my home and say Joanna will bear another child and mine will never be born! Do you hear me?"

"Mara-Joy, I was just kidding. You know, like we always do," he said, becoming frightened. He hadn't seen Mara-Joy this angry since Joanna had run off with Chad. He realized he had gone too far.

He stood up and went to her. He tried to comfort her by placing his arms around her shoulders. It didn't work. Mara-Joy turned on him, striking Alan-Michael forcefully around the head.

"Get out of here before I call the police! Do you understand, Alan-Michael? I never want to see your pitiful face here again." She whirled on him, once more hitting him around the ears. Alan-Michael lamely tried to shield himself with his hands, too stunned to do anything more.

"You are so pathetic, Alan-Michael, with the way you moon around me!" Mara-Joy said, face full of rage. "What are you thinking in that sick mind of yours? Huh? Do you actually think I don't know how you feel about me?"

Alan-Michael began to turn red with shame. He hadn't known he was so transparent with his lustful feelings.

"I don't know what you mean," he said, playing dumb in his drunken stupor.

Mara-Joy tilted her head back and laughed her cackling, evil laugh.

"You poor fool. You really think I don't know how you lust after me? How you desire your own sister."

"Don't be ridiculous," Alan-Michael said with little conviction.

"Ridiculous!" Mara-Joy said, pushing her fevered face into Alan-Michael's pasty one. "'Ridiculous' is you thinking it could possibly happen. That is what is 'ridiculous'."

He could take no more. He pushed Mara-Joy out of his way and fled the house, humiliated.

Alan-Michael ran until his lungs felt like they would burst. He stopped, crouching forward, his hands on his thighs, panting and spitting saliva that formed in his mouth.

He stayed in the same position for some time, until finally he could catch his breath. When he felt he had some control, he straightened his spine and breathed deeply of the cool night air.

His thoughts were dark and hateful. How could this be happening to him?

He had lost Mara-Joy forever. She had ridiculed him worse than an animal.

Why? Why had Mara-Joy turned on him?

It was plain for him to see. So obvious in his twisted mind.

It hadn't been because of him and the things he had said. They had always been close and would have always been that way, if it hadn't been for *her*.

Alan-Michael let out a deep belly yell that echoed throughout the neighborhood. Dogs began to bark and someone yelled out the window for him to leave or they were going to call the cops.

He began to walk. His feet moved faster and faster. His brain kept pulsating with hatred. The more he thought of it, the more it seemed to make sense.

He had lost the only person that mattered to him, Mara-Joy, and it was all Joanna's fault.

Joanna didn't hear Alan-Michael creep through the front door of her house.

How could she? She was sound asleep beside Chad in their bed. They slumbered peacefully, unaware of the uninvited guest sneaking up their staircase to their bedroom.

Alan-Michael stopped in front of Joanna's daughter's room. Jena slept peacefully with a doll snugly tucked under her chin.

She should have been Mara-Joy's daughter, he screamed in his head.

He then slowly crept to the boy's room. Charles slept with his bottom up in the air, his legs scrunched beneath his tummy.

How sweet," Alan-Michael said sarcastically. He shut the door and walked quietly to Joanna and Chad's room.

There she lay: the one who had destroyed Alan-Michael's life. Rage surged through his body like never before. His mind could see nothing but hate.

The tramp! The trollop! Look at her! He screamed in his head.`*Look at her lying with another woman's husband. Jezebel!*

The malice Alan-Michael felt for Joanna was overpowering. It consumed his mind. Everything in his life that had gone wrong was associated with the woman who lay in that bed, oblivious to it all.

If it hadn't been for Joanna, Mara-Joy would not have abandoned him. Everything was Joanna's fault, everything.

He didn't even think twice when he raised the butcher knife above his slumbering sister; and he didn't stop plunging the knife into her soft white flesh, even when she screamed out in terror. He kept on thrusting his dagger into her body over and over again, blanking out the sounds of her screams and those of her husband. Nothing would stop him from finishing what he had started.

Nothing.

A sharp object struck his head forcefully from behind and everything went black.

— Chapter 47 —

Startled awake by Joanna's screams, Chad woke to see his wife being stabbed to death by her own brother. At first he didn't know who the assailant was, only that he wouldn't stop plunging his knife into Joanna's already bloodied body.

Chad leapt from the bed, terrified. He yelled out for the intruder to stop, but the man seemed unable to hear him, intent on his job of viciously slashing Joanna. Quickly scanning the room Chad grabbed a crystal vase off of the dresser and smashed it on the back of the aggressor's head. He dropped like a log to the ground.

Chad rushed to the silent Joanna. Her body was riddled with stab wounds, each gushing with fresh blood. She made no noise as he knelt down beside her bloody form. A sob escaped his mouth as he looked at Joanna's blue quivering lips.

"Joanna, hold on baby, hold on," Chad trembled. She nodded and looked to the door.

"The children," she mouthed.

Chad turned to the bedroom door. Jena and Charles stood huddled together in the corner across the hall. They had heard their mother's screams and had rushed to her rescue only to witness her being stabbed to death. Horrified, they hid together in the corner, crying as they clung to one another, not knowing what to do.

"Jena, run next door and get help! Tell them to get an ambulance and fast!" Chad yelled with panic in his voice. He knew he was frightening the children more than they already were, but his mind was focused only on saving Joanna.

Jena sat frozen in the corner, clutching a crying Charles tightly. Her face was a mask of fear. She had just witnessed her mother being stabbed. It would be a sight she would never forget for the rest of her life.

"Jena! For Christ's sakes, go now, before your mother bleeds to death!" Chad hollered, cradling Joanna's head in his arms.

Jena jumped up, still holding onto Charles' hand and ran down the stairs and out the front door, dragging her weeping little brother with her.

Chad peered down on his wife's pale face. Her green eyes were beginning to glaze over. He smoothed back her light brown hair and kissed her bloody forehead.

"Hang on, babe. The kids have gone for help." Chad choked, full of emotion.

Joanna looked bad. He could no longer tell where the stab wounds were, because her whole body was covered in blood.

She began to choke, spitting up blood from her blue, shivering lips. She tried to speak.

"Don't speak, save your energy," Chad said, smoothing back her blood soaked hair.

"Why?" she mouthed a wet sound coming from the back of her throat.

"Don't think about it. Just stay calm until we get some help here." Chad raised Joanna's head on top of his lap. It felt limp and heavy. "You have to stay still until help comes. Do you hear me? I can't lose you. Jena and Charles can't lose you."

A drunken moan came from the floor. Chad looked down at the man who had turned his life upside down in a matter of minutes. He couldn't believe his eyes. It was Alan-Michael.

"You son of a bitch!" he said, gently placing down Joanna's head and turning on Alan-Michael. Chad began to beat the slumped form with all his might. Pounding Alan-Michael into unconsciousness. He couldn't help himself. All he kept thinking of were Joanna's screams as Alan-Michael stabbed her over and over again.

"Chad," the bubbly voice called weakly from the bed.

Chad looked up from the beaten piece of meat that had been Alan-Michael and went to his pale wife. The blood was starting to congeal and the flesh he could see was bleached white.

"Hold on, Joanna!" he begged, feeling her slip away from him. "I can't live without you. You're my life." He bent his head clutching her hand in his own. It was ice cold with a bluish tinge to it. "Please!"

"I...love . . . you . . ." she said thickly through blood stained teeth. "Never . . . doubt that." Her hand went limp in his grasp and Chad felt the life run out of her.

"No," he sobbed in an anguished wail, pressing her frozen fingers to his lips. "Nooooooo!"

Joanna was dead and Alan-Michael had killed her.

When the ambulance and police arrived, they found Chad still clinging to his dead wife's hand and Alan-Michael unconscious on the floor beside them.

Later at the hospital, Alan-Michael awoke from his coma, babbling rubbish.

Jobeth, mortified, had gone to her son's room demanding to know if it were true. Did he kill Joanna?

She stood pale and trembling, unable to show any emotion. This could not be happening to her. Of all the things that had happened in Jobeth's life, this was by far the worst.

"Alan-Michael?" she called, looking at the stranger lying on the hospital cot. "What have you done?" She was unable to control the shaking in her voice.

"I sent the devil back to hell, Ma. We can all go back to the way things were now. The she-bitch is dead," Alan-Michael snarled viciously, insanity visible behind his words.

"Do you even know what you have done?" Jobeth raised her voice. Images of Jena's and Charles' haunted faces filled her mind. The sight of her two grandchildren sitting with their father, holding on to him for dear life, suffocated Jobeth. She felt she couldn't breathe. "Do you realize Joanna is dead?" The moment the words were out of her mouth, Jobeth felt a curdling moan escape her throat. She cried out in grief for the daughter she had just lost and the horror in how she died.

Alan, red-eyed, came charging into Alan-Michael's room in time to catch the collapsing Jobeth into his arms. He held Jobeth firmly, her body and his own grief weighing him down. They both fell slowly to the ground, overwhelmed by sorrow.

"Alan . . . He's craaazzy," Jobeth wailed, pounding Alan on the chest. Alan could do nothing but cry openly into her arms. "He admits it, Alan. Our son admits to killing his sister. What have we created? What kind of monster would kill his own sister in cold blood and have no remorse over it? What, Alan? What have we done?"

They held each other tightly, both unable to contain their raw emotions.

Alan-Michael lay confused on the gurney, not comprehending his parents' behavior.

"Stop it, Ma, Pa! Stop it! What are you crying for? What's the matter?"

He tried to get up to go to them on the floor, but found that his arms were handcuffed to the bars of the bed. He pulled at his arms to free them, making sick, clanking sounds.

"Let me go!" Alan-Michael hollered, confused.

An orderly came running into the room, followed by two police officers.

Seeing the scene before them, sedatives were ordered for Alan-Michael and his parents.

Alan-Michael was admitted to a hospital for the criminally insane, without hope of ever leaving the institute alive. Jobeth had gone to the head administrator of the hospital and had informed them of her son's mental health. Under no circumstances was Alan-Michael ever to leave the hospital facilities.

He was a prisoner, sentenced to life.

They stood in two groups huddled together beside the open grave. One group included the parents and sisters, the other group, her husband and children.

Shawna and Oliver left with the rest of the mourners, leaving the immediate family alone to say their good-byes.

Both groups couldn't hold back the wave of tears that fell freely from their souls. How could such a tragedy happen?

Jobeth clung to Alan's chest, unable to look at the gaping hole that was to be her daughter's permanent resting place.

"How did this happen?" She sobbed uncontrollably. "How?" Alan couldn't answer Jobeth as he clung tightly to her for support. His heart was breaking inside for the daughter and son he'd lost. Never would he be the same again. He couldn't grasp the fact that he had lost his daughter at the hands of his own son. All he could think of was what he could have done to prevent this massacre from happening. If only he could have seen it coming, he could have saved both Joanna and Alan-Michael.

Constance, unable to stand seeing her mother so filled with grief began to leave the devastating scene. She couldn't stand to witness the events taking place. She had just gotten Joanna back. Now she was putting her into the cold ground, forever gone from their family.

Mara-Joy watched Constance flee and bubbled with rage. How dare she leave the family at a time like this? Could she not see that their parents needed the two of them more than anything now? Pauline was still in Africa, unable to return in time for the funeral, though she was making arrangements to come home as soon as possible for a short stay. Frederick, who was becoming more than just a friend and co-worker, was accompanying the devastated Pauline to her family. He didn't want to let her go back to the life she once led, and Pauline had no plans to ever return after she paid her respects to her sister. The memories were too painful and life too wonderful in Africa to want to linger anywhere she felt pain.

That left only Mara-Joy and Constance; and it was plain to see that Constance was going to be of no help.

Mara-Joy fastened her mink coat tightly around her collar, desperately wanting a cigarette. She felt terrible.

Her eyes were swollen nearly shut from all the crying she had done and seemed to continue doing. She hadn't even bothered with any makeup to hide her bad appearance. She just didn't have the energy to make herself presentable. Larry did not know what to do and had called Dr. Avery. He'd never seen Mara-Joy so distraught before. He knew she was close to her brother, but she had always claimed to hate the sister who had died. Frightened, he asked Dr. Avery to help Mara-Joy, which he did by sedating her. It had helped, but had by no means cured Mara-Joy of her sorrow.

Mara-Joy was grieving. Grieving for the brother she had loved all her life and the sister she should have. She had not expected to feel the way she did over the death of Joanna. She actually felt a yearning to tell Joanna that she had forgiven her for stealing Chad from her. But it was too late for it all now, and that saddened Mara-Joy the most.

She looked across the grave at Chad as he stood grasping his small children close to him. He looked horrible. His face was crumpled with grief and he looked older than she remembered.

Placing a gloved hand on her small mound of a stomach, Mara-Joy took a deep breath and walked over to the bereaved Chad. He stood clutching his children tightly to him. The little girl could not stop crying into his hip, while the boy stood solemnly and eerily still.

Mara-Joy pressed her lips tightly together. She had never seen Chad and Joanna's children before. They were beautiful. The girl, Jena, looked like their side of the family. She had the olive catlike eyes, with blonde soft curls like Constance's. Charles, the boy, he was the spitting image of Chad: a handsome boy with light mahogany hair and chestnut eyes.

Mara-Joy's breath escaped her and a throbbing sensation developed in her throat.

These were her sister's children. These two darling children were her niece and nephew.

"Chad." Mara-Joy mumbled, her fingertips lightly brushing her quivering lips. Her lips expelled words before she knew she was going to speak.

Chad looked up from his distraught children. His face white with shock and grief drained of the little color he had left as he began to register Mara-Joy's presence.

"What do you want?" his voice stung with venom. Jena and Charles cowered behind his legs, confused by their father's hostility.

Mara-Joy bent her head low, understanding Chad's reaction to her. After all, she had made it clear to Joanna that she would never be forgiven by Mara-Joy. There had been no love lost between the two for some time.

"I just wanted to say how sorry I am for you and the children," she said, peering at the two terrorized youngsters concealed behind their father. Little hands clutched the hem of Chad's coat tightly. "Despite everything that has happened, Joanna was my sister and I am horrified by the events that have transpired."

Chad looked at Mara-Joy in disbelief. His mouth fell open and his ashen face began to show red spots, beginning under his shirt collar and creeping up his neck.

"How dare you," he said in a calm voice. "How dare you come and stand at my wife's grave and say you are sorry for me and my children's loss? You, of all people."

Mara-Joy looked at Chad, bewildered, her heart beating madly in her chest, banging relentlessly against her rib cage.

"Chad, it is time to bury the hatchet. I realize Joanna and I should have resolved things sooner, but—"

"Resolve things sooner?" Chad said incredulously, "You have got to be kidding. Do you really believe the crap that comes out of your mouth?"

Mara-Joy clamped her mouth shut and breathed deeply through her nose.

She could sense everyone looking at her. Out of the corner of her eye she could see her parents in the background. They stood silently, holding onto each other, watching Mara-Joy from a distance.

"Chad, I am trying to tell you I forgive you and Joanna," Mara-Joy said through clenched teeth. "I understand now that you two loved each other and didn't mean to hurt me in the process."

Chad began to laugh a sickly, cackling, sobbing laugh. His hand clasped his forehead open-palmed and roughly pulled back his bronzed hair from his wrinkled brow.

"You forgive us?" he said, unable to digest what Mara-Joy had said. "You forgive us for what we did to you? You have got to be kidding me."

"I assure you I am not kidding in the least," Mara-Joy said. Unable to refrain from smoking any longer, she pulled out her cigarette and lit it, blowing out a puff of white smoke.

"Well," Chad's hands flew into the air dramatically, "everything is just swell now that Mara-Joy has forgiven Joanna and me."

"Chad, your behavior is inappropriate. Think of your children. They have been through enough already without you frightening them also," Mara-Joy said before inhaling deeply from her cigarette. A dull ache was beginning to form in the pit of her abdomen and she was becoming tired of this display with Chad. If he couldn't accept her forgiveness, than that was fine. She had enough for one day. All she wanted to do was go home and lie down for a while.

Chad swung on Mara-Joy like a jackrabbit.

"My children have been through what?" He leaned in close to Mara-Joy, looking into her sapphire eyes with hatred.

A chill of fear ran up Mara-Joy's spine and she felt the urge to bolt away from Chad and his repellent eyes. He grabbed Mara-Joy harshly by the shoulders and began to shake her savagely. Mara-Joy's head rolled back and forth painfully on her neck.

"My children watched their mother being stabbed to death by a madman. A madman you helped create out of hate and revenge against Joanna. They watched in horror as their father could do nothing to save their mother from this psychopath who had invaded their home and their lives."

Alan grabbed Chad around the shoulders and yelled at him to stop. Chad released Mara-Joy and pushed her away. Jena and Charles were now held protectively in Jobeth's arms, sobbing.

"You!" Chad pointed with all his might at Mara-Joy who stood, rattled and confused. Her neck hurt and her body was beginning to break down. She was weak in the knees and felt she might faint.

"You are the reason Joanna is dead in that grave. You are the reason those two children no longer have a mother." Chad gestured to the open grave and the two horrified children in Jobeth's arms.

"You poisoned your brother against Joanna and you have been doing it for years!"

"No, it is not true!" Mara-Joy protested with fear in her voice. It couldn't be true. "Alan-Michael is sick. What he did to Joanna had nothing to do with me. I would never kill my own sister!"

"Don't you see that you did!" Chad said, feeling defeated, his voice full of emotion. He couldn't bear the thought of Joanna gone. "You corrupted your brother. You were the one who had the most influence on him, Mara-Joy. It was you. You killed my wife and our unborn child."

"No." Mara-Joy said, wanting to run. "I didn't have anything to do with Alan-Michael killing Joanna."

Jobeth began to wail painfully. Hearing her two children's names together was too excruciating. She held Joanna's children tightly to her chest, afraid to let them go for fear she would lose them too.

Mara-Joy ignored her mother's cries. Her mind was occupied with the last memories of Alan-Michael leaving her house the night Joanna was killed. She shook her head.

"Nooo," she said, she knew she had shared her hatred of Joanna with Alan-Michael and sometimes she had gone a little too far with her anger, but she hadn't wanted him to kill her. "I am not responsible for Joanna's death."

Chad shook his head subdued. "You can say whatever you want to make yourself sleep better at night, Mara-Joy; but that will never change the truth. You helped drive your brother insane, and you helped him kill Joanna." He turned away from Mara-Joy's protest and retrieved his children from a shattered Jobeth. Without looking back, he walked away holding on to each child's hand.

Mara-Joy ran to her mother who sat on her hind legs gawking into space.

Alan went and placed a hand on Jobeth's shoulder. Neither one could believe what was happening to their family.

"Mama!" Mara-Joy begged, crouching down to Jobeth's vacant gaze. "Mama, please, it isn't true! Tell Chad it is not true! I didn't do the things he said."

Jobeth's eyes flickered for a moment, but didn't focus on Mara-Joy's frantic face. She stood up slowly, putting her arm around Alan's waist and resting her head on his shoulder. Alan wrapped his arm protectively around Jobeth's back and gently kissed the top of her head.

"Mama?" Mara-Joy said, distraught. Jobeth and Alan's backs were turned towards her.

"Take me home, Alan," Jobeth voice said vacantly. Alan nodded and they began to walk away without a glance back.

Mara-Joy stood watching her parents leave in disbelief. Her abdomen tightened and instinctively she placed her hand over her small mound to settle it. She stood, alone, frozen to the ground, eyes resting on Joanna's open grave.

"I am not to blame," she said out loud. "I'm not."

— Chapter 48 —

She is dreaming.

Joanna stands beside her bed looking down at her accusingly.

"No!" Mara-Joy calls out in a distant voice. "It was not my fault. She scrunches up in a tight ball, wrapping herself protectively around her growing belly. Something feels different. Something is not right. A pain rips across her abdomen and Mara-Joy cries out in pain.

Joanna floats out of the room and Mara-Joy lifts her stiff body out of bed to follow. She looks over at Larry's sleeping form and kisses him warmly on the cheek. He smiles as he slumbers and Mara-Joy can't help smiling back at him.

"I love you, Larry. I honestly do," she says, holding a hand under her belly. The churning sensation is getting progressively worse.

"Mara-Joy," a floating voice calls out. She turns to the sound and follows it, her bare feet lightly touching the ground. Her white gown flows around her legs freely as they follow Joanna's ghostly form down the stairs and out the front door, into the calm night.

She doesn't know where she is going. All she knows is she must follow Joanna. Nothing is more important than trailing after Joanna.

"Joanna! Wait!" Mara-Joy calls out. She winces in pain as she tries to run and catch up to her.

She can't do it. Joanna is too far ahead. A mere glimpse of her is seen through the dark night.

Panting, Mara-Joy continues to push after Joanna, in spite of the increasing bolts of pain that attack her midsection.

Suddenly she stops.

There she stands.

Joanna.

She is looking down upon her own freshly dug grave.

Mara-Joy swallows the hysteria about to emerge from her throat. How did she end up at the graveyard?

She stands behind Joanna's form, her hands pressed protectively on her tummy. The pain is persistent and continually increasing.

"Joanna!" Mara-Joy calls out in agony. The spectral form of Joanna turns slowly and smoothly around, facing the distressed Mara-Joy.

She is beautiful.

Joanna's face is heavenly and void of anger and hate. Her hair is long and flowing, seemingly floating around her angelic features. She reaches out loving hands to Mara-Joy's tortured figure, welcoming Mara-Joy to her.

Mara-Joy falls to the ground sobbing, her insides twisting in agony.

"I didn't want you to die, Joanna," Mara-Joy cries. "I know I thought I did, but I didn't really. You are my sister and I have always loved you deep in my heart. I am so sorry for what I have done to you and to Alan-Michael. I didn't mean for this to happen. I just wish I could take it all back."

Joanna touches Mara-Joy on her head. The moment her fingertips brush Mara-Joy's damp curls, she feels her distended stomach harden. A sharp popping sound gurgles from the depth of Mara-Joy's belly and the pain has stopped. She feels a surge of warmth begin to envelop her mid-section and gently move up her entire body. She looks down at her white gown. Between her legs, blood is quickly spreading over her gown. She touches the dark spot and lifts her bloody fingertips. A panicked sound escapes her lips as she looks to Joanna for help.

Joanna seems to float in front of Mara-Joy, her hair cascading around her soft face.

"Don't be afraid, sister. All is forgiven," Joanna says in her heavenly voice.

Joanna seems to glow as she reaches a hand down to Mara-Joy. Mara-Joy takes a gulp of fresh air and feels freed of pain, freed of anguish and hate and anger as she takes Joanna's airy hand in hers. She rises to her feet easily, as though she is weightless and stands equally with Joanna, both looking into each other's eyes without trepidation or hostility.

"Why are you here?" Mara-Joy asks in a faraway voice. She feels weightless, the pain she was feeling forgotten.

"I have come for you," Joanna says, and turns them both toward a bright light. She smiles at Mara-Joy and holds tightly to her hand as she leads her into the temperate illumination.

The groundskeeper found her body the next morning. Curled up in a fetal position on Joanna's grave, Mara-Joy was blue from the blood loss. Clutched in her stiff fingers she held a flower, a peace offering to her sister who rested beneath her.

Cause of death was hemorrhaging, due to the placenta covering the cervix. The baby had become heavy as it grew larger and placed too much pressure on the cervix, causing Mara-Joy to rupture and bleed to death. How she had ended up on Joanna's grave, no one knew. All that was known was Mara-Joy had died with a smile on her face and a peaceful expression that no one had ever seen on her before.

Jobeth and Alan, along with their remaining children and their extended families, buried Mara-Joy beside Joanna. It seemed appropriate that the two women spend eternity together. Even though they didn't know what had transpired the night Mara-Joy had died, they knew some truce had been made in the war between the two sisters. Jobeth planted flowers on her daughters' graves that spring. The seeds she used were the seeds she had once salvaged from another grave so long ago. When she visited, she felt peace in her heart as she weeded the tiny buds that seemed to bloom so quickly from the rich soil that held Mara-Joy and Joanna. By summer, the flowers were in full bloom and the two gravesites were alive with vivid color.

Pauline, back for a visit from Africa and now married to Frederick and tranquil in the life she had chosen, examined the red flowers carpeting the two graves. She stood up from her crouched position and dusted off her trousers.

"Mother, why these flowers?" she asked Jobeth, who stood silently, watching Pauline.

"It was the flower Mara-Joy held in her hand, the night she. . ." Jobeth stopped, placing her knuckles to her quivering lips. It was also the flower she had planted on her beloved baby's grave. "It seemed right."

Pauline nodded and hooked her arm in the crook of her mother's.

"Let's go home to Dad," she said warmly. Jobeth nodded her approval and began to walk toward the car parked at the front of the churchyard. They were just about to leave the cemetery when Jobeth stopped Pauline with a light touch on her arm. She looked back at the two resting places. A sea of red immediately caught her eye, signifying Mara-Joy and Joanna's permanent home. Jobeth smiled to herself. She knew her daughters were together finally, loving each other, as they always should have. Jobeth had no doubts that the wars of the past were finally over.

She knew it because Mara-Joy had told her. Why else would she have clutched a poppy in her hand on her sister's grave? The very flower Jobeth had retrieved and saved for all these years. She had never planted the tiny gems held captive in the dried head. Not once did it feel right to do so. She had waited for the right place and the right time. It was over. The war was over.

"What is it Mom? What's the matter?" Pauline looked to her mother, concern written plainly on her face.

Jobeth patted Pauline's hand lovingly.

"Everything will be fine, dear," Jobeth said with sincerity. "Everything will be fine."

— About the Author —

Deena Thomson grew up in Ontario, Canada where she still resides. She and her husband, Todd, have five sons: Anthony, Aidyn, Ansen, Arris and Avery.

She is currently working on her second and third novels "The Last Boy" and "Colors of Mavi".